MW01515397

C. C. MILLER

Shedding

Acknowledgement

I would like to thank my wonderful husband, **S. Miller**, for all the support he provided throughout the writing of this book. You are a beautiful person, and your support means everything to me. It has certainly been a unique experience bringing this book to fruition. I also want to thank my two beautiful children for bearing with me as well. They would sometimes just appear out of nowhere to make me laugh and to check on me as I worked tirelessly on my novel *Shedding.* I also want to thank my friends and family members for all the brilliant suggestions and insightful knowledge they have provided to assist with completing my second novel. **Amelia White**, you were my rock and my muse and my inspiration throughout this entire production. I also want to thank the creator of the universe, for his many blessings as I wrote my heart out to deliver one of my finest work yet.

Prologue

"This is it, right?" Brooke asked looking at the apartment number on the door. Her face was hidden by her large oversized hoodie as was her partner's.

"Pretty sure it is. Step back!" he told her and after he surreptitiously looked around to make sure no one was present in the main hallway; he gave the door a good kick and it swung open. He then quickly made his way inside, with Brooke following closely behind him. Her partner flipped on the light. Dianna's apartment was neatly organized and furnished with good taste. Brooke ran her hand along the top of the turquoise armchair before violently flipping it over, creating a loud booming sound as it hit the floor. Brooke looked at her partner and gave him an evil smile.

"Are you ready to trash this shit?"

"Ready as I'll ever be!" he responded.

They went around the apartment toppling furniture, scattering paper, breaking glass and doing a good job of wrecking Dianna's apartment. She went into Dianna's bedroom where she roamed, searching her drawers for anything interesting. She noticed a large bottle of vodka on the floor next to the nightstand and she picked it up and smiled at the heavenly find. She then noticed a picture of Dianna and her mother on the nightstand. Dianna must have been about 6 years old and her mom was holding her protectively in her arms. Brooke picked up the picture and threw it against the wall where the glass inside the picture frame broke into small pieces. She then kicked over the nightstand and removed the covers off Dianna's bed. She opened the bottle of vodka and poured some of it on the carpet before taking a big gulp. The alcohol burnt her chest in a good way. She leisurely strolled back to the living room where she watched her partner ransacking the kitchen without interrupting him. She then looked around at the disgusting mess they made and felt immensely satisfied with their handy work.

"You think she will get the message?" her partner asked as he walked back to the living room to meet Brooke.

"It doesn't matter. This is just the beginning."

"What do you have there?" he asked her, looking at the bottle in her hand.

"Just a little sumpn' sumpn' I found." She took another swig and then gave him the bottle. He took a swig himself and then placed his hand around Brooke's waist, leaning in for a kiss. Brooke giggled as he kissed her neck, then she pushed him off her.

"Let's get the hell out of here before someone gets suspicious!" she told him. As they were about to leave, Brooke stopped as if she remembered something. She turned around, leaving her partner hanging at the door. She turned off all the lights, relishing the unpleasant surprise they were leaving for Dianna to find, then she rejoined her partner at the door. They both covertly exited the apartment, barely closing the door behind them, feeling exhilarated from the break-in. Brooke more so than her partner. She felt her heart racing as she thought about how close they were to their goal. This was what she was waiting for. She had finally found Dianna after years of searching and it was only a matter of time before she caught up with her mother too. When she was ready to turn them in to highest paying bidder, there was only one thing she wanted more than anything else in the world after that, and that was for Dianna and her mother to be dead.

Shedding

BY: C. C. Miller

She sat at the bar, her iridescent green nail delicately circling the rim of her unfinished glass of vodka. The bartender had asked her for her ID, before serving her the hard liquor and she obliged him with a fake one. This was routine not only because it was legally mandatory to verify a drinker's age but also an added safety measure since she looked like a 22-year-old gothic girl asking for a world of trouble. Her green eyes and jet-black, curly hair with streaks of green made her stand out anywhere she went which was hardly what she wanted. She wanted to be inconspicuous and off the radar as much as possible in the way her mother wanted to be inconspicuous and the same way her grandmother had been inconspicuous, and the list went on. She hissed in silent disgust. She hadn't chosen this life for herself. She didn't want any part of this generational curse and she sought to end her lineage with herself. She didn't want kids, a husband, none of it. She just wanted to be a reclusive loner until her dying days. The problem was, even though she wasn't immortal, she was burdened with longevity of life. She was in fact 54 years old with a supernaturally long life ahead of her…maybe 250 more years or so.

"Fucking aye!" she mumbled to herself as she raised her glass, "Cheers to that!" her words slurred, and she downed the drink in less than a second. She motioned to the bartender for another round, her plan was to binge drink herself to death tonight…*well not quite*. The corner of her mouth curled into a cruel smile. "Yeah right!" she muttered with cutting sarcasm. "Bitch, you couldn't kill yourself if you were blindfolded in front of an oncoming train". The bartender eyed her warily as she spoke a little too loudly to herself.

"Inside joke," she explained.

He looked at her askance, "with the other personalities in your head?" he quipped and poured her another. Dianna smirked, admiring his dark humor...her kind of humor. He winked at her then left her to the privacy of her depressing thoughts once more. She started talking to herself in public after the seventh drink or so and this was her tenth. She made a mental note to work on drunken rants as well as her drinking problem, but the truth was, she had a long list of personal issues to iron out with her suicidal tendencies topping the list and her drinking habit coming in second.

However, as much as her suicidal inclination was an issue for her, it wasn't an option, and it wasn't for lack of trying. Her breed wasn't immortal, but they were resilient. If they got hurt, even extremely hurt they could regenerate. Their cells simply could not die unless it was through the natural aging process.

"So, fucking generous of you, oh almighty and powerful one!" she shouted, raising her hand to the ceiling. Then she downed the drink in one gulp.

"Yeah, I think that's enough for you tonight, sugar," the bartender said walking back to check on her. He was a white guy with pastel pink hair. He seemed to be in his mid-20s and strikingly prepossessing.

"You're cute," she smirked at him.

"Hmm...in a hamster kind of way or I'm-making-your- panties-wet kind of way because either way I'm gay," he responded without missing a beat, punctuated by his pursed lips. They both laughed at his quip. "But seriously, I think you're over your limit," his words had taken on a nurturing tone. She could tell that he was a sweetheart. She really wasn't over her limit. The fact was, she could go 50 gallons more if she put her mind to it.

"I'm just having a very depressing night," she confided. "Please don't cut me off yet."

"How are you getting home?" he asked her. He seemed genuinely concerned and she was pretty sure it was driven by her youthful face. A young girl, alone in a bar was not a good look. She sighed heavily. She wasn't finished drinking but she couldn't create a scene.

"I already called my bestie," - she said 'bestie' like an annoying teenaged girl while batting her eyes for effect - "she is on her way and will be here in half an hour. I promise." She slid her empty glass toward him. "Please, sir. Give me more." She gave him a sexy pout. He scoffed. He stared her down, seeming to calculate something in his mind and then softened.

"Alright. Only one more. After that, get the fuck out of here. I don't need you on my conscience if you get hurt, kidnapped, raped or whatever it is these perverts do to young girls these days." He was animated as he said this which made Dianna smile.

"What is a pretty girl like you doing alone at a swanky bar like this anyway?" He ventured as he poured her some more vodka. The bar was far from swanky. More like a grimy hole in the wall. Just then another customer beckoned to him.

"Hold that thought. I'm still on the clock," he said walking off. He had momentarily taken her mind off her cesspool of depression. Sometimes, she wished she had close friends, but she was always hopscotching from place to place. If anyone found out her secret, she had to go into hiding again. She knew she was an anomaly. A creature that didn't belong. There were names for people like her. Aliens, demons, reptilians, hybrids, gargoyles, Medusa...The last one made her sneer. It was the closest thing that could describe who she was, but she knew it wasn't the answer. Medusa was a myth, she wasn't. She was a living, breathing, strange thing. She decided to sip slowly on her drink since it was her final one. She laughed inwardly at the social constraints and rules that bounded her even though she knew she had the power to turn the world on its head. That, however, was not in the divine scrolls which pretty much stipulated that her kind assimilate or better yet, remain as hidden as possible...*at least, according to her mother anyway.*

"Moronic!" she muttered. As far as she knew, it was just a long lineage of women, getting pregnant and running off to raise their daughters single-handedly in seclusion. They never got married. They never had more than one kid and they never had sons.

Damn shit show! she groused inwardly.

She was certain this needed to end with her, and she wasn't sure why any of the women didn't just choose to end it themselves...*oh, yeah. They couldn't.* Her mother was still alive, aging somewhere in isolation. Dianna told herself that she didn't care. She hated them and all the ancestors that did this to her.

"I see you're still on this one," the bartender said ambling over to her.

"Things picked up, didn't it?" she said diverting the conversation from herself as she peered around the bar which was slowly getting crowded. He exhaled loudly.

"It's almost 11:00. We are about to be slammed." Just then, another customer caught his attention. She winked at him as he went to serve the customer. Oddly, she wanted to be his friend. It was the way he cared about her without even knowing who she was. She decided it was time to hightail to avoid the crowd he was talking about. She finished her drink and waited about five minutes for him to return.

"Hey, what's your name?" she said, taking $250 out of her purse.

"Are you hitting on me again?" he had to shout as the noise level got louder.

"I promise I am," she said.

He laughed light-heartedly. "You must be really desperate to be making moves on a gay bartender," he threw back at her.

"Something like that, plus I like your hair," she complimented him. He chuckled. She did, her green streaked hair didn't come close to the flamboyance of his silky, pink, perfectly cut hair.

"Simon."

"Hi, Simon. I'm Dianna." She scribbled her number on a napkin and handed him the crisp bills. "We should hang out sometime." His smile broadened from the hefty tip. He laughed when he read the words under her number. *No funny business, just friends.*

"I do like new pets! I'll call you," he said with seeming sincerity, but she was almost sure he wouldn't. She waved to him then walked out in her patent leather stiletto boots, green mini dress, and brown leather jacket.

She walked briskly to the parking lot and found her motorcycle. It looked like a dangerous raven, black and sleek, coruscating under the parking lot lights. This was her one, true love. Her baby was an unfailing, reliable, and majestic object of her affection. She hopped onto it gracefully and skillfully, smoothing her curly hair before putting on her helmet. She turned the key and revved it a few times for her satisfaction and then took off, bobbing and weaving through the busy streets. She was tipsy on alcohol and high on her adrenaline but in full control. Her heart soared and sang as the wind ruffled the parts of her hair the wasn't covered by her helmet as she blurred past cars on either side of her. She was unafraid, mostly because she knew even in the worst accident, she wouldn't die.

***

Her alarm jarred her rudely awake. She felt the blood rushing to her head and her pupils were mere slits as her eyes adjusted to the sunlight beaming in from her apartment window. She had forgotten to close the blinds from the previous night.

"Too much light, too much noise!" she muttered. She quickly turned off the alarm, then buried her head under her pillow. She wasn't ready for the day, but she had a Skype meeting to attend. She was a video editor that worked from home and didn't have to interact much with her clients except over the phone and through emails, but this particular client suggested a Skype meeting with her boss to discuss her latest work, since Dianna flat out refused to attend an office meeting.

Annoying! She had to move, as painstaking as it was, despite her horrendous hangover. The Skype meeting was at 9:00 a.m. It was 8:45. She needed to make an effort to look somewhat professional. She threw on her leather jacket from the night before and slicked her hair back in a bun to hide her natural green streaks. She also dabbed on some foundation and lipstick to rid herself of the gothic look. She looked in the bathroom mirror and was satisfied with her appearance except for one thing...her eyes. She closed the blinds in her living room and turned on softer lights so her pupils could dilate to their normal size, double checking herself in the bathroom mirror to make sure her eyes had adjusted.

Finally, five minutes before the meeting, Dianna was turning on her computer and logging into her Skype account. She pulled up the commercial she had edited on her computer screen and got her note pad ready so she could write down their complaints because she was certain that the meeting was nothing more than a grouse fest. Then came the incoming call. She accepted.

"Hello, Dianna. How are you?" Susanne greeted her, all bright-eyed and bushy tailed. A morning person, no doubt. She was African American with straightened hair that passed her shoulders. She had colored it auburn which went well with her dark complexion.

"I'm well. How about yourself?" Dianna bantered less enthusiastically.

"Same. This is Mr. Ashton, the C.E.O of Ashton Advertising."

"Hello, Dianna," he followed quickly.

"Good morning," Dianna responded, her words dripping with as much honey-sweetness and feminine charm as she could muster. She really wanted to get the meeting over with. It was already too long.

"Well, let me just cut to the chase. I really love your work. This was by far the best editing you've done for us yet." This took Dianna off guard. She bowed her head slightly to hide her sudden arrest of bashfulness, but she quickly composed herself. It was indeed a rare thing for anyone to Skype her to tell her they loved her work. They usually sent it in an email.

"Thank you, sir."

"I do have a few suggestions," the part she knew was coming. She squared her shoulders and prepared to take notes as she braced herself for the criticisms. "We thought the second girl was a bit underdressed. We're advertising beer not porn, so we want her part cut completely out of it". This was not a problem. She didn't shoot the video, nor did she choose participants for the video. She just edited. That was her sole job. She would have cut the scene out herself. The girl's nipples protruded proudly through the raunchy mesh top she was wearing, with a nipple ring to boot, but she felt they were going with the theme 'sex sells' so she blurred them instead.

"I can do that," Dianna responded.

"Also, if you could pace the voiceover a little more," he said seeming to be reading from a to-do list. Without realizing, Dianna narrowed her eyes.

"Is that a problem?" Mr. Ashton questioned catching the sudden change in Dianna's expression.

"Oh, no! It's just usually... any additional instructions and changes are sent via email to save the client's time," she responded sweetly. She saw him put his pen down. *Oh, shit. Had she said too much?* She winced inwardly. She didn't want to lose them as her client. They paid her a lot of money and was a guaranteed job.

"You are right. This was sort of an excuse for me to meet you since you've been our contractor for almost a year now and we have never spoken." Dianna felt awkward. She wasn't sure which direction he was going or where the meeting was crash landing.

"I also wanted to offer you a job in-house, working full time for our company," he said.

"Oh. Thank you for the offer but I'm a freela--"

"-- a freelancer, yes, I know. Susanne informed me that you were very, what's the word, 'underground'. Scheduling this meeting with you was damn near impossible," he said eerily.

"Yeah...sorry. I'll look into that," Dianna said noncommittally.

"Correct me if I'm wrong but most of your current contracts are procured by 'word of mouth'?" She could tell that he had been researching her near nonexistent LinkedIn profile. Dianna took the chance to focus on Mr. Ashton features. She realized that he seemed a bit young to be a CEO. He seemed to be about 25 years old. He was African American with chiseled features. His eyes were dark, and his lips were inviting. He was pretty put together, easy on the eyes and great visual for new fantasies she would imagine later while doing dirty things to herself. She smirked, cleared her throat and focused.

"Mr. Ashton. Again, thank you for the offer but I must decline. I have my reasons," she said skirting his question.

"...and what reasons are those?" he pushed. *If there was ever such a thing as not taking a hint or not accepting flat out rejection for that matter,* she thought to herself. Even though it was a three-way conference call, Mr. Ashton had homed in on her so much that the call seemed to reduce to only the two of them.

"I do not wish to disclose them, if you don't mind." She was getting agitated. She felt as if he was trying to corner her.

"... and if I offered twice what you are making now, plus benefits?" He was doubling down, but Dianna was uncertain of the reason. She felt very uneasy and Mr. Ashton was striking her as a man with ulterior motives. However, she had to play her cards right. She still wanted to maintain their business.

"That's a pretty good offer, I would advise you to at least think about it." Susanne chimed in. Dianna had a good repertoire with Susanne and wondered if she was in on this surreptitious coercion.

"Another company is planning on making a similar offer, but we wanted to nab you first," Mr. Ashton explained. Things were starting to make a little more sense. Her work had gained such popularity that she was in demand.

"I promise you that my answer will be no to them as well, Mr. Ashton," Dianna said without hiding her amusement.

"May I invite you to the office to have a look around? You might like it once you've seen it," he offered. Dianna could see he wasn't ready to give up, but she wasn't going to concede. The office life wasn't for her. Bright lights and too many people. She didn't need to work in a high-stress environment that could trigger some of her physiological reactions. She would only be placing herself in mortal danger.

"Mr. Ashton, my mind is made up. It's not about the money. You can say, it's more of a... precaution." Dianna noticed slight disappointment on poor Susanne's face, but Mr. Ashton's expression was unreadable. She had no intention of enlightening them any further on the subject.

"Okay, Dianna. We hear you loud and clear. I made you an offer and you made your point. I'll have Susanne email you with the rest of the instructions," he said gathering the stack of paper in front of him. "I'm looking forward to the grand finale."

"I won't disappoint you."

"Okay. Good to hear. Susanne, come to my office once you're finished. We have to catch up on a few things." He then refocused his attention on Dianna. "It was nice meeting you, Dianna," he nodded politely.

"Okay, sir," Susanne responded with so much enthusiasm that Dianna questioned the sincerity of it. *Must come with the job description of being Mr. Ashton's main assistant.* He disappeared from the screen leaving Dianna to speak with Susanne.

"I wish you had taken the offer," she remarked. All signs of perkiness vanished.

"I'm sorry but I couldn't accept it."

"I know, I know. You have your reasons. I'll send over the information to you within a few hours," Susanne said, clearly heartbroken.

"I am sorry. I hope this doesn't change anything."

"Don't worry. It won't. You are still hot commodity around here," she responded returning to her usual perky nature. Dianna envied Susanne's enthusiastic disposition, which was growing on her each time they interacted. *She gave off such a positive vibe...unlike her moat of depression that spread wide and deep around her.*

They ended the meeting and Dianna quickly threw off her Jacket. Her pores needed to breathe. She felt as if she was overheating. She went to the kitchen and got an ice pack and placed it on the lower back of her neck. The meeting was somewhat intense for her. She pulled her hair free of the bun and pulled at a strand, grateful they hadn't noticed her hair grow a few inches longer. She was pretty sure her pupils may have constricted a few times. A few more minutes of Mr. Ashton's insistence and her hair would have gone full Medusa on them both out of sheer agitation. She needed to learn to control herself better. Thankfully, the meeting had ended on a calmer note.

It was for this reason interacting with the outside world on a regular basis was a huge no-no. One Skype meeting and she was ready to bare her fangs and attack. She laughed at the thought. "Calm down, love. No need to show your ugly side...literally." She smiled in personal amusement. She decided to take a cold shower once the ice pack thawed on her skin.

Mr. Ashton had her emotions a bit scrambled. His forcefulness riled her, but his dark eyes aroused her. It was strange since she had been emotionally dead for such a long time. She figured it had something to do with her hangover. She wasn't herself completely, maybe a little messed up from the drinking. Yet, when she thought about his handsome face, her body warmed, and her heart raced. It was necessary that she never laid eyes on him again but somehow, she knew that this was unavoidable.

About five minutes later she was walking into her bathroom. She turned on the water and allowed her robe to fall around her ankles and she tentatively stepped inside. The water was ice cold. Exactly what she needed. She wet her hair and felt it shrinking to its normal length. She used the sponge to lather her golden-brown skin as her body temperature seemed to be returning to normal. The shower felt good.

She noted to herself that she didn't know his first name. Sliding her hand across her soapy breasts, she allowed her head to fall back as the powerful stream of water washed over her. The last time she liked anyone was about 20 years ago. Then, she looked like 18 and was dating a 21-year-old. He was a really nice guy. Even though he was mature for his age, he was still too young for her. The relationship lasted a whopping six months, more than any of her previous relationships. He hated her secretive ways or that she didn't want to go anywhere with him in the daytime. He thought he embarrassed her. He also thought she was cheating. She saw that they were headed toward an explosive train wreck and fast, so she ended the relationship and moved away from the area so he wouldn't come looking for her. It was tumultuous. The constant arguing, the secrets she kept from him which fueled his insecurities. The first time he saw her pupils constrict was when he overslept at her place. Of course, he wanted to know why her eyes were like that. She told him that she had cat eye syndrome. He noted that it was the first time noticing the anomaly and she told him she had the selective type. *Completely ridiculous* but he believed her... *or at the very least, he wanted to believe her*. She hated lying to him and hurting him. She turned off the shower as her essence and peace were restored.

After her shower, she cooked a hearty meal of eggs, toast and grits and drank some cold orange juice. She ate it on her couch as she flipped through the channels on her flat screen. She stopped it on a reality show, 'Housewives of Denton County'. She liked these types of shows because she could live vicariously through the boisterous women. She knew their dialogue were scripted but it didn't matter. It was a life she couldn't have and wanted so badly instead of a life of hiding and secrets. She enjoyed her breakfast leisurely, occasionally laughing at the overstated drama unfolding on her television. Within an hour, she was back in front of her computer working. She wouldn't move until evening where she would take a power nap then head to the bar.

It was about 6:30 when she was finishing up one of her projects. She was so proud of the edited work. The short three-minute video was polished, high-end and she loved it. She was rotating her neck and massaging her shoulders to relieve the tightness when she heard her ringtone going off. She assumed it was a telemarketing call but checked just to make sure it was no one important...*like her mother*. It wasn't a saved number. She threw her phone back onto the bed and let it go to voicemail.

She went to the kitchen and poured herself some wine. She was hungry but she would eat out tonight...alone. She usually chose a hibachi dinner, that way, she could sit at the counter and watch with intrigue as they prepared her food without worrying too much about seeming alone. Her phone alerted her to a voicemail. She picked up her phone and listened.

"Hi, Dianna. It's Simon. I'm just checking on you to see if you got home safe. Also, some friends and I are going bar hopping tomorrow. Not sure if that's your scene but it's going to be a group of us and I figured if you wanted to drink like a marine, you might as well drink with us. Anyway, let me know. Byyyyyeee" He dragged out the word 'bye' and Dianna laughed. It sounded like he would be good company and she really wanted a friend, so she quickly warmed up to the idea.

***

Dianna was in a dimly lit bar booth with her newfound friends Simon, Eric, Alicia, and she forgot the other girl's name, but she was sure it was K-something. She had been drinking all night and was already losing her grasp on her inhibitions. She couldn't tell the last time she laughed this hard. Simon was a hoot, always taking jabs at his parents for not observing his gayness.

"I won't say a thing for as long as they act like I'm not. I still think they are hoping I'm not because they want a grandchild so bad." He took a sip of his drink then whipped his neck dramatically. "When they finally acknowledge my orientation, I'm going to say 'really, I hadn't noticed',". The group erupted in a roar of laughter. He was so unapologetic, and she had to admit that she was envious of his freedom. "What about you, Dianna... holding any grudges against your parents?" he asked her, shifting the conversation.

She shook her head, pretending to be preoccupied with her drink. She took a big gulp and slowly swallowed. "Super shy, isn't she?" Eric said to Simon motioning his head in her direction. Eric was Simon's boyfriend and they acted like each other. Honestly, except that one was blond and the other had pink hair, in her drunk state, it was hard to tell the difference. She knew they wanted her to open up more but after years of closing off, it came to her naturally. Furthermore, she didn't have too much normal things to share anyway.

"I'm a video editor," she said to smooth over the awkwardness.

"Really? I work for Ashton Advertising Firm. I could probably help you get a job there," Eric responded, his eyes wide with excitement as if he had found a gold mine.

"You're the second one to offer me a job from that company, today. Must be a sign," she joked without thinking.

"Who was the first?" Eric probed. She felt her brain swimming in a sea of alcohol inside her skull. She must have been on her twentieth drink.

"The CEO himself, ...Mr. Ashton... I think his name was." Dianna shrugged to show her disinterest and she knew that by the time she was having a problem remembering his name, she was tipping over her alcohol limit. "But I told him to shove it up his rear...well, not exactly. I told him I just wanted them as a client."

"You turned down Mr. Ashton?" Eric seemed bemused.

"Yeah..." Her words were slurring, "Did I commit a crime or something?" she said sarcastically. Simon was laughing a little too hard at her joke. He was drunk as a skunk like her, which made her giddy. She was misery and he was company.

"Drax offers you a job, you take it!" Eric was the only one not impressed with her drunken jokes.

"Drax???" She almost bellowed at the discovery of his name.

"You didn't even know his first name? You're a hot mess!" Eric said disapprovingly.

Fuck him!" she said. The alcohol had given her enough fuel for an over show of bravado. She was feeling really good, too good.

"Ooooooh," came from the group in unison.

"I'm surprised you didn't want to fuck HIM," Eric said. He seemed put off by Dianna's nonchalance about Mr. Ashton. Dianna was getting the feeling that he was being a degree too sensitive about the issue.

"Who said I didn't want to?" she quipped flirtatiously.

"Oh, my gosh Dianna. You are sloshed. Simon please take her glass!" K-something said. Dianna made an effort to try to remember her name...*was it Karen? Karen the alcohol police.*

"No, I'm, not 'sloshed'. What the hell does that even mean, Karen!" she defended herself. Simon took her drink from her hand.

18

"Yes, you are honey. You have outdrank us all and it's pretty much closing time." Simon, the nurturer, kicked in again "She's my pet. I've got this," he told the group apologetically, but his words were slurring too.

"Tell your 'pet' my name isn't Karen," K-something taking full offense, her blue eyes were burning with annoyance.

Dianna chuckled at her remark. "See, that's why I like you Simon," she said pouting her lips. "You're not sensitive."

Eric addressed her promptly, "Girl, he's taken and he's right. That's your last one."

"Yes, fawtha!" Dianna said in an exaggerated British accent, rolling her eyes, oblivious that she was spiraling. She got up and staggered.

"Simon, please take her home. She's done!" Eric said staring at Dianna concerned.

"I don't know where she lives. She came here on her motorcycle, remember!"

"Does that mean she's coming home with us?" Eric stared at Simon and got his answer. "Shit! Okay."

Chapter 2

She rolled and fell onto the white shaggy rug on the floor. "God!" she moaned, feeling like an overfilled trash bag being crushed in a compactor. She sat up and immediately realized she wasn't home but, where was she? She grabbed her purse which was on the table and rifled through it for her phone, finding it in no time. She had a missed call from Susanne. Her head was swimming as her stomach churned somewhere in her intestines. She was nauseous and wanted to throw up. She looked at the time. It was 8:30. Eric came out from nowhere in a shirt and tie, dressed for work. He looked like he had an easy night unlike her. The lights were coming in from the ceiling to floor glass windows of his apartment. She quickly lowered her gaze and pretended she was searching for something in her purse. She came across her sunglasses. Dianna shoved them on her face.

"Why are you wearing sunglasses?"

"Too much light," she responded.

He gave her a quick uncertain laugh. "Whatever! So, Simon is passed out. He couldn't even crawl to the bathroom if he tried. I could take you with me to work and get you to your motorcycle during lunch or you can stay here and wait for me to get back," he suggested.

She didn't like either choice. She couldn't be around anyone right now...not during the day.

"Taxi!" Dianna said softly.

"Suit yourself. Do you remember the name of the bar?" She shook her head since she didn't, but the movement only made her head pound.

"I don't remember the name or the address, but I can drive you there which is a lot better that searching for an underground bar in Las Vegas in a taxi." On account of the fact that they were bar hopping last night, she didn't remember names or streets either. Her options were getting smaller. She needed to go home, get away from people. She felt panicked and nauseous.

"Where's the bathroom?" she asked as bile began erupting in her throat. She gagged then covered her mouth hoping she wouldn't vomit. She needed the bathroom now.

"Not on my expensive rug! It's that way." He pointed frantically to the hallway. She dashed like a tornado was chasing her. As soon as she bent her head over the toilet, all her shame, sins and indiscretions of the night came up, over and over again. When she was finished, she flushed and watched with disgust as her green stomach acid swirled down the toilet. *This is my life* she bemoaned. She needed to leave now! She rinsed her mouth at the sink and placed the glasses back on her face. Then, she returned to Eric in the living room.

"I'll go with you," she told him.

***

She sat in Eric's office. It was pretty nice with a spiral-shaped design, dark blue desk, and a large flat screen monitor inside. He also had a wide lounge chair which elegantly matched the desk. Ads were playing in a repeated sequence and she even got a glimpse of a few ads she had edited.

"What do you do here?" Dianna asked. Eric smirked at her.

"Senior editor, I finalize the decision after your work gets sent to me." Dianna nearly coughed up her lungs.

"What?!"

"Small world. I know." Dianna was cringing from embarrassment because of the tasteless things she said the night before.

"I did, I-I didn't--" she stuttered.

"Girl, please. I don't even remember half the things you said," he lied to her and blew her a kiss. She relaxed. She couldn't believe she was inside the building of the company that she so confidently turned down yesterday.

"I think I can sneak away before lunch," Eric said reading something on his computer. "My schedule looks clear and I know you want to get out of here," Eric said eyeing her sympathetically.

"I do," Dianna admitted.

"Why don't you want to work for us?"

Dianna touched her sunglasses as a nervous gesture. "It's complicated," she responded.

"Sure, it is." Eric seemed to be getting a little short when it came to her enigmatic nature. Just then, Mr. Ashton walked into his office. "Eric, I'm going on a rushed trip to Beijing for a few days, so don't miss me while I'm away," he joked. Eric gave him a stiff smile as he eyed Dianna nervously. Mr. Ashton hadn't noticed her yet as she was just a smidge out of his view. "Anyway, just a few clients on that side of the world that I want to speak with personally. Please send me the approved cut from that beer commercial for the Milver account as soon as possible. I want to put my eyes on it one more time," he said all-business, opening the door a little wider. Just then he spotted Dianna in her sunglasses with her head down in the lounge chair. "Well, hello! I didn't see you," he said genuinely surprised. He leaned his head to the side assessing her. "Have we met?" This was bad...really bad! Dianna felt herself warming as she lowered her head further, it was only a matter of time before her snakes appeared baring their ugly fangs.

"Aaaah, I'll definitely get on top of the Ad," Eric responded, saving her from having to explain herself. "I'm sorry, Mr. Ashton but this is my friend, and she isn't feeling too well. Do you mind if I take her home? It won't take but a minute," Mr. Ashton continued to survey her. Dianna wasn't sure if he recognized her, but he didn't say anything.

"Yeah...sure. Just make sure you get back to me on that commercial today. They're waiting on it." He popped his head back out and left. Dianna breathed a sigh of relief.

"Girl, that was too close. Fucked up is no way for him to see you." Dianna showed her agreement by nodding her head. She didn't even want to speak in case Mr. Ashton overheard her voice and recognized her then. Eric was right, everything was too dangerously close, and it wasn't because she was looking a little hungover. Her green streaked curls were slowly uncoiling, and she was feeling the change creeping over her just at the sight of him. She found a scarf inside her purse and quickly placed her hair in a messy ponytail, then tied the scarf around her head to cover her hair, breathing in and out slowly, vowing to never return to Ashton Advertising Firm.

***

Eric and Dianna rushed out as soon the opportunity opened itself and not a minute too soon. Dianna's discomfort was at the pinnacle. Luckily, the scarf in her purse, hid the changes taking place on her head. He took her to the last bar they had hopped the night before. She marveled at how unassuming the club looked during the day. She was excited to see her motorcycle where she left it...untouched. Her world began to feel right again.

Dianna got out of Eric's black Bentley and ran to her baby, placing her purse in a small compartment on her bike. She then checked it thoroughly and after assuring herself that no harm had come to it, she swung her leg expertly over her motorbike, straddling it with ease. She inserted her key inside the ignition but waited to turn it on. First, there was something she needed to get off her chest.

"I'm sorry I said those things about Mr. Ashton last night."

"We don't call him Mr. Ashton behind his back, sweetie," Eric said amused.

"What do we call him?" Dianna said taking the bait.

"Drax."

"Oh...yeah. Well, I didn't mean those things. I don't want to have sex with him, and if things were different, I would take him up on his job offer." She glanced away, "Things are just a bit incompatible in my life right now." She refocused on Eric. "I hope Mr. Ashton--"

"Drax. His first name is Drax," he reiterated, deliberately flustering her as he sat in his car with one of his arms resting on the car door.

"Drax!" she reminded herself. "I hope he understands."

"First of all, you're lying about not wanting to have sex with him because everybody does. Secondly, I'm sure he isn't sweating it. No offense, but I can tell you personally that he doesn't have the luxury of crying over people who reject his job offers. That man is out here saving lives."

Dianna smiled, knowing Eric was right about both things, although she wasn't quite sure about what he meant by 'saving lives'. "I'll see you around and thank you for bringing me to my baby," she said patting the front of her motorcycle as if it were a loyal dog. Eric waved and drove off in his black current year Bentley Continental GT. It wasn't long before she was riding her baby away from daytime, away from her embarrassing night and away from her near encounter with Drax...

***

Dianna had completed the beer commercial. She realized just how important the commercial was and now that she knew Eric was going to approve the project and send it off to Mr. Ash--Drax, she made certain her finished project was meticulously perfect. It was different when she knew the faces of the people looking over her work. So much more seemed to be at stake. She was now working on another project.

Yesterday was a strange day. Waking up at Simon and Eric's apartment. Seeing Drax again. It was one of those days where everything was following its own accord and you just had to go with the flow. She never felt so out of her element. She had lived a long time, but yesterday, she felt like 22 again. Young, naïve, and unfamiliar.

She paused her work. She needed a drink, but she promised herself she wouldn't touch another glass anytime soon because of the way she acted at the last bar she went to with her friends. She wouldn't be bar hopping soon either for that matter. She couldn't afford to wake up at other people's homes again. This had to be the last time. She looked like an idiot sitting in Eric's office disheveled with sunglasses on.

"Ugh," she lamented, cringing at the memory.

She looked at the time on her phone. It was almost 2 a.m. She decided to get back to the editing. She wanted to get as much done by 3:00 a.m.

As she worked, she thought about Drax. She wondered if he had a wife… *kids maybe?* She wouldn't be surprised. Young and successful, he was definitely a catch, which was more than she could say for herself. The thought was a stab through the heart. She couldn't date anyone in the true sense of the word 'dating'. She had too many secrets. Furthermore, she didn't want children. She didn't want to carry on her cursed genes that strung her together like a Frankenstein experiment. She hated living like this. Why would she subject her kid to her personal hell? It was evil and she hated her mother for doing it to her. She reached for her stress ball on her side table as her mind went back to her childhood. She slowly started compressing the ball as she thought how different things were then.

"Why can't I go to public school?" She had asked her mother.

"No one would believe you were 15. You look like 8. You would bring too much attention to yourself," her mother responded.

"I have no friends, mom. I have no life! This is far outside the reaches of normal!" she screamed at her mother angrily.

"It's for your own protection. You don't know what people would do to you if they found out who you were…what you were."

She was right, she wasn't a person. She was a thing. A monster of sorts. Medusa was a monster too and look what happened to her. She was beheaded by an overzealous warmonger. Her mother was right, but it was a life she never asked for or wanted. If someone gave her the option to continue living a life of loneliness, lies and seclusion or death, she would've instantly chosen death. She was squeezing her transparent stress ball aggressively by now.

Even if she was ever accepted by humans for what she was, outliving her partner and others around her would be pure misery. Her mother was 150 years old and looked like 50. She lived somewhere in Alaska. Dianna wasn't interested in visiting her. She preferred it here in Las Vegas, but she was prepared to pack up her things and start her life again elsewhere if she had to. So far, she had lived in twenty States.

"Twenty...shit!" She threw the ball on the floor and it rolled under her turquoise armchair. She rubbed her eyes as she felt herself getting tired. She left a piece of herself in each state, sometimes literally. Small pieces of shed skin in dumpsters, woods, wherever she could hide it. With the exception of her hair being able to transform into snakes, her eyes slitting when there was too much light or her skin shedding or fangs protruding, she was basically human. She scoffed. Those were the things that prevented her from living a normal human life so maybe her human side wasn't anything to celebrate. She had no idea of her history or what could have caused this type of mutation. She didn't know if she was created by man or nature. She had no answers for who she was except that her family and ancestors were in hiding for centuries.

She guessed she fared better than her ancestors. The green streaks in her hair could pass as hair dye and her eyes could be passed off as contacts...*or cat eye syndrome* in the year 2019 but centuries ago, they would have been accused of being witches and burnt alive.

Her mouth thirsted for some vodka. Whenever she started thinking deeply about her life, she wanted to binge drink. It was better to be depressed and drunk than depressed and sober, but she resisted. *I'm stronger than my weakness,* she told herself. She decided to take the work to her queen size bed in her bedroom, where she could lay comfortably on her bed.

After an hour, she had gained some headway with the new project. She decided to take a break. She grabbed her phone and decided to check out her social media account. She created one for her work with only a picture of her logo which was a green coiled snake with hypnotizing green eyes. She posted short clips of her work as samples but that was about it. She received a lot of business because of it. It also helped her to keep up with current events. She decided to search for Drax Ashton. She found him easily. He was already in her list of contacts. She must have added him when she started to freelance for the company.

She scrolled through his timeline…pretty professional, standard, boring stuff. She saw that he had a master's in business marketing and that the company had received the outstanding business award for their impressively high business standards. He also did a lot of charity work by constructing a halfway house for homeless people. No doubt for public relations purposes. She rolled her eyes cynically.

Typical poster child!

She couldn't tell if he was married or if he had children. His personal life wasn't something he divulged on his social media account either. She scrolled through some more until she became bored. As she was about to exit his timeline, she saw that he had posted a picture of him and other business partners on his timeline with the Chinese World Finance Center in the backdrop. Susanne was also there, standing next to Drax and beaming from ear to ear. The caption read; *Beijing trip was a success*. She clicked on it and accidentally reacted with a heart emoji. As quickly as she clicked it, she unclicked it, but it was too late. He would receive the notification. She hoped that he didn't manage his own page and had a PR specialist that handled his account. She immediately came off his page and ended her browsing for the night. She was bringing too much attention to herself and it wasn't intentional. Her phone vibrated. She checked it. It was a social media message from Drax. She threw her phone on the bed in a panic and hugged herself as if to protect herself from his message.

"You're acting silly, Dianna."

She mustered up the courage and decided to view the message.

"Was that you in Eric's office yesterday?" The question was direct. Her body warmed.

"Yes, it would seem we have mutual acquaintances," she responded, trying to play it cool.

"Were you there to see me?"

"Narcissistic much!" Dianna muttered to herself.

"I had no idea you would be there," she explained. She chided herself for not having a more intelligent response. Of course, he would be there, he was the CEO.

"What were you even doing there? I thought you weren't interested in stopping by," he typed.

"Long story. Eric was helping me with something personal."

"I see. Judging from the sunglasses, it seems you had a rough morning...or night." She smiled...mission accomplished. It wasn't a lie. She did have a rough night.

"You could say that." There was a long pause but the ellipses on his end told her he was typing. He was thinking about something.

"May I take you out to dinner?"

"I'm sorry, but I think it's best not to date clients," she responded promptly.

"It's not a date. We could renegotiate your contract." She wasn't sure what that meant. Furthermore, her contract was fine and didn't need *renegotiating*. She wasn't wet behind the ears; she knew what he was doing. She sparked his interest and he wanted to unravel the mystery that was her. She laughed to herself biting her bottom lip, knowing that she desired to meet him in person. She didn't want to seem like the shy, skittish deer she was projecting. It was far from who she was. She was daring, loved to take chances...spunky even.

Give him a chance...even for one night, she chided herself.

"Did I lose you?" Popped up on her phone screen.

"No. Just thinking," she told him.

"About?"

"Why I should let you wine and dine me under the guise of renegotiating my contract."

➤ Smiley face emoji< "Guilty"

"I'll let you this once," she typed back flirtatiously. *You are making a mistake, Dianna but the good kind,* she told herself.

"Good. Is Saturday a good time for you?"

"I might change my mind before then."

"I would be okay with that." She breathed out. She needed the option of forfeiting their date. It made her feel less obliged.

"The later, the better," she added.

"Darkness is our friend. Send me your address...and phone number. I'll pick you up." He instructed. Dianna was trying to grapple with his statement. What did he mean by darkness is our friend? But more importantly, was exchanging numbers even necessary?

"My phone number?" she inquired. She noticed the running ellipses from his end again and knew he was trying to figure something out.

"Seems logical. How am I going to let you know I'm outside?" It was crazy but even giving him her number seemed like a big jump. She felt herself retreating from her daring spirit. She sent him her address but held on to her phone number.

"Pick me up at 9:00. Don't be late. I'll be waiting"

➢ Laughing emoji< An address but no phone number? Okay. I'll be there."

She keyed the words, "Good night," then sent it as she licked her top lip with the tip of her tongue seductively.

"Sleep well, Dianna," was his final message to her.

Dianna placed her notifications on silent and placed her phone gently on the nightstand. She had a lot to think about. Things like, why did she agree to dinner with Drax Ashton?

Because you're bored and desperately need to get laid, she snuggled herself and covered her face. She hadn't had sex in years. She chastised herself on getting ahead of herself. Sex didn't seem like it would be on the menu, if he was as professional as he appeared, but she wouldn't mind if it was. If he wanted to slay her vagina, it would be a fun cat and mouse game with him trying to get into her pants and she pretending as if she didn't want him there. She already turned down his job offer, there was no way she would turn down an opportunity to have sex with him at this point. She would only play coy enough to seem like a lady. Her grin became devilish.

She worried about her appearance. She didn't want to seem like a dark gothic teenager. He was a worldly man of class. She went to her bathroom and reviewed herself. She lifted her hair on top of her head. *Maybe an updo, a high bun?* It would hide her green streaks enough. Or maybe she could straighten it, putting her green streaks on full display and just let him think she was a wild child...*a demon child* was more like it. She knew she needed to stop doing that...berating herself but she couldn't help it. It was years of self-loathing that made her self-critique second nature. Her thoughts were turning dark again.

"Snap out of it, Dianna," she told herself. "Just enjoy yourself with a good-looking guy for one night...it's just one night." She decided to straighten her hair and let the green streaks accentuate her sheer, dark green dress that she had hidden away in her closet.

"He might like it...who knows," she tried to convince herself. She was feeling excited again. After making a mental note of how she would dress, she decided to call it a night. She was exhausted from the eventful week she was having. Her week hadn't been this eventful since the car accident two months ago when she woke up in a hospital with bandages wrapped around her head and monitors beeping. According to the nurses, the car accident was so bad she shouldn't even be alive. They advised her against checking out against medical advice, but she knew that it was only a matter of time before they started digging and probing and asking questions. Then the police kept showing up at her apartment because it was a hit and run. They eventually stopped when they realized she wasn't being cooperative, and the case became a cold case.

She turned out the lights and closed her eyes, thinking about the possibilities with Drax. Her nether region throbbed from the thoughts of all the naughty things she wanted to do to him. If they wound up in bed together, she was going to have fun... real fun to make up for her dry spell. The thought sent a warm feeling coursing throughout her body. It would be a night to remember for them both.

Chapter 3

"I was homeschooled and in my later years, I picked up classes online to earn my degree," she told him. The dinner was going well. His eyes glowed when he saw her step out of her apartment building in her form- fitting sheer dress that gave the appearance of seeing her nude body underneath.

"Seem extremely sheltered...almost like you're hiding from the world," he said to her. She looked into his eyes, but his expression didn't really tell her much. Yet his comments seemed omniscient. He wasn't gathering information about her, in fact, it was the other way around. It seemed as if he was confirming details. His words were perfectly placed like he knew things about her.

He chose the perfect table, a little separated from the high traffic area with low lights which she hoped would minimize the lighting effect on her eyes. She detested the fact that while others worried about restaurant seating for other reasons, she primarily worried about restaurant lighting fearing it would trigger natural responses she was powerless to control.

"If I didn't know better..." She paused. She decided against finishing her sentence.

"What?" he pushed her.

"Nothing." She delicately sliced through her Kobe steak. Then placed the diced piece of morsel in her mouth. She savored the juiciness on her tongue. Her meal was euphoric or maybe it was Drax's presence that was causing her dopamine level to spike. She let her gaze linger on his torso a little over a second. His shoulders were broad under his suit. She wanted to see him naked.

"Don't undress me all at once, Dianna." She coughed on her saliva then swallowed the rest of her wine to wet her throat. Drax smiled. She needed to keep her horniness in check.

"I'm sorry. I didn't mean to stare like that."

"Don't apologize. We're both adults here," he said clearly amused by her.

"I promise I'm not here for that," she assured him. *Lies!*

"Okay. What are you here for?"

"I needed to get out of the apartment. Get some fresh air and enjoy some good company," she lied even more. Two nights ago, she was making love to herself thinking about him. She was a horny mess.

"Fair enough. I would still like to renegotiate your contract, Dianna. I can't afford to have another company whisk you away because I'm not on my A-game." Her libido took flight. He was talking about her contract again. Maybe he wasn't attracted to her or maybe he was like Simon. She stared at his masculine features. He exuded power and sexy maleness. She highly doubted he swung that way. In fact, he looked like it would be easy game to dominate her sexually in bed. His mouth on her inner thighs, his tongue on her forbidden places. She felt the wetness on her Panties as she imagined him performing cunnilingus on her.

"Do you want to head back to my place?" he asked her. She woke up from her fantasy and considered his question. However, after what happened at Simon and Eric's apartment, she shut the thought down. It would've been too risky. She tried to gather her thoughts to remember his previous sentence.

"No. We can renegotiate the contract here. What are you offering?"

"The offer still stands at doubling your current salary from our company."

"I'd like that." She was happy with her contract the way it was, but she wasn't going to turn him down again. He just wanted her loyalty to the company.

"Clearly, I didn't prepare the contract for you to sign tonight. I was kinda trying my luck again, but you could come by my office on Monday. Also, how do you feel about picking up a heavier workload?"

She laughed, "I should have seen that coming."

"More money, more responsibilities," he bantered.

"Something to think about," she said noncommittally.

"Sounds like we are getting somewhere. Tell me more about yourself. How old are you?"

"25 but people say I look younger"

"Good genes I presume." There it was again. Another loaded statement. It could be that she was reading too much into it since that wasn't uncommon for people to say but combined with other loaded words, it was driving her a little crazy. Again, she attempted to ignore her intuition.

"What about you?"

"Wiser than my years but 28 is my number." *His number?* As sexy as he was, there was something about him that wasn't sitting right with her, but tonight was a night to enjoy. She had decided she would leave her paranoia at her apartment and throw caution to the wind. Whatever he had up his sleeve, he was only human, and she was stronger than him in every way, so it didn't matter. She was in control. After a few more wine, laughter, and secret lusting on her part, they decided to end the evening.

On the ride back, they chatted some more about places that they'd been to. She confessed to him that she lived in twenty states, each time due to a personal family crisis.

"Sounds like you guys were on the run. What did you guys do that was so bad?" he said it as a joke, but it hit home for her.

"Exist," she responded, feeling herself getting emotional. His eyes softened and he reached over and covered her hand with his. His hand was large, warm...and comforting, engulfing her smaller hand. She liked the safety she felt with him. By the time he arrived at her apartment, she didn't want him to leave. She wondered if she should throw herself at him and forget about being a lady. She wanted a one-night stand so bad. However, he was about to become her boss, and she didn't want to make things awkward between them in case he didn't want her.

"It was a lovely night, Dianna. Thank you." *Don't be a gentleman. I want you in my bed, her* inner voice was screaming.

"Same. We should do this again." *Wait, no! Not that! Just invite him up.* Her inner monologue was warring with her spoken words. He stared at her and she could tell that he wanted to ask her something. She didn't want the night to be over and maybe he didn't as well.

"Do you want to come up?" she said, casting her line.

He bit, "are you sure?"

"Yes," she responded too quickly but at this point, she didn't care. She just wanted to have sex with him. Her attraction to him was getting the best of her. He could come up, have a romp, and then leave. That's all she wanted and needed from him tonight.

"I'm wondering if this is the wine talking," he said to her. *Was she unmanageably drunk again?* She didn't drink that much. She felt fine.

"No, it's not the wine." She leaned over and kissed him gently...then seductively. *What am I doing?* She prayed he didn't reject her. That her come on wasn't...overbearing. But he responded. He kissed her back deeply. His tongue exploring her mouth as he gently placed his hand on her right thigh and caressed her warm skin. *Yes.* He smelled like heaven and man. Her body was ready for him. His hand had slid up to her butt cheeks and cupped her. She smiled. She wanted him to touch her like that all night.

"I want this, Dianna," he said to her in between kisses.

"Yes, I want this too," she told him. She pulled away and licked the taste of him off her lips as he watched. She let herself out and he followed after her. She might never get the chance again and she just wanted to know what he felt like inside her. She held his hand as they got onto the elevator to her floor, letting go when she fidgeted for her keys inside her purse, outside her apartment door and then as she opened the door, he closed in behind her. She moved her head to the side so he could have access to her neck, and he sucked on her skin, first gently, then a little harder. She moaned. Then he spoke, "Are you sure? I don't want you to regret this. This could change our professional relationship," he whispered to her, but she didn't want him to speak. She wanted more of what he just did to her neck.

"Be honest, Drax. We both wanted this since the first time we laid eyes on each other and I'm too old for regrets," she said sucking in air as he squeezed her breast through her thin dress and as he slipped his other hand inside her underwear, touching her sensitive spot.

"Too old, huh?" he teased her. She wanted to care that her words were a dead giveaway to her secret, but she couldn't think past her desire. She pulled away from him. Climbed out of her underwear, slipped out of her dress easily, unstrapped her bra and let it all fall to the floor. She stood gloriously naked in front of him.

"Put it this way. I've NEVER been surer in my life!" She walked back over to him and began undressing him. First, his pants. She wanted to taste him. After she unfastened his belt, she pulled his pants and underwear down, staring at his penis with unbridled desire. She licked it then sucked on it. He moaned and ran his hand through her hair as he gyrated in her mouth. She removed his hand, worried he might trigger her snakes and stood up.

"That's just a sample, Mr. CEO!" she teased him. She almost tore his clothes off him as she pulled off his jacket, shirt, and tie as quickly as she could and backed him up against the wall. She was aggressive but she didn't care. She was calling the shots. She figured since she was a lot older than him, she was going to dominate him. She put her hand around his neck and squeezed gently. She bit his bottom lip so it could hurt a bit then kissed him. He gave her the power to control him in that moment. She loved it. He grabbed her butt cheeks again squeezing possessively, both their naked bodies warm and ready for each other.

"Bitch!"

"What did you say to me?" She breathed her words into his mouth.

"You heard me!" She pulled away from him again, then slapped his face playfully. It caught him off guard only for a moment as his eyes smoldered. She gave him a devilish look pulling him towards her as they both walked their way to the bedroom, bumping things in the darkness. They got to the bedroom, but he lifted her and threw her on the bed. He had turned things around making it obvious that he was in charge now. She was so heady she couldn't protest or resist. She wanted him any way she could get him. He climbed over her and restrained her wrists with his hand. She wrapped her legs around his waist.

"Not yet," he told her spreading her legs wide apart. He started kissing her from her lips, sucking on her breasts, dipping his tongue in her navel until he reached his destination.

"I know this is what you want," he said to her returning her devilish stare and without any warning, he delved his tongue inside her. She gasped loudly and then moaned in satisfaction. He strummed her like a delicate guitar note and she writhed in pleasure.

"You read my mind. Don't stop!"

"This is an all-nighter, Dianna." It was music to her ears. She wasn't even considering what things would be like if she woke up next to him in the morning because her mind was so wrapped up in the here and now. She hadn't felt this good in such long awhile. Her body was craving the high. She was coming. She tensed, arched and climaxed in his mouth. Her pupils fully dilated; she closed her eyes in pleasure. Her scalp tingled from the explosion. When she opened her eyes, she found him staring at her with a nefarious grin on his face. She jumped up and threw him on his back. It was his turn. She followed suit, kissing from his inviting lips to his stomach. She licked the pathways between his muscular abs which gave her extreme pleasure. His body was a temple, she was a worshipping fool. She traveled down to his groin which was excellently manscaped.

"I like," she told him. She sucked on his chocolate goodness eliciting moans from him that satiated her soul. She wanted him to say her name, but he didn't. She wanted to own him, but it would take more than a good romp in the bed to own a man like him and she didn't have the time or the capacity for commitment but tonight, TONIGHT! she would make him remember her forever.

Again, he tried to run his fingers through her hair so he could guide her mouth down his joystick but again she removed it.

"No hands," she joked. She stared at him as he looked into her soul. She pleasured him without breaking his stare.

"You're a beautiful green haired woman, Dianna!" he said to her. He pulled her toward him, guiding her on top of him. He lifted her hips and gently eased himself into her. An inner heat radiated from her walls closing around him like perfect fitting gloves. His eyes darkened, as the pleasure increased in increments, one pleasure wave followed by another. She sped up and slowed down based on the way his body spoke to her. It was a beautiful give and take polyphony.

"... and you're a beautiful chocolate man," she said to him. He laughed. Her long green nails dug harder into his skin as she felt her body climbing to the top of her climax, hoping to crash into ecstasy on the other side.

"Are you close?" Her voice was breathy and seductive.

"Don't worry about me," he told her. "I have plans for you," he said, equally breathless. It was a promise. She whimpered in satisfaction as she came again and again. He was right. He had a lot of stamina and he held out for as long as he could. When he finally arrived at his climax, he almost roared his pleasure, and the bed shook from his own convulsions. She didn't remember any of her past lovers climaxing so powerfully. It was otherworldly, to say the least, but it was one of the best nights she ever had. She was so drained by the end of it all that she could do nothing but collapse on top of him and close her eyes. As reality was about to fade into her dreams, she felt him tracing his fingers gently along her spine.

"We're not done, are we?"

"I did say this would be an all-nighter." He rolled her onto her back, then kneeled over her. "Let's finish what you started.

***

Her eyes flashed open. Her pupils constricted as they adjusted to the lighting. He was staring at her. She looked at her clock. It was 8:30 a.m. He had to go! Her room was barely lit but it didn't matter. Things would start happening to her body and he would start asking questions. Their beautiful night had ended... now, today! She quickly got up and grabbed an oversize T-shirt from her clothes drawer.

"Mr. Ashton, I know this is abrupt and maybe a little rude, but you have to leave. Now!" She left the room quickly to go to her bathroom, locking the door. She sat on her toilet and waited for him to respond. She heard him shuffling around with little to no urgency. She heard his footsteps headed her way.

"What the fuck!" she whispered to herself. "Mr. Ashton, please leave!" she said sternly and loud enough for him to hear.

"Mr. Ashton...I thought you were calling me by my first name?"

"Please go!"

"Dianna, why are you hiding?" Something was off. His tone sounded unnervingly casual for someone being kicked out. "Come out," he coaxed her. He sounded like he was just on the other side of the door. She could hear his slow breathing.

"If you don't leave, I'm calling the police!" she threatened him, feeling like an eel but she had to say something drastic because he was not getting the picture. She became anxious that he was some type of psycho deviant.

"With what? Your phone is out here!" he said even more calmly. He wasn't affected by her words which only served to confirm her thoughts that he was probably a psycho. "What did I do to warrant this overreaction?" he said. His voice was patronizing her. She didn't like the direction the events had taken. She was full-fledged agitated. She tried to calm herself but between Drax refusing to leave and daylight spilling in through her blinds, she couldn't help her emotions. Her hair was beginning to awaken.

"Come out, let's talk...like two normal adults," he said to her.

"Look! Mr. Ashton...Drax. I don't know what you have going on, but you have to go. You are creeping me out!" She heard him sigh deeply. Then she heard him walking off.

"Okay. We'll do it your way." She heard him opening her blinds. Some more shuffling and then the door slammed. She listened some more and heard silence. To be sure, she waited a little longer. She opened her bathroom door and looked around. There was a lot of light in her living room with Drax letting in the sunlight, her eyes were mere slits. It didn't matter. He was gone. She sighed relief. She felt terrible but she had to get rid of him.

"I'll apologize later," she mumbled to herself.

"No need." She heard his deep voice and looked around. He was waiting behind the door. Her reaction was immediate. Her green streaks became menacing snakes. Her eyes widened and her fangs grew. She hissed and backed him into the wall, squeezing his neck with all her strength.

"I told you to get out!" she roared at him.

"There she is!" He smiled in deep satisfaction. The rise and fall of her chest were evident as her eyes raged like a venomous snake ready to strike. She was pissed. He had disobeyed her and now he knew what she was. She leaned in closer. She was intimidating. She knew this, but he didn't look frightened. In fact, he only looked like he may have been struggling to breathe a bit. She loosened her hold.

"What the fuck is your problem?" she hissed angrily. "One night not enough for you, creep?" There was no seduction in her voice. The 'Dianna' he was with last night was a snake-haired hag staring at him now. He reached his hand up and with a strength that rivaled hers, he pulled her hand away. She dropped her hand by her side and backed away. He rubbed his neck and breathed in deeply.

"Problem solved." He stared at her, his expression unchanging.

"Who are you?" she asked him, backing away even further. She was slowly realizing that he wasn't who she thought he was.

"Don't look so scared, Dianna. If I wanted to harm you, I could have done so while you were sleeping." He walked past her and sat on her couch. "Let's talk".

"Something isn't right!" she mumbled; panic was slowly setting in but maybe talking was the only way out of this confusing moment. "Why aren't you running away from me?"

"Because you are beautiful when you're angry. Snakes everywhere!" He gestured his arms in a circular motion "hissing and seething. Pretty cute display," He stretched his legs out on her center table making himself comfortable. Dianna's snakes were snapping and hissing wildly around her face, ready to strike at any minute. She was a wild element and he called her...beautiful.

"Put your pets away!" he commanded her.

"You need to-- "

"STOP FUCKING AROUND, DIANNA!" he roared. He was on his feet, his skin had changed to a silvery scaly coat, his fangs were dripping with saliva. Her snakes had recoiled submissively, and she fell backward. He walked over to her and lifted her chin as he looked down at her.

"What? You thought you were the only one?" His eyes hadn't changed to slits from the sunlight. He took out his contacts and she saw them. His pupils had constricted like hers. She covered her mouth with trembling hands.

"But there are no-- "

"Men! Is that what your mother told you?" He went back to the couch and his features began to return to normal just as quickly as he had changed. "I bet she also told you to remain in hiding, the way you've been doing all these years". He sat down. "I didn't mean to scare you," he said eyeing her apologetically. She calmed. Her hair began to return to normal and her fangs retracted.

"It's okay," she said, regaining her composure. She slowly walked over to the couch and sat a little distance from him making sure there was just enough space in case he did anything rash.

"Don't be shy now, not after last night." He smirked. He reached over to touch her hand resting on the couch, but she pulled away.

"Did you know…about me?" she asked.

"I had an inkling, but I wasn't sure." He closed the space between them. "I had to be sure."

"What gave me away?"

He gave her an endearing smile. "Your eyes. Your eyes, Dianna. They always give you away. They gave you away last night too." She winced. As far as she could remember, she was giving everything away, but it was worth every moment. She smiled at the memory. He was watching her closely. "It's really hard to hide who you are around any of us." Dianna stared innocently at him. He had said 'us' which made her a little hopeful about meeting others like her. "Want to go on a trip with me today? I have some folks I want you to meet."

"Wait! I have so many questions."

"I know you do. Get dressed!" he said to her patiently. "I'm sure I have the answers you are looking for."

***

On their drive to God knows where, Dianna was pensive, her mind was racing. It was all so much to take in. Her mother either lied to her or was dead wrong about their kind. There were others and there were men…at least there was Drax Ashton.

"How old are you really?" she asked him.

"Seventy-four."

She looked him over carefully. "Shouldn't you look older?" she asked him.

"Trust me. I'm going to look this way for a very long time." He looked at her like a teacher schooling a student. "We are alike in some way but I'm also different from you."

"How so?" She was perplexed.

"I'm an original," he said to her casually.

"A what?" she said with some resentment. She wondered if this was some type of hierarchy bullshit.

Drax laughed. "Relax, Dianna, it's not what you think. Both my parents are pure breeds. They are originals; therefore, I am an original." Dianna couldn't believe what she was hearing. *Pure-breeds, originals*...she gathered that she probably didn't know even a small percentage of what she needed to know.

"You're a half breed," he offered. "Your dad is human and your mom, well she is like you. Naturalistic eugenics, you could say."

"What do you mean?" she pushed. "How do you know I'm not a pure-breed...like you?"

"Your lineage and others have been diluting their blood for years, thinking this was the only way." He caressed her face. "I know because your traits are limited." She knew this wasn't something she could grasp in a passing conversation and a lot of the things he said was going over her head.

"The only way for what?"

"To safeguard themselves from extinction," he said staring at her, gaging her reaction. She stared back wondering if there was a speck of truth in what he said. "But it only weakens you. You can only live up to 250 years. 300 if you are lucky," he explained.

"And you?"

He refocused his attention on the almost empty road before announcing, "Up to 1000 years!"

Dianna was floored. She thought her torment was unforgiving and cruel but as it turned out, the gods were merciful. What she thought was a curse was an actual blessing. She didn't have to live as long as the purebloods...pure breeds whatever. She laughed at the thought that she had actually dodged a bullet. "Shit! And I thought I was cursed," she retorted. "You make being a half breed sound like bad thing. At least I won't be trapped in this existentialistic hell for 1000 years!" she spat with pure disdain as she stared dreamily out the window.

He weighed her words. "I'm guessing you don't like who you are?" he said giving voice to her self-loathing.

"Do you? By the way, you mean what we are. We are freaks. We are never going to be normal or accepted. And worst, we are going to be subjected to human experiments once they figure out, we exist."

"THEY already know we exist...but let's leave that for another discussion." His voice was soothing and deep. She looked at him, studying his youthful face. Had she not seen him transformed before her very eyes, she would have never believed he was...like her. Her heart skipped a beat. She wished she could deny it, but her heart swelled with emotions. For the first time since she was born, aside from her mother, she had someone that could relate to her...understand her.

"What are we?" she asked, eliciting a smile from him.

"You, my beautiful half-breed princess, are a Nagalian." She let the information soak in. *Not Medusa, not a reptilian, not an alien.* She was Nagalian. There was actually a name for her. She embraced the inner peace that washed over her. Her origin surpassed that of fearful women raising their daughters in secrecy and shame. The highway they were driving on had narrowed into a two-lane empty road. The landscape changed from the scenic city to mountainous terrain. She wondered where he was taking her. She turned to see him gazing at her.

"It's going to be okay. You can let your hair out, literally. Be who you truly are around me." She gave him a half-smile. He touched her hair, and it came to life. Her snakes answered his call as they slowly wrapped themselves around his hand and wrist as if he was their master. She was completely enthralled and flummoxed by the fact that they didn't attack him.

"How are you doing that?" It was all so strange to her. He was so strange...*but inviting.*

"I'd like to think I can charm both women and snakes," he joked. It was good to finally meet a man...*Nagalian,* she corrected herself, that wouldn't run away from her, not that she gave the others a chance to run. She never revealed herself to anyone like this. He pulled his hand away and her snakes limped with disappointment, a disappointment she shared. She liked him playing with her snakes and her other parts. She smirked.

"We'll be there soon," he mentioned to her.

They had sex last night and this morning he figured out who she was, but she honestly didn't know what would happen next? Would they go back to a normal client-contractor relationship? Would they be friends…lovers? She wouldn't push it. She would be okay either way. She still had the memory of his mouth on her, his body moving in sync with hers as he drove her to the edge time and time again. That glorious memory would be lodged in her mind decades and possibly centuries from now.

Chapter 4

"Drax, oh my goodness! You're here. Why didn't you tell us you were coming?" The woman who appeared to be in her mid-40s came over to where we stood in the foyer, with quick steps to hug him. She was wearing a thick white robe and house slippers, a towel wrapped around her head to dry her hair.

"I'm sorry, mom. This was sort of a last-minute decision. I want you and dad to meet, Dianna." The woman looked at her.

"Hi!" Dianna waved shyly.

"She's the company's video editor and she's also one of us." His mother's eyes widened.

"A Nagalian?"

"Well, yeah. Technically, she's a half breed." Why did that make her feel inadequate all of a sudden?

"Oh, Drax. We don't use that language to describe our brothers and sisters. She's one of us. Nice to meet you, Dianna." She hugged Dianna warmly. Just then, Drax's father came out with a large mug in one hand and the newspaper in the other. They looked like typical parents. She couldn't tell that they were anything like her. She was marked by green streaks, green nails, and slitting pupils, all of which were things she couldn't hide, especially during the day.

"Son, dropping by?" his father asked raising a quizzical eyebrow at Drax, then his eyes lingered on Dianna. "Who is this?"

"Marvin, this is Dianna. She is one of us," Drax's mother explained.

"Pleasure, Dianna. I can already tell that it must be difficult to blend in," he said looking at her hair and eyes.

"I don't usually come out during daylight. I think I have a few people convinced that I am a vampire." They erupted in laughter.

"Far from it," Marvin chuckled.

"I thought she would appreciate being around her kind for a change," Drax said graciously.

"Well, let me get dressed so we can get acquainted then," Drax's mom said sweetly. This was a good start.

"Are you hungry, Dianna? Do you need anything to drink?" Marvin asked, his show of hospitality was endearing.

"We haven't eaten. I'm starving as well," Drax chimed in.

"I'll take care of it," his dad responded then disappeared leaving both Drax and Dianna alone.

"Is he going to cook breakfast?" Dianna asked curiously staring in Marvin's direction. Drax laughed.

"Don't be ridiculous, Dianna." He then led her to the living room. It was oversized and extravagant. Like a drug dealer's dream house.

"Make yourself comfortable," he instructed her. She sat awkwardly looking around.

"Do you like it?" he said observing her awe.

"It's not bad. You guys have done quite well for yourselves."

Drax smiled. "I would say we did more than well for ourselves but that's not why I brought you here. You had questions and we have answers." Just then, Drax's mother came waltzing in, wearing what appeared to be tennis clothes, with a sweater tied around her shoulders and a white pleated skirt that stopped at her knees. She sat on the other end of the couch smiling brightly. Dianna felt as if she had stepped into a sitcom of the 'Fresh Prince of Belaire'. They almost seemed too good to be true.

"Um, okay. How did we get here? On Earth," she asked naively.

"You think we are aliens?" Drax said giving her a serious look. Dianna felt foolish but it was a serious question she had. How could they even be from the same planet as these humans? Drax's mother laughed delicately.

"You must be listening to those reptilian conspiracy stories," she joked. They were so casual about their reality as if they belonged here, just like anyone else. She didn't share that false sense of comfort.

"I didn't have much to go by. My mother didn't seem to know much herself. I narrowed it down to either aliens or splicing of human DNA."

It was Drax's turn to laugh. "Well, technically you are spliced with human DNA," Drax joked. "We aren't that different from humans though. Their race and our race were created the same way, only by different Gods." Dianna looked at them both incredulously.

"Gods, you say?" She was right. They were too good to be true. The family was nuts and may even be occultists. Dianna flung her head back and breathed in deeply. "Okay. I guess this is where we end the conversation," Dianna said getting up.

"Sit down, Dianna," Drax commanded her. She didn't want to admit it, but she was a little afraid of him, which was strange since she wasn't afraid of many things, not even death but Drax was clearly a hundred times more powerful than she was and could easily overpower her. "Just because you don't believe something doesn't make it any less true. Listen to us," he told her.

"I just don't believe in polytheism and myths, Drax. The next thing you are going to tell me is that Medusa is real," she fired back.

"You've been hiding all your life, Dianna. It wouldn't hurt to hear what we have to tell you." She realized that he was right, she wouldn't lose anything. She may be more convinced that they've lost their marbles, but she wouldn't lose anything. She sat down.

"Okay. I'm all ears," she conceded trying not to be disrespectful even though every bone in her body was rattling with skepticism.

"So, these Gods. They came together and created creatures in their images. Humans, Nagalians...others."

"Others?" *Great, there are more freaks among us! She thought to herself.* She sighed. "Go on." It was his mother that continued.

"We were all beautiful and powerful in our own right. We were all perfect according to our makers, but we all lacked something the other beings had. The humans had numbers. They reproduced quickly and spread across the globe, settling in different places and thriving. Our kind didn't thrive so well. Plagued by fertility issues, we couldn't reproduce as quickly but we lived longer, we were stronger, physically dominant, able to shape shift and roam the Earth as man or beast. The humans saw this as a threat and before we realized it, they had learned the secrets of our weakness and started hunting us down wherever we gathered. Killing the men, capturing and weakening the women by raping and reproducing with them."

"Why didn't the Gods do something?" Dianna's words were dripping with sarcasm.

"The same reason good people die; bad people get away with immoral deeds and innocent children are harmed. Free will, character flaws and life encompassing all that's good and evil," Drax supplied sternly. She could tell she was getting on his nerves.

"Outside of reproductive issues, I assume we have no other weaknesses. I don't know if you guys notice but nothing can kill us," she said to them. She wondered fleetingly about letting them know that she tried to kill herself a few times but decided against it. That wasn't really a dinner table topic.

"Almost nothing, Dianna. There is a type of chemical if you will, capable of destroying every living cell in our body within a matter of hours," his mother explained.

"A chemical? What is it called? How can I --errr-- we access it?"

"Apoptosyde. We have samples," Drax told her unknowing of her devious thoughts. Dianna started scheming. This was it. This was the option of instantly choosing sudden death...well more like lingering death if it took hours to take effect. Drax dragged her from her suicidal thoughts.

"We have dwindled down to maybe 1000 pure-breed Nagalians remaining in the world. You can say we're sort of endangered. All the other kinds of beings were slaughtered by humans. The few Nagalians that remained, majority women, a few men, were so scattered, there was no unity among us. We were all left to our own devices, left to figure our way out. The women decided the best option was to assimilate by becoming as human as possible."

"Like my mother. What was different about you guys? She hadn't noticed Drax's dad walking in and having a seat.

"We were lucky. We were a part of the monarchy. We had wealth and so could buy our safety, immunity within society. If it's one thing the humans loved more than slaughtering and pillaging, is wealth and power."

"Which is why they slaughter and pillage," Marvin chuckled to himself. He sipped some coffee then as if it were an afterthought. "Alice is going to make something quick for you guys to eat."

"Thank you, Mr. Ashton," Dianna responded. *Who the hell is Alice?* Dianna thought fleetingly to herself. She didn't realize she had a confused expression on her face.

"Calling me by first name is completely acceptable, please," Marvin told her. "And Alice is our household associate." Dianna nodded...clearly *you meant your maid, Mr. Ashton,* she thought to herself, amused at his political correctness. But her attention was once again submerged in the free history lesson she was getting when Drax started speaking.

"Things and times have changed but we kept our lineage going ... and pure. We made sure we had the right connections to ensure our survival. Being from a monarchy means little and nothing to people of today but we've still managed to keep our wealth and maintained some of our status," Drax grinned.

"Our son is one of the few younger males, especially one that leads such a public life. The others are much older, tired. Worn out. Hiding... like you," Drax's mother informed Dianna. It was a sad story. It didn't make her feel any more powerful, any more belonged than she hoped she would but at least she knew now. *On the bright side, there was a way out...a way to end it,* Dianna mused inside her brain.

"Are you up for a tour?" Drax asked her, seeping into her thoughts once more. He stood up in front of her and extended his hand to her. Dianna hesitated.

Sometimes she wished he wasn't such a gentleman. She looked shyly at Drax's parents who she was sure were getting ideas by now.

Drax's mother lifted an assessing brow. "We'll check on you both later," she said getting up and casting hints to Marvin.

"But I just got here," Marvin said staring back at Drax's mom in protest with his unfinished mug of coffee.

"Story time is over, Marvin! Let's go!" Her tone was firm but loving.

After they walked out, Drax led Dianna by the hand down the passage to a staircase leading to an enormous underground cellar of the house. As they walked down the dark staircase, Dianna held on tightly to the banister watching each step. It was dim and seemed to go on forever. She stared at Drax's broad shoulders as he guided her. They were the same yet so different. He was proud of his heritage, proud of his genetical purity, saw power in his kind while she only saw despair. She could understand his empowerment and privilege but for her, the damage was rooted and nothing they told her today could change her attitude overnight.

A light flickered on once they arrived at the bottom of the stairs and what Dianna saw left her speechless. Relics, armor, old weaponry, cases and cases of artifacts, shelves of old dusty books. She slowly walked over to the shelf to her right and ran her index finger along the spine of a large book that caught her attention. She pulled it out. It was an encyclopedia of sorts, written in an old likely dead language. "She looked up from the book to Drax's watchful eyes. "Do you understand this language?"

He scoffed. "Yeah, right. Maybe a few words like 'Nagalian'." She laughed at his light humor. As she flipped through the pages, her eyes darted over the images of snake-like humans. Some looked like her, others looked like Drax and there were so many more other forms.

"What determines our form?" she asked him curiously.

"Our gene pool. It's like pulling straws sometimes. We take what we get."

"I look like my mother and my mother looks like her mother," Dianna countered. It didn't seem that random to her.

"Your gene pool isn't really much to speak of... considering." Dianna winced.

"Careful. I have feelings," she chucked.

"I didn't mean it like that."

"Yes, you did. You've been doing it all day." She sneered and gave him a sideway glance. She returned the book back to its place. She pushed past him to continue her browsing. "Why are you telling me all of this?"

"You wouldn't be the first. Plus, you seem a little ... lost." She sensed his pity. She was lost. She was pretty much an alcoholic, workaholic, suicidal recluse. She couldn't shake the darkness that followed her everywhere, even here. She walked over to a small refrigerator. She looked inside. There she saw beakers, vials...a claw. She stared at him questioningly.

"Experimental purposes."

"For what?"

"An antidote."

"For the Apoptosyde?"

He nodded and then reached for a large beaker. It had a transparent red substance inside. He held it in front of her face. "It doesn't kill you right away but trust me, you will wish it did. The pain is excruciating."

"Have you ever tried to...y'know, to die?" she asked him.

"I'm digging the longevity thing. You?"

Dianna chose to let her silence speak for her. His eyes looked at her with sympathy again. He touched her face.

"You shouldn't do that," he told her. She backed away.

"Forget I even asked you!" He clearly didn't understand, and she wasn't going to explain herself. There were other vials in the refrigerator. She pretended to be preoccupied with the artifacts as she thought of ways to get her hands on one. She leisurely touched and inspected other items in the room. It was literally a treasure trove of Nagalian heritage. She imagined warriors, kings, and queens in their eras. Happy beings with normal lives, far removed from how Nagalians lived today. She thought of a way to distract him. She highly doubted he would leave her alone in the cellar unless… She laid eyes on a large ax-like weapon. She quickly walked over to it and picked it up.

"Careful!" he said walking worriedly over to where she was standing. She ran her hand over the sharp blade carelessly slicing her hand open. She dropped the weapon in pain, and it clanged noisily on the hard cement floor.

"Shit!" she yelled holding her hand to her stomach as she doubled over.

"What did you do? Let me see it." She showed him her bloody hand and he grimaced.

"It hurts pretty bad," she told him, and she wasn't lying. Her skin paled as sweat poured from her face. He pulled a chair and made her sit on it.

"I'll be right back," he said, completely distracted by her wound. He ran up the stairs and out of sight. Checking furtively to make sure the coast was clear, she got up quickly and ran to the refrigerator. She didn't want them to notice anything missing so she grabbed an empty beaker from the top of the fridge and awkwardly poured a little of the red substance in the narrow container. She closed it and shoved it deep inside her front pocket before she noticed blood dripping onto the floor. She quickly stripped off her white oversized t-shirt, showing her skin-colored sports bra underneath and wiped up any evidence of blood, then used the shirt to wrap her hand. It would heal soon. She wasn't worried about it. She returned to the chair and waited for him to return. He seemed to be taking a while. She decided to go look for him. She returned to the living room area and was about to call his name when she heard hushed speaking. He was speaking to his parents in the kitchen. She walked over and listened.

"Are you guys dating?"

"No, not really," Drax responded.

"We like her," his dad said.

"Yes, but not for you, honey," Drax's mother lectured. "Remember, you're Full Nagalian."

"I know. You guys are thinking too far ahead."

"I don't think so, Drax. I can tell that you are already attached." Dianna felt a sickening feeling in her stomach.

"I'm not talking about this right now!" Drax snapped at them, cutting the conversation short. Dianna tiptoed with super speed back to the hallway. She saw him coming toward her with some type of bag. As he got closer, she could tell it was a first aid kit.

"I'm okay, Drax. I think it's already healing," she assured him. He looked at the shirt she had turned into a makeshift bandage. It was soaked. She had cut herself deeper than she intended to. He unwrapped the shirt in silence and she stared at him as he looked at her wound.

"You did a number on yourself," he said to her. "But the bleeding has slowed down. I'll put some clean bandage on it. You should be fine within an hour or so." He looked up at her and caught her staring. She looked away.

"I have something for you," he said to her. "Give me your other hand."

She instinctively gave it to him out of curiosity. He placed a tiny, light blue case in the middle of her palm. "What's this?" she said, looking from the object to him.

"Open it." She quickly did and saw that inside, there were dark green contacts. "I tried to get a color that closely matched the natural color of your eyes."

"Wow! Do you have these just lying around or something?"

"My mom does."

"I've tried contacts before. They irritate my eyes," she complained.

"Not these. They are specialized for us. Try them," he implored her. She inspected them closely. They looked really thin compared to the ones that she tried. They were moist and looked organic. She rubbed one between her index finger and her thumb. It felt like a thin delicate membrane with a smooth texture. She awkwardly tried to put one in her eye, considering that she didn't have much experience doing it and her other hand was

54

incapacitated. Drax realized her difficulty and assisted her. His face was so close to hers that she could see the pores on his skin as he delicately inserted the contacts. They naturally molded to the curve of her eyeball. It felt as if she wasn't wearing a thing. "Now you don't have to go inside buildings wearing oversized sunglasses." She laughed at the memory he conjured up of her when she was at his firm that crazy morning. "These will make your life a lot easier." Her eyes were so reactive to light, they were always a tell-tale sign. She was pretty sure these would make a world of a difference. "How do they feel?"

"Not too uncomfortable." She smiled up at him, grateful for the little hack.

He smirked. "Told you so," he teased her affectionately. His face was still extremely close to hers and she was getting turned on. *No! Fight it!* She admonished herself. *It was no use getting further entangled.* Her smile disappeared and she closed the tiny box and placed it in one of her back pockets. She knew it would come in handy when she needed to store her new contacts safely away later. "You shouldn't get *attached*," she scolded gently, repeating the gutting words spoken earlier. His smile dissipated as well. He refocused on her wound. He wrapped the gaping slit and then he took off his shirt and covered her body.

"You overheard my parents, huh?" he said to her.

"I didn't mean to," she told him.

"It's complicated," he told her.

"I get it," she said but she was ready to leave. It was just another reminder that she was somewhere stuck in the middle. She couldn't assimilate into the human world and she wasn't good enough for his world either.

"It's a survival thing but-- " it was obvious that he wanted to explain but she placed her finger over his lips to silence him.

"It's not you. It's me," she winked playfully letting him off the hook. It wasn't as if he had promised her the universe and failed to deliver. It was simply one beautiful night...*that was all...but why was she hurting?* She thought about the beaker of Apoptosyde in her pocket. By tomorrow she might not be here anyway. She found solace in the thought. Who would miss her? *Not a damn soul!*

Chapter 5

"About earlier--"

"Don't worry, Drax. I know why having a child with another pure breed is important to your family...to you," she told him while looking out the window of his car as he drove her back to her apartment. She didn't need a long dragged out explanation. He practically said they were endangered and as exclusive, primitive and ritualistic as it sounded, they had to reproduce with their own kind, or they would essentially die out. She snuck a glance at him. He looked straight ahead but she could tell his mind was elsewhere.

"I'm drawn to you and I don't know why?"

"The sex...was mind-blowing," she said almost fishing for a compliment.

He grinned. "Agreed, but even before that. I had to know who you were and what you were about. I couldn't dismiss you from my mind. I tried and I just came back around to the thought of you." Dianna was affected by his words, but it wasn't enough to change her mind. Tonight, was the night. She was going to drink some Vodka, lay in her tub, drink the Apoptosyde and wait for death to come.

"You're sweet but you have your obligations, Drax. You know this," she reminded him like an overbearing mother. He parked the car outside of her apartment building. "Let's get one thing straight though. Until I marry or have kids, I screw ...and care about whoever I want, whenever I want." She could see in his eyes that he wanted more. He leaned over and kissed her. The weight of him pushing her against the car door made her gently brace her hand against his chest. She wanted to tell him to stop but instead found herself responding to him, just like her snakes did on the ride to his parents. It was as automatic as the attraction between two unlike poles of a magnet. Whenever he summoned, she answered. His hand ran along the side of her arm, then down to her hip area. She felt a pause from him. He pulled away and looked down on her jeans where he saw the imprint of the beaker.

"What's this?" he asked her, feeling the shape of the small beaker in her front pocket. She realized in hindsight that it was stupid to put it in her front pocket. She pushed him away.

"It's nothing," she said opening the car door before he could figure out her plans to end her life. She stepped quickly out of the car; she wasn't even concerned about the traffic as she crossed to the other side to get to her place.

"Dianna!" he shouted after her. He was trailing her and actually gaining on her. She picked up her speed running up to the entrance of her apartment building.

"Leave me alone, Drax!" And before she knew it, he was right behind her and violently pulling the beaker from her pocket, roughing her up a bit. Once he saw that it was the Apoptosyde, he glared at her with such rage, she turned away from him...ashamed.

"What were you going to do with this?" she remained silent. He turned her around to face him.

"ANSWER ME!" he barked, his eyes becoming dark under his contacts, and she thought he was going to change into his true form, but he didn't.

"You don't understand. You might want this mockery of a life, but I don't. No one should have to live like this. I HATE IT!" she told him. "Unlike you, I don't want to continue my 'lineage'." She made air quotes as she said the word 'lineage' with disgust.

"So, you were just going to exterminate yourself?" he responded rhetorically. He opened the beaker and poured the content out on the ground in front of her. She watched as the red substance fizzled then vaporized on the ground. "This is what you do with the information I give you." He leaned closer to her ear. "You're weak," he said in a controlled whisper, "and unworthy". He threw the beaker and it shattered loudly against the red-bricked wall of her apartment building. Dianna flinched from the sound; her face was drenched with tears.

"I'm sorry," she said lamely. He stared at her with a distant and cold look in his eyes and then left her standing alone as he headed back to his car.

"I HATE MYSELF!" she shouted at him, then fell against the rough wall as she sobbed. She heard him drive away and she cried some more before she finally decided to go inside. She regretted her actions, mostly because she knew Drax felt betrayed. She wished she could make him understand anything was better than being a half-breed Nagalian.

***

She hadn't heard from him in a month. Susanne had sent over the new contract for her to sign which was a good indication that he still wanted her to work for him, but she hadn't signed it yet. She also decided to wait before accepting any more workload from his company. Just as Drax had predicted, another company had made an offer and she was thinking of accepting it. Drax's offer was better, but she couldn't face him again, not after the way she took advantage of his openness. She was convinced he was disgusted by her. She wouldn't be surprised if he had decided to eradicate her from his memory.

However, life was looking better. With the contacts that Drax had given her, she braved the outside world a little more. She even adopted a café on her block where she drank her coffee while soaking up the morning sun on the terrace. She was able to think about a lot of things. Her mother...her father. Even though she was sure he had died by now, she wanted to know more about her human side. She decided that she would give her mom a visit and also take a break from her life in Las Vegas. She took out her phone and rang the last known number she had for her mom.

"Hello!" Her mother's voice sounded frantic as if she couldn't believe Dianna was calling.

"Hi, mom," Dianna responded calmly. She heard a gasp, then sniffles.

"I'm so happy to hear your voice. Are you okay?"

"I'm ok."

"Are you still angry with me?" Dianna allowed her silence to respond. "Why?" her mother continued. "Are you still punishing me for giving birth to you?"

"Mom, just...don't." She pinched her nose bridge squeezing her eyes shut to get a handle on her stress level. "I wanted to see you this weekend," Dianna told her.

"Really? Of course!" her mother stated excitedly. "Dianna...I-- I miss you," her mom said, her words hesitant. Dianna's rejection of her really hurt her and she tried to heal the divide every chance she got but she couldn't. Dianna wouldn't allow it. She was right, it was punishment for bringing her into this world, for raising her in isolation and for leaving her to die alone and sad when the time came.

"I'm taking a flight to Alaska; can you pick me up at the airport?"

Her mother was silent. Then she finally spoke again. "Why are you visiting?"

"Something has come up...and we need to talk about it."

"In person?"

"Yes."

"Okay. Have you already booked the ticket?"

"Not yet but I will send you the inform--" Dianna spotted Eric inside the café waiting in line to purchase his coffee. "Shit!" she said turning her back to him. She lived on the other side of town from his apartment, it was certainly strange seeing him here.

"Hello!" her mom responded. "Is everything, okay?"

"I can't talk now, Mom, but I'll let you know my arrival time. Bye." She hung up the phone and grabbed her coffee. She sprinted to the door as quickly as she could before he spotted her. She didn't want to talk to him. He was very shrewd and would figure out in no time that she had sex with Drax. She didn't know how long she could keep herself under the radar from her new friends. She had been avoiding their calls and had tons of voicemail from both him and Susanne. It made her realize that if Drax wanted to call her, he could have gotten her number from them. The thought made her heart ache. *You violated his trust, what did you expect?* came the voice in her head. Once she was outside the café, she started to briskly walk down the sidewalk. She heard running footsteps behind her. Then heavy panting.

"Damn, you're quick!" She heard him say behind her as he huffed out of breath. "Hold up!" She turned around.

"Eric! Hi!" she said with exaggerated cheerfulness.

"Stop faking with me! I know you saw me in the cafe?" Dianna slumped her shoulders and let out a sigh of surrender. "What's going on with you? Why are you avoiding your friends?" She didn't expect him to use the word *friends*. It was...sweet.

"I got caught up, Eric."

"With Drax?" He sucked his teeth unsurprised. "That was bound to happen sooner or later, honey. You weren't fooling anyone."

"I'm a horny slut!" she joked. Eric laughed at her.

"Anyway, I don't care about that. Why aren't you answering work calls. You can't just disappear off the grid like that." *But I could,* Dianna mused to herself. She could disappear from Las Vegas and no one would be able to find her. She was such an expert at disappearing *off the grid* she could make money teaching her methods. "Or are we just not worth the trouble?" Eric said, prompting her for a response. Dianna hadn't realized she spaced out for a few seconds.

"That's not it. I told him I would sign the contract."

"That's good news." He read her doubt, "...or not. Did you change your mind?"

She grimaced. "Another company offered me a contract." He pinched her arm painfully.

"Ow!" she howled.

"Is this the part where I'm supposed to give you a long speech to convince you to stick with us? Because if you don't, that's fucking bullshit!" he said candidly.

"I think I've ruined my professional relationship with the firm."

"Is the other company offering you more money?"

"No! But it's not about the money."

Eric closed his eyes and waved his hand dismissively as if he was mentally trying to block her words out, "Look! Just think it over. It looks like things got a little complicated between you and Drax, but if it's one thing I am positive about is Drax is a good businessman. He won't let personal issues create conflict at work. Plus, I'm sure if it gets too hard for you to work at the office, he'll let you work from home but don't make a bad decision because you made a previous bad decision to have sex with him."

Dianna swirled her coffee with a contemplative expression on her face, knowing it was a lot more complicated than what he thought. "I'll think about it, but I have to go. I'm going to be out of town for a bit."

"Where?"

"Family out of state," she said cryptically.

"Okay. You don't want to tell me. I can take a hint. Enjoy your trip and call me as soon as you get back." He rubbed her arm comfortingly. "Simon was worried about you. You know you're his little pet."

Dianna laughed. "I'll call him later," Dianna promised. Eric hugged her, then he walked back to the cafe. She continued her path to where her motorcycle was parked by a parking meter. She poured out the remainder of her coffee and threw the cup in a nearby trash can. She slipped a few quarters in the meter, then jumped on her motorcycle and rode away thinking about her trip to Alaska.

***

"You look amazing sweetie. I guess your new life agrees with you," her mom, Irene, smiled sweetly after receiving a stiff hug from Dianna.

"Thank you. You look great too, for 150," Dianna demeaned her.

"That was a little mean," her mom said giving her a half smile, only too happy they were on speaking terms. She was wearing a tie-and-dye t-shirt that was a tad too big over a long shapeless jeans skirt that stopped at her ankles. A pair of pink Nike tennis shoes with a white baseball cap. It was obvious that her mother favored practicality over good fashion sense unlike her, who sported who usual brown leather jacket along with a knee length beige sweater dress and knee length boots. Irene lifted one of Dianna's suitcases and led her to the parking lot. Dianna grabbed the other and followed her. They found the red '95 Nissan Maxima quickly and placed the suitcases in the trunk. They both got into the car and started their trip to Irene's home.

"Are you staying long?"

"I'm thinking about it. I need to get away for a while," Dianna told her mom.

"Are you pregnant?"

Dianna felt revulsion at the thought. "Hell no! You know better than to ask me that," she said to her mom. Irene looked a little embarrassed.

"Just checking. Usually, running away to an isolated place is something we do when we're pregnant," her mom explained in her maternal way with a knowing smile on her face.

"We? You mean the half Nagalians," Dianna shot back. Her mom's smile faded as her eyes remained locked on the road. Her seat was adjusted too high and too close to the steering wheel and she held the wheel with a death grip as if she was afraid to drive the car. "Why have you never told me anything about our kind?"

"I don't know much myself, Dianna. I told you that," her mom said looking at the long distance ahead. "It's just our way."

"Mom, it's your way. You and grandma decided this was the way," Dianna said angrily. She looked out the window at the lush green Alaskan landscape. "I met another Nagalian." Dianna's mom turned her head sharply.

"Are you sure?" her mother asked flabbergasted.

Dianna scoffed. "Oh, I'm sure. I slept with him." Irene gasped and then covered her mouth.

"How is that possible, there are no-- "

"Men. That's what I said to him, then he showed me his Nagalian form. He scared the shit out of me!" Dianna said remembering her encounter. After about forty-five minutes of driving, Irene turned off on a lonely unpaved road and finally pulled up to a small house at the dead end. It was the only house on the road.

"Go figure," Dianna said to herself. They both got out of the car and got the things from the trunk. They walked in solemnity to the house. When they entered the house, Dianna was a little dismayed by the small, tight space, hideous floral wallpaper and worn out hardwood floor, but checked her snobbery. Her mom was probably struggling financially. It's not as if she had anyone to help her and she was pretty sure whatever job she had was barely paying the bills. She felt some guilt for not at least helping her when she could more than afford to. Irene brought her to a room. It was the only bedroom in the tiny house... needless to say, it was the size of a matchbox. Her queen size bed at her apartment certainly wouldn't fit. Dianna paused before entering.

"Is this your room?" Dianna asked.

"Yes, but it's okay. You can have it for as long as you need."

"No mom, I'll sleep on the couch," Dianna said graciously. Irene dropped the suitcase and cupped her daughter's beautiful face. She smiled warmly.

"Please take my room, sweetie. Let me do something to make YOU happy." She could see the wrinkles slightly creasing her mother's pale skin. Her mother was white which gave her a clue that her father was African American since she was mixed. They never talked about him...*literally never! She* sighed deeply at the frustration that was her life.

"Okay," Dianna responded feeling the effects of her long trip. She stepped into the room which was very neat and cozy. She saw a few pictures of her and her mother in separate locations around the room and there was a television. She placed her suitcase on the bed then turned to look at her mom. Her mother was putting away the other suitcase in the closet.

"Do you have any pictures of my father?"

"No."

"Nothing?"

Irene contemplated for a bit. "There's something." She reached for an old box in the closet and took it out from the top shelf once she found it. She walked over to Dianna and sat on the bed. She looked at Dianna, silently willing her to sit as well. Dianna sat slowly beside her. Her mother opened the box and took out an old folded piece of newspaper. She unfolded it and showed it to Dianna. It was an article of some type of protest or march with a picture of a group of marchers under it.

"This was during the civil rights movement in the 1960s." She pointed at a black man at the front of the march. His face was circled with a black marker. "This is your father." Dianna took the clipping and stared. The newspaper clipping was old, but she could still make out his features slightly. She may have looked like him, but she wasn't sure. "I really loved him," Irene told her.

"Did you tell him?"

"No. I was young and afraid. Experience had taught me that you live to regret such actions," Irene explained. There was speck of sadness in her eyes. "So, I did what I thought was best for us."

"Is he still alive?"

"I don't know."

"May I have this?" she asked her mom. Irene nodded and Dianna folded the paper and placed it carefully in her suitcase protecting a piece of herself. "What else do you know about the Nagalians?"

"Just old myths and folktales about Gods and our origin. Mumbo Jumbo," Irene said fanning her hand dismissively.

"It's not mumbo jumbo, mom. Drax seems to think all this shit is our true origin."

"We'll never know for sure, will we? No God has ever spoken to me about it," Dianna had to agree with her mother.

"So, this Drax. Is he your boyfriend?"

Dianna got up and decided to start unpacking her things. "I don't want to talk about him."

Irene assessed her daughter. "What did he do?"

"He didn't do anything except save me from myself, literally."

"What does that mean?" her mother demanded. Irene knew Dianna's little secret. Growing up, she caught her a few times in the bathroom slicing her wrist. Dianna stared resentfully at Irene and her anger came back in full force.

"It means I tried to kill myself for the hundredth time!" Dianna yelled.

"Why do you do that? YOU CAN'T!"

"Actually mom, as it turns out, I can!" She sneered as she thought back to the moment Drax drained the Apoptosyde out of the beaker. "...but he stopped me," she said in a low sad voice. Irene hung her head, distressed by what she was hearing. This only served to enrage Dianna even further. "Disgusting isn't it?" She felt suffocated by her emotions. "I'm sorry I'm not enamored with this mystical lifestyle!" Venom was in her eyes as her body started to awaken to her other form. Irene started sobbing. But the sight of her mother's tears was only adding fuel to a blazing fire. "Give me a fucking break!" Dianna said, storming out of the house with angry snakes hissing around her face, before she said something else, she would regret. She needed to take a long walk, so she could get a handle on her emotions and get away from her mother.

They always fought and Dianna always instigated the arguments, but so much resentment had built up over time, she couldn't avoid letting her mom have it. She didn't know where to go but figured all she needed to do was follow the path to the three-way ahead of her and something would reveal itself. Her boots stomped loudly as she neared the turn off. By the time she got there, she had calmed down quite a bit and her snakes had disappeared. She looked across the street and saw that there was a mechanic shop, a bar and a diner that she hadn't paid attention to driving in. She decided to go to the bar. It was evening and nearing her drinking hour. She had promised herself that she would stop drinking but this seemed a good night as any to relapse. Being stuck in the boondocks with her mom was beyond exhausting for her.

"Hey there," she turned to see a greasy looking old white guy staring at her from inside a rundown car at the mechanic shop. She guessed he was the mechanic that worked there. She thought he was catcalling her, "buzz off creep!" she mumbled to herself and kept walking as she proceeded to ignore him.

"Are you walking from Irene's house? Did something happen there?" he said a little louder. Dianna stopped in her tracks. She looked at the mechanic curiously as he exited the car. She couldn't take her eyes off his round beer belly.

"You know Irene?" she said, finally prying her eyes away from his engorged stomach to look at his concerned expression.

"You could say that, yeah. Is she okay?"

"We had a fight," Dianna divulged, offering a reason for why she was out alone walking in a place she barely knew.

"Sorry to hear that. I just wanted to make sure she was okay."

Dianna stared at him a little longer and then snickered as she realized he wasn't just being nosy. "You got the hots for 'Irene'?" Dianna said mockingly making air quotes with her fingers. She found it a little hilarious.

"What makes you say that?" He then conceded. "Is it that obvious?" he said a little embarrassed.

"To me, yeah". Dianna was amused. Despite his dirty blue overalls, he looked a little vulnerable. *Poor guy,* Dianna thought to herself. She decided to be nice to him. "I'm her daughter, Dianna."

"Nice to meet you!" he said walking towards her so he could shake her hand. Dianna took one look at the black grime on his extended hand and shook her head.

"Oh, sorry. Got to get cleaned up," he said wiping his hand in a dirty rag which didn't help. "Are you headed to the bar?"

"Is it that obvious?" The mechanic smirked at her cleverness.

"Yeah, but you're going to be disappointed. It's closed today. The owner had an out of town emergency."

Dianna cursed, pulling her hair back in frustration. She really needed something to take off the edge.

"I got a beer and a chair if you want to join me," he offered. Dianna had warmed up to him a little in that short time and she desperately needed a drink. She decided it wouldn't hurt to hang out with a quaint dirty fella'.

"Sorry I look so unpresentable. Wasn't expecting outsiders today." His statement made her think that outsiders visiting his part of the world must be a special occasion to him. He proceeded to drag two white, plastic chairs from the back of the garage placing them side by side. He then selected an ice-cold beer from the cooler and handed it to her.

"You hold on to that one," she said not wanting grease to transfer to her hands. She bent over the cooler and got her own bottle of beer. He sat in one of the chairs and waited for Dianna to sit in the other. She plopped herself in it, exhausted from her trip combined with her little disagreement with her mother. She quickly opened the beer with her teeth, watched as it fizzled, then she took a large gulp. It was weak in comparison to anything she preferred, but it would have to do. The mechanic watched her in amused curiosity. He took a bottle opener attached to his keys and lifted the beer cap off with ease which made Dianna feel a little silly. He took a long sip, then wiped his mouth with the back of his dirty hand.

"You don't visit her much, do you?" he probed.

"Our relationship is in a bad shape to put it simply," Dianna admitted.

"It happens." He took another sip of the beer. "I fixed her car a couple of times. She's struggling a bit, so I didn't charge her my usual fee." Dianna stared at the gravel as he spoke. "Not sure if you know but she works part-time at the diner. I don't think tips are so great there." Dianna hummed her response. "I tried asking her out a few times, but she turned me down."

Dianna gave him a hard look over. Then scoffed. "I guess you're never too old to date."

"Not when you're lonely," he responded. Dianna had to agree. "Could you put in a good word for me?" Dianna laughed loudly. He was so desperate. Her beer was finished so she rested the empty bottle on the ground, then she got up to leave.

"I never got your name."

"I'm sorry. It's Mack."

"I'll see what I can do, Mack," she said slapping him gently on the arm. "Guess I'll be seeing you. Thanks for the beer."

 "Do you want me to walk you back? It's gotten dark." Dianna looked up at the sky. The sun had completely set, and since it darkened early there, it was already black except for the light from the mechanic shop, the diner and the widely spaced out streetlights.

"I'm okay. Trust me, I can handle myself." She started walking away and he followed behind her. She was standing in the middle of the street when she turned around to let him know that his chivalry wasn't needed. Suddenly, she heard a horn blowing loudly and she turned to see a pick-up truck with blinding headlights speeding toward her. Before she could react, Mack had pushed her out of the way. She heard a loud banging sound as she fell on the other side of the gravel road. She had hit the ground hard and scraped her skin in different places. When she got over the shock, she got up to see where Mack was. The pickup truck had sped off. She heard moaning and she saw him rolling onto his side a little distance from her.

Dianna raced toward him. She gently rolled him onto his back. He moaned louder, letting her know he was in a lot of pain. It was obvious that he was in no shape to move. He was losing blood from a gash on his temple, and blood was also leaking from his mouth. When she touched his chest, he howled in pain. She didn't know if he would survive the trip to the hospital.

"Help me!" he gasped through uneven breaths. It horrified her to know he could die because of her. She needed to call her mom, but she didn't have her phone and she hadn't committed Irene's number to memory to call from Mack's phone.

"I have to get my mom. She used to be a nurse. Maybe she can help," she sobbed.

"Don't leave me! I think I'm dying, please!"

"I promise I'll be back," she assured him, resting her open palm on his chest. He coughed up more blood and she knew she had to move quickly. She picked herself up and ran as quickly as she could. The gravel crunched under her heavy shoes as she propelled herself closer and closer to her destination. When she finally got to the house, she banged violently on the door. Her mother came rushing to the door wide-eyed and terrified.

"What's the matter Dianna, you gave me a scare!"

"Mack got hit by a car," she spurted.

"Mack the mechanic?"

"Yes, I think he's dying. Help me save him!" Dianna's hair looked like poofy cotton candy because of her high-speed running.

"We can't save him, Dianna. Why didn't you call the police?"

"Mom, please. He doesn't have time. You have to do that blood transfusion thing you did with the jogger."

"Are you insane/! He will go running to the cops and they will capture us!" Irene whispered angrily as she pulled Dianna into the house.

"He's lying on the side of the road. Please! Don't let him die." Dianna was hunched over trying to catch her breath as she pointed in the direction of where Mack was waiting. She was sweaty and distraught and at that moment, something broke inside Irene. "He tried to save my life. It's my fault!" Dianna explained.

"Okay, okay. I'll get my stuff!" Irene went into the room and came rushing out with IV tubes and some medical needles visible from her large tote bag. "Let's take the car!"

After speeding back to Mack's exact location, they lifted him inside the house and Irene went to work.

"Help me find some type of pole to hang this," she said handing Dianna the IV tubing. She looked around the house. It smelled of diesel oil and old furniture. She found an old coat rack and brought it close enough to Mack so they could hang the tubing which made things less cumbersome.

"Don't want to move him too much," Irene said resting his head on an old dirty blanket that was close by. She tied the latex ribbon around his biceps and began instantly searching for a vein in his forearm. Mack's color had paled to a pasty white. It was obvious he would have died at the hospital or on his way because of the blood loss. Irene inserted the needle into his barely visible vein then tied the latex ribbon around her own arm, quickly inserting the other end of the tubing into hers. Then they waited. Dark red blood coursed its way through the narrow tube and began filling up the bag before continuing its journey through the second tube. Mack's breathing was so slow, at some moments, it looked as if he wasn't breathing at all. The blood finally reached his arm. Dianna dashed the tears from her face and looked with relief at her mother. She mouthed, "Thank you", then reached for her mom's hand to squeeze it. Irene smiled, happy that there was something she could do right to gain her daughter's respect. They both looked at Mack, whose color was slowly returning. He was still unconscious, but they knew he was going to be all right. His wounds would heal within a few hours and his body would renew itself.

Dianna thought about how strange it was that their blood type was compatible with humans. It worked like a serum, healing them even if they were on the verge of death. Humans would have a field day with that type of discovery. She knew if Mack told anyone about what they had done for him…it would end badly for them both.

"Are you okay?" Irene's movements now appeared to be lethargic probably from the blood transfusion process. She wiped sweat from her face with the back of her hand, leaving a streak of black grease on her forehead.

"Yeah, just thinking about what you said, about being captured." Dianna gently rubbed the dirty spot on her mother's forehead with her thumb, removing most of the grease. The small gesture made Irene cup her daughter's face before returning her attention to Mack.

"It's too late now," she said tilting her neck and rubbing her muscle. "Besides, it was worth it because you're no longer mad at me," her mom smiled, and Dianna returned her smile.

"Remember the jogger?" Her mother nodded. "It was the most miraculous thing I had ever seen. A person who was taking their last breaths suddenly healing right before my eyes...and you did that." She was 8 years old when it happened, and it stuck with her forever.

"This is my first time doing it since then," Irene shared. Just then, Mack stirred. He gave them a puzzled look, then became unconscious again.

"Should we leave him on the couch? Maybe he won't remember," Dianna suggested.

"I think it's the best plan we have," Irene said, removing the needle from her arm. "We'll wait until the remaining blood is inside his body, then we'll head out."

Mack was still unconscious by the time he received the last of the blood. They found another blanket and covered his body as he slept. They were relieved that they had saved his life but prayed that he wouldn't remember when he came to. They eventually left him alone in the house like two mercy angels in the middle of the night.

Chapter 6

"What do you think you'll find in Alabama? Your father is likely deceased and all we have left of him is a newspaper clipping," Irene said the next day as she washed the dishes.

"It's worth searching," Dianna countered.

"The entire state of Alabama?" her mother rebutted.

"I don't know, mom," Dianna said indifferently. "He was in Salma, right?"

"The march was in Salma and he was there for the protest," her mother corrected her. Irene grabbed a kitchen towel and dried the soapy water from her hands. "Hold on, I think I have something that might help." She went into her bedroom. Dianna heard things being moved around and drawers opening and closing so she waited a few minutes before deciding to check her phone. She had about fifteen missed calls from Susanne and none from Drax. This angered her. He didn't have her number, but he could've gotten it from Susanne...*if he cared.* There were also missed calls from Eric and Simon. Her only two friends right now. She had to get back to Las Vegas and face her life. She knew Drax wouldn't let her secret escape, after all, she was one of them, even if it was only by half relation. She didn't know why, but she didn't want to resort to her typical approach of uprooting her life and starting over. She wanted to fix things or at least try.

Her mother returned with something in her hand, as Dianna sat on the couch checking her emails on her phone. She handed the small square plastic card to Dianna. It was a driver's license for her father.

"Where did you get this?"

Irene's eyes gleamed with cunningness, "Memorabilia I stole from your father before I ran off."

His name, Jonathan Montague, was printed under his picture and it had his Alabama address on it. Dianna focused her attention on the man's face. This was a huge help. "And you didn't think to give me this first?" she said, carefully placing the driver's license inside her purse. She was relieved that she now had a specific place to start.

"I forgot about it," Irene shrugged and went back to washing dishes. "A thank you would be nice," she said placing the plates in the dishwasher. "Mack came by this morning when you were at the store."

"Really? What did he say?"

"That he knew something happened at his place and he wanted answers."

"What's the last thing he remembers?"

"Us standing over him with medical supplies."

"Shit! What did you say?"

"Nothing happened. He probably fell, hit his head and had a bad dream."

"Really? You couldn't fabricate something better than that?"

"He was accusing me; I said the first thing that came to my mind."

"He's on to us," Dianna stated with growing consternation.

"Well, let him drive himself crazy trying to figure it out!" Irene said.

"He likes you, y'know," Dianna told her.

"I'm not sure 'like' describes how he is feeling about me right now." They both laughed in unison. The deed was done, and moping wasn't going to undo the damage. Her mom joined her with a warm cup of tea in hand. She inhaled the strong aroma before sipping. Dianna wrinkled her nose recognizing the smell of Cerassee which seemed to be her mom's favorite herbal tea.

"That stuff is awful! Why do you insist on drinking it?" Dianna blurted out in disgust.

"Because of its health benefits. How do you think I maintain my girly figure and youthful glow?" Irene quipped. Her response caused Dianna to feel a rare sense of appreciation for her mother. It was weird that everything that happened in the past few months forced her to view her mom in a more humanly way, *half-humanly way to be exact.* Irene struggled to deal with a life she was dealt as well. It was likely she didn't want to get pregnant but chose to be an adult and deal with the consequences of her actions. She, too, may have wanted a normal life but could never have it.

"Do you think about, grandma?" Dianna asked her.

"Every day," she admitted. "I loved that woman." She turned to look at Dianna. "Did I ever tell you about how she met my dad?"

"You never tell me anything about your life, remember?"

"I know and I'm sorry. I just figured I was protecting you."

Dianna tilted her head with an askance expression on her face, "protecting me by keeping me in the dark?" Dianna's voice had a slight edge to it. She sighed. She didn't want to instigate an argument today. "How did they meet?"

"He was a pianist at a brothel."

Dianna eyes widened. "Grandma was a prostitute?!" Dianna couldn't believe what she was hearing.

"Not for long. She fell in love with the way he played the piano and he fell in love with her affections. He took her away from that place and married her." Irene stirred her tea slowly.

"What? I thought having a husband went against the code?" Dianna said sarcastically.

"Well not for them. He was blind."

Dianna laughed heartily, "A blind pianist and a prostitute. Sounds like the perfect love story."

"Yeah...until she killed him."

Irene had Dianna's full attention by this as the story became more interesting.

"It was an accident. They were arguing one day. She became so angry, she transformed and accidentally pushed him down a flight of stairs and he broke his neck." Irene stared at her cup for a while. "I don't even know what they were arguing about. She was probably drinking." This sparked a little bit of guilt in Dianna since her drinking problem was a bit out of control. Her heart bled for her mother and she was surprised that she was even able to hold back the tears. "I saw the entire thing," her mother finished. It was no wonder to Dianna now that Irene chose not to talk about her past. She scooted a little closer to her mom and wrapped her arms around her.

 "I'm sorry for neglecting you," Dianna told her. She began stroking her mother's short graying hair, streaked with green. Just then, there was a loud knock at the door. Dianna and Irene stared at each other mystified.

"Are you expecting company?" Dianna whispered. Irene shook her head then got up and went to the door. She peeked through the side window. She quickly drew the curtains back and turned to Dianna.

"Cops!" she mouthed. Dianna sat in the couch frozen with her facial expression mirroring the fear she saw on her mother's face. The knock came again snapping her out of her frozen state.

"Fuck!" Dianna cursed, frantically searching her purse for a hair tie or scarf. Anything to control her snakes which was damn near impossible. Thankfully she was wearing the contacts, but Irene wasn't. "Should I speak to them?" Dianna asked her mother frantically. "No!" her mother said, motioning her to stay. She grabbed her baseball cap and placed it on her head, hoping to shield her eyes. Even though she was better at masking her own physiological transformations, like her snakes, she still struggled with the unpredictability of her reactionary changes. Irene breathed in deeply and composed herself. She opened the door.

"Hello, officers. How can I be of assistance to you?" she said sweetly, almost flirtatiously. If not for the circumstances, Dianna would have been thoroughly amused.

"Good day, Ma'am. I'm officer Drummonds and this is Officer Baker. We would like to speak to you about a hit and run incident that happened at the three-way last night," Officer Drummond asked professionally.

This was all too familiar to Dianna. Cops had shown up at her Las Vegas apartment just like this trying to solve a hit and run case some months ago. She told them she didn't remember anything and stuck to her story.

"May we come in?"

"Not without a warrant, but we can talk on the porch if you'd like," Irene replied maintaining a polite tone. The cops looked at each other, clearly getting suspicious.

"Is there someone else in the house, ma'am?" Officer Baker asked her.

"Yes, my daughter. She's visiting from out of town and as you can imagine, she's jetlagged from her flight." Irene stepped outside and closed the door behind her. "You said there was an accident?" she said refocusing their attention.

"Aaaah, yes, last night. We found a pickup truck abandoned by the woods nearby. There was some blood on it, but we aren't sure who the truck belongs to. We were able to trace the incident back to Mack who came into the station this morning saying he was hit by a pickup truck that matched the description of the vehicle."

"Okay. I don't mean to be rude but what does that have to do with me?" Irene said coyly.

"He said your daughter may be able to provide some details because the last thing he remembers was pushing her out of the way of the truck and then being struck. He said everything else was foggy until he woke up with barely a scratch and a bruise," Officer Drummonds explained.

"My daughter didn't mention anything like that to me," Irene commented.

"What's even more strange is that the police weren't called, and Mack didn't even go to the hospital to get himself checked out," the officer continued.

"Sounds like it may have been minor. People around these parts don't go to the hospital unless they vomit a kidney or something," Irene said evasively. The cops looked at each other skeptically.

"Doesn't explain the shit load of blood on the fender. Was your daughter with you the entire time yesterday?" Dianna could tell that Officer Blake was a hard ass.

"As far as I know, yes!" Irene said folding her arms defensively. Dianna had been watching from the window. She saw that the off-the-cuff interrogation wasn't going well. She didn't want her mom taking the fall for something she dragged her into. She opened the door cautiously. The cop stared at her.

"Are you Dianna?"

"Yes. I can answer your questions."

"Dianna, you don't--" Dianna touched her mother's arm gently.

"It's okay, Mom." She then turned her attention to the cops. "Yes, he pushed, me out of the way and the truck hit him. He was unconscious for a brief second but when he woke up, he seemed fine. We didn't notice any visible bleeding, so I helped him into his house."

"And none of you thought to call an ambulance? It's possible he could have gotten a concussion or even internal bleeding."

"Did you get a look at the driver?" Officer Drummonds followed up immediately sensing his partner's distrust.

"As I said, we both determined he was fine, and after I helped him into the house, I went my separate way. The truck had already left, we didn't get a license plate number, so it was a lost cause. If there was a lot of blood on the fender of the truck you found, it's possible it wasn't the same truck," Dianna suggested, deliberately trying to confuse them. Officer Blake narrowed his gaze at her not believing a word she was saying, but she kept her composure.

"Is that everything, officers?" Irene asked with a stiff smile.

"It's a small town, we could've apprehended the driver quickly if you had reported the incident to us," Officer Blake pushed, failing to hide his agitation while tapping his note pad.

Officer Drummond stepped in, "we just need a description of the truck that almost hit you to corroborate your story." Dianna complied and eventually the cops left after promising to keep in touch. Both Dianna and Irene went inside and let out a sigh of relief.

"You need to talk to Mack," Dianna said. "At least he didn't mention you."

"Only because he wasn't sure I was there."

"Whatever. Talk to him and see if you can get him to change his version of the story."

"Dianna, I don't want to call you naïve but that's wishful thinking."

"Well, the cops are going to keep asking questions if we keep giving them different stories."

"Damn it! This is what I didn't want." She said, turning her back to Dianna.

Dianna could hear the frustration in her mother's voice. "I think you need to come live with me in Las Vegas. Stay low for a while."

Irene was silent. Her back still turned. She shook her head slowly. "I think it's better I stay here. They don't know I was involved so that might work in my favor."

Dianna walked around so she could face her mother. She noticed the glow Irene had in her eyes earlier had faded. She rested her hands on Irene's shoulders before telling her, "You can't stay here."

"It will look suspicious if I leave right after the cops questioned us, Dianna."

"And we don't look suspicious now?" Dianna said with sarcasm.

"I promise if things get really bad, I'll come to you." Her tone was resolute. "But I'm riding this out for now." Dianna realized that it was useless to try to change her mother's mind. This was how she always handled her problems...alone. "Go to Alabama. I want you to get your closure." Dianna's thoughts shifted. She had to admit that Irene was right. She had other priorities right now. "Don't worry about what's happening here. I'm sure it will blow over."

"I hope you are right?"

"Me too, baby. Me too..."

***

She had gone to the address printed on the ID to face the unknown of her father. She stood outside the wire fence looking at the yard overgrown with weeds. Peering at the ranch style house she figured that like her mother, her father hadn't fared too well financially. She thought for a while at the things he might say to her, denying her if she told him she was his daughter. She had aged well...too well to convince anyone she was born 50 years ago. Her nervousness caused her palms to sweat as she struggled with following through with her plan or bolting back to Las Vegas. Her crave for closure however, kept her feet anchored. The sensible thing to do was to walk up to the door and knock but she was honestly terrified.

"Can I help you?" Dianna hand clutched her chest as she gasped. She turned around quickly and came face to face with a tall, dark-skinned man in his 40s. He stared at her expectantly.

"I'm sorry. I am here to see..." she trailed off as she gazed at his features. She was shocked at the uncanny resemblance. He looked like a darker version of her. His beautiful big brown eyes staring at her with peculiarity.

He looked away into the distance and his eyes glazed over. "He passed away."

Dianna regrouped her thoughts, "how did you-- "

"You're here to see my dad, right?" he said fastening his gaze on her making her feel like an ant. There was a recognizable pain in his eyes. She wasn't familiar with the pain that came with losing someone, but she knew pain to the depth of her core. Once you've felt it, it becomes an unspoken language to anyone else who knows it. Dianna's heart sank for the man that stood in front of her who was clearly her brother, and for herself since she missed her chance to get to know her father.

"Yes."

"How typical. A bastard child trying to find their absent father?" His harsh words were unexpected and struck her like a jagged knife through her heart. She stared wide-eyed and speechless.

"Don't worry, I'm also a bastard child... with less questions considering I knew him." He gave her a wry smile, but she still needed a minute to gather her wits. *He called her a bastard child for crying out loud.* He had a dark sense of humor like her, but it still caught her off guard. He chuckled at her prolonged astonishment.

"I'm sorry. I should be nicer. I'm Quinton." He extended his hand to her and she lightly shook it, feeling like an ass for showing up like a bad memory. "Come on in. We can talk inside." She relaxed and followed his lead.

Inside was much more appealing than the exterior. In fact, it was cozy. A cushy brown couch positioned against the wall of the living room with a low wooden center table in front of it. There was an open beer can and an unfinished game of chess. There were a couple pictures of a young boy with a smiling face and a proud father by his side. There were no pictures of his mother. However, there were pictures of Quinton with a woman and child...a perfect family. She was jealous. Snapshots of a normal life she couldn't have. She surmised that they lived at the home with him.

There was one picture that looked a bit disturbing. It wasn't in a frame. It looked worn out and it was placed carelessly on the center table with the unfinished chess game and open beer can. The same little girl in a few family portraits was the same girl in this one. Yet even though her mouth had a bright smile, her eyes were faded and haunting. She was in a hospital gown and her long curly hair was now short feathery tufts of hair on her scalp. It gave her an eerie feeling.

He went to the kitchen and came back with a glass of water.

"No tha--" she thought against her original response as he tilted his head slightly to the side, daring her with his eyes to refuse the drink. Already she could tell that he was a blunt no nonsense type of guy. She took the glass and held it.

"Thank you."

"Have a seat." He flopped himself into the brown couch and she sat in the adjacent armchair. "Do you play?" Dianna placed the glass on a coaster on the center table. She had enjoyed a few games of chess in the past, but she wasn't here for games, *so to speak*. Yet she found herself nodding her head simply to be cordial.

"Good. You could say I dabble." He started moving the pieces around and she realized that she was about to be his opponent. She wasn't in the mood. She placed her hand over his.

"I just want to talk," her eyes pleaded. She never met him but now she knew she had a brother. She wanted to know more about her extended family. A mental battle in a game of chess was the last thing she felt like doing.

"I'll try my best to go easy on you," he responded. His words seemed foreboding. Her throat felt dry and she decided to drink the water after all.

He moved his chess piece forward. Dianna didn't know if he was being strategic or friendly. She was beginning to feel as if she was under a microscope.

"You never told me your name." Dianna cleared her throat.

"Dianna...Dianna Montague." She moved her piece forward as well.

"I figured you had his last name." Dianna thought this was a weird statement to make.

"Pretty sure I'm his kid, if that's what you are insinuating," Dianna stated assertively. Her brother stared at her silently which sent a chill up her spine. She trudged on. "Anyway, was our father married?" she pressed.

"No. My parents broke up when I was pretty young. My mother married a man I couldn't stand so I ran away to live with my dad." He slowly moved another piece. "Best decision I ever made. I respected my father as a parent and even more so as a man." Dianna could see the pride shining in his eyes. "He was an advocate. Fighting for rights and equality, that kind of thing. One day, he just got too sick to fight anymore." She could see him struggling to contain his emotions. The wound was still fresh, but she had to continue pushing.

"Too sick?" she probed.

"Yes, he had a rare form of hereditary cancer." He moved another piece quickly after she made a move.

"Wow!" Dianna shoulders felt weighed down. Maybe she was jetlagged or maybe it was just the sudden burden of knowing how her father died. Quinton watched her as she rubbed her shoulders, then she made a careless move on the board.

"Sorry you couldn't get to know him. He was a great guy." He made another carefully calculated move, "you look incredibly young, how old are you?" Quinton assessed her from her feet to the curls on top of her hair. Dianna cleared her throat and made another careless move. She was finding it more and more difficult to focus on the game and the conversation at the same time.

"25"

"Really, that would mean I was 15 when your mom got pregnant. He told me he never had any more kids after me. Guess he lied." He moved another chess piece. Dianna's heart raced. She didn't know what to say. She hadn't gotten her lie together and now she felt as if she was getting entangled in a web. She had no recourse but to continue with her lie.

"Well, y'know. He was a single man. Things happen," she said trying her best to play it off.

"Right…right. But by the time I was 10, he stopped all of that. His cancer kept coming back so he was mostly focused on raising me, working and fighting his cancer."

"So, you're 35?" She initially thought he was older. She studied him briefly. No, it wasn't age she saw. It was an overwhelming exhaustion. She moved her piece and it fell, rolling across the board. Her head felt like it weighed a ton. She rested her face in the palm of her hand. She was struggling to keep her eyes open. She looked at Quinton again but this time she couldn't focus her vision. She needed to leave. Her instincts struggled to grapple with what was happening to her as she began standing to her feet. Something was wrong.

"I think I've overstayed my welcome here," she slurred. Before she could think of her next move, she felt herself crashing to the floor, hitting her head on the edge of the center table as the dead weight of her body fell like a freshly axed tree.

"TIMBER!!!" was the last thing she heard before she succumbed to the abyss.

***

A sharp pain shot through her brain as she mentally begged for the buzzing to stop.

"Where's my phone?" she mumbled as she slowly opened her eyes.

"Looks like you have a few people trying to get in touch with you. Drax? Your boyfriend, maybe."

Dianna looked up at her captor. Quinton was holding her phone staring at the screen. He turned it around and showed it to her and she saw Drax's name in capital letters and his handsome picture on the screen as the vibration continued incessantly. It finally stopped and she felt a sense of despair. She looked around. She was sitting on a chair with her hands tied behind her back. Even though she was waking up, whatever was in her system still slowed her motor and sensory skills. She moved slowly trying to minimize the achiness in her arms.

"What do you want?" she demanded, realizing that Quinton...her brother...had done the unthinkable and detained her.

"Also, your mom called. I didn't want her to worry so I used your fingerprint to access your phone and sent her a message that you were fine." His tone was too relaxed. She began to think he was a crazed lunatic. She hung her head. *What the heck had she gotten herself into*? Her mind started to rationally assess her situation. Maybe he was one of those hunters that Drax was talking about...*Drax*...he had finally called her. Maybe he missed her. Maybe he noticed she was gone for days and was worried. She should have told him she was leaving for a few weeks. But his feelings weren't her immediate concern. Her escape from her deranged brother was the only thing that mattered now.

"I feel like I'm talking to myself here," she heard Quinton's words piercing her thoughts. *Shit!* He had asked her a question, but she hadn't heard it...she heard him talking but...she was struggling to keep her thoughts straight. The drug he used on her was extremely powerful...*but how?* She grimaced as she thought about the glass of water, he gave her.

"Why? What do you want from me?"

"Good! You're ready to talk. Let's bypass the chit chat. My daughter is in the hospital dying from the same cancer my father had, and I need you to cure her."

Dianna stared at him as if she was seeing him for the first time. "What the fuck are you talking about?" Her words were slow. She braced against the restraints hoping to break them, but she couldn't find the strength because she was too sedated. Whatever he gave her had her senses reeling.

"Sorry I drugged you by the way, but I couldn't risk you getting away."

"You're a pig!"

"I can understand why you would feel that way. You're tied up in my basement." He stared at her almost looking remorseful, but Dianna wasn't buying it. "Nothing personal but I can't let my baby girl die. She's only 9 years old and nothing is worse than a parent outliving their child."

"WHAT MAKES YOU THINK I CAN CURE HER?" Dianna shouted. Her anger was beginning to seep into her veins. It was only a matter of time before her snakes revealed themselves with a hissing and venomous force as the sedation wore off.

"Must we do this?" He grabbed a chair and dragged it across the floor. Dianna cringed from the grating noise it made which worsened her migraine. He turned on the light. It flooded her eyes and forced her eyes shut. She wished she wasn't wearing her contacts so she could look even more frightening so she could scare the shit out of him. "I know who you are...but, I haven't quite figured out what you are. Maybe reptilian?" Dianna's hair began to uncoil into angry snakes thrashing at him, but he was just out of reach. He inched the chair back a few inches just in case.

"My God! My father told me he saw you like this as a child, but I thought the cancer was making him lose his mind a little." He looked at her transformation in awe.

"I'm going to FUCK YOU UP, Quinton. You're going to wish you never met me." He could do his worst to her, but she would come back, and she would destroy him.

"Yes, but before you do that. A little back story. So, my dad, your dad went looking for your mother years after she ditched him for no reason. Don't ask me why considering it's pretty irrelevant now. Anyway, I don't know how but he found her. When he found her, she had a daughter...you. He knew immediately that you were his kid. He was waiting at the house when your mother popped up looking completely freaked out. She was so caught up in her emotions she didn't even notice him standing at the corner. But as soon as she went into the house; she came back out and ran into the woods. He followed her, taking cover behind a tree and there you were waiting for her with a man lying on the ground. My father said the guy was beat up pretty badly. But then your mother did some type of blood transfusion and healed him." He was speaking even faster now. "He said, it didn't end there. He said that you were so scared while your mother was trying to save the guy that snakes started growing from your head." Quinton chuckled softly. "Dad said he nearly shit himself; he ran away thinking you guys were some sort of aliens."

"So, you think my 'alien' powers can cure your daughter." She let out a soft laughter. "Well, bad news for you, Quinton. I CAN'T! You need my mother for that."

"That's it, Dianna. Your mother doesn't want to be found. Years later, my father started getting sick and we found out that he had stage three cancer. He did chemotherapy and got rid of it, but it kept coming back." Quinton stood up and walked away from her with his back turned as if he was thinking about something. "You should've seen him. He looked like a dead man walking. He lost weight and his hair."

"I'm sorry he died like that, but I can't help you."

"LET ME FINISH!" he ordered. "He went back to search for your mom, but you guys were gone. Completely vanished. He knew that if he found her, she could help him." Quinton rubbed his chin pensively. "Before he died, I thought he was crazy. Until my daughter got the same type of cancer." He started looking around searching for something. "It's hot as shit in here!" He rested his eyes on something behind her. Dianna followed him with her eyes as he went to get the standing fan piled on top of some more junk to the back of the basement. He took it back to the chair he was sitting on, plugged it in and turned it on. He set the settings on rotate and as it spun around, the cool breeze hit her face. She had to admit that it felt good. He sat down, seeming to calm down.

"I researched and came across a lot of myths, but I did find enough convincing information that everything he said was probably true. So, I searched, and I looked but I couldn't find you guys either which was expected. Then this morning, you showed up in front of my house. Like a sign from God." His eyes were hopeful.

"Quinton, listen to me. I can't save your daughter. My mom, she's the healer. I can only heal myself."

"You are her daughter. You can do anything she can do."

"No. I can't. I'm sorry."

"Don't be sorry. Thankfully, now, I know where your mom lives. I know that the CIA would love to get their hands on her."

"You just said she doesn't want to be found." Dianna sneered at him with murder in her eyes. She had never killed anyone before, but she would gladly make him her first victim.

"About that." He walked over to the corner of the basement where her purse was resting on the floor. He picked it up and walked back toward her. He opened it and took out a plane ticket stub and some receipts. He looked at the ticket stub. "Says here you were in Alaska. I'm betting she might live there." Then he straightened out the receipts, "Gas station receipts from 8520 Algrange Street, zip code--"

"They won't believe you!"

"Oh, really." He took his phone out. "Say cheese, sis." The light from his phone camera flashed. Dianna blinked her eyes rapidly. He stood up and showed her a photo of herself tied up, her snakes gnashing, and her fangs bared. She was a beastly sight!

"Looks convincing enough. Do you want to test me?" He tucked the phone away in his back pocket. "Don't force my hand, Dianna. I will cut off one of your fingers if I have to and send it to whoever I need to, with more pictures of you to make this case as convincing as possible." He was a desperate man and willing to do anything to save his child. With her already in his possession, he had one chess piece to make the most desperate move of his life. He would stop at nothing. She sighed in defeat.

"My mom...I have to call my mom. She can be here in a day."

"No time! You need to do the transfusion today."

"Do you hear yourself? How are we going to do an unauthorized blood transfusion at the hospital?" She hung her head again, this time more defeated than before. She came to Alabama on a prayer and fairytale ideas of meeting her father and instead, met his lunatic son. She made one last effort to change his mind. "Quinton, this isn't going to work. I am not a panacea for diseases. I've never done that kind of thing. What if we inadvertently poison her blood? You might harm your precious daughter instead of helping her," she reasoned.

His eyes quickly teared up. His five o'clock shadow made him look scruffy. He rested both his hands gently on her knees. "It's a risk I'm willing to take. She's the most important thing in the world to me. My wife thinks I've lost it talking about half humans that can cure cancer. The insurance from my job can barely cover my daughter's medical bills so now I'm on government assistance. The doctors say she only has a few weeks left...if that." He dropped his head into his hands, hiding his frustration.

Dianna understood how it felt to be so hopeless that praying for a miracle was the only option left. "I'll see what I can do but I can't do it at the hospital."

"I understand." He stood from his chair and flicked out a swiss army knife. "I'll take care of that." He paused as he was about to cut the zip ties from her wrists. She could sense his hesitation. She smiled reassuringly.

"I promise I won't bite," she said to him. He smiled back with uncertainty but cut the bondage from her wrists and ankles. Dianna rubbed the bruised areas, relieved she was out of the restraints. He stood in front of her and as she stood to meet his full height. With her true terrifying form revealed to him, she grabbed him quickly by the throat and threw him across the room into the wall with pure, unadulterated rage. She could hear him writhing and moaning in pain as she sat back on her chair and calmed herself.

"I needed to get that out of my system," she told him.

"I deserved that!" he said, wobbling as he picked himself up with support from an old washing machine next to him. Dianna rolled her eyes with annoyance, but she would help him. After all, his daughter was her niece. They were blood and she knew that her conscience wouldn't allow her to let her family die.

***

Dianna stared at her phone. Drax had called. *What did he want?* She wondered if it was about work. She had already sent the final completely edited copy to Eric. Maybe he had more complaints. She had put her heart and soul into the editing. It was perfection yet knowing Drax and the anger he felt towards her, he may have found a few flaws.

Knowing Drax??? Dianna, you slept with the man once. That certainly doesn't qualify you as an expert on his character. Dianna sighed at her thoughts. He was like her. He was someone she would never have to hide herself with as a person, or as a half Nagalian. But he saw her as only as a flawed version of himself. She didn't want to admit it but that hurt her sorely.

She heard Quinton's car pulling up outside the house. She placed her phone back into her purse and went to the window to observe. She saw him carefully helping his daughter from the car into the wheelchair. She saw a woman taking a medical bag and some supplies from the trunk. Then, they started walking to the house. She went to the door to let them in. Quinton carefully pushed the wheelchair over the door's threshold, jerking his daughter forward and she grimaced from the sudden movement.

"I'm sorry, Adisa. Are you okay?" he said in a soothing tone.

"You have to be careful, Quinton!" the African American woman said fussing at Quinton. She was beautiful. She had long gold dreads that were in a ponytail. Her skin was caramel, and beautiful full lips. However, you could tell that beauty was not a priority for her. She wore no makeup, and her eyes were sad and tired, no doubt from caring for a terminally ill child. She turned to look at Dianna. She looked unimpressed and just a tad disgusted. Exactly what she didn't need right now.

"Hi!" Dianna greeted as upbeat as possible.

"You know I think this is a bad idea, right?" the woman said to her.

Quinton intervened. "Dianna meet my wife Audrey." Dianna extended her hand but realized soon enough that Audrey needed help more than a hand to shake and took the medical bag from her, setting it down on the center table.

"Are you going to help me get better?" came the feeble voice of their daughter. Dianna shifted her attention to Adisa. She kneeled to meet the child at her level resting her hand on the girl's hand reassuringly.

"We are all going to do our best to help you get better," she smiled. Adisa responded with a smile that could light up the galaxy and she flung her arms around Dianna's neck. Dianna was taken off guard, but she returned the hug. "It's going to be okay." She felt a little guilty for lying to her. No one knew how safe the procedure was or what the outcome would be. They could kill her. She stood and straightened herself. "Let's get started!" she said to them.

"Wait! Adisa is my daughter too. I need proof that you aren't just some random person with an agenda. I'm going to take some blood from you for testing plus…" She paused as she stared at Dianna skeptically. "I need to see you…you know…change."

"In front of your daughter." Audrey looked from Dianna to the kitchen.

"In there," then she led the way with Dianna trailing behind her.

"I'm sorry but did you say you want to take some blood for testing?"

"I'm an RN. I just want to run some quick basic tests to make sure you don't have any STDs, drugs in your system, things like that."

"I thought…"

"Look!" Audrey interrupted slamming both of her hands on the kitchen counter. Dianna could see her hands shaking. She knew she was scared of what the outcome would be. "I don't like any part of this. I don't even know why I agreed to this. This is crazy!" Dianna grabbed one of the kitchen knives artfully arranged in the knife holder near the sink. "What are you doing?" Dianna sliced her wrist. "No, stop!" Audrey begged a little too late. Dianna quickly turned on the sink faucet and started rinsing away the blood. It was only a superficial cut that would heal fairly fast.

"Watch!" she told Audrey. Audrey stared at the small cut that had stopped bleeding.

"My skin regenerates just like everything else on my body. You cut me, break my bones, burn me, scratch me, stab me, I won't die!" Dianna said emotionally. By now her cut was completely healed.

"What are you?" There was a harrowing look on Audrey's face as if she was seeing some type of monstrosity.

"Just found out last month that I'm a Nagalian." She then held Audrey's hands firmly and looked into her eyes, searching for even a small ray of faith. "I've never done this so I don't know if it will work but I can tell you that your husband drugged and detained me because he was willing to risk it all to save Adisa."

Audrey looked at her hands entwined with Dianna's then laughed, "I'm sorry about that. His mind has been a little corky since Adisa's diagnosis."

Dianna looked behind Audrey at Adisa, then back at her. "And after seeing my beautiful niece, I get it. I'm ready to risk it too."

"But it's not your life that is on the line." Audrey reminded her.

"True but it doesn't benefit me to do this either. I just want to help." Audrey calmed bit, then breathed out.

"Okay. No tests. We don't have enough time for that anyway. I'll get the things set up."

It only took a few minutes for them to set the medical supplies up in Adisa's room. Quinton's home was wheelchair accessible, so it didn't take long to get Adisa up the stairs using the stairlift. Dianna stood close by Adisa who was lying on her bed, weak and burnt out from her day's activities. As Audrey inserted the tubing into Dianna's arm, she said a prayer. Then went on to insert another tubing into her daughter's arm, whispering another prayer. As she was about to turn the machine on, Dianna stopped them.

"What are you going to do if this doesn't work?" She was staring directly at Quinton.

"It's going to work!" he said with conviction.

"Yes, but what if it doesn't!" his wife cornered him.

"I'll let Dianna go and we'll just have to try something else," he said staring reassuringly at Adisa. He folded his trembling lips and stepped away to give them space. Dianna knew he was also trying to put on a brave face for his daughter. Audrey turned the machine on. The low vibration had a hypnotic effect. They waited for Dianna's dark red blood to start making its way through the long-elongated tube. None of them knew what they were waiting for but hope mixed with anxiety was palpable the room.

"Mommy, I feel cold," Adisa murmured. Dianna's blood had reached her arm and the transfusion was underway.

"Is that normal?" Audrey asked Dianna who was just as concerned.

"I don't know. Like I've said a million times, I've never done this before." It was basically trial and error.

"Quinton get a blanket!" Audrey ordered. "Sweetie, are you in pain? If you need us to stop, please tell me."

"It's okay mommy. It doesn't hurt. It just feels like ice going through my body." Her eyes were drowsy. Quinton came back with a blanket and tucked her in. She was slowly nodding off while Audrey was slowly losing her mind with worry.

"How much blood does she need?" Quinton asked Dianna. But Dianna didn't have the answers.

"I'm giving her the same amount she would get from the hospital." Audrey provided. Her eyes darted to Adisa's arm. Something had caught her attention. "Look! Look at the rash on her arm. It's disappearing."

Both Quinton and Dianna stared at Adisa's arm. Audrey was right. The dark purple medium size rash was slowly vanishing. Audrey let out a sob and tears welled up her in her eyes. She turned to Quinton who had begun tearing up as well. She hugged him with trembling hands. She let out another sob. "It's working! I can't believe you were right."

After a few more minutes the procedure had ended but all the rashes and any sign of bruises had completely disappeared and Adisa's skin was visibly healthier. She was sleeping peacefully on the bed, but they could tell she was getting better because her color was no longer ashen, and her lips were no longer pale.

"Thank you. You don't know how much--" He couldn't get the words out. It didn't matter. The gratitude in his eyes was enough. Dianna was emotional too. She had never saved a life before and it was...gratifying.

"Let's give her some time to rest," Dianna said pulling the tube from her arm but before she could leave the room, Audrey hugged her, tears from her face wetting Dianna's blouse.

"Thank you. I can't-- I can't thank you enough. You are an angel." She lifted her head and stared up at Dianna who was about 2 inches taller.

"I'm just happy it worked," Dianna said. Just then her phone rang. "Excuse me."

She took the phone out of her pocket and stepped into the hallway for privacy. It was Drax. She didn't know what to say to him. She had never been this nervous about anything in her life. She let the call go to voicemail. She didn't want his contempt for her to take away from the beauty of the moment. For the first time in a long time, she felt good about herself. She felt like a healer instead of a monster.

***

Dianna hadn't had a drink in about a week now. She had a new lease on life and wanted to keep the positive energy going. She was still staying at Quinton's house, spending as much time with them as possible before she went back to Las Vegas. Quinton rehashed old stories of their father and they watched home videos especially of Adisa when she was a baby. Sometimes she found herself laughing so hard, her stomach muscles ached. Other times she was fighting back tears in her stolen moments of nostalgia. She felt like Jonathan was more Quinton's father than he was hers. As if she had no business longing for his laughter or life lessons or fatherly love. As always, the connections she yearned for, felt inherently undeserved but finally she allowed herself to miss the father she never had. She really wished he could've been in her life.

She also spent a lot of time with Adisa. She realized that Adisa had been a lot of things before the cancer took over her body. She practiced martial arts, was on the softball team and her favorite thing to do was ballet dancing. Cancer had taken all of that away from her and even so, she never lost her passion for life. Dianna decided to appreciate and enjoy her niece one second at time to stretch their moments a bit longer. Adisa was a reminder of her lost childhood. The naivety of wanting more from life but only getting less and less. But Dianna had given her niece more and regretted nothing. She wished she had arrived sooner but was happy she hadn't missed the train to something as big as saving her niece's life.

She wanted to stay...*could I...* this was the closest she would ever come to a family that gave her unconditional acceptance. Granted, Quinton drugged her, tied her up and kidnapped her. Then threatened to report her and her mom to the CIA, before he forced her into a Jekyll and Hyde experience of a lifetime. Most interesting ice breaker she ever had the displeasure of enduring but as she stared at Adisa, she was happy her brother was able to pull off his scheme. She was happy he believed in her.

"Mommy said your blood type is universal. Is that true?" Adisa's little voice broke into her inner thoughts.

"You could say that," Dianna responded as they swung slowly on the large patio swing.

"I'm so lucky you are my aunty," Adisa smiled up at her. "I know everyone thought I was going to die but God wasn't ready for me yet. I have way too much to do."

Dianna hated that her tears were just a knee jerk away. Every little thing made her emotional. She wasn't used to being so emotional when it came to other people's life issues.

"You're right! Recitals, championships...prom." Dianna poked humorously at her.

"No, I mean bigger than that. I want to be a doctor." The knee jerk tears were threatening to spill over.

"That's ambitious Adisa...and admirable...and beautiful"

"Thank you. You're so beautiful," Adisa told her.

"Awwwe. You like green or sumpn'?" She was never one to take a compliment gracefully not even from a kid.

"I do. I want green streaks like you." Dianna wondered if Adisa's mother would let her get some temporary hair dye. She made a mental note to ask. She touched Adisa's short feathery hair. Quinton had explained the chemo had thinned her hair immensely.

"I'll see what we can work out." She realized that she had struck gold because Adisa's face brightened like the full moon on a cloudless night. Dianna couldn't help laughing. Audrey came out dressed for Adisa's appointment at the pediatrician.

"Come on Adisa, it's time to go."

"Okay. Let me get my bag!" Adisa said whizzing pass her. It was almost impossible to tell that she was recently stricken with terminal cancer or was nearing the end of her life a week ago. Audrey's face had changed too. She was glowing and relaxed as if she was just coming back from a long vacation. She was even wearing lipstick.

"I keep telling myself, I'm going to wake up from this dream," she said, her lips quivering slightly.

"But it's not a dream," Dianna assured her.

"It's a miracle. I mean, they are still running tests on her, but the cancer is completely gone."

"That's good news."

"I know. They don't know what to think. They want to know if I did anything differently."

"What did you tell them?"

"Nothing. I told Adisa not to say anything or we might get aunty Dianna in trouble." The tears came rolling down. She searched her bag for tissue and started dabbing at her face. "She loves you so much, she's guarding this secret with her life," Audrey laughed through her tears. Dianna laughed with her. It was unexpected when Audrey gave her hug. This was her second time hugging her.

"Thank you!" Dianna felt Audrey's body shivering with emotions. "Please stay as long as you want. You're family." But as much as Dianna wanted to escape her trap of a life and live with them, she knew she had to go back to face her demons. *Doesn't mean you can't extend your stay* came her inner voice. She pulled away.

"I can only stay one more week," she told her. "I've got to get back to work...to my friends," ... *to Drax.*

"Can I be honest," Audrey wiped away the remaining tears. "It doesn't seem like you want to go back home, and just in case you change your mind, mi casa es su casa." By that time, Adisa came out. Audrey straightened herself as Adisa handed her a small brush and a hair band with a large green bow on it. Audrey quickly brushed her hair and delicately placed the glittery hair band on her daughter's head. It was more decorative in purpose since her hair was so short and thin. Audrey appeared grateful for the distraction.

"Could I get her some green streaks? I promise it will only be kid friendly products."

"Please, Mom!" Adisa quickly chimed in. The bombardment took Audrey by surprise and she became flustered.

"I - -"

"Pleaaase, Mom! It will probably wash out within a week." Adisa's eyes were pleading.

"Okay!" Audrey raised her hands in surrender. Then her eyes softened. "Anything for you, baby." She planted a kiss on her forehead. "Now, let's go or we're going to be late!" They walked off briskly, leaving Dianna on the porch waving. She then returned inside the house. She checked her phone. Ten missed calls and two text messages. Her phone hadn't been this busy since...ever. She went through it. Her mom was the reason for at least eight of the calls. Drax was the reason for the rest. She checked her messages. They were also from Drax.

Text No.1

"I'm worried about you, Dianna. No one has heard from you in weeks. Praying you didn't take more of the Apoptosyde. Just let me know you're okay."

Text No.2

"Dianna, although I meant every word I said to you--"

"Asshole!" Dianna hissed.

"-- My delivery may have been harsh. I'm worried about your state of mind right now since we didn't quite end things on a good note. Call me or my personal assistant Susanne. I just need confirmation that you didn't... you know what I mean."

She decided that it would do her soul justice to let him worry even more. Who did he think he was anyway? *'I'm not worthy.'* "Worthy of what anyway?" she asked herself. *Of acceptance from the privileged high society family of Nagalians? Think I'll be fine,* she mused to herself.

"Hey why are you in here talking to yourself?" Quinton swung around the corner from the kitchen with some kind of sandwich in his hand. She could tell that he made it because it looked quite unappetizing.

"I thought you were sleeping. What did you hear?"

"Nothing interesting," he said before taking a big bite out of the sandwich. "I did want to talk to you about something do you have a minute."

Dianna's curiosity was piqued as his tone took on a serious foreboding air. "Yeah, sure. What do you wanna talk about?"

"Do you know why I believed my father about you? Or why I was willing to take a chance and kidnap you?"

"I guess desperation makes you do crazy things." Dianna shrugged nonchalantly.

"You could say that, but something had to convince me without a shadow of a doubt that you were capable of healing my daughter before I took a chance. So, for years I heard my father talking about you and your mother and what your mother could do but we all thought that he was, as you know, coocoo. A few years after he died some people came to my house. They looked like government agents, but you could tell that they weren't good people. They asked me about my father and my mother and if I knew anything about my father's ex... your mother. They wanted to know if I knew what she was. I lied and told them I didn't know anything and even started asking them questions to make it look convincing, but they weren't convinced. They wanted to take a sample of my blood to test me or something. At that point I told them to get the hell out of my house."

Dianna couldn't believe what she was hearing. "So, you're telling me that people are actually looking for my mother." *Shit! Her mom was right.*

He nodded his head slowly, "that was all the confirmation that I needed that my dad was telling the truth." He started walking towards the door. "Come with me. I have something to show you." She followed him silently outside then to the back of the house. He had finally cut the grass and cleaned up around the house.

"I think your property value just went up marginally," she said looking around at the yard that was seriously neglected about a week ago.

"HAHA!" His laugh was loud and also exaggerated, and he playfully shoved her. An old rusty wheelbarrow, a rake and a pitchfork were leaning neatly against the shed at the back of the house and she wondered about what was inside. "I got rid of the hobo beard too," he said pointing at his face. "Keeping up appearances hasn't been one of my priorities in the last year or so dealing with cancer and all."

"I get it."

"I'm pretty sure the neighbors hated me." He laughed sardonically. He stopped and pointed above the back door.

"I had security cameras installed here and a couple of other places along the side and even in the front." He walked to the side to show her his security equipment. "All of this is transmitted to my phone, so I get an alert every time someone thinks to set foot on my property." He walked to the front of the house. This camera can pick up footage within 20ft radius in this direction." Then he walked back to the backyard. This time he went to his shed. When he opened it, it was dark and dusty. She tried to fan away some of the dust and coughed a little after she accidentally breathed the particles in her lungs.

"Sorry about that. Might be some spiders in here too." He stepped inside and switched on a lightbulb that hung from the ceiling.

She saw at least six rifles and a shot gun and some smaller guns. Quinton had an arsenal.

"Why are you showing me this?" She inquired.

He walked to her and placed his hand on her shoulder. She could smell beer on his breath.

"Because dear sister. If you do decide to stay with us, I've got your back!"

Chapter 7

"*Are* you sure you don't want to get your hair done, too?" The beautiful African American hairstylist inquired.

"No, thank you." Dianna shook her head emphatically. "Trust me, I would hate for my hair to bite you," she joked.

"No hair is too untamed for me to handle, sweetheart," the stylist said taking Dianna's words at face value. "This is my profession, and hair is what I do." She reached her hand toward Dianna's hair, then paused. "My apologies. May I touch your hair?" she said, catching herself. Dianna was beginning to get a little anxious.

"I--"

"Aunty Dianna, should I get green and blue or just green?" Her question temporarily distracted both Dianna and the stylist.

"Sweetie, we can get any color you like," the stylist offered walking toward Adisa who was at this time being prepped by another stylist. Dianna also walked over to Adisa.

"Are you sure you don't want a more girly color? Maybe pink or pastel purple?" she said lightly tapping the tip of Adisa's nose. Adisa broached a thoughtful expression on her face. Then as if a light bulb went off inside her mind.

"I think I'll stick with dark green. I want to look just like you." Dianna blushed at the compliment.

"Aren't you a cutie and a sweetie!" The stylist responded, clearly touched by her words. But no one was more touched than Dianna. The words stole her very heart. She had never had anyone openly admire her like Adisa did. Her niece looked at her as if she was a heroine from a Marvel comic book. It was the purest thing she had ever experienced. "As long as that's what you want." Were the only words she could muster.

"It's so pretty in here," Adisa said looking around. The 'Hair Glam Hair Salon' was extremely popular in Montgomery especially because they styled Afro hair. Dianna surveyed the expansive shop as well. Light colored glossy hardwood floors, crystal chandelier, beautiful black leather styling chairs. They also had a few massage chairs for waiting customers. Large portraits of beautiful women with lavish hairstyles and all the seats were full. The ambiance was calm and relaxing with Zen music and just the right saturation of fruity fragrance. They had good business.

"How about I wait for you in one of those massage chairs?" Dianna cued Adisa. Adisa nodded as the stylist began her work.

Dianna sat in the leather chair and started fiddling with the remote console on the arm of the chair. She chose a low setting to get started with the massage and then rested her head lightly on the back of the chair. The low vibration was paradisiacal to her tense back muscles. She began to relax, and her mind wandered into an erotic fantasy of her and Drax.

They were back at her apartment naked in bed with the sun light glowing from the windows, warming their naked and exposed bodies. His chest to her back as he traced the curve of her bountiful hip. He was kissing the side of her neck and she hissed in pleasure as his long tongue tantalized the smoothness of her warm skin. She moaned out loud.

"That massage chair must be what the doctor prescribed!" she heard her stylist saying. Her eyes shot open as she had completely forgotten where she was for ten seconds.

"Do you have water?" she asked the stylist.

"Of course."

"Three bottles would be fine. I'll pay," she said a little embarrassed she was entertaining wayward fantasies in a salon shop.

"No need," the stylist responded kindly. When she returned, Dianna emptied all three bottles to quench her thirst. She then took her phone out and checked. No calls from Drax but one from her mother. She decided to call Irene from outside and briskly exited the shop.

"Dianna! Thank God!" She heard her mom exhaling heavily, no doubt to calm her nerves. "Are you okay?"

"Yeah." Dianna cleared her throat. "I'm fine."

"Did you find out anything about your dad?"

"Yes. You were right. He died...from cancer," Dianna said. A sad feeling came over her.

"I'm so sorry, Dianna. He was a good man."

"I know." Dianna held back the tears because she knew she would have loved him so much. "The good news is that I have a brother, a sister-in-law and a niece." This brought a genuine smile to her face. Dianna shot a quick glance in the direction of Adisa to make sure she was okay. She looked completely engrossed in the hair coloring process as she watched her reflection in the mirror. "You could say we're having some bonding time," Dianna told her mom. Her mom was silent.

"Are you there?"

"Yes. Don't get your hopes up too much...Just in case," her mother cautioned. There it was. Every time Dianna tried to be normal or do something that required getting close to humans, her mother would snatch her back to reality under the guise of tough love.

"I don't think you have to worry about these humans. They already know I'm a Nagalian." She fired back much to her mother's surprise. It gave her immense pleasure to vanquish her mother's worst fear which was exposing their secret.

"That doesn't sound safe, Dianna. How do you know they can be trusted?"

"Because Quinton knows where you live and hasn't contacted the CIA," Dianna said confidently. "Anyway, enough about me. What's going on in small town, Alaska?" she said switching the subject.

"I--I moved to Canada."

"What! Why?!" Dianna's confidence turned to bewilderment.

"I was planning it for a while now but now that things are a little hot here, I decided it was the best thing to do right now."

"What about your house?"

"I put it up for sale."

Dianna took a deep breath and then leaned her back against the wall. This was the only life her mother knew, and this was their way, but Dianna hated it. She didn't want that life. She was finally settled in Las Vegas. She had a beautiful apartment, a decent career and now she dared to hope for a damn sex life with someone that was nearly identical to her own genetical makeup. She wanted to go back to that. She wanted to see if she had a chance at a normal life.

"Mom, I wanted you to stay with me," Dianna said, disappointed that her mother chose to move to Canada instead of living with her in Las Vegas.

"Honey, you know I can't. It's safer this way." Just then, Adisa came out and showed Dianna her hair.

"Do you like it?" Dianna looked at Adisa's new green streaks in her short hair.

"It's gorgeous. Now people will really think I'm your mother." Adisa chuckled at the thought. "Go back inside and wait while I finish up my call, okay, sweetie." Adisa nodded then went back inside.

"Was that her...your niece?"

"Yeah."

"She sounds cute…I'm going to change my number. I kept this number long enough for you to call me back. Keep your phone close. I'll call you once I change my number."

"Fine!" Dianna quickly ended the call and went back inside the hair salon. The feelings she thought she had resolved in Alaska were slowly coming back. The feeling of being sick and tired of her mother.

***

It was Dianna's idea to take the bus and do some sightseeing in Montgomery since she only had a few days left in Alabama. She and Adisa had eaten lunch at a popular restaurant, hit some tourist sites, bought a few souvenirs and taken a lot of pictures. The sun was on the verge of setting behind the skyscrapers when they decided to go home.

They had been walking a few meters from the bus stop when Dianna noticed a black car driving slowly on the other side of the street.

"Adisa, let's walk a little faster since it's getting really dark," Dianna implored secretly begging God to keep them safe. If Quinton was telling the truth, the car may be the agents that had visited his home a few years back.

"Okay." Adisa squeezed her hand and picked up her pace. Yet when they picked up their pace, the car continued to trail them. As soon as Dianna could see Quinton's house, she paused.

"Adisa, run home without me and tell your dad to check his cameras. Okay!" Adisa's forehead creased with evident confusion but she did as she was told. As her niece ran home, Dianna's pace became slow and deliberate all while she was searching her purse for her mace. The car came to a complete stop, but Dianna kept walking. She heard quick steps on the concrete behind her. She quickly turned around, pulling out her mace ready to spray any attackers. "WHY ARE YOU FOLLOWING ME?" she shouted at them.

"We don't want to hurt you. We just want to talk," one of the two men said to her raising both his hands in the air to show he wasn't armed. "Are you Quinton's sister?"

"I'm a family friend, what is it to you?"

"Quinton owes us money...again!"

"Money! That's what all this is about!" Dianna let out a sigh of relief. It seemed Quinton's personal problems was catching up with her. She laughed at the irony since her personal problems had caught up with him.

"We have a message for him."

"A message?" she derided. "How much does he owe you?"

"Look, we just want you to send him a message."

"You know his daughter had cancer, right?" she said with incredulity at the nerve of them to kick a man while he was down.

"That is the only reason we haven't sent him a stronger message...yet. We know times are hard, but he should have given us the money back months ago. At some point, sob stories become just that...sob stories."

"How much does he owe?"

"Are you going to pay it?"

"If it's low enough, yes."

The men looked at each other skeptically.

"Fifty grand!"

"Woah...can you guys go any lower?" Dianna tried to bargain.

"Fuck no! That's what he got from us and that's what he should pay... with interest!"

Dianna couldn't believe Quinton borrowed so much money, but it made sense since Adisa's medical bills were so high. "I was hoping you guys would say $4000 or something in that area." Her jab had only served to annoy them.

"Look, bitch! This is not a joke. We might be coming off as friendly right now, but we are not. Tell Quinton to pay us what he owes us or he's going to notice some changes in his life very soon." She decided against annoying them any further. The one that called her a bitch, the one with the tear drop tattoo and the scar on the right side of his face looked like he would shoot her without blinking an eye. She wouldn't die but it would certainly be a world of hurt that she was not in the mood to endure since she was having a good day.

"I'll pay you but not today. I have to make some calls, get some things together. I don't just have that kind of cash lying around." Dianna was lying through her teeth. Thanks to a year of hoarding her hefty salary, she had more than plenty to pay them off...with *interest*. But she could tell they were seedy, and she didn't want them thinking they could start extorting her. Do you know Bella's Restaurant on Dexter Ave, in the capital?"

"No not really, but we'll find it."

"Meet me there two days from now at 4:00 and I'll have your money."

Again, they looked at each other. They laughed and the guy with the tear drop tattoo walked a little closer to her.

"If you are fucking with us, we'll hurt you and Quinton." Dianna had no intention of taking their threat lightly. She had nothing to lose but Quinton had an entire family depending on him.

"One more thing. Don't tell him anything about what I said to you," she demanded.

"You think this is a negotiation or something?" They laughed at her. "We don't give two shits about what goes on between you and Quinton. Just bring our money."

"HEY! GET AWAY FROM HER!" Quinton's voice bellowed loudly in the night. Dianna and the two men looked around to see him walking speedily to them with a shotgun. Dianna's heart raced.

"Quinton! We don't want any problems. We just want our money," one of the men shouted back.

"Leave! Please!" Dianna begged the two guys, but Quinton had already gotten close enough.

"I told you two that I'm working on it. Leave my family out of it."

"If you'd paid us when you were s'pose to, your family wouldn't be in it." The guy with the tear tattoo then directed his attention to Dianna. "Don't stand us up!" The two men then quickly crossed the street, jumped into the black Charger and drove off.

"I'm sorry about them. Did they hurt or threaten you?"

"I'm fine!" She wiped her clammy hands on her hips. That was terrifying to say the least, but she made sure they saw her grit...*or foolhardiness.* "You owe them money?!" she said in an accusatory tone.

Quinton rolled his eyes. "They shouldn't have told you that! Please don't tell Audrey. She would leave me."

"You don't deserve her with all the illegal shit and lying you're doing behind her back!" Quinton kicked some nearby bushes in frustration. "And that's the least of your worries!" she said closing in on him so she could poke his chest hard.

He rubbed the spot soothingly. "Damn!" he cursed walking away from her.

"How much do you owe them?" Dianna closed the gap between them again. She wanted to get into his face. He did something stupid and someone had to let him know.

"Not much. Five grand."

"They said fifty!" Dianna counteracted, fuming at his bald face lie.

"Okay, you're right. I'll handle it."

"With interest!" Dianna added. He paused and placed his hands on his hips, with his shotgun pointed upwards, looking into the dark sky as if he could find the answers to his problems there. Then he turned to face her.

"I'll handle it," he repeated more emphatically.

"How?"

Quinton took a seat at the edge of the sidewalk, resting his shotgun beside him. "I'll take out a loan against the house."

"Audrey would leave you for sure then," Dianna told him as she sat beside him.

"She won't know. The house is in my name."

She realized that she had to tell him about her plans to pay off the money he owed before he did anything else more stupid. "Look, I've got some important friends. I'll take care of it." She really didn't trust Quinton when it came to money and she didn't think he could pay the money back either. The reality was, he couldn't afford it. His plan, put simply, was to borrow from Peter to pay Paul which meant that he would still struggle to pay a loan. Only with a bank loan, he could potentially lose his house.

"No! You've done enough." Dianna could see embarrassment in his eyes. "I wish we hadn't met like this."

"Like what? Struggling to save your daughter from a terminal illness?" Quinton scoffed. Then shook his head in exasperation. "It's handled. Just do me a favor and get the rest of your life together and no more loans from goons," she advised him. He flashed the *okay* hand sign. She leaned over and hugged him. He was reluctant at first but eventually he returned her hug. She used the moment to drive home her sentiment. "Next to my mom, you guys are the only family I've got." She looked at his sweaty face. "You guys mean everything to me," she told him and meant it with every fiber of her being. "I swear on my father's grave, I won't let them hurt your family and I've got your back too."

"You just found out your father was dead two weeks ago! Now you're swearing on his grave."

"Time has no concept here!" They both laughed as she broke the tension.

They eventually left their secrets at the pavement and headed home.

■ ■

***

Dianna sat nervously inside 'Bella', a family style restaurant, at 3:30 p.m. with her luggage and an envelope full of cash. She was constantly checking her phone. Her flight was at 5:00 p.m. and she hoped she gave herself enough time to do the transaction with the perps headed her way. However, she also feared that the guys would be a 'no show'. They weren't upstanding citizens and this little meeting they were having could result in nothing. A server came over to her interrupting her thoughts.

"Just checking to see if you might be interested in our *Wednesday Special* or even a refill on your iced tea?"

Dianna wasn't hungry but figured a little appetizer could settle her upheaved stomach.

"Actually, how is the clam chowder here?"

"It's pretty good. We've added our signature herb blend to give it a unique flavor that I think you might like." The pretty, blonde girl stated with just the perfect amount of enthusiasm. She reminded Dianna of Susanne, but the waitress's name tag said Penny.

"Oh really? Why is that Penny?" Dianna goaded her.

"Because everyone does!" It was such a simple yet convincing response.

"In that case, I would like a small serving please. I'll also take that refill," Dianna told her. The waitress scribbled something on her note pad, stuck it in her apron pocket and took Dianna's half empty glass away. Dianna didn't have to wait too long before a handsome young waiter returned with a fresh glass of iced tea and her clam chowder. The aroma caused her stomach to gurgle. Dianna focused her attention on the delicious warm creamy broth to get her mind temporarily off the little rendezvous she was supposed to be having a few minutes from now. Dianna was about six spoons in when a familiar voice stole her attention.

"I'm just going to grab a quick bite, then head to the hotel," he spoke into the phone.

"This way, sir." Her waitress, Penny, was showing Drax to a booth. Dianna spit some of her chowder back into the ceramic bowl.

"Shit!" she muttered. She tried to face away from them but this was an impossible feat since her seat was facing their direction so there was pretty much no hiding from him. She decided to pretend that she was preoccupied with her phone and began swiping and clicking.

"Not sure what street I'm on," he shifted the phone away from his ears, "ma'am, what's the name of this street?" he said directly to the waitress. He was standing about two booths away from Dianna.

"Dexter Ave," she told him quickly. Drax mouthed a *thank you* to the pretty waitress and Dianna thought she detected a glint of flirtation in his eyes, but she quickly admitted to herself that she was just being insecure...*or jealous.*

"You heard that? I should be on my way in maybe 15 minutes or so," he said as he walked past Dianna's table. He quickly glanced at her then kept walking.

He didn't recognize her. *Ouch!* She didn't know whether to be thankful or insulted. They shared a moment...*in bed,* and she was even introduced to his parents, the least he could do was notice she was sitting in a restaurant full of strangers. Her body slowly heated at the thought.

"Dianna!" came his voice as he doubled back with his phone still to his ears. "Hey, let me call you back." He ended the call and placed the phone inside his jacket. *Does he always wear a suit?* Dianna found herself wondering especially because it was hot as hades outside. She had chosen to wear a strapless floral romper because of the escalating heat.

"What are you doing here?" he asked taking the seat facing her. The waitress didn't seem to know what to do.

"Sir, is this where you want to be seated?"

"I'm sorry, yes. I'll have what she's having."

"So that will be iced tea and our signature clam chowder?" The waitress started scribbling immediately.

"On second thought, no!" He quickly grabbed the menu and surveyed the choices. Dianna guessed clam chowder was not his preference which amused her. "I could eat a damn horse!" he commented to himself taking a little time to make up his mind. Dianna felt bad for the poor waitress. "Hmmm…The angus steak looks good with the spinach rice and the mango sweet tea," he finally decided.

"Will that be everything?" the waitress was scribbling on her note pad some more trying to keep up.

"Medium rare and yes, that completes it," he responded, handing the waitress the menu. He then fixed his eyes on Dianna. His medium brown contacts stirring her emotions. *If he wasn't so deliciously--*

"And you ma'am, was there anything else I could get for you?" Penny said giving her attention to Dianna who tried to clear her throat, but the frog remained, making her sound like an old man.

"No, no, thank you. I'm fine. You can bring the bill."

"Put it on my ticket," Drax intervened. "In a hurry, Dianna?"

After watching Penny walk away awkwardly, Dianna checked the time on her phone. It was 3:45. "As a matter of a fact, I am." She flashed him a curt smile and started gathering her things.

"To do what exactly?" He sounded annoyed. "Why didn't you at least let me know you were okay?"

Dianna didn't like his interrogation and forwardness and his timing couldn't be any worse. "Drax, what are you doing here? Did you know I was here?"

Drax seemed slightly stunned by her question, then he smirked. "I see where this is going. Don't flatter yourself, Dianna. I'm attending an old business partner's funeral. Believe it or not this is a crazy coincidence," he said to her while taking an observatory glance at the surroundings, as if he was looking for someone.

Dianna was a little embarrassed at what her questions seem to be insinuating. "I wasn't suggesting you were stalking me or anything," she said straightening her shirt. "This is just a bit weird."

She could see that his hackles were calming. "I'm guessing I'm the last person you wanted to see, after the way our previous encounter ended."

"I really don't want to talk about it," she warned.

"Fair enough. Can we move past it?" he said eyeing her expectantly.

"I suppose we can. I'd like to think we both were in the wrong," she told him. "Enough blame to spread around."

"You're delusional, Dianna. I saved your life," he said in his usual direct manner.

"Didn't ask you to!"

"You're a fucking piece of work. If I didn't enjoy the sex so much, I would've dropped you like unwanted baggage."

His arrogance incited her even more. "And I'm a piece of work? It seems you speak English and *asshole quite proficiently*?" she retorted sarcastically.

"Here you are, sir." The same handsome waiter from before came back with Drax's order.

"Wow! You guys must have a super chef back there!" Dianna complimented the server, impressed with their short wait time. Drax's food looked mouthwatering, but she didn't have time to savor the sight of the food or to extend the tense moment they were having. She needed to be in front of the restaurant now with the money.

"Don't go," he asked her nicely as he read her mind.

"I've got a flight to catch back to Las Vegas. I don't want to miss it," she stated.

"Cancel it. I'm going to be in Alabama for a few days. I'd like to spend it with you."

"As sexy as that sounds, I've got more important things than your hormones to attend to. I'll see you around." She picked up the envelope and quickly made a dash for the exit. She heard him calling after her. She prayed he didn't follow her, but her attention was now focused on the black Charger pulling up to the curb. She paused at the door to check the time on her phone.

"Right on time."

"Right on time for what?" Drax's warm breath caressed her ear and she felt the hairs stand up on the back of her neck.

"Damn it, Drax! Not now!" She quickly stepped through the glass doors. She waved urgently as the men exited the car and was successful in catching their attention. They strode over to her quickly. She noticed how they looked even more shady during the day. She hoped this would be the last time she ever saw them. The one with the single tear drop tattoo on his face spoke first.

"You got it?" His voice was low and discrete.

"Yeah, right here," she responded looking nervously at the people walking past them.

The second one spoke. "Over here is better," he motioned his head to the alley on the side of the restaurant. She stepped forward but felt a strong hand on her wrist.

"Dianna, what's going on?" Drax asked her while looking suspiciously at the men.

"Drax, I told you not now!"

"Who's this guy?" Tear drop tattoo guy asked sneering at Drax. "You didn't tell us you were bringing company?"

"Drax, trust me. I've got this covered."

"Fine. I'm coming with you," he insisted.

"Drax-- "

"Look we don't have time for this. Let's roll!" Tear drop tattoo guy commanded his partner. She was beginning to realize that he was the more vocal of the two. She guessed he might have been the one in charge.

"No, wait!" She showed them the envelope. "It's here!" She walked briskly to the alley and everyone followed. They gathered near a green dumpster. She shoved the envelope at tear drop tattoo guy. He ripped it opened and five neat stacks of $100 bills fell onto the ground.

"Slow motherfucker!" the other guy sucked his teeth before quickly grabbing the money and flipping through each stack. He then quickly shoved the money back into the envelope. "Looks like it's all here. Great doing business with you." They started walking off.

"Wait!" she shouted after them. The two fleeing individuals stopped in their tracks. Drax grabbed her arm again. She looked up at him angrily.

"Let then leave, Dianna!"

"I can handle myself!"

"Can you?" he pushed, not caring about the two men waiting in front of them. She seethed at his remark and snatched her arm from him. Then she faced the men. "This ends now, right? You won't bother them anymore?"

They laughed at her mockingly. "That's up to Quinton. He's always coming back for something." They walked off.

"Dicks!" She looked at her phone and checked the time. She didn't want to miss her flight. "I've got to go."

"I don't get you. Who were those guys? Are you in some type of trouble?"

"This is none of YOUR business!"

He stood in front of her, blocking her path. "I don't want to fight." He gently caressed her face with the back of his hand. Her skin heated where he grazed her. He touched her hair and snakes came to life as if he had summoned them. She couldn't resist him. His aura enveloped her and while she was within it, she could only succumb to it. He kissed her tenderly. His lips were soft and inviting. She moaned as her fantasies came to life. He was here, in front of her, kissing her sensually...and she wanted more.

He broke away. "Forget your flight!" Then, he kissed her harder and she felt it between her legs, what they wanted to do and needed to do. She would regret not giving in. He cupped the back of her head as their tongues played tug of war in the alley. His mouth went down to her neck and he unraveled her. Her legs weakened and she fell forward onto him, but he stood firmly, supporting her weight.

"Okay," she conceded quietly. He won and she wanted to celebrate his victory in his bed, much sooner than later.

"Thank you," he said when he finally finished his onslaught of kisses. She could tell he was sincere in the way he looked at her with gratitude and humility which was a pleasant surprise. She kissed him. "You're welcome. Hopefully this will be the last time we make out next to a dumpster."

"The only reason I didn't strip you naked in the alley."

"In broad daylight? You're daring." She flirted as they walked back to the restaurant together.

"A minute ago, I was a fluent speaker in *asshole*," he quipped. Dianna laughed as she acknowledged just how much she had missed his...*everything*.

 "But don't detract from our conversation. You still have a lot of explaining to do."

"Do I?"

"YES!"

***

Drax, a king size bed, an executive suite with whipped cream, strawberries, a chocolate fountain, unlimited wine and soundproof walls was the perfect firestorm for multiple mind-blowing orgasms. They both knew how to make the most out of sexual pleasure and now that Dianna didn't have to hide who she was, she had no reason to restrict herself. Dianna had never felt this free, relaxed, open and satisfied with anyone. She always had to contain herself, to make sure nothing frightening happened like one of her snakes biting her partner. With Drax, a snake sinking their fangs into his deliciousness was tame game. Pleasure and pain that heightened his arousal. He would playfully spank her for being a *bad girl doing bad things to him* which was delightful to Dianna. She realized she was only experiencing an inch of the pleasure she was capable of feeling. It made her dread ever having normal human sex again.

As her naked body lay along the length of his, his head and shoulders up. She squeezed him tightly to make sure he was hers...even for a night.

"I've been doing it wrong this entire time," she confessed.

"I know."

"How?"

"Your body told me. Little things I did made you react as if it was your first time."

"You could say somethings were "a first.""

He grinned. He lay on his back so he could look up at her while she was straddling him. His hand transformed into an iridescent scaly claw with long nails. He scraped the smooth skin of her breast with it as he trailed it down to her nipple. She moaned unabashed. Those were the *little things* he was talking about.

"I want to stash you away like a relic in my parents secret show room, enjoying you as much as I can, while I can.

"Good thing I can't be 'stashed away'," she flirted.

"Hmmm," he responded. Something was on his mind.

"What is it?" she asked, grinding his pelvis as she teased him, not wanting the mood to end but it was too late. His tenor had changed and there was a sudden heaviness in the room. His aura was so strong, he didn't have to say anything. She could feel it.

"I want to trust you, Dianna. You can't try to kill yourself again." She closed her eyes and sighed heavily, then got off him wrapping the sheet around her body. She lay next to him, staring at the high ceiling.

"You're killing the vibe," she finally said. She didn't want to talk about her suicidal tendencies. Not to him. She loved the way he looked at her when he wanted her, not when he was fearful that she might hurt herself.

He rolled onto his side and turned her face to his. "You're not alone," he said to her. "I know that's what you're thinking in that crazy head of yours...but you're not," he tried to assure her.

"Yeah, until you're married to a full Nagalian with a kid on the way. Trust me, I'll be the least of your worries then," she reminded him.

"Nobody is getting married. At least not yet. So, for now, I say fuck old rules and traditions."

"Yeah, that part of it. You know...the centuries of traditions your family clearly live by." He smiled. She then saw his transformed, scaly hand slide under the sheet. She thought he was going use his sharp claw to explore the inside of her, so she closed her eyes and tensed herself, but she only felt his warm human fingers massaging her erogenous pearl gently. He smiled more broadly at her reaction.

"I thought-- "

"--I know what you thought."

He wasn't an amateur. That was certain. Times like these, he made her want to live forever. His massage intensified sending waves of pleasure throughout her body. She tightened her legs around his arm.

"Besides, I've got someone to live for."

He slipped two of his fingers inside her which caused her to bite her bottom lip.

"Who?" he asked expectantly.

"Quinton and Adisa."

He stopped himself, slowly removing his fingers. His creased forehead looked like he was trying to calculate a hard math problem, and something burned behind his gaze. She couldn't tell what it was...anger, jealousy.

"Who is Quinton?" he asked in a controlled but edgy tone. She realized it might have been both.

"My brother. Adisa is my niece," she explained. Then she saw it all coming together in his mind.

"Your father had a son?" he asked. She nodded in response. "Was that what the money was about today? Is he blackmailing you?"

"No, no. Nothing like that." She touched his face gently and she could see his nerves visibly calming. "I have a brother and a niece!" She smiled at him. "I have a family."

He returned her smile and stroked her hair. "I'm sorry I assumed the worst. I know that's a big deal for you." His words were sweet, but they didn't reach his eyes. She could see that there was something bothering him.

"What is it?" she probed.

"You just need time."

"For what?"

"To get it."

"I don't understand." He was being cryptic but before she could probe him any further, he planted a kiss on her forehead, then her lips, then her neck and she quivered.

"Hmmm. Your weak spot." He breathed into her neck.

"Didn't even know I had one."

"You have a few," he said smiling flirtatiously. Then he jumped out of bed. "I've got a dinner thing to go to. Wanna come?"

"Strangers make me uncomfortable."

"Y'know, you need to get over your social anxieties. I promise it will improve your quality of life," he advised her.

"Or trigger an entire episode that sends the FBI or CIA straight to my front door."

"Then what, you'll move again? You've already lived in almost half the entire US."

"Which means there's another half of the US I haven't explored." She clambered out of the bed and blocked his path so she could rest her head on his chest. She wanted to soak him up as much as possible.

"I can help you."

She stared up at him, "How so?"

"I can help you control your impulses" his face transformed into iridescent silver scales, his eyes were mere golden slits, his teeth were long, sharp ivory fangs. She touched his smooth scales then his fangs. "I can teach you to turn it on and off." The scales disappeared and then she was stroking his chiseled jawline.

"You're addictive." Her words were breathy as she stared into his eyes. He ran his fingers through her tendrils, awakening her snakes.

"So are you," he told her without breaking her stare. "You can feel just as in control as I do. Instead of hiding in the night or moving from state to state." The slim green snakes entwined themselves through his fingers, hissing gently as if they were following the tune of a snake charmer's pipe.

"How do you do that?"

"Biologically speaking, we mated. I'm your Alpha. It's almost impossible for you to resist me."

She cringed at the thought. "My God! You're insufferable!" she said as she backed away from him, full offense taken.

"I thought that's what you wanted to hear… that I've marked you." She realized he was teasing her.

"I hate you." She smiled up at him.

"And I dislike you even less." He pulled her to him again. "I really can't get enough of you, but I have to go."

"Okay, okay! I relinquish you to your social duties," she joked. "Take a shower. You smell like sex!" she said as she led him to the bathroom.

"Yes, ma'am!" he replied obeying her orders.

***

They finally arrived in Las Vegas and were headed to his place with his personal driver. He was able to convince her to go home with him under the guise of 'unfinished business'. She knew the unfinished business was more late-night sex which she was always up for with him. However, she knew the real reason he wanted her at his place was that he didn't want to let her out of his sight since he was now convinced, she led a reckless lifestyle. She also was convinced that he thought she was still looking for a way to harm herself. She wished he hadn't known that about her, but he did and now he was like a doting parent. She decided to indulge him to regain his trust even though she couldn't believe he was still interested in her. Even for a Nagalian, it must be energy draining and worrisome for anyone who genuinely cared for a person with suicidal tendencies. The thing is, she felt so alone for such a long time, she figured the only person she would be hurting was her mom and in fact, it wasn't just a way to end her misery but also to make her mom pay for being who she was and forcing her into this life but after the time she spent with her mom in Alaska, she knew it would be unusually cruel to punish Irene by killing herself. In a way, she was happy she didn't get the chance to go through with it.

"What are you thinking about?" he said stroking her cheek gently. She grabbed his hand and slowly sucked on his finger. His eyes became a burning inferno. He used his other hand to unbutton the top of his shirt, trying to cool himself. "You are going to run me into the ground," he admitted to her. She gave him a naughty giggle enjoying the effect she had on him then released his hand. He took hers and kissed it romantically. "What were you thinking about?" he asked her again knowing that she was only trying to distract him from the question.

"You don't have to protect me from myself."

His gaze softened. "Yes, I do. You're always getting yourself into trouble. Besides, you heard my mother, I'm 'attached' now."

"Is that so?" She withdrew her hand, but he captured it and brought it to his lips again. She had told herself that what they were doing was casual, but this didn't feel casual in the least. It felt as if they were falling into... a beautiful pattern...an unspoken understanding...an alliance of sorts.

"Don't question it. This is good," he said catching the skepticism in her voice.

"Have you ever been in a long-term relationship before, Mr. Ashton?"

"A few."

"With someone like me?"

"Yes...humans, pure-breeds...half breeds."

"I hate it when you call me that. Makes me feel half worthy."

He contemplated her words, "I'm sorry I said you weren't worthy at your apartment. It's just..." He let go of her hand and stared out the window as they drove past the myriad of casinos and clubs in the better part of Las Vegas. "It enraged me that I could've enabled your suicide and I felt like an idiot for allowing you to dupe me like you did," he confessed. She liked that he opened up to her.

"You're not an idiot. I took advantage you. I schemed and I stole from you and I'm sorry." She placed her head on his chest and he kissed the top of her head. "I was so wrapped up in the type of thoughts that pulls you into the most destructive part of yourself."

"Yeah, well I was wrapped up in myself too. Had to put myself into your shoes for a minute which was hard. I don't want to die young and I love the perfection and the brokenness of life."

"'The brokenness'? I hope you aren't trying to fix my 'brokenness'. That's like falling into quicksand."

"I wouldn't give myself that much credit to be able to *fix* you. Some things you gotta fix on your own." She looked up at him again.

"Where have you been all my life?" she said in pure admiration.

"I guess, hiding in plain sight...speaking of which. Have you signed the renegotiated contract?"

"Naw. I've been a little busy." She responded. He quirked a smile and she felt his long Nagalian nails gently scraping the side of her leg.

"Ouch!"

"Sign it!"

"Damn, Drax! Couldn't you at least try to be subtle."

"I tried, remember. I offered you a lot of money."

"You can't buy me, sweetie." He kissed her semi-open mouth. Tasting her tongue, putting an end to her useless protest.

"I'll sign it," she agreed as her body started craving him again.

"Tonight!"

"It's very important to you, huh?"

"You're important to me," he said to her, kissing her again.

He stopped briefly to tell the driver to drive around the city a second time. He then wound up the tinted screen for privacy.

Dianna's eyes glistened with anticipation as she realized what was about to happen to her in the back of the Mercedes limo which oddly enough didn't look like the typical limo. Its design was very refined. "Is there any place that's off limits to you?"

"Can't say there is," he gave her a devilish smile as he lifted her black mini dress higher and used his sharp nails to rip off her silky underwear. He then spread her legs wide, making sure she felt completely exposed to him, stripping away any need for modesty.

"Your driver-- "

"-- is minding his business," he finished for her. She shot him a wanton look. She couldn't deny that Drax made her body come alive and her mind enraptured. He was a promise she wanted a keep, an experience she wanted to explore and a man she wanted to tame. He was a part of her in so many ways ancestrally and genetically and yet he was like nothing she had ever tasted, wanted or enjoyed. As she stared at his face between her legs, tasting her, she knew that no matter how much of herself she gave him, he wouldn't be satisfied. He wouldn't be satisfied until he had her undying loyalty and unfaltering trust. She had shown him she couldn't be trusted and that's where he was trying to meet her now, within that circle of trust.

She closed her eyes as her body convulsed from the pleasure, he was feeding her and the power he was giving her as she pressed her vagina against his face and rode his tongue. The car made a sharp turn and Dianna fell onto her back, but he was holding her legs firmly and didn't miss a beat as she climaxed loudly.

"I wanted to let you have that but…you're so ready," he said rising from his knees with his pants slightly down so he could guide himself inside her. Once he was inside her, she locked her legs around his waist and pulled him into her as his thrusts became stronger and stronger. Soon, he too was in the throes of a gripping climax. His grunts of pleasure were like a hungry bear on a chase. He finally relaxed before he sat up, zipped up his pants and tightening his belt. He opened the sunroof, letting the cool air in and Dianna slid into his arms as they silently watched the flashing neon lights on the high-rise buildings go by.

"Las Vegas is beautiful and sinful at the same time," she whispered. "I don't ever want to leave." It was an innocent statement, but it was almost a Freudian slip since she had a habit of leaving whenever things became too heavy.

"I'll make sure you don't have to," he said to her.

"You can't promise that!"

"It's not a debate." Fresh from an organism, she wasn't in the mood to debate either, so she decided to let his statement slide but she knew better, and she wasn't a hopeful. If things got too hot or chaotic, she would have to find a new home...*maybe move to Canada with her mom.*

"Hey, can we stop by my place so I can grab a few more things?"

"Can it wait until tomorrow?"

"Not really." She showed him her torn underwear.

He feigned remorse. He let down the partition and instructed the driver to stop by her address.

They arrived about 15 minutes later and she instructed him to stay in the limo. He obliged. She quickly crossed the street and went to the garage to check on her motorcycle. It was still intact and untouched even though she was away for so long. She ran her fingers over the smooth metallic surface.

"I missed you baby," she whispered. She jumped on it, turned on the ignition and rode in circles in the near empty parking lot, creating smoke from the friction between the tire and the concrete.

"I used to have one of those," Drax said a few feet from her.

This startled Dianna since she thought he was waiting in the limo. It made her jerk the motorcycle forward.

"Don't do that!" she chided him.

"May I?"

"Um..."

"I won't break it." Dianna stared at him hesitantly before relenting. He got on it and revved it.

"A little small," he told her.

"I'm a little small," she quipped making him smirk. He gassed it and sped the motorcycle around in circles like she did. Then, he rode it up to her hitting the breaks a few inches from her feet.

"Woah there, cowboy!" she said clearly impressed. "Is there anything you can't do?"

"When you've lived as long as I have, you pick up a few interests and learn a lot of things." He swung himself off the motorcycle so she could get on it and park it.

"You say that as if you're that much older me. You intrigue me more and more each day," she told him as she walked past him to the garage elevators. As she waited for the elevator, he came and stood next to her.

"You were supposed to be waiting in the car."

"Guess I got bored while you were in here joyriding instead of getting fresh undies." The elevator door opened. "Ladies first."

"You need to stop pretending to be such a gentleman when we both know you're a fake," she teased him.

"Woah! Where did that come from?"

"Don't act as if you haven't been an asshole to me just because you're being nice today," she instigated.

"Like you haven't been a bitch to me." She chuckled, pleased with herself, as she watched the numbers change above the elevator door on their way up. When they stepped out of the elevator on her floor, they sauntered slowly to her front door, his arm around her shoulders possessively but when they finally got to her apartment, they found the door slightly ajar.

"I thought I closed it when I left," she said looking confused. She cautiously stepped inside with Drax following closely behind her. She could hear the faucet dripping. She stubbed her toe on something. Something wasn't right. She quickly turned on the light only to find her apartment ransacked. Furniture flipped over, clothes and paper everywhere, broken glass on the floor. With her heart racing, she tried to run to the faucet to turn it off, but firm hands held her back. He held his finger to his lips to indicate that she should be silent. He lifted his pant leg and pulled out a gun. Dianna stared at it in shock as if it was her first time seeing one.

"Stay close," he whispered slowly. He went through and inspected every room and the hallway to make sure no one was hiding or lurking in any spots. He turned on all the lights as he went through thoroughly, checking under beds, inside closets, bathroom shower. By the time they circle back to the living room, he was positive whoever did this was long gone.

Dianna went to the kitchen and turned off the faucet. They both sat at the kitchen table, trying to calm their nerves from the jarring ordeal.

"Who could've done this?"

"I've got a few ideas!" Drax responded unable to contain his ire.

"Maybe I should call the police in case it was a robbery."

"Did you notice anything missing?"

"Not really but I haven't checked my jewelry."

"I don't think this was a robbery, Dianna." His words were foreboding and ominous. He was right. Everything was out of place but there was no real damage. It was as if they just wanted to let her know that someone was there...like a warning. She dropped onto her couch.

"Maybe those guys in Alabama did this?" he asked her.

"How would they even know where I live? Quinton doesn't even know where I live."

"Are you sure?" Dianna thought for a while. Her experience with Quinton taught her that he was a calculating and a desperate man sometimes. He had been through her purse when she was unconscious. He could have easily spotted something in her purse that gave her address away. Her ID had an old address on it and she never changed it to keep herself off the radar but maybe an old piece of mail or something. *Why would he do that though?*

"Quinton wouldn't do this. I saved his daughter's life!" she convinced herself, immediately dismissing any thoughts of betrayal.

"What do you mean by that?" Drax eyes were demanding.

"Nothing. Besides he told me that men had showed up at his house looking for my mother years ago. I wouldn't be surprised if it was them," she said, quickly shifting the blame. She knew Drax wasn't fond of Quinton in the least. She knew it, the night they were in his suite in Alabama. His entire persona changed when she mentioned him.

Drax rubbed his temple as he felt a headache forming in his skull like a tsunami bringing the pain.

"Get your things!" he commanded her curtly.

"I've got to-- "

"It's not safe here. We have to leave now." His tone remained stoic, and she could see he wasn't inviting a debate, so she decided against protesting any further. As she walked towards her bedroom to collect some items, she paused.

"What about my motorcycle?"

"That's not important..." he said distracted as he sat on the chair holding his gun in one hand and his head in the other. His body was slumped forward. Dianna could tell he was exhausted and that his mind was preoccupied with the events of the night. He looked at his watch then at her keenly, trying to read her expression.

"What is it?!" His agitation was evident. But she didn't care. If her motorcycle didn't come with them tonight, she wasn't leaving. She knew Drax would never come back for it. He didn't trust her, and, in that moment, she realized that deep down he shouldn't. She needed her motorcycle just in case she needed to take off and go into deep hiding. It didn't matter that she had connected with him or anyone else, she would disappear like she always did.

"I'm not leaving it!"

"FUCK! You're a pain in the ass!" But he saw that she meant business. "Okay! I'll put it in the trunk or something." He waved his hand flippantly as he walked toward her bathroom. "You got any aspirin?" She could hear him loudly rummaging through her medicine cabinet. He finally found something in a prescription bottle and returned to the kitchen where he downed it with a glass of water. It was probably the oxycodone, the only useful thing she had gotten from the hospital when she met into the accident months ago. Dianna turned around and quickly ran inside the room. She started packing a few of her things but she had always been a light loader. She was in and out in maybe five minutes. She ran to where he was standing in the living room.

"Ready!" she told him. Then she hesitated again. "You should know this arrangement isn't permanent," she added.

"We'll revisit this once we figure out what's really going on," he said dismissively. He pulled her close to him gently. He no longer had his gun in his hand and Dianna assumed that he placed it back in the holster under his pant leg. He kissed her hair soothingly, "In the meantime, I just need you to trust me." She nodded her head, but she knew that they were both a long way from any true concept of trust.

***

It was day two at the office after she had signed the contract. She still wasn't fully adjusted to the constant bright lights that flooded through her window when the blinds were open or the fluorescent lights that flooded her office when the blinds were closed. It was a stark difference from being able to control the lighting at her apartment, to being flooded with it at her job. She also wasn't used to having an assistant at her beck and call and she sought to avoid requesting Jana's assistance at all cost. This wasn't who she was, but she had to get used to it. Drax wouldn't have it any other way since he wanted to keep an eye on her as much as possible. He didn't even want her to go to lunch alone. She was beginning to wonder if he ransacked her apartment as a form of subterfuge to become his casual prisoner but had to admit to the fact that Drax had too much integrity to play such juvenile games.

"At least he didn't assign me a damn, bodyguard!" she said taking a sip of her coffee and opening her laptop to see what her tasks were for the day. She had enough work to keep her busy night and day. She still had outstanding projects from when she was a freelancer that she needed to complete ASAP plus the new workload that he generously piled on her. She was appreciative that he didn't smother her at work. In fact, she hardly saw him since he was barely there. He popped in for morning meetings, stayed long enough to approve budgets and projects and then he was gone. She figured if she didn't get used to it in a month, she could go back to freelancing. Her work spoke for itself and she didn't have to work too hard to build clientele. In the meantime, a 9 to 5 job and living arrangements with Drax, was something she had to get used to while they sorted out what really happened at her apartment. After that, she hoped she could revert to her normal life.

"I've got a whole mess to clean," she said bothered that her things were still strewn all throughout her apartment. Her obsessive compulsiveness wouldn't let her forget about it. But she knew that was the least of her worries. Somebody broke into her home, went through her things and destroyed the small sanctuary she had created. *Maybe going back home WASN'T a good idea.*

She played an ad she was working on. They were selling high tech security equipment that could change any regular home into a smart home. This made her think of Quinton and all the security cameras he had installed around his house. She wondered if he was telling the truth about people looking for her mother. *Maybe, he had the cameras installed because he was mixed up in bad business.* She racked her brain trying to remember any clues that could prove he wasn't lying but she couldn't think of any. He said he had her back but now she had to wonder. In her guts though, she knew it wasn't him. *It couldn't be.*

"I want to fuck the boss too!" Dianna looked up from her laptop. It was Eric. "Damn, your office is as big as mine and I'm in charge of you," he joked. Dianna laughed.

"I'm not fucking the boss…anymore," she responded with a guilty look on her face.

"Of course not. You're just spending a lot of time playing mommy and daddy."

"Okay! You're right! I'm screwing his brains out." She feigned a dramatic confession. She slicked her tongue on the roof of her mouth and nodded her head salaciously. "uh-uh."

"You...screwing his brains out...okay, whatever makes it sound good and feel even better." They both laughed boisterously at their dirty jokes but quickly contained themselves after remembering where they were.

"Girl, don't get me fired!" He smacked her playfully on her hand. "Anyway, I just wanted to check on you and tell you congratulations."

"Thank you," she said getting up to hug him graciously. "How is Simon?"

"Still working night shift at that awful bar. I can't get him to sell the damn thing."

"He's marching to the beat of his own drum, like I was," she admitted to him.

"...and now?"

"Someone else is playing the beat," she confessed.

"Don't sound so sad. I thought you liked Drax."

"I do. I guess it's the change I'm afraid of."

"Change can be a good thing," Eric assured her.

"We'll see." She flopped back into her chair and pulled herself closer to her desk. "But I have to get some work done. It's piling up," she told Eric.

"I know and I'm going to be riding you if you don't meet those deadlines. We should do lunch," he offered. She knew Drax was a tad territorial now but as long as she wasn't eating alone, she didn't think it would create too much friction between them.

"Okay. Come get me at 1:00!"

"Will do. Byyyeee!" he said dipping out of her office, leaving her alone to ruminate on their conversation. Things HAD changed. Drax was being a little closed off and overly protective as if she hadn't been risking the elements since she was sucking on her mother's breasts. She didn't need his protection, but she wasn't fighting it which made her even more confused. Usually, she followed her own accord when it came down to her survival but this time, she was going against her better judgement. Truth be told, she was tired of running...*like her mother.* She still couldn't believe her mother jumped borders and went to Canada. "Will that be me...for the rest of my life?" She breathed out exasperated. She decided to focus on her work and suspend her self-searching for the time being.

She was working ferociously when she saw five men in black suits exit the elevator on the opposite end of the main lobby area from her glass door. She noted that one of them was Drax. The others were large and burly and very intimidating. She saw Drax point them to the conference room following behind briskly. Her hackles were up, and her intuition was off the rails. This didn't look like a typical business meeting in the least. She grabbed her phone and called Drax. The call went to voicemail. She used her office phone to call his office assistant, leaning to the side of her chair to dial her extension.

"Hello, you've reached the office of Drax Ashton, how may I direct your call?"

"Samantha, it's me, Dianna Montague. Was Mr. Ashton booked for a meeting today?"

She heard the assistant's nails clicking away at the keyboard. "Um...not with any clients but...he is having a personal meeting in the conference room and he asked not to be disturbed."

"Do you have any idea what the meeting is about?"

Samantha chuckled. "That's above my pay grade, Ms. Montague, but would you like to leave a message. I can have him call you back when he comes out."

"No, thanks." She hung up the phone. "Damn it!" She swiveled her chair back to her laptop frustrated. After brainstorming for a short while about how she could get some information on Drax's little informal meeting, she gave up and continued working even harder on her editing to distract herself but there was no escaping the strange feeling that sat at the bottom of her stomach like an ugly, bulbous frog.

***

She was sidetracked all throughout lunch, chiming into the conversation between Eric and Simon when it was appropriate and toying with her salad as they sat at the far end of the vegan restaurant. Eric had told her that the food was so good she wouldn't be able to tell it was vegan, but she was so absorbed in her own thoughts that she wasn't even hungry.

"You have got to be the most uninteresting lunch date I have ever lunched with!" Eric said to her picking up on her disinterest. His blond hair was neatly swooped to the side as he pierced her with his blue eyes.

"Um…did you see those men come into the office with Drax today?" she said with her arms folded on the table inches away from her Caesar salad.

"Yeah… what about them?"

"Do you know them?" Eric looked at Simon and Simon averted his gaze. The exchange did not miss Dianna.

"Eric, who were those men?"

"I don't know but I do have my suspicions," Eric said cryptically.

"What suspicions?" she asked, her heart racing as she waited for an answer.

"That you need to mind your business and eat that damn salad!" Simon went into a fit of laughter.

"I'm glad you are enjoying this," she retorted feeling dejected at the fact that Eric had her going only to leave her empty-handed.

"Girl, who do you think they were?" Simon inquired completely amused at her curiosity.

"I don't know…they just looked scary."

"Well, one thing you're going to find out working for Mr. Ashton is that his clients are on a spectrum. Some of them are normal and others are not so normal. Don't let it bother you."

"I don't think they were clients," she pushed back.

"What else could they be, IRS, FBI, CIA?" Dianna went silent. "Let it go. I'm sure it's not what you are thinking."

"I hope so," she responded feeling even more frustrated that Eric couldn't provide her with more information. Then her phone rang. It was Drax. "Hey," she greeted him none too enthusiastically.

"It's good to hear your voice. Sorry I missed your call today."

"It's fine." She paused then decided that she might as well bulldoze ahead. "By the way, who were those guys in your office today?" She caught Eric rolling his eyes dramatically as she waited for Drax to answer. She decided to step away from the table since clearly both her lunch dates were listening intently to her conversation.

"Business partners." Her heart sank because she knew he was lying. "I've got to travel out of town today," he added.

"Why?"

"There are some things I need to take care of."

"So, this is what we're doing? Secrets?" She heard a heavy sigh on his end.

"It's a family thing."

"Like the funeral thing?"

"Yeah."

"Y'know, Drax. A part of building trust is being open with each other. If you can't open up to me, then how can I trust you?"

"Di--" She hung up the phone and went back to her lunch.

"Everything okay?" Simon asked. His nurturing side resurfacing again as he noticed Dianna's wet eyes.

"I'm fine," she lied blinking back the tears. She was mad at herself for even wanting to cry. She composed herself quickly and forced a smile.

"You're really not," Eric told her.

"Dianna!" She heard Drax's voice and thought she was imagining it, but Simon and Eric were staring into the distance behind her, so she knew she was not hallucinating. She turned around quite ungracefully, making a raucously loud sound with her chair to see Drax standing a few feet from their table.

"Give me a second," she told her friends as she got up and walked over to Drax.

"Weren't we just on the phone?"

"I was outside. I was going to come in to surprise you."

"How did you know I was here?"

"Your assistant told me." She cleared her throat. This was the second time she insinuated that he was stalking her, but she couldn't help it. He just kept popping up conveniently.

"Of course!" But she wasn't ready to let go of her anger. "What do you want?"

"I don't like leaving you alone like this, but this trip is important." His voice was deep and controlled.

"Y'know, I've been taking care of myself way before you came along!" she snapped. He rubbed her arm and it soothed her.

"Don't get upset. You know what will happen." She was getting so used to being out in public, she almost forgot that she wasn't like him. She couldn't control her transformations entirely like he did. She looked around nervously to see if anyone was watching and she resolved to calming herself. He took her hand and led her outside. "Let's talk in the car," and he opened the door of his limo so she could get inside, and he followed behind her. He instructed the driver to let up the partition for privacy.

"There are things I want to tell you but it's too soon. It doesn't mean I'm lying or keeping things from you."

"It feels that way. You've been so closed off since I moved in with you. What's really going on?" Her eyebrows were knitted together as her eyes begged him for answers.

"Can you honestly say that you see any of this being long term?" Dianna was silent. She stared at her fingers clutched tightly together in her lap. "Exactly! I'm all for revealing things about myself to you and I hate to say this, but you have to earn it," he told her frankly. "You think I don't know why you insisted on taking your motorcycle with you to my place." He paused and lifted her chin so she could face him. "The real reason you practically begged me to lift your heavy ass motorcycle in the back of my limo." She sighed heavily as she contemplated his words. "Or the reason you still haven't told me what went down in Alabama." She looked down at her hands again. He was right. She was keeping secrets that she had no intentions on sharing them with him.

"When the time is right," he told her.

She nodded her head slowly. "Okay." She breathed out to release the tension. "When are you coming back?"

"Thursday."

"That's three days from now!" she said incredulously.

"You can handle it, right?" She nodded again. Just a minute ago she told him she could take care of herself but now she felt scared, alone and vulnerable without him. She couldn't believe she was surviving without him all these years, but she was. Yet she was changing, becoming dependent. She squared her shoulders and put on a brave face.

"I'm good," she said resolutely. He smoothed her curly black hair away from face. He knew she was pretending.

"Call me if anything happens. Anything."

"Okay."

"And control that feisty spirit of yours or you'll give yourself away," he reminded her.

"Okay."

He studied her face. "I don't want to leave you like this," he told her. "Have you ever shot a gun before?" She stared at him silently as she tried to gather his meaning. He took his gun out of its holster and handed it to her. "Take this."

"No!"

"Take it!"

"Where am I going to put it?" she asked looking at it as if it was about to grow fangs and bite her. He pulled out her neatly tucked in shirt from her work pants and pushed the gun in the waist of the back of her pants. He then covered it with her shirt. It felt cold and heavy on her back.

"Slip it into your purse as soon as you go inside the restaurant. I'll go in with you." She nodded her head. If someone had told her months ago that she would be willing to do almost anything Drax told her without question, she would've laughed them to scorn. He kissed her again and her longing for him increased but she had to return to her friends.

By the time she was back at the table where her friends were waiting, they gave her a knowing look when they saw her shirt hanging outside of her pants. She realized that they had the wrong impression, but it was a good cover considering she was hiding a gun in the waist of her pants. She grabbed her purse and took it to the bathroom with her. She placed the gun inside her purse, fixed her clothes and freshened her dark brown lipstick. Then she went back out where she saw Drax carrying on a conversation with Eric and Simon. Once he saw her, he politely ended the conversation and allowed her to sit at the table. He placed his hand over hers and bent to whisper in her ear.

"I'll see you Thursday." He kissed her ear and then walked out. She had inhaled his scent and locked it in her memory. She refocused on her friends.

"I'm hungry all of sudden," she told them.

"I bet you are."

She pondered for a bit at the fact that neither Eric nor Simon seemed uncomfortable with Drax's affection toward her. "Doesn't he care if people...know about us?"

"Do I look like I care? And what is Simon going to do…snitch to the CEO of the company?"

He was right, "Point taken," she responded.

She looked behind her through the glass of the restaurant. Drax's limo was gone. She had a strange feeling. She couldn't remember ever being this happy but also this scared and it wasn't only because Drax was meeting with unscrupulous looking men, or that she was possibly being hunted by people who may want to kill her. She was afraid of what her future would look like with or without Drax.

Chapter 8

Blood and brain matter from Charlie's head splattered against the wall. Jinn wanted to run but he couldn't. There were at least three of them inside the dingy apartment. Sweat was pouring from his forehead and all color drained from his face as a tall white guy with brown hair placed his gun right under his eye where he had the tear drop tattoo. At first, he thought they were the Feds but after they shot his partner, there was no doubt in his mind that these men were not working with the government.

"Let's try this again. Do you know this woman?" He held a picture of the girl that paid them the $50,000 in front of his face. They had asked Charlie first but instead of complying, Charlie wanted to play tough guy and ended up with a bullet through his head.

"Listen!" he begged frantically. "She was walking with Quinton's kid. We figured she was his sister or sumpn' and we were going to intimidate her enough to scare Quinton into paying us what he owed."

"Go on!" the man who was clearly the leader urged.

"She told us she would pay us the money and to lay off Quinton and his family,"

"Did she give you the money?"

"Yeah, yeah! She paid in cash! Please don't kill me!" he groveled. His heart was beating out of his chest, and he needed to urinate.

"Was she alone?"

"No, some guy was with her. A black guy. He didn't seem to like the fact that she was paying us money, but she told him to back off." He started to sob uncontrollably. "And that's it, man! We left with the money. We haven't seen her or Quinton since."

"Is there anything else you want to tell us?"

"No! Wait, yes! She had a suitcase; she may have been travelling. I don't know where but -- Look, is this about the money?"

"No, It's not about the money. You did good. You won't end up dead like your partner here."

"Thank you, man!" The man lowered his gun.

"Yeah, I think that's all we need." They began leaving, then the leader turned around and stared coldly at Jinn.

"One more thing." He lifted his gun and shot a bullet into his forehead and red droplets of blood and flesh splattered across the wall.

***

"First, before we start this meeting. Let's congratulate Dai Chung's son and Rendu's daughter on their beautiful wedding this week!" Marvin announced and the room erupted in a round of applause and cheers.

The stocky Asian man stood up at the announcement which prompted Rendu to stand up as well. They both looked immensely proud of the union and they shook hands amicably and sat down.

"Such a beautiful couple. This means our kind has another pureblood to look forward to." There was an uproar as the men banged heavily on the table in agreement.

"What about Drax? He's been delaying the inevitable with my daughter for years now. It's becoming insulting!" Norlan belted out. The roar died down and was replaced by an awkward silence.

Drax stared at the old man dead pan. He was not in the mood for his shit today. He had been trying to get him to marry his daughter for over a decade now. In fact, the damn thing was pretty much arranged and just needed to happen. Since Norlan was Marvin's right hand, there was really no way around it and it was very obvious that Drax was stalling. Norlan returned Drax's stare undaunted.

"Y'know how young men are, Norlan. My son is trying to live out his bachelor days. He's well aware of his obligations to us."

"Is he? We don't have time for bedroom games and skirt chasing. We need to strengthen our kind with strong families and future heirs. Drax's gaze never faltered. He couldn't stand Norlan and quite frankly didn't trust a bone in his body.

"Y'know father, I can speak for myself," he said to Marvin leaning forward to get closer to Norlan's face. "There are other single Nagalians that are more than willing to marry your daughter, Norlan. No need to sit around waiting for me to get my act together."

"Now, now Drax. That's no way to talk to an old family friend and ally. Plus, his daughter is amazing. She has a PhD. in Astrophysics and works for NASA. You'd be a damn fool to turn that down," Marvin stated.

Norlan grinned. "Such an arrogant fucker! Exactly why I want you as my son-in-law." The room erupted in laughter. Drax scoffed not finding the exchange the least bit amusing. Marvin patted his back good-naturedly.

"My son will make a great son-in-law. Patience, Norlan. He'll come around." Marvin cleared his throat. "On to more important business." He turned to Drax's personal assistant Susanne. "Did you take down anything about Norlan's daughter?"

"No, thought that was off the record."

"It was but make sure you get the minutes of what we are about to discuss."

139

"On it!" she said enthusiastically.

"Okay, what do we have to report!"

"More half breed Nagalians showing up dead. Found two dead bodies in Georgia floating in the Chattanooga River, A mother and her young daughter. And two more found dead in Texas in their home."

"What's their relation?"

"Doesn't seem like they were related. Probably just friends."

"Were they women?"

"Yes, at this time, it is without any uncertainty that all half Nagalians are women."

Drax listened keenly as Dianna came to his mind. Dianna didn't even know half the danger she was in and he couldn't tell her yet. He knew she would try to go into hiding again which only served to expose herself more to the men hunting her. It was becoming more and more indubitable that her apartment was trashed by bounty hunters, but he wasn't absolutely sure. She made a few connections with outsiders, including her brother, Quinton, who probably knew she was a half breed, so he wasn't ruling him out.

"Drax has located one more alive…. brought her to the house," Marvin revealed to the fraternity members. "Do you still have eyes on her?"

"Huh…yes. She ran into some problems. Her apartment was broken into. I think it may have been the bounty hunters, so she's under my protection now." He was caught off guard with his father bringing her up. Drax shifted his weight in the chair as an uneasy feeling came over him knowing fully well that he was doing more than just protecting her.

"Under your protection? Since when has fraternity members started offering personal security?" Norlan inquired. "Isn't that what we hire people to do?"

"She was freelancing for my company before I knew she was a half breed. I offered her a position at my firm so she could continue working for me and a place to stay since her apartment clearly isn't safe." Norlan eyed Drax suspiciously. "She does good work. One of the best editors on my team," he stretched on. He lowered his gaze as he tapped the point of the pen pensively on the wooden surface of the long conference table. "It's the least I could do." He placed the pen down carefully; aware he was under Norlan's scrutiny.

"Had a chance to meet her. Pretty nice girl. A bit uncultured, oblivious of our traditions but y'know, they do what they do." The men murmured in agreement. "A little clumsy too. Sliced her hand really bad on an old ax in our cellar. Ain't that right, Drax?" His father's eyes were laughing from his amusement.

Drax gave him a half smile, "Yeah... clumsy." He picked up the pen and started tapping it again on the table. Something he did whenever he was uncomfortable. Technically, he wasn't lying about Dianna, but he knew he had crossed the line with her on so many levels. He had become attached and that was dangerous.

"Have we traced any of the hunters," Marvin continued.

"No, but we have eyes everywhere, or in all the major cities at least."

"Of course, but you know the half breeds...aaah, excuse me. Half Nagalians," Marvin corrected himself. "The wife keeps telling me that the term 'half breed' is offensive." The men laughed.

"The wife isn't here!" another guy shouted from the back. They continued laughing and hooting raunchily.

"Yeah, but she wanted me to retrain you guys. She says y'all are a bunch of uncouth savages!" Drax laughed along with them feeling the camaraderie in the room. "Okay, simmer down, simmer down. Let's not get sidetracked. So, it doesn't seem as if the half Nagalians are mutating beyond what we already know." There was a lone chuckle in the back.

"No, sir," his informant pressed on.

"My wife is still working on finding an antidote," Marvin alerted them. The room became dead silent.

"No offense old friend but she needs to work faster. The humans have an arsenal of Apoptosyde that could wipe us out in the blink of an eye," Norlan commented.

"I know, she and her team of biologists are working hard." There was a low murmuring.

"I know. It's quite disconcerting."

"Apoptosyde is the cause of death for all the bodies we have found, so far. Seems like that are injecting it into their blood stream."

"It's the only way they can kill us," Marvin agreed.

"We can't just wait like sitting ducks!" Rendu belted out.

"Yes, we can. We'll wait patiently but not like sitting ducks. We are more organized and militarized than before. Our militia is more than prepared to take on these bounty hunters and once we have the antidote, we will have more leverage to protect our kind."

"My dad is right!" Drax added. "Our numbers aren't large, granted we are a larger organization today than we've ever been since the war, but we have centuries of training when it comes to handling our human enemies. We also have human allies who are aiding us plus our financial power is growing which means more safe houses, more weapons, more prominent communities, more clout with the US government. We are far from sitting ducks!"

Marvin patted his son proudly on the back. "So, remain vigilant. Let's save as many half Nagalians as we can. Let's continue to build our numbers... and brothers...let's continue to stay safe!"

The meeting went on for another half an hour before ending. Drax was about to leave when his father pulled him to the side outside of the conference room.

"Drax, I'm trying to take the heat off of you, but you have to at least show some interest by dating Norlan's daughter." Drax hung his head and rubbed his temple as he felt his ire rising. He then slowly faced his father with frustration evident on his face.

"I'm not interested in his daughter," Drax clarified through gritted teeth.

"You know it's not about that. It's about tradition and honor and keeping promises."

"You should check yourself before you make unguaranteed promises, Father," Drax challenged Marvin which was something he rarely did but he didn't like being manipulated in this way. He owned his own conglomerate, proved himself to be an outstanding leader time and time again and here he was having a tedious conversation about whom he should or should not marry.

"Is it that half Nagalian girl that's making you confused? There's nothing serious there, right?" His father said looking around anxiously to make sure no one was listening to their conversation.

Drax diverted his gaze. He had to be honest with his father. "I don't know!"

"Damn it! Look, just forget her!" Marvin said gesturing his hands dismissively as if by magic he could make Dianna disappear from his son's mind. "You have more important fish to fry. Go on a date with Norlan's daughter as a show of good faith and see how that works out for you." Drax studied his father's face. Marvin was about 500 years old. He'd seen a lot. Been through a lot and it was finally catching up with him as his youthfulness was now cracked by tired wrinkles. He was halfway through his lifecycle, the last thing Drax wanted to do was disappoint his father or create an enemy out of him. He conceded.

"I'll go on a date but don't expect much!"

"I do expect much! I expect a lot from you son." Drax was going to be the next president of the Nagalian Fraternity. He knew the responsibilities that came with it and he knew the other members were watching his every move. He had to admit that getting wrapped up with a half Nagalian woman would only make him seem dismissive of important Nagalian traditions. It could also dictate whether the other members respected him as a leader or not. It was the last thing he wanted to do but he had to at least give Norlan's daughter a chance to change his mind about marrying her.

***

She was a tall beautiful brunette. She was wearing a shimmering skin colored dress and long beige stilettos. She held her clutch daintily as she walked towards the table. He got up and pulled her seat out as she seated herself.

"Well hello, stranger," she said sweetly to him.

"Long overdue, right?"

"Right," she agreed. She placed her bone straight hair behind her ear then placed her clutch on the table.

"So…I've heard so much about you. A PhD. in astrophysics. A physicist at NASA and you have a startup company." He led into the conversation. She smiled proudly.

"And you, a multibillion-dollar advertising agency. Next in line to be president of the Nagalian Fraternity and quite handsome I must add," she flirted. "It seems we are sort of even keeled. Why has it taken so long for us to get together like this?" she inquired innocently.

"The playboy life never grows old when you are young," he supplied, but he realized too late that his statement may not have been the classiest thing to say. She was only slightly taken aback but then she smiled.

"I get it," she told him. "Get it all in while you can before you're knee-deep in marriage; right?"

"Something like that." He took a sip of his water. "What about you? Young, beautiful, and successful. You're every Nagalian's dream," he flattered her. "Excuse me for not sounding progressive but why don't you have a man?"

Dianna chuckled. "Well, I mix and mingle here and there but my work keeps me busy."

"Same," he told her. He noticed she had a tattoo on her wrist. 'Clive'. It was in cursive.

"Who is Clive?" he asked, motioning his head toward her tattoo.

She slid her bulky bracelet over it self-consciously. "Just an old friend from the past," she explained.

"Nagalian or human?"

She sighed heavily. "Human." She gently reached out to his warm hand and held it. "He's no longer in my life and... I don't want to talk about it," she said kindly. Her brown contacts glistened under the soft light. In a way, he was grateful. He could use this information to his advantage, but he would keep the charade going for tonight since he had to report the outcome of their date, back to his father.

"Love isn't easy for our kind. It's a luxury," he told her. She visibly stiffened then pulled back her hand.

"Who needs love when you can have stability, a lifelong partner and an heir to carry on your legacy?" she told him. Drax wasn't stupid. He could see that she was dragged here as much as he was, but she was going to make the best out of it to appease Norlan.

"Don't look at me like that," she admonished, gently slapping his hand. He gave her one of his infamous wry smiles.

"Like what?"

"Like you're reading my mind and you know my secrets."

"Let's just say, you and I have more in common than you think."

"Well, that's a good place to start. We can maybe...build from there." His gaze became smoldering as he considered her words, which sparked fire in her eyes.

"Let's see where things go," he told her.

***

As he lay next to Jasmine, her tall, sexy body, fast asleep alongside his. He pulled the covers over her and she snuggled up closer to him. She was perfect. She was his equal in bed, intelligent, and beyond attractive. She was also a gentle spirit, even though he liked his women a little...fiery. But that was the least of his concern. He was perceptive enough to know she was still in love with Clive, and they both knew that this was a union simply to bring their families together with little to no emotional attachment. He turned onto his back and stared at the ceiling. He didn't have a tattoo of Dianna on his wrist. It wasn't his style, but she was certainly tattooed on his brain.

He hadn't heard from her and he hadn't called her, but he was watching her. He had cameras installed in her office and at his apartment. The camera in his bedroom was installed before she came along but the one in her office was just recently installed. They were mainly for her safety but if he was being honest, he knew it bordered on the edge of obsession. He practically knew her every move. He knew when she stood by her window looking out at the view in front of her that she was missing him. He watched her pleasure herself a few nights in his bedroom. He knew she was a workaholic, staying up until the wee hours of the morning trying to meet her deadlines. He had told Eric to load her up with enough work to keep her preoccupied. He also told Eric to keep an eye on her and he was playing the role perfectly. He was practically her best friend. He gnawed on the side of his lip. If she knew he was manipulating her life like this, he could send her packing for sure but like his father said, she was pretty oblivious to the depth of her situation. Half breeds were being slaughtered all over the US because they chose to lead isolated lives that left them vulnerable with no protection, but this was only after many of them were repeatedly raped and experimented on for vaccines, cures, and biological weapons.

He carefully got out of bed and went to his travel laptop. He logged into the surveillance system and selected the bedroom. She was sleeping peacefully. He rationalized that he wasn't really stalking her, and he laughed inwardly when she thought he was. He didn't know she was in Alabama. That was pure coincidence, but he was happy he bumped into her there. Once they patched things up, he decided to play his hand a little better, a little smarter. She was strong but extremely fragile at the same time. She could handle herself, but her emotions were consuming her, eating her alive and trapping her in darkness. She drowned it out with work, but he was afraid of what she would do in her darkest hour. In that moment when she didn't feel good enough or when she felt her loneliest. He didn't want to marry Jasmine but what if he had to? What if he could no longer be there for her? He wouldn't let her get around the batch of Apoptoside at his parents' home anymore but there were other ways to get it. She just had to ask the right person or research places she could find it. He could only hope that she could overcome her demons on her own. When it came to her life, his protection could only go so far. He couldn't be with her every day or have eyes on her all the time. He hoped that she recognized in time that as short as her life was, it was worth living. She woke up, tossed, and turned for a second then checked her phone. She pulled her legs close to her chest and rested her head on her knees as she swiped through her phone.

"You're lonely," he said as he observed her. He checked to see if Jasmine was still sleeping then crept out to the hallway with his phone. He called her.

"Why are you still up?" he said smiling into the phone.

"I miss you."

***

"When are you coming back to visit us?" Adisa's tiny voice traveled through the line.

"It might be a while, baby."

"I bought something for you," she told her. "It's a surprise but you will like it."

Dianna's heart melted.

"Keep it and when I come to visit, you can give it to me."

"Can you visit on Thanksgiving?" Thanksgiving was a few months away. She figured she could, but she didn't want to make any promises.

"I think I can. But enough about me. Did your streaks wash out?"

"Yeah."

"Are you going to get more?"

"Mommy has a lot to do and daddy just got another job so they're both kind of busy right now."

"Really?" Dianna said excitedly, "what kind?"

"At the post office," Adisa divulged.

"That's awesome. Are you home alone now?"

"No, there's a babysitter here." Dianna didn't like Adisa being home without her parents, especially since Quinton had a knack for attracting the wrong crowd.

"Well, do as your babysitter tell you and I'll call back later tonight, okay?"

"Okay."

They ended the call and Dianna was once again forced to face the silence in Drax's house. It was Friday night and Drax still hadn't returned from his trip. It made her anxious. His large, custom built home was too spacious for her comfort. She felt like an ant in its vastness. The master bedroom where she slept was big enough to fit her mother's entire house. It was self-contained with an adjoining bathroom, bedroom bar and an outfitted workstation, so she mostly isolated herself to that area. There was not much reason to explore the rest of the house except to see what it looked like. As far she could see, there were four bedrooms, split levels with an open floor concept with elevated ceiling and spiraling stairs which made her feel as if she might miss her step and fall onto the white marble floor in the living room below. There was also a home theater which she never used. She, instead, opted to catch up on her reality shows on her laptop. From the lower floor, she could see the well-lit outdoor pool in the back and manicured grass of the courtyard to the side through the expansive glass walls, cornered with custom cut bricks. The house was perched about 50ft back from the edge of the cliff which overlooked the main less-traveled highway below.

"Who gets a house on a damn cliff!" she said as she stared out through the glass walls. *An other than worldly creature that doesn't want neighbors in his business* came the voice in her head. She didn't like the silence or the feeling of being left alone in the middle of nowhere. She was a loner, but she preferred being a loner lost in a sea of people than a loner secluded on a precipice.

Drax's words, *I just want to stash you away like a relic in my father's showroom,* replayed in her mind. "You have managed to do that all right!" she ruminated to herself. Even if she wanted to get on her motorcycle and ride out, the trip to any grocery store was so far, she usually ended up deciding against it. She opted to work from home three days out of the week just to avoid the hour-long trip into the office. She liked long rides for the purpose of scenic therapy but getting to and back from work was a whole other matter.

She might have thought he was overcompensating for something, but her psychoanalysis would be off base. He had everything, was well-bred and was the product of excellent and meticulous parenting. He was so used to wealth and power, none of this luxury and prestige was probably a second thought for him. If anything, she may have been the one overcompensating with her motorcycle... the need to be tough and daring when deep down inside, she was always scared... her dark thoughts were plaguing her again. She went to the bar, pulled out a glass and made herself vodka on the rocks. She stepped out of the bedroom and went to the bottom level of the house. She spotted a few cameras installed in strategic locations of the house on her way down. She wondered if there was a camera in her room. If there was, it might have been one of the tiny ones. She thought of the two nights she was spread eagle, masturbating on his bed. A devilish smile played across her lips. She bit her bottom lip at the thought of him watching her please herself.

"That's what you would get for being a paranoid pervert," she joked to herself. She went to the pool area and walked around the deck a few times as she sipped her drink. She then walked back to the sliding doors and noticed yet another camera.

"Damn, Drax! I can't escape you." Then a thought snuck into her head. She was wearing her pajamas. It was anything but sexy, just the regular ones she always wore when she did her night work. Never once taking her eyes off the camera and after placing her drink on the ground, she slipped off her slacks and then the top. She didn't have a bra underneath, but she had her Panties, and she 'sashayed' her way out of that too. She started squeezing both of her breasts erotically and gyrating her curvy hips to a song in her head. She spun around a few times so that the camera could capture every nuance of her body under the fluorescent lighting. She was so caught up in her own little dance that she didn't notice Drax coming around from the courtyard at the left corner of the house. She didn't see how frantic his expression was because she wasn't inside the house and he thought his worst fears had come to pass or when he stopped in his tracks to watch her dance for the camera or when he snuck up behind her until she could finally feel his breath on her neck. She gasped audibly but recognizing his smell, which flooded her senses, she immediately turned around and jumped on him with her legs around his waist.

"What took you so long?" she whispered, her mouth only half an inch from his. "I told you that I fucking missed you!" her voice was raspy and aggressive. She bared her fangs and her snake-hair hissed in a frenzy from her excited emotions. Drax had gone through almost every single emotion in less than fifteen minutes but now he just wanted her, every part of her, everything about her. The fire she ignited within him was a first for him and even though it threatened to consume him, he embraced it because it made him feel every bit alive. He cradled her ass as she held the back of his head and bit his bottom lip enough to draw a small amount of blood.

"Ouch!" he said deliberately, seeming to enjoy the small pain. "Why are you so good at being bad?" he whispered in her mouth. She kissed him deeply and unrelentingly. "I'm sorry I made you wait," he told her when he was able to speak again, but she captured his mouth once more. She started unbuttoning his shirt while kissing him. She wriggled out of his arms and finished undressing him.

"Change!" she said, her eyes were penetrating his soul as he processed what she was asking him to do. He had never completely changed for her and she wanted to see it happen now.

"Do you mean--"

"I mean... I want you to show me your true self!"

"I might hurt you, you're still half human," he reminded her, clearly shaken by her demand.

"I don't care. I want to make love to you this way... in case we don't work out so I can remember this moment." Her lips trembled slightly. "I want to make love to the ONLY Nagalian male I've ever met in my entire 50 years of life. That's a long time to live without knowing what or who you really are..." she unloaded on him. She could've been drunk; she was drinking but she needed him to hear this. "The only person I could have sex with without hiding who I truly am. The only person I've met that I know for certain isn't afraid of me no matter what I do!" Drax remained silent as he absorbed her words laced with a deep haunting pain.

"You were right when you said I was lost. When you found me, I found myself." She closed the gap between them. She stared up at him, her eyes shining like diamonds. She lightly touched his left shoulder running her fingertips over his hard muscles. "I'm not stupid, Drax. I know what you must do, for your family, and it doesn't involve me. But while I have you, while I'm here, I want to give you almost everything I have, and I want you to give me you." She kissed him tenderly. Then she backed away "Change!" she ordered him pretending to crack a whip.

"You don't know what you are asking me to do." She could see that he wanted to give her what she wanted but he was afraid. So, she silently waited for him to see that she wasn't going to change her mind. Then he started to change right before her eyes. He grew a little taller, more muscular. He was hairless with silver scales from head to toe. His hands and feet became large claws, his eyes and mouth widened, and his tongue became longer and slenderer. His fangs were sharp and glistening. He was terrifying and gorgeous at the same time and he was right. He was enormous compared to the average man. She could feel the strength in his arms as he lifted her carefully and took her inside. He placed her gently in the bed and lay on his side beside her fully Nagalian. He was so large his feet hung several inches off the bed.

"Did I scare you?" he asked searching her eyes for any fear...or even disgust.

She smiled patiently. "No."

"I'm not sure how this is going to work."

"I'll get on top so I can look at you."

After she climbed on top of him, he gently guided himself into her until they were a perfect fit and then, she proceeded to work her magic. He held on to the sides of the bed so he wouldn't hurt her with his claws. She leaned forward as her hard nails pressed into his chest. His tongue extended as he tasted the salty sweat from her face.

"Feels better, doesn't it?"

"You know it does," he growled. He had stripped away a layer of himself to the deeper part of himself emotionally and physically. He tightened his grip as his thrust strength increased. His loud moans could be heard throughout the house, but it didn't matter because no one could hear him, and no one could hear her. The sweat glimmered on her body and her breasts bounced up and down as she rode him harder and harder. He watched her, hypnotized by her movements while she watched him, hypnotized by his transformation. The way his body stiffened and the way he sped up his upward thrusts, she knew he was close. If he lost control in the heat of pleasure, he could shred her half human form. She wouldn't die but she would have a lot of healing to do.

He finally climaxed, but he didn't lose control...and yet she could lose all her self-control. She let her head fall back as she loudly announced her orgasm. She tightened her grip with her long Nagalian nails digging hard into his chest and she let it all go...the anxieties, the tension, the lost feeling that haunted her deep down inside. Then she fell forward on top of him. He slowly changed back to his human form as he wrapped his body around her.

"I'm going to be sore for a while, aren't I?"

He laughed at her question. "Yeah, your legs are going to be useless for a day or two." She kissed his chest.

"Thank you!" she told him.

"No need. This was good for both of us." She wasn't sure what he meant by his words, but It gave her a reassuring feeling. "I want to have a future with you in it, Dianna." His words sounded sincere, but she knew better than to rely on wishful thinking.

"That bite mark on your neck contradicts your words," she responded. He quickly touched his neck and rubbed the area of the bite mark and then he released her and sat up. "Spotted it before you transformed. Kind of why I said the things I said." Her tone was even, and she was being very mature about the fact that he apparently slept with someone else. "Who is she?"

She sat up and inched away from him pulling her knees to her chest in a protective manner. He appeared conflicted.

"Tell me."

"I'd rather not, Dianna."

"Is it serious?"

He stroked the soft skin on her cheek.

"Not in the way you're thinking."

"I think I have fallen for you...I just feel it." Her voice was sad but steady. He stared at her knowingly. Everything was coming at him so fast. "But I think it's better for both of us to--" His eyes immediately narrowed and darkened like midnight, before she could even finish her sentence. There was that rage again. He had clearly read her thoughts.

"Over my dead body, Dianna, and since it's a certainty that I will outlive you, I wouldn't hold my breath!" He roared authoritatively at her. It was Dianna's turn to get angry.

"You can't lock me away while you go fulfill your family obligations, or sleep with people or whatever you do when you are not with me, Drax."

"I wasn't planning to. I just need more time," his voice softened. "I'm sorry you feel like I have imprisoned you." He instinctively touched her hair and a few of her snakes wrapped themselves affectionately around his hand. It was a gift he had with her and a gift he relied on to confirm that she had feelings for him. If she was frightened, so were they. If she was angry, so were they and if she was attached, so were they. He pulled his hand away and they disappeared.

"My father wants me to marry her. Pretty sure it won't happen," he told her.

"You don't have a choice."

"I disagree." He wiped the moisture from her face. "I promise you I'll fix this." She saw the integrity of his words in his eyes, but it only made her hurt more.

"Fix your family tradition?" she shot back. "Or your parents? Or the fact that I'll get old and die way before you do?" Her tone was biting. She lay back on the bed. She didn't want to expect anything from him but being with him required too much and she didn't want him to wreck his life for her, especially when she was a wreck herself.

He snuggled up behind her and it felt so good to be in his arms that she just gave in and started sobbing. He was her safe space now that her world had been turned upside down again. "You're right. But I'm not going to let you leave so we have to figure it out." He kissed the back of her neck.

"I don't know if I should be grateful or scared that you are holding me hostage." He laughed softly.

"I'm not holding you hostage. You came here willingly, remember?" he whispered into her ear seductively. "Tell me when you're ready to go."

"I just tried."

"You didn't try hard enough," he taunted. He ran his long finger languidly along her spine, then he rested his hand on the side of her hip. "You may not believe me now but a part of it is for your own good." His speech was slowing. He was falling asleep. "The Fraternity alone won't be able to protect you like I will." Dianna was confused by his statement.

"What fraternity?" she asked. He didn't answer and she realized that he was already dead to the world and there would be no use pressing the issue tonight. She decided to put it off until the following morning.

***

His eyes shot open to glaring sunlight. They had fallen asleep without closing the blinds. Usually his eyes would be mere slits but so much happened last night that he forgot to take his contacts out before falling asleep. He swung his legs over the side of the bed, getting up to manually close the blinds as the sun bounced off his skin, giving him the appearance of a golden God glowing in the radiant rays of the sun. He tried to recap the events that took place the night before. He had come home to find Dianna missing from the house which sent him on a frantic hunt throughout the house. He found her outside naked and drinking, which calmed him, but he was confronted by a new set of emotions as they were about to make love. She had spilled her soul to him. He figured the drinking had something to do with it since drunk lips tell no lies. These were the thoughts in her dark mind that either gave her clarity or drove her over the cliff and she made him privy to them. He touched his neck, he figured by now, the bite marks had healed but she had seen them and made love to him anyway. She wasn't angry or jealous and he unfortunately knew why. She didn't think he was worthy of the fight within her and had given up which was a blow to his ego since he was ready to put everything on the line for her. It was such a blow, he threatened her that he wouldn't let her leave which in hindsight seemed really selfish and controlling but that wasn't his intention. At the very least, he wanted to make her safe until he knew the full story of her circumstances. *If everything was kosher, then she could go back to her normal life,* he tried to convince himself.

He stared at her naked body entangled in the red sheets. He stroked her cheek and she stirred but he failed to rouse her. After the way they made love last night, he knew she was probably going to remain in bed all morning. He, on the other hand, was ready to start planning his day, which today, would mostly revolve around Dianna. He had promised her that he would help her tame her impulses which really was a difficult feat since she was such a free-spirited person with very little concept of controlling anything. Her idea of control was running and hiding. He could control her snakes better than she could, but she had to learn or she was going to reveal her true nature every single time she lost control of her emotions and yet, there was a part of him that loved her rawness, her authenticity and he didn't want to change her.

He needed some coffee in his system before he could think any further. He headed to the bathroom where he rifled through the medicine cabinet for a bottle of aspirin. His muscles were aching. He hadn't completely transformed like he did the night before in ages. It was a different time now, where humans and Nagalians alike relied on modern technology and strategy for protection to win fights and wars. He was strapped, all his properties were outfitted with the latest security cameras and surveillance utilities. His headquarters were only accessible through ID chips and the Fraternity headquarters were only accessible through biometric scanning. A full transformation hadn't been a necessity in decades for him and an entire century for many. He flexed his muscles and rotated his shoulder joints. His human form was in shape, but he was completely rusty in Nagalian form. He grinned as he admitted this to himself, but it was worth it. His orgasms were ten times more explosive when he was in his true form. He had gotten so used to sex in his human form that he had forgotten how exceedingly satisfying it felt. Just the memory made him want seconds from her but as sore as he felt, he knew she was going to feel it ten times worse when she woke up. It took a lot more energy and ... *stretching for a woman to pleasure him* in that form. It was easier for a Nagalian woman, twice as hard for half Nagalians and impossible for human women. He felt a tiny tinge of guilt, but he was more so amused. He made a mental note not to appear too pleased by her physical anguish when she awoke. *But you asked for it, Dianna,* he mused to himself with a glint of mischief in his eyes.

After brushing his teeth, he grabbed a pair of grey slacks and some clean socks, quickly slipping them on and then descended the flight of stairs to the kitchen. He quickly got some coffee started. His clothes from last night, his keys and phone were all left on the pool deck and he wasted no time in retrieving them. When he checked his phone, he wasn't at all surprised to see that his dad and the entire metro area was calling him. He called his dad first.

"You were supposed to call to give me the status on how things went with Jasmine after the dinner!" his father reminded him. Drax peered upstairs to make sure Dianna was nowhere in sight and even with that, he still played it safe by keeping his voice low and his words concise considering she had a knack for eavesdropping on conversations that were damaging to her self-esteem.

"I've got company, dad. I'll update you later," he euphemized. Dianna wasn't guest; she practically lived there.

"Is it that half Nagalian girl?"

The coffee machine beeped and Drax poured himself a cup.

"Uh-uh."

"When are you going to stop messing around with that chick?" Drax laughed inwardly at his father's use of the word *'chick'*. It amused him that his 500-year-old dad was picking up modern day lingo.

"Not any time soon," he said bluntly, he pulled out two aspirins, dropped them in his mouth and took a few sips of the hot coffee.

"You're going to compromise our connection with Narlon!"

"Already compromised dad, his daughter is in love with somebody. Got his name tattooed her wrist," Drax said casually all the while keeping a sharp eye out for Dianna.

"Like you can't charm her out of her panties. You're good at that!" his father responded bluntly.

"Is mom around?" Drax chuckled at his father's boldness. "Besides, I know when someone is emotionally unavailable and quite frankly, dad," Drax strolled over to his gym area where he turned on the treadmill. "I am too."

"Drax, get this shit together and make it work between you and Jasmine or you're going to cause friction in the Fraternity and we definitely can't afford that right now." Drax didn't want to argue with his father this early but he couldn't resist provoking his dad for the heck of it.

"Think I'm going to skip next week's meeting," Drax provoked.

"You must attend all meetings; your presence is vital so the brothers can see that you are serious about the organization. You're the youngest of everyone there which is already creating murmuring. They need to know you're young not dumb and right now you're being young and dumb!"

"21st century and arranged marriages are still a thing," Drax said sarcastically. "Gotta go!"

"Drax--" but Drax disconnected the call before his dad could dig any deeper under his skin. He placed the phone on the top of the treadmill console. He sped up the machine at the highest speed and ran for a few minutes until he was good and sweaty. His phone rang again. He wanted to ignore it in case it was his dad, but he had other businesses that needed his attention too. Thankfully, it was the retired officer he had hired as his private investigator and a fellow Nagalian.

"Yeah!"

"Bad news, Drax. Those two guys you told me to look into, got their brains blown out last week," the private investigator said, getting straight to the point since he wasn't one to mince words. He was all about his job.

"Damn! Who?"

"Pretty sure they were bounty hunters." Drax shook his head at the confirmation. Unknowing to Dianna, her trail was so hot that she wasn't even aware of the aftermath she was creating around her.

"Killing humans? They are not usually this messy. What's changed?" There was a pause on the other line. "Spill it!" Drax insisted.

"Think this might be personal." Drax walked to his glass door facing the edge of the cliff and stared into the distance as he fathomed the gravity of Dianna's circumstances. "Something to do with her mother. Can't track down the mother though. Traced her back to Alaska but she skipped town after police started investigating a mysterious hit and run. The guy remembers being hit by a car and two women helping him. No bruises but a shit load of blood on the pickup truck they found." Drax's mind was in overdrive. *What the hell have you gotten yourself into Dianna?!*

"What about her brother?"

"He's clean. No criminal record, decent husband, great father. Just seem to be in a little debt." Drax heard shuffling of paper on the other line before the retired cop resumed. "But get this. The daughter."

"Adisa?" Drax briskly walked back to the living room to looked upstairs. No sign of Dianna.

"Yeah...had a rare form of hereditary cancer. The cancer was so aggressive there was no recourse. Your girlfriend showed up at their home and Adisa's cancer disappears. Doctors have no explanation how a girl that should've died in a few weeks was completely cured of terminal cancer overnight!"

"Drax?" He spun around to see Dianna slowly and painfully hobbling her way down the stairs which should've amused him but after what he just heard, all humor had dissipated.

"Gotta call you back. Send over everything you have to my email." He threw his phone onto the white plush couch.

"I'm down here!" he alerted her as he headed in her direction. He saw her gripping the stairs with both hands as she grimaced with each step.

"I got you," he said running up the stairs to her. He lifted her in his arms and carefully walked the rest of the way with her.

"You didn't tell me it was going to be this bad," she said resting her head in the crook of his neck.

"Didn't want to ruin the moment," she chuckled at his humorous response. He took her to the living room and gently placed her on the couch.

"Coffee?" he asked her. "I've also got some orange juice?" he said sweetly. Looking at her now, wincing and grimacing, confirmed the reason he was having sex lesser and lesser in his Nagalian form as cataclysmic as it felt.

"I like the sound of orange juice."

It took him less than a second to get the orange juice. He handed her some aspirin also. "They should help with the soreness."

She mouthed a quick 'thank you' and then gulped down the pills with some juice. He sat on the floor in front of her and gently placed her left leg on his right shoulder.

"Ow! Ow! Ow!" she yelled.

"Shhh..." he said soothingly and started gently massaging her leg. "Is this helping?"

She nodded her head with an appreciative look on her face. "You've got the hands of an angel." He smiled handsomely at her. "And the sexiest smile in the world," she finished.

"Sounds like you woke up on the right side of the bed this morning," he said as his smile brightened to show his immaculately straight, pearly white teeth.

"Can you blame me? Last night was tantric!"

"Glad you enjoyed it. Up for another round?" he teased.

"Yeah, next month!" He laughed at her response. But his joy was short lived as he wrestled with himself to tell her what he knew and to get more answers from her. Yet, she was so happy within this moment that he just wanted her to bask in her euphoria. He kissed the inside of her leg tenderly. He then placed her leg on the couch and fluffed a pillow under it as she rested her back on the arm of the couch before starting on her other leg.

She was staring at the ceiling when suddenly she shot straight up. "Adisa!" she murmured. Drax heart raced as he wondered if she overheard his conversation with the private investigator. "I forgot to call her back!" She tried to get up but immediately plopped back down in the sofa from the severe soreness. Drax's phone was still on the couch and she contemplated it for a second. Her reservation was obvious so Drax picked it up, unlocked it and handed it to her.

"Use it," he coaxed her.

She dialed the number, placed the phone to her ear and waited. Then her face lit up. "Adisa, it's me."

She rose tentatively and started walking toward the kitchen where she could sit at the island. He used the opportunity to sprint upstairs and opened his laptop perched on the edge of the self-serve bar counter in his bedroom to see if the email had come in. It had. There were pictures of the two dead men she was trying to pay off in Alabama, pictures of her niece and her parents, and the victim of the hit and run accident in Alaska. There were medical records and police records, home addresses, phone numbers, place of employment for both Audrey and Quinton. It was all there. He should've felt guilty that he went behind her back and did this, but she left him no choice.

Besides, what's the point of being so rich and influential if you can't abuse your power every now and then, he thought to himself and had to admit that he was showing signs of megalomania. However, in his defense, he didn't care. *Some things you can't take for granted,* he thought to himself.

He zoomed in on Adisa's hospital discharge papers. There were the red flags. Renal Cell Carcinoma... one kidney completely destroyed, cancer had infected her second kidney, multiple kidney failures followed, stage four cancer, waiting on kidney replacement. Post cancer screening results showed negative for cancer cells, left kidney shows scarring, but she tested negative for infections, no additional abnormalities. Proper diet, regular hydration and monthly checkups were recommended... the list went on. Her chance of survival was bleak before Dianna showed up and yet she was the sign of perfect health in pictures of her at the playground. It really didn't add up. When he had time later, he would scan through some more to see what else he could find about Adisa's cancer healing miraculously and the hit and run victim. He closed his laptop and went back downstairs. Dianna was still sitting at the island staring at something in front of her. He followed her gaze. It was a picture of him with his father standing behind him hung on the wall inside the foyer. Both of them dressed in a suit with the green Nagalian emblem emblazoned on it. It fell right in place with his home décor unless you were privy to information about the Fraternity, then it would stand out like a clue into his behind the scenes life of a secret organization of powerful and influential Nagalians spearheaded by his father.

"Y'know, I assumed this was some type of family portrait."

"It is," he stated in a matter-of-fact manner.

"What does that green symbol mean?"

"Secret society stuff," he said nonchalantly. Dianna stared at him wide-eyed. "So gullible..." He laughed. She scowled at him in return, lifting her chin and clenching her jaw to show she wasn't amused. "My father and I are a part of a country club," he lied. Honestly, he was too good at lying he thought to himself. She seemed disappointed.

"Last night before you fell asleep, you said you could protect me better than the Fraternity." Last night, he was exhausted after their love making. It came as no surprise that he was revealing well-guarded secrets to her. His gaze was unfaltering as he prepared to lie some more through his teeth.

"I misspoke. I probably meant to say the Federal Bureau or something...I was sleepy." He shrugged.

"You were quite lucid, Drax," she argued.

"Even if I did say that, it sounds like you are looking too deeply into it."

"Am I?"

"Yes. Drop it!"

Her quizzical expression told him she wasn't convinced but she handed him his phone. "Thanks!" she said to him before slowly getting to her feet. "Guess I won't be riding my bike for a few days," She held on to him for support. He was relieved that she wasn't going to push the subject any further, but he knew this wasn't the last of it.

***

Drax was at a meeting listening to a pitch from one of the creative team employees. Usually he was as sharp as a tack, but today, he couldn't focus. Dianna was still playing coy and withholding information about her past. Every time he tried to interrogate her about what happened in Alabama, she deflected his question. She had also become more insistent about the Fraternity after she searched the internet and found some information from a noncredible website about Nagalian fraternities. Whereas he could easily dismiss the content as junk considering that the website also talked about the existence of aliens and Bigfoot sightings, he knew it wasn't enough to curb her tenacity for the truth.

The young man presenting his pitch, dropped one of his charts, bringing Drax back to the present. Susanne his personal assistant, who was always present at any of his meetings, was sitting to his right. He leaned forward enough for her to hear him.

"What do you think?"

"He's nervous. Not really selling me on his pitch."

"Is he new?"

She nodded.

Drax sat back and tried to listen to what the young man had to say but he simply had too much on his plate and the young man's monotone voice was losing him. He soon started thinking about Dianna again. The only thing he had to go on was when she slipped up and told him, that she healed Adisa. He couldn't wait for Dianna to confess. He needed to know why she was so important or special to the bounty hunters, so he did what he had to do.

"Mom, I need you to run some tests."

"You've never needed me to do that before. What's the occasion?"

"Not for me, personally."

His mom looked up from the medical journal she was reading. "Dianna..." He handed her a bag with a few bloody cotton balls inside.

"How did you get those?"

"Long story." It really wasn't that long. He bit her lip a little too hard when he was kissing her, and it was no accident.

"Have you ever tested a half Nagalian before to see in what ways they were different from us?"

"Yes, and the results were as expected. Significantly more human DNA than Nagalian DNA. But I know that look in your eyes so what are you trying to find out?"

"Do you think they have the ability to heal humans?"

"Well, the humans seem to think that, that's why they are hunting half Nagalians and us alike, but their biological system has always rejected our blood type and tissue cells. We are only compatible enough to procreate."

"And if they mutated?"

"No evidence so far that they have. Do you think Dianna's DNA has mutated?"

"I don't know but whatever you do, don't tell dad about this."

She looked at him with a slight scowl. "You do know I'm with your father about Jasmine." He gave her a peck on the cheek.

"Tell me what you find. I'm heading back to the office."

"Son, don't you think you are in too deep with Dianna?" his mother cautioned as he left the house.

She was right. He was in too deep and couldn't pull out. He laughed at his own pun. He didn't realize that he was tapping the pen point loudly on the conference table because he was so lost in his thoughts.

"Uh…Mr. Ashton, did you have any feedback on the presentation?" the presenter asked nervously. Drax stared blankly at him with no idea what his presentation was about. But he remembered Susanne's comments.

"So, I was not 100% sold on the concept. Maybe it's because your nerves got the better of you, but I do want to authorize that you proceed with the project to see if you have what it takes to pull off your idea," he said vaguely. He could afford to blow the company's budget a bit on a nervous hopeful hungry for an opportunity. He looked at the other staff present. "Did anyone have any other feedback?" he asked the table.

"I think he should tone down the complicated banking terms and stick to catch phrases like "banking made easy." Drax had no idea the pitch was for a banking ad.

"I see what you are saying," he said slowly catching on.

"Also, even though the target market is between 35-60. Still try to appeal to a younger demographic," Eric continued. "Like a college student getting quick cash at an atm for a competitive fee." Drax had to admit that he was really impressed with Eric's perceptiveness. Had he been paying attention; he probably could have provided similar feedback, but his personal life and obligations were pulling him farther and farther away from his functions at the company. He owned the firm but he started considering that maybe it was the right time to become a silent board member and hand over the position of CEO to someone he could trust and someone who thought like him...someone like Eric.

Just then, the phone in the conference room rang shrilly. Susanne answered it quickly.

"I told you to hold all calls!" Susanne said a little agitated. Then she paused. "Okay. I understand."

She then handed Drax the phone. "It's for you Drax. It's urgent," she said with worrying eyes. Drax grabbed the phone.

"Yes!"

He heard the voice of his office secretary. "Mr. Drax, your mother is waiting in your office and she says it's important."

"Tell her I'll be there in a few minutes." He quickly hung up the phone and stood. "Please finish the presentation without me. Eric, I would like to have a word with you about it later."

"Okay," Eric said looking bewildered.

Nearing his office door, he knocked, then poked his head inside so he wouldn't alarm her. "Wow Drax! Do you really need this much space for an office chair, desk and computer?"

"You say that every time you come here, and my answer is always the same. It's a power move," he pointed out with an air of arrogance. Drax's mother was a woman of essentials not exorbitance, so he understood why she was put off by his extravagant style.

"You could literally fit an entire animal shelter in here and do some good for society," she said, looking around tentatively.

"I think I do my fair share of 'good for society'," he quipped.

"I felt the same way when you bought that massive house overlooking the cliff so you can spend one day out of the month there. Ridiculous!" Drax walked over to her and hugged her lovingly.

"You should be happy to know that I practically live there now."

"Is that so?"

"I'm hosting a temporary house guest so I would say that buying said remote property came in handy." He sat on the edge of the desk and grabbed a handful of nuts from the decorative crystal bowl on the table. "Anyway, I know you're not here to criticize my eccentric taste in real estate. Did anything interesting come back from the lab results?" He said, popping the peanuts into his mouth. His mother breathed out. Walking around to the other side of the desk, she took a seat in his office chair. She then pulled out a flash drive from her purse.

"I need access to your computer." Drax circled around his desk to where he could stand behind her. He entered his password and watched her insert the flash drive into the PCU. After a few clicks from her, he could see some microscopic images on the screen. She zoomed in. "This is the sample of Dianna's blood that you gave me." Drax looked carefully. He wasn't quite sure what he was looking at, but he waited. "This is a blood sample of a full Nagalian." He noticed the cells were larger in size, more robust and more packed together. "Our blood cells generate at a faster rate and is about one and a half size larger to give us more energy, nutrients and oxygen to shape shift. We also age more slowly because of the regenerative qualities of our blood." Drax was already aware of this from private schooling. "This is a human blood sample," she said clicking on another image. He noted they were much smaller in size compared to the Nagalian's cells. In fact, about half the size and more spaced out. Nothing spectacular yet.

"This is a fourth sample." She displayed all four images on the screen at the same time. Drax looked carefully. Dianna's blood seemed closer to the human blood type except that the color became much darker where the cell concaved. He then looked at the fourth sample, analyzing it. There seemed to be two types of cells. The larger Nagalian cells with the human cells separated, similar to white and red blood cells in humans. "The fourth sample is another Half Nagalian."

"Why doesn't it look like Dianna's blood cells?"

"The question is why doesn't Dianna's cells look like sample four? I took some more samples from other half Nagalians that work for me. They all look like sample four. Sort of the reason why their blood and tissue cells are rejected by humans. Humans cannot produce the Nagalian cells to support the tissue during transplant or transfusion."

"So, Dianna's blood has mutated?"

"Yes, but it's more than that. The reason her blood cells look darker in the center is because the nucleus of her blood contains Nagalian DNA which, for lack of a better term, teaches the human blood cell how to regenerate. Dianna's blood is not only compatible with humans, but it can allow damaged human tissues to regenerate." It all came together in Drax's mind. The test results explained so much. It explained the way she healed Adisa, and why the man in Alaska, who lost a lot of blood from being hit by a car, could get up and walk around the next day like nothing happened.

"Another thing. The blood cells also mimic the blood cell of the host. So eventually, in a human, the regenerative properties of Nagalian blood will wear off because the blood cell will start behaving like the human host's cells once inside the human's body."

"What about Nagalians?"

"Same. The regenerative capabilities will not only mimic but amp up once inside a Nagalian's body." Drax couldn't believe what he was hearing.

"I think she's tried to heal humans before."

"That's not good. That's bringing unnecessary attention to herself!" Drax was silent. "They are after her, aren't they?" His mother covered her mouth slowly as fear crept over her face.

"I have reasons to believe this, yes."

"You have to tell your father, Drax."

Drax walked around to the front of the office desk and dropped himself into the chair, exhausted from the information. He pinched the bridge of his nose.

"Dianna, what the hell have you done!"

Chapter 9

Drax had been very evasive for about a week now. He was always busy at work and whenever he was at the house, he was preoccupied. She wondered if confronting him about the Fraternity had driven him away. Maybe it was the fact that she didn't believe he was telling her the truth, especially when he was trying to garner her trust. He was so good to her that she found herself being afraid of losing him. It felt good to have someone in her corner. Someone who cared about her so much. It felt good that he was defying family pressures just to keep her safe and his body was a drug she couldn't get enough of. She liked that he spoiled her, not with things but his affection. The way he touched her hair, caressed her skin, stared unfaltering into her eyes, squeezed her much smaller hand, wrapped himself around her when they slept together, kissed her weak areas, and nursed her slightest injuries. Yet, this week, he withheld his affection. She barely got a peck from him. Now, she was anxious and off center because of it. She wasn't sure if her growing emotional dependency was a red flag to budding toxicity. Yet, it didn't feel that way. Her feelings hinged on a certain entitlement...she not only wanted him to care, she basked in the privilege and the benefits of it. In a twisted sense, it empowered her.

He whizzed past her in the kitchen with a manila folder in his hand. He placed the folder down on the counter as he grabbed a cup from the overhead cabinet to pour himself some coffee. He was dressed in a suit she assumed for work. He took a few gulps of his coffee before setting his half empty cup on the counter. Picking up the folder, he was about to make a mad dash to the front door when Dianna grabbed his arm which stopped him in his tracks. "Did I do something?" she asked softly.

He gave her a blank stare. "What do you mean?"

"You've been avoiding me."

His confusion was replaced by a look of understanding. "I've just been busy," then he kissed her tenderly on the forehead. Dianna became irritated. She pushed him away.

"Stop lying! Are you being this way because of my questions about the Fraternity?"

He paused, anticipating more animosity from her, "Is this an argument?"

"No, but we need to talk. You've barely said a word to me all week," she tried to take the folder he was holding from him with the intention of setting it aside so they could converse, but he instinctively pulled it away from her. This caused the file jacket to open and paper flew wildly all over the kitchen floor. "I'm so sorry, I didn't mean to do that!" She bent down quickly and immediately started stacking the sheets paper together.

"Dianna, Wait! Don't!" He knelt beside her taking the stack of paper from her. A picture of Adisa slid from the stack. Dianna picked it up and stood slowly as she examined the photo. Drax cursed and continued to pick up the other scattered paper. Dianna quickly grabbed some of the other loose paper on the ground and began looking through them. "Medical records of Adisa!" she read with a mixture of confusion and disbelief. She looked at another one with labeled images of her cell on it. "What's this?" Her knees felt like buckling. "Have you been investigating me behind my back? Why do you have these?"

"It's not what you think," he said rising to his feet with the rest of the paper neatly organized in his hands. He placed them back in the folder and closed it away from her prying eyes.

"Give that to me!" she demanded.

"Calm down!" he told her resolutely. She wrestled the folder from his hands. "Cut this shit out, Dianna!" he warned her. Afraid she would rip the file, he released his grip and she slapped it loudly on the surface of the kitchen island before opening it. She angrily separated the paper as she sieved through the information furiously.

"This damn sure looks exactly like what I think!" she foraged further searching for answers. "You even have a picture of Quinton?!" Her eyes narrowed as she looked at a picture of the bloody crime scene of the men, she had given money to. She covered her mouth, and her legs gave out, she grabbed on to the counter but Drax was immediately at her side supporting her weight. "Please Drax, please tell me you didn't..." she questioned feeling helpless as she stared up at him with disbelief shrouding her expression. "Please tell me you didn't kill them." She was weak from shock. He lifted her up and she struggled against him, but his strength overpowered her.

"Put me down!"

"You're blowing this thing way out of context!"

"Where are you taking me?!" Her eyes became wild as hysteria was taking over. She struggled harder.

"You know it's futile to struggle," he told her. "You'll only succeed in hurting yourself." His voice sounded eerie and for the first time since she met him, she was in fear as she thought of the fact that he might be a murderer. She started replaying moments in her mind. Moments with him that she couldn't explain. *Why was he in Alabama? Why did he let her stay in such a secluded area? Why was he risking everything to protect her?*

"I don't understand. Are you studying me?" she questioned naively. He finally got to the bedroom and laid her gently on the bed. He also closed the door in case she tried to get out.

"Who are you really?" she demanded.

"First off, I'm not a murderer. I didn't kill those men," he tried to assure her.

"Then who did?"

"Likely bounty hunters."

"Why should I believe you?" she said, her hands flailing.

"Because you know me! You know I wouldn't kill anybody unprovoked."

"But you've killed before?"

"Yes... and I'll do it again if it means protecting the people I care about."

"So, you are a murderer! Oh my God, Drax. You're wrong. I don't know you. I've been living in a bubble you created for me. I'm such an idiot!" He walked back toward the bed, but she flinched away. Her snakes gnashing at him. "Don't come any closer! What do you want with my brother and niece?"

"Nothing. I know you healed Adisa of her cancer." She became silent. "And I know you had something to do with healing that man in Alaska," he said as calmly as he could, "and I know why the bounty hunters want you more than they want me or any of half or full Nagalian out there... because of your ability to heal humans."

Dianna tried to think of something to say but she had nothing. He knew her secret and she never felt more exposed than she did now. "And I know all of this is shocking to you now, but if you leave, you are putting yourself in so much danger." But everything was hitting her all at once and it was making her panic.

"When did you find out?"

"Last week."

"Is that why you were avoiding me?"

"Not intentionally. The information is just a lot to process." Drax said eyeing her warily. She folded her arms across her chest protectively.

"Did you have to do this behind my back?"

"Yes. You weren't very forthcoming."

"What else do you have on me?"

"You've mutated. We think you are the only one at this time that can heal others."

"Others know about me?"

"Just my mother. She ran the tests."

"So, no one else knows?"

Drax shook his head in response.

Dianna unfolded her arms as she thought for a while, "that's not true, y'know. What you said about me being the only one," she said as she sat on the edge of the bed. Drax waited for her to finish. She steeled herself to divulge her more of her secrets. The secrets that she had guarded with her life and planned on taking to the grave.

"My mother healed the man in Alaska, and she healed a hiker back in the 70s."

"Fuck! Where is she now?"

"Safe...In hiding."

"She is not safe...She needs to be here with you. I can protect her." He stalled momentarily. "We can protect her."

"We? Who is we?"

Drax hesitated but knew he had to tell her the truth sooner or later. "The Nagalian Fraternity." Dianna sprang to her feet.

"I knew you were lying!" she said angrily.

"To be fair...you weren't truthful either." He remained calm as he defended himself.

"Are you going to tell them about me?"

"I need to so I can gain some perspective... I've lost objectivity," he said breaking her stare. She could sense a tinge of frustration in his voice and she calmed. She knew he was talking about her and at this point he was confirming what she already knew...she was his kryptonite.

"It's all a big mess, isn't it?"

"Bigger than you know. You've placed humans and Nagalians alike in danger including your brother and niece. Bounty hunters will do whatever it takes to get to you, and they will hunt us more aggressively to get their hands on someone with your blood type whether half Nagalian or full. They won't discriminate!"

Dianna felt deep regret. "I'm sorry," she said pathetically. "I had to save Adisa and even though my mother warned me, I forced her to save Mack. I couldn't watch either of them die."

"Dianna, you might have saved their lives but a lot of Nagalians are losing theirs because of what you and your mom did," he explained.

"But I thought you said they've been hunting Nagalians for centuries," she said hoping to relieve her guilt even in the slightest.

"You're right. It's gotten worse."

Dianna scowled wickedly, empowered by a fresh batch of rage. She refused to be blamed for something she didn't intend to do or even knew about. She refused to be the scapegoat for cruelty of heartless blood thirsty bounty hunters, when she only tried to show compassion. She understood that she exposed them, but he was placing years of murderous genocidal human behavior square on her shoulders, or at least that's what it felt like. "What the fuck have you and your merry band of reptilians done except to hide behind privilege and wealth!" Drax patience was running thin with her ill-advised insults. "All you idiots do is flaunt your wealth and power around gullible humans and downtrodden half breeds, separating yourself from us as if somehow we are beneath you motherfuckers!" she spat venomously at him. "You are all a bunch of assholes masquerading as good Samaritans."

"Dianna, STOP!"

"Screw you, Drax!" She flung her arms forward and pushed him with everything she had, and he fell backward into the wall causing the structure to quake. "You're not the only strong one here!" she bluffed knowing fully well that he was at least two times stronger than her. "I'm leaving! If you come near me, I will fight you and I will hurt you!" She grabbed her purse from the white nightstand and stormed down the stairs fearing he would be on her tail. She just needed to get to her bike and maybe she could run off to Canada with her mother. They could get menial jobs and make it work but anything was better than being around her insufferable boyfriend right now.

She scoffed at her own thoughts, "boyfriend my ass! More like psycho pervert, obsessive control freak!" She didn't slow down until she got to the garage area where his collections of cars paraded like precious art in a museum. This made her even more annoyed because he stunk of high-class advantage.

"How could I have even fallen for him!" she said with disgust. She usually went for nice, humble guys that could connect and relate to the struggles of life. Not some imperial heir tied to a Nagalian Fraternity. She went around in a confusing circle in the underground garage, but she couldn't find her black motorcycle. She stilled her movements and her mind so she could think clearly. Then it hit her that Drax would've moved it to another place because at the very root of it, he didn't trust a bone in her body. She yelled loudly in the garage, letting her frustration be heard. With her heart pounding in her chest, she retraced her steps back to the master bedroom since he hadn't followed her. She found him where she had left him sitting at the edge of the disheveled bed with a calm demeanor holding the motorcycle key in his hand.

"Looking for this?" he taunted without looking at her. She dashed over to him and grabbed them from him easily. He wasn't fighting her.

"Where is my cruiser?"

"Not here," he said continuing to taunt her.

"Are you proud of yourself?" She started to walk away from him with her back turned then in an instant, he was behind her, holding her hands behind her back. Dianna gasped loudly, as she instinctively struggled against him. He brought his other arm across her chest, restraining her further. Not only was she in slight discomfort, he had her immobilized.

"Listen to me you selfish bitch!" he whispered menacingly in her ear. "I don't give a fuck about what type of crusade you are on but what you have done, whether you want to take responsibility for it or not! is make us even more of a target." He tightened his hold causing her to cry out. "They know about you and the only possible reason you are still alive is because they want your blood, or you would be dead in a river like the others we've found!" Her eyes were stinging with tears as his words sank in. "They WILL try to wipe us out and in case you haven't figured it out yet, the only thing slowing them down is my organization and others like it." She could feel his warm body behind her, her arms painfully taut between them and his slow and deliberate breathing, on her neck. Under ordinary circumstances, she would've been immensely turned on, but this wasn't sex games. He was angry at her. She moved her head to the side since that was the only part of her body, she could move without being in excruciating pain, but he only pulled her arms tighter.

"You're hurting me," she whimpered.

"You're hurting all of us!" he roared at her. "You're so ungrateful. You think riding around on your little motorcycle from state to state is going to save you? They've already found you. They were at your apartment. Wake the fuck up!"

"You don't know that!"

"Are you willing to bet your life on it?" She didn't respond. "Or is that what you want? To be murdered so you won't have to do it yourself?" he spat at her. She closed her eyes trying to shut out his words and her snakes began to uncoil.

"That's not fair."

"It's not? I have to babysit you to save you from your damn self and bounty hunters. Maybe I should just give you what you want," he responded frostily. He let her go and walked away from her. She rubbed her wrist without maintaining eye contact as she composed herself.

"I don't want to die," she admitted to him. "Not anymore."

"Well that's a fucking relief!" he snapped at her bitterly.

"Thank you," she told him. He looked at her, searching for a spark of sincerity.

"Do you even mean that or is this some ridiculous mind game?"

"I mean it! I meant it that night by the pool and I mean it now." She placed her keys in her pocket. "I don't need you reminding me that I wanted to die. That was a dark place in my life." She turned her head to the side, finding it difficult to tell him how she felt. "Before you came into my life...so thank you."

"Good to hear. A little gratitude goes a long way," he said harshly. His nerves were raw. He stared at her wrist as she massaged it. It was red from his tight hold. "Sorry I had to manhandle you."

"I was actually sparing you!" she countered.

He managed a half smile, then, he became serious again. Dianna could tell he was on an emotional roller coaster dealing with her. He walked over to her and lifted her, so her legs were wrapped around his waist. It was obvious that he liked it when she did that. She held on firmly, resting her head on his left shoulder and just like that, everything was back to normal as if they didn't just have a vicious argument. "I've fallen for you," he confessed. "The mistake of a lifetime."

Dianna winced as she stiffened at his words. "Not sure how to interpret that."

"No...I mean..." he sighed, "falling for someone whose idea of safety is going into hiding." He braced her back against the wall. "I'm pretty sure you are going to leave me hanging. I guess I could handle it if you did." Dianna breathed in his smell. It was the ultimate high. "But in good conscience, I can't let you." She lifted her head so he could lay his on her breasts.

She kissed his forehead, "Are we together?" she probed.

"Meaning?"

"Are we in a long-term relationship?" He went silent and Dianna found herself cringing in those few seconds. She didn't want him to reject her. She wanted to take back the question. It was too heavy and too soon. "I mean, if that's not what this is, I'm okay with--"

"Shut up!" he said with a little amusement in his voice almost like he was enjoying her discomfort. "I guess I thought it was understood." He finished. Her body relaxed.

"Is that what young people say these days?"

He laughed, "I think they still say *boyfriend.*" Dianna rolled her eyes, wondering if he had heard her self-rant earlier. "But to answer your question more directly. I would like that if you're a willing participant-- "

"Completely willing!" She didn't want to stop holding him and she didn't want him to stop holding her. She was letting him reside in her soul, the deepest part of her. The room was silent, but their internal voices were loud as their emotions spoke to each other.

***

Dianna had decided to go with him to his Fraternity meeting, but she was so nervous her hands were shaking. She knew this was a major undertaking. From what Drax had told her, these were old men, stuck in their old ways *'oozing with toxic masculinity I bet'* she said to herself. They had only allowed a few women to attend the meeting, let alone speak since its inception. Being half Nagalian, Dianna was beyond unwelcomed, but it needed to be done. "Are you sure you can't just explain it to them without me being present?" She queried as they drove in the back of the limo to the spot. She was dressed in a suit, trying to appear as professional as she could.

"You need to speak. Plus, you're kind of a big deal now. You deserve to be at the meeting."

"I'm a big deal now?" she said incredulously.

Drax smirked at her, satisfied that he had goaded her.

"Honestly, probably the most important Half Nagalian to ever exist."

"How reassuring," she said rolling her eyes as her words dripped with sarcasm.

"Besides, this is your story. I can't tell it for you."

Dianna exhaled loudly trying to ease her tension, but it was impossible. She honestly felt as if they would rip her to shreds so they could laugh at her innards, once they laid eyes on her. He didn't even tell them she was coming. It seemed like the perfect storm for impending chaos.

They pulled up to what seemed to be an old monastery at the edge of Reno. It was archaic in its design and quite imposing among the other more modern architecture. Yet It fit right in as there was a Methodist church just a few yards away. There was a large monument sign on the lawn that read "Arthur Ashton's Academy."

"Is this a school?"

"A private boarding school for Nagalian children," he informed her.

"Are there more like this?" she said as she stared in awe at the magnificence of the place.

"Only a few more. They're scattered across the country." Dianna thought back to her childhood. She hated homeschooling. She had wanted so badly to be around other kids and do normal things like cheerleading. She would have loved to attend a school like this.

"Who is Arthur Ashton?" she asked without thinking.

Drax grinned at her and she was reminded that Drax came from generations and generations of Nagalian aristocracy. She knew and immediately felt out of place.

"I'm not doing this!" she said as her soul crawled back into its shell. These were wealthy, sexist stuffy old men that could potentially destroy her pathetic little life. Drax held her hand, something that always comforted her.

"You can do this." He encouraged her. She knew he wouldn't let her sit this one out. He opened the door of the limo and got out, holding the door while assisting her out of the vehicle. They both walked up to the large iron doors. There was a security device on the side of the door with buttons. Drax placed his thumb on a small screen of the device and it flashed a green light. The door opened and they both walked in. They seemed to walk into a large hall area that resembled a library. There was a receptionist sitting at the counter. The man looked briefly at them and then returned to his work. Dianna expected Drax to walk up to him to make some type of announcement or request, but he didn't. Instead, he continued to walk to the opposite end of the hall. He then swerved down to a narrow corridor with pillars, lining the left side of the walkway, spaced out enough to see the courtyard outside. It was beautiful. Kids of all ages peacefully communing or reading on benches or feeding ducks. It was very exclusive, and she began rethinking her previous ideas of her childhood self, wanting to attend a school like this. They went down another corridor and then arrived at another large wooden door. There was another biometric scanner. This time, Drax scanned his retina. The machine flashed green.

"I can see why you are a paranoid pervert."

"Pervert?" he inquired raising a quizzical eyebrow at her; disregarding the part she mentioned about his paranoia.

"Yes. I know about the camera in the master bedroom."

Drax gave her a lopsided smile. "That camera was installed years ago. Maybe it's you who shouldn't be so horny, love."

Dianna gave him a devilish grin, "I'm betting you couldn't peel your eyes away? I believe the real issue here is you watching me getting my rocks off."

"Very conceited of you to think I'm watching."

"Isn't that what perverts do?"

"A pervert. I. Am. Not. A little kinky…maybe," he said seductively. They finally came to another door. Again, Drax scanned his eye and Dianna heard a click. Drax placed his hand on the doorknob and turned it, "Are you ready?" Dianna's mood changed to fear.

"No but whatever."

They walked in. Men sitting at a long table turned around and stared at them wide-eyed with their mouths agape. A few of them shot to their feet.

"Drax! What the hell do you think you are doing?!" Marvin barked. His eyes were molten lava.

"Dad, sit down, you need to hear this."

"Who the hell is she?" Norlan blurted out. "What is the meaning of this?" he demanded.

"Drax this better be fucking good!" Marvin seethed.

"Everyone, please calm down. I'm only requesting a minute of your time." he commandeered, shaking a few hands before leading Dianna to the head of the table. Dianna's eyes almost rolled out of their sockets when she saw Susanne sitting in the corner with pen to paper staring back at her. *What the hell?* Was all she could mouth to her and could only briefly ponder on her presence at the meeting. It took no time for them to get to the other end of the table where Marvin sat infuriated. Drax then stared at her calmly, with his expression telling her that everything was going to be okay. She breathed in deeply, ready to follow his lead. He reverted his gaze to the men in the room. "This is Dianna Montague. She is half Nagalian and what she has to say is crucial so if you could just lend her your ears."

"I don't want to hear this!" Norlan said getting up from his chair ready to storm out.

"You walk out that door, you will never be allowed back in," Marvin told him coolly. "Don't forget who is in charge of this operation. You will leave when I dismiss this meeting."

Norlan stared from Marvin, to Drax then to Dianna.

"So be it!" he continued to walk out. Marvin watched him silently leave. The door clanging heavily as he exited the room. Marvin immediately picked up the phone punching in some numbers with his large fingers. "This is Marvin Ashton. Jason from the IT department, please!" There was a long pause. "Yes, Norlan Fisher is no longer a member of this Fraternity, please have his credentials deleted from our system immediately and I mean in the next five minutes!" He slammed the phone down. "Is there anyone else who wants to leave? Now is the time!" he said staring emotionless at the remaining

Nagalians. There was a slight murmur, but everyone remained in their seats. "Good! Drax, please go on."

Drax had never felt such pride for his father as he did in that moment. Norlan was always a point of grievance between them and the way his father stood up to him solidified his respect and loyalty.

"I can only hope to be half the man my father is. I love you dad!" He patted his father on the shoulder. "And trust me...Nate, Andrew, Mr. Chung, and everyone here today, I would never do this if my reasons weren't exigent." Marvin nodded his head as he waited with his leg resting impatiently on his knee. "But first, Dianna has a few things to say so I'll let her get to it." He walked over to his chair next to his father, giving her the floor to say her peace. Dianna's heart was in her throat as she stared at the individuals before her. Just last week she was speculating that the group existed and now there was living, breathing proof right in front of her. If they were all like Drax, she suspected that they could all transform and annihilate her. She decided to imagine them naked instead to ease her nervousness.

"Wow! Pretty intense, right." Dianna started out awkwardly. "Hi, Mr. Ashton," she said waving at Drax's dad. Marvin shifted into a different position.

"Hi, Dianna. As you can see, we are all waiting," Marvin said a little impatiently.

"Yes, of course. So, I was born 1964. My mother, Irene, is 150 and the only thing we've ever known was seclusion. I couldn't even go to a normal school, let alone a school like this because we were always trying to stay out of sight. About 1973, we were living in Alabama. We lived near a wooded area and we were just walking back home when we heard someone yelling a few feet into the woods. We went to see who it was and apparently it was a lone jogger who fell and was bleeding out from a stomach wound. Think he fell onto a sharp object. I don't know. I was eight. I was so scared I became hysterical and started crying, begging my mom to do something. I could tell she wanted to walk away but I guess she didn't want me to think she was a bad person. She was a nurse when she was younger, so she had the expertise and she always kept a fresh supply of gauzes, IV lines, things like that just in case. She went back to the house and got some things while I kept watch. He barely had a pulse by then and had lost so much blood. My mother performed a direct blood transfusion and healed him. Even his wound closed up in a matter of minutes." She was interrupted by the loud murmuring that suddenly erupted.

Marvin banged the table, "Brothers, let her finish!" Dianna continued, telling them about the mechanic and Adisa.

"How do we know you aren't lying for attention! Or to impress Drax. Clearly you know who HE is!" Nate shouted out of turn. The murmuring started up again.

"Quiet! Quiet!" Marvin shouted. "Nate has an excellent point, Dianna. We've met before and this wasn't information you gave us at the house."

"I thought this came with being Nagalian or half Nagalian or whatever... After I found out I could do it, I concluded that we all could do it. I'd never met another...creature like me... to tell me what we are capable or incapable of doing. I'm sure you can understand the disadvantage of that."

"I am sorry about your secluded childhood, but I am sure you don't expect us to believe you without proof!" Marvin said harshly. The men mumbled in agreement.

Drax stood up. "I'm glad you asked, Father." He walked over to Dianna who was clearly becoming overwhelmed. He kissed her. "You did well." He then pulled out Norlan's chair so she could sit. He started setting up the projector in the center of the table with great skillfulness and then he dimmed the lights. The images of the cells appeared on the wall.

"So, I had mom run some tests."

"You involved your mother?"

"The best damn biologist I know."

"You both have some explaining to do."

"She wanted me to tell you sooner, but I decided it was best to wait. Don't blame her."

Marvin squinted his eyes, "How long have you had this information?"

"A week but that's beside the point."

"Expect a long discussion about this later," Marvin said sternly. Drax continued, explaining exactly what his mother had told him. When he was finished, he could hear a pin drop as the men were devoid of rebuttals.

"There's more." He looked at Dianna and his expression seemed apologetic. "Mom thinks that Dianna's blood type can help us create an antidote for the Apoptosyde." At this point, the uproar was so loud, Marvin's voice was barely audible above it. He got up and went to stand beside Drax.

"Really?" she whispered to him in shock. She didn't know what the information meant for her. Dianna's mind began to race with questions. *Was she immune to the poison or did they want to use her for research purposes, why didn't he tell her before?*

"Simmer down, simmer down!" Marvin voice boomed interrupting her mental breakdown.

Drax was staring at Dianna the entire time. "I didn't want to tell you because I didn't want you to think we were like the humans but it's true."

"Am I immune to the Apoptosyde?" she asked, her eyes were questioning.

"No. But if a Nagalian has it in their system, a blood transfusion from you can provide him or her with fresh blood with healthy cells that could help to flush the Apoptosyde."

Dianna suddenly felt trapped and wanted to leave. She was trying to figure out how to get out, but she was locked inside the room and she realized that she had to get past a dozen Nagalian men to even get to the door. She began to feel dizzy as the room spun and her body heated. Her snakes slowly uncoiled as she began to lose control of her emotions.

"Dianna are you okay?" came Marvin's voice. She stood up swaying as she did so.

"Is that why you want to be with me? Because I can help you create a cure?" All eyes were on Dianna but before Drax could respond, she fell into the seat of her chair then slid to the floor.

"Shit!" was the last thing she remembered Drax saying before she succumbed to unconsciousness.

***

"Don't you think you should have warned her first or even us before you brought this display here?"

"It wasn't meant to be a display. I didn't think she would take the news this hard."

"How does she even know about the Apoptosyde?"

The conversation was happening somewhere close by. Dianna could feel a splitting headache tearing her head apart as she awoke to hushed voices. The room was brightly lit as she opened her eyes. She looked around. She was in another room on a bed. The room was cozy compared to the conference room. She saw Drax and his father a few feet away, their backs turned. They were so deep in conversation; they hadn't noticed she was awake.

"It's a long story. I don't really want to explain it," Drax told him. His voice sounded tired.

"I don't think she'll want to stick around after this shit show," his father advised. Drax didn't respond. "I wouldn't blame her. Imagine being the answer to everyone's problem and thinking that's the only reason you're fishing around her," Marvin continued. Drax was still silent. He placed his arm on the wall and rested his head on his forearm, his eyes closed as his breathing paced. She could tell he was extremely stressed. She closed her eyes and pretended she was still sleeping, hoping that the conversation would reveal something about his inner thoughts.

"Think we should get mom here. She's taking a while to come to."

"What are you going to say to her when she wakes up? You're going to need something good."

"Don't concern yourself," Drax said dismissively. "I'll handle it."

This triggered an annoyed tone from Marvin. "I guess my real question is how exactly do you expect me to handle this situation?"

"What do you mean?"

"You just told fifteen Nagalians that she is a potential cure to the one thing that can kill us all. Am I to leave the Fraternity members hanging?"

"Tell them whatever you want but I think we all know that her participation in creating the antidote is entirely up to her." Dianna could hear the finality in his voice.

"In that case, you should have just kept what you know about her blood to yourself. What's the real reason you brought her here?"

"I didn't want to risk you and the other board members finding out from anyone else. As bad as this went, today, it would have been disastrous if you found out any other way."

"I might be old Drax but I'm not an idiot. You wanted Dianna to be accepted by me and the other board members and you made a hell of a gamble with that shit!" Dianna peered through her slightly opened eyes. Marvin looked angry. "I lost my right hand and best friend today over this and now my board members have more questions than answers. So, you need to think very carefully before you tell her shit that she wants to hear instead of the hard reality."

"Which is what exactly?" Drax interjected.

"We need that damn antidote! Now, if you don't mind. I'm going back to the meeting to do some damage control while you brood over the chaos you created today." He then walked away heated from the conversation. As soon as she was sure he was gone, Dianna sat up. Drax walked over to her briskly with worry etched on his face.

"Dianna, before you say anything, you're right. I am an asshole for telling you like this!" he said as he knelt in front of her. "But I would never expect you to sacrifice yourself for the possibility of an antidote."

She touched his face gently. "I know." She responded. "I think it was just the shock of it all. I'm not usually a fainter," she said deciding to take it easy on him. She understood the position he was in. "What's going to happen now?"

"Doesn't matter but I think I've at least given them enough reasons to make your protection the number one priority."

"Is that why you told them?"

"A part of it." He kissed her hand.

"What's the other part?" she probed almost afraid of his response.

"I'd hoped you knew," he said holding her gaze… and she did. Exactly what his father had said. He was setting the stage for her. She couldn't help wondering if her blood wasn't the answer to the antidote, would he still be willing to risk everything for her. She prayed he wasn't manipulating her for the antidote because she was ready to risk it all too.

"What would I have to do if we were to start working on the antidote?"

"No!"

"I'll speak to your mom," she continued.

"This isn't your cross to bear."

"Kind of sounds like my purpose." She didn't believe in so-called purpose before. Once, she wanted to end her life because she thought she had no significance to the planet but now her entire life had shifted, gained meaning and seemed like a testimony to her purpose. To add, this was the only way to get the heat off of Drax, so the answer seemed clear to her. She started to get up.

"Give yourself a minute," he told her; his eyebrows knitted together intently.

"Where's this?" she said narrowing her eyes to see through the small exit. It looked like a small medical station.

"School nurse."

"You're kidding; right?"

"Well...we are at a school."

"On the surface of things." She smirked. She managed to get to her feet without stumbling. She squared her shoulders and smoothed her suit. "Can't believe I fainted. I probably confirmed why you all don't need to mix with us weaklings." She damn sure made herself look like a fragile damsel passing out like that. Even she felt a little disgusted with herself.

"Don't beat yourself up. Besides, things were extraordinarily crazy in there. It's not every day you get to speak in front of a bunch of overprivileged Nagalian men."

"Hopefully the last!" She could see why women wouldn't want to attend a meeting even if they were invited. Even Drax's father was an asshole which was surprising since he seemed so nice when they had just met. She made a mental note to herself that moving forward, the only Nagalian prick she wanted to deal with was Drax.

***

Dianna sat at her desk with a lot on her mind. Drax had stepped down as CEO and promoted Eric to the position. Even though he was in their bed most nights, it still felt out of place for him to not come into his meetings or to lurk around the office. He informed her that he needed to focus more on Nagalian business which was his true work. He opened up about his charity work which she came to understand wasn't actual charity in the traditional sense of the word. His fraternity created temporary and permanent domicile to Nagalians who were down on their luck, hunted or just needed to be a part of a community through housing projects. She realized that the fraternity's network and investment ran deep, hidden under the guise of charity work. It was more than just helping; it was strengthening their community that they strongly identified with. He told her that for years he had only been half involved, even when it was in his power to do more. He had become an advocate of sorts over time. While she was proud of him, he was bit more hands on with the rescues and providing a sanctuary to women and children like her, which made her more of a spectator to his life but she didn't want to complain because she knew he was passionate about changing the way things were between the half and the full Nagalians...*lessen the divide* were the exact words he used to describe what he wanted to do.

She also decided it was time to be upfront with what really happened in Alabama. She explained how Quinton kidnapped her and forced her to cure his daughter using desperate strategies. Of course, this only fueled his hatred for Quinton, even when she tried to assure him that it was something she was happy he did because she would have never done it otherwise and she also wouldn't know she had the capabilities to heal humans. Drax humored her but she knew it was futile to make him see the good side of Quinton.

However, that wasn't the only thing on her mind. She also hadn't heard from her mother or Quinton in weeks. She made a mental note to call Quinton, but it wasn't as easy to contact her mom since she changed her number and was living, only God knows where, in Canada. When she had the argument with Drax, her first instinct was to go to Canada and find her mom. Thinking back, she felt stupid for even thinking she could find her mother let alone rely on her to create any modicum of stability. This was always how things were. Her mom would run off to a new place, change her number and she would have to wait weeks, maybe months to hear from her. Usually, she wasn't worried about her mother's safety but now that she was aware of the extent of the danger, she was anxious.

She wondered when it was that her mother first discovered that she could heal people. What was the big event that forced her to even try to do something so selfless to a kind that hated and hunted her? She never spoke about it. In fact, the time she had saved that jogger was something of a dormant memory triggered by the accident in Alaska. Her need to save the mechanic sent her in a panic similar to when she was eight years old. Then, she begged her mom to do something too, without caring about the consequences. Eric knocked on the door before walking in.

"Hey, Eric," she greeted him reining in her thoughts.

"Hey beautiful. I'm here on business!" he said in a professional tone.

"Yes, sir!" she said, militantly holding her hand to her head like a soldier acknowledging their superiors. Eric rolled his eyes amused by her silliness.

"Sorry, I've just been in CEO mode all day. This stuff isn't as easy as I thought," Eric said whipping his hair from his face with a twist of his neck. "Brrrr. It's cold in here." He wrapped his arms around himself. "Anyway. You haven't been meeting your deadlines since of late."

"I'm sorry. I just have so much going on."

"It's really not an issue. We kind of overloaded you with work on purpose when you started working here."

"We?"

"Girl, you know it was under Drax's orders. Anyway, I'm going to delegate a percentage of the assignments to some of our junior employees to narrow down your workload."

Dianna wanted to argue but she wasn't in the position to. She was finding herself to be tired all the time and she could barely focus. "Okay," she said in a docile tone.

"Are you okay? Maybe you need less work plus a vacation," Eric suggested.

A vacation was actually sounding really good to Dianna. "No. I'm fine. I think it's better for me to work on just a few projects at a time right now," she said feeling a little flushed.

Eric eyed her skeptically. "From a friend to a friend, you don't look yourself, Dianna. Maybe you should take the rest of the day."

"I'm fine. I promise." Besides, she would just be going home to an empty house anyway. "I'll send over the list of projects I'm transferring and work a little faster to meet those deadlines for the projects I'm keeping."

"If that's how you want it." Eric proceeded to walk out.

"And Eric?" He turned around at the sound of his name. "Thank you."

"I care about you, Pet. Don't forget that." He turned again to walk out. It was Simon who usually called her pet, but she was finding that her relationship with Eric was strengthening and quickly surpassing the bond she had with Simon.

"Can you do me one more favor?"

He let out a dramatic sigh, then winked playfully "Yes, anything!"

"Turn down the thermostat on your way out." She pleaded with puppy eyes.

"It's so cold in here, you're saving the ice caps in Antarctica." He walked over to the thermostat. "This thing is literally on 40 degrees. What are you trying to do?"

"Set it to 35 degrees," she asked politely. He stared at her with uncertainty then adjusted the temperature.

"If you die of hypothermia, it isn't my fault." Then he walked out. Dianna was thankful she could go back to her thoughts. She began thinking about the antidote. She wasn't a scientist so she wasn't sure how it would work. For humans, a direct transfusion seemed to work and only about a pint of blood was needed. Would it be the same process for Nagalians, or would they need more blood? Would she have to do a transfusion each time? What if more than one person were poisoned, would she need to supply fresh blood to of all them? It seemed very dangerous from where she stood with a lot of blood donations. She needed to contact Drax's mom, but she did not have her phone number. She decided to call Drax. He picked up on the second ring.

"Hey baby." Her heart did a jig in her chest at the sound of his soothing voice. She wanted to be his *baby*.

"Hey." She croaked into the phone. She cleared her throat and realized she had mucous in her throat. This was definitely new.

"Are you okay?" His voice was heavy with concern.

"I hope so. Feel like I'm getting a cold."

"Doesn't sound right."

"No."

Drax was silent. "You might need to visit my mom's medical facility. Maybe she can figure out why you're getting sick."

"That's why I called. I need her number." Drax gave her the number by rote.

"Okay. Thanks."

"Wait! You don't need to talk to her about anything else."

"You mean the antidote?"

"Yes."

"I'm curious and I have some questions."

He sighed. "Okay." Dianna ended the call and dialed Drax's mom. An older woman's voice greeted her after a few rings.

"Hi, Mrs. Ashton. It's Dianna."

"Who?" Dianna felt silly for expecting Drax's mom to even remember who she was. She began feeling like an insignificant bug. "Oh, yes! You're Drax's girlfriend; right?" A feeling of relief came over her.

"Yes! You did some lab work on my blood," Dianna explained.

"Pardon me for the memory lapse, Dianna. I know who you are. How can I help you?"

"Drax told me that you may be able to figure out the antidote... y'know, because of my blood type."

"He told me not to push the issue," she responded curtly.

"I know but he doesn't speak for me. I have a few questions."

"This isn't something you discuss over the phone, dear," Mrs. Ashton continued with a curt tone. Dianna was beginning to think that everyone in Drax's family were not as nice as she thought. But she surmised that with bounty hunters always hunting them, maybe being nice wasn't a luxury they had. "Would you like to meet for lunch?" she continued. Dianna thought for a while. Maybe lunch was not such a good idea either.

"Can we meet at your lab? I'll pick up some lunch on the way, but I've been feeling a little sick and it's honestly my first time so...if you don't mind, I'd like to have some more tests done."

"That does sound strange," Mrs. Ashton agreed. I'll be working until 8:00 so anytime is good." Dianna was relieved to hear that. She did not want to talk about things over a quick lunch. Maybe this could also be a good opportunity to get in his mother's good graces as well.

Chapter 10

"Are you sure?"

"Does this look like something I would be unsure about?!" Mrs. Ashton snapped slapping the document on the desk in front of Drax. He scrutinized the results. "It took me a while to figure it out. I figured maybe since she had mutated, it was possible she could get sick as well. The pregnancy test was just an afterthought."

"Well, thanks for being thorough." Drax was experiencing a whirlwind of emotions as he was still trying to get over the shock of Dianna's pregnancy. He had to admit that they had thrown caution to the wind and had not even discussed contraception because he thought it was highly unlikely for this to happen so soon. His own mother did not conceive him until she was 250 years old.

"I thought it was best to tell you first." Mrs. Ashton's words seemed heavy with something underlying…something ugly and sinister.

"She doesn't know!"

"Drax, don't take this the wrong way but there's still a chance for you to still marry a full Nagalian woman."

"What are you suggesting?" His mom walked around to her neatly organized white office desk and sat with her back straight with her hair pulled back neatly in a bun. She was a graceful beauty even though she wasn't too much behind his father in years. She was wearing her white lab coat with the green Nagalian crest proudly visible just a few inches below her right shoulder.

"I could take care of it...and she wouldn't know." Her voice was soothing, but her words were like a serrated knife tearing through his flesh. He stared at her in complete awe, sickened to the pit of his stomach by her words.

"Take care of *it*...are you saying what I think you are saying?" Drax's facial features slowly contorted into a nasty scowl.

"I can see that this vexes you," his mother said gently, "I just want you to know that you have options." But he could tell that she was unfazed by what she saying which made her appear colossally heartless.

"So, we are clear...you are talking about aborting my child." His jaw was clenched as he walked towards his mother's desk, with one hand inside his pants pocket and the other holding a pen he was clicking at an even rhythm.

"I know you are noble at heart, Drax. You clearly love her and you...mean well but have you considered that you will outlive them? You won't have someone to continue after you. You could literally end your legacy with this woman and her baby."

"OUR BABY!" He corrected her, inserting the pen on the outside pocket of his jacket and placing both of his hands flat on his mother's desk. He hunched over the desk so he could level his gaze with hers as he stared squarely into her eyes. "So, let me get this straight. She is good enough to save the Nagalian race, but WE get to deliberate behind her back whether OUR child deserves to live or die?"

"You are looking at it the wrong way!" She implored.

"I think my vision is a perfect 20/20 on this, Mom!" he said through gritted teeth, but Mrs. Ashton didn't even flinch. "You so much as speak like that about my child again, you will definitely have to worry about passing on a legacy because I can promise you this. I'll flip this entire Nagalian operation on its head in a nanosecond!"

His mother grinned wickedly undaunted by his threat. "How do you even know this is what she wants? When I first met her, she didn't seem that thrilled to be half Nagalian." Now his mother was twisting the serrated knife in the deepest part of his soul as her words hit home. Dianna had admitted that she would never want to sentence her child to the life of a half Nagalian. He cringed at his mother's words. He stood up straight, grating his teeth over his bottom lip in an attempt to get a hold of his emotions. "If you think murdering my child is the solution to any problem we are facing, then you are no better than these fucking bounty hunters!"

"Let me tell you what a good mother does, Drax." Mrs. Ashton sneered at him. "A good mother tells you the truth even when it's a hard pill to swallow!"

Drax sniffed derisively. "Unbelievable! Don't worry about telling her about the pregnancy. I'll tell her myself." He snatched up the paper with Dianna's lab results, then he walked out of his mother's office. He was beyond livid and disappointed in his mother. He had never found the need to check her this severely before but that was the least of his worries. He was more worried about his child's safety. He hated to admit it, but Dianna was or used to be suicidal and clearly his mother had no qualms about selective breeding. There was no question in his mind what he needed to do. Protect HIS child at all cost! He shuddered to think of how Dianna might react, but he would lock her in an iron suit if it came down to it, because he would be damned if either of these women intentionally harmed his kid.

**

He had decided to be upfront with Dianna instead of waiting for her to discover that she was pregnant, ultimately hating him in the process for keeping something as important as a person growing inside her body from her. Eric had told him that she seemed really distracted and tired at work. He figured a little change of scenery would do her good, along with a bout of fresh air. He would have loved to book a trip to Costa Rica, but things were too hectic for him to travel out of the country now. He settled on Luxury Cabins in the mountains where she would be away from everything except staff at her beck and call. Surprisingly, she had not put up any of her usual protests. Usually, she would decline, using work as an excuse but even a workaholic like Dianna could not resist a weekend trip to Gaitlinburg.

They were at dinner, away from listening ears and prying eyes, where they could admire the night breeze by the lake and the beautiful starry sky. He could tell that the trip was what she needed because she was already looking more rested. She was wearing a scarlet spaghetti strap tightly fitted dress with matching heels. She had not worn her contacts and he could see the dark green specks in the natural coloring of her eyes. It was highlighted by all the red she was wearing. Her hair was pulled back in a curly puff with long elongated diamond earrings that cascaded elegantly down her long neck which made him think that dinner was such a waste of time when he could have been tasting her neck instead. He breathed in heavily, preparing himself for any type of reaction from her. The more he thought about the pregnancy, the more he began to rethink telling her in public over dinner. At least, if things went south, no one would notice since their seating was so private...*or that's what he hoped,* he thought to himself as he looked around tentatively.

"What's going on in that busy head of yours?" She stroked his chin sensually. Her pouty lips silently begging for a kiss. "You've barely said a word to me all night."

"How is everything?" he asked courteously. She stared out at the lake where a mother duck was leisurely swimming with her ducklings. She shrugged her left shoulder seductively.

"What more could I ask for?" she said sincerely. His heart picked up pace. He could not believe he was so nervous. Thankfully, he masked it well with his handsome smile.

"Exactly what I needed to hear." He responded. He pecked her lovingly on her lips and then picked up his knife and fork to begin eating. "Shall we?" he prompted her. She looked at his steak with utter disdain. She had gotten herself a salad to start off, saying that she might get something heavier later, but he knew her appetite was changing. It was strange to know and understand her changing habits while she was completely clueless. Her body had not changed, just her behavior. She was more docile no doubt due to her always being tired.

"I thought you liked steak," he goaded her.

"I do! I just-- I don't know." She gave up trying to explain what had changed within her. She stared out at the moon. "I just haven't been myself lately." She then began to eat her salad.

"How was your meeting with mom?" She widened her eyes at the reminder.

"Oh, I completely forgot to tell you about that. Your mom is nothing short of a mad scientist!" Drax chuckled at her excitement.

"Why do you say that?"

"Well...she explained that making the antidote wasn't as complicated as I thought. After the necessary testing and trials, she said she would make synthetic blood that would be readily available for transfusion. She pretty much said that I wouldn't even need to be present once they started producing the synthetic blood."

Drax had to give it to his mother. Her brain was indeed one of the marvels of the universe.

"Wow! Sounds promising...safe...less demanding than I previously thought," he responded with uncertainty.

"I think she's trying to create as minimal inconvenience for me as possible." Dianna smiled appreciatively. Drax licked his lips and then drank some wine, ready to dish it out. It was torment waiting for the right moment when he knew the right moment would never come.

"Dianna-- "

"I told her I would do it!"

"Do what?"

"Help her make the antidote. I hope you aren't upset," she said reading his expression with fervency.

"Why would I be upset?"

"I guess the word I'm looking for is 'guilty'," she continued.

He scoffed. "If anything happens to you or --" he stopped himself before he said, 'the baby'. "I mean, if you ended up regretting it, I might have a hard time forgiving myself," he continued. He was genuinely concerned that any type of medical research or testing might be harmful for Dianna now, in her condition.

"It's for the greater good," she reassured him. She covered his hand gently. He sneered at her and pulled his hand away, "Did my mother tell you that?" He was barely able to disguise his animosity towards his mother. "Sounds like some bullshit she would say!" He placed his fork down loudly, stunning Dianna. She cleared her throat at the sudden awkwardness and placed her fork down gently. He could tell she was little confused.

"I'm sorry. We got into a fight before we left Nevada."

"Why?" She was searching his eyes for answers. The longer he waited to tell her, the more difficult it was becoming to tell her about her pregnancy. The irony wasn't lost on him that usually, it was the other way around. If she did not want to keep the baby, it would create so much friction between them, but she had to know. "Did she say something to you about me?" He had to take the plunge now.

"Nothing bad," he said reassuringly. "You know mothers. Always think they know best."

"I know what you mean. My mom can be a pain in the ass too!" Dianna laughed but Drax wasn't feeling humorous.

"I can understand why you wouldn't want to have kids." He was avoiding eye contact as he played with his food. She stared at him quizzically.

"I told you that?" she said trying to recall.

"Yeah, you were pretty adamant."

"Well, yeah. I mean...being one of us is a little crazy don't you think?" she said unsure how they even arrived at this topic.

"Not really. We have good schools, a good support system," he countered.

"For wealthy, full Nagalians like you. Of course, it was easy! For me, it was a nightmare!" she said nonchalantly.

"But your circumstances have changed. It would be easier for you…to have a baby."

"Why do I get the feeling that you're trying to make me want a child?" she said astutely.

"I'm just curious. Now that you know things aren't so bad…and you have me…would that make you change your mind?" Dianna was quiet as she studied him. She was no fool. He saw she was putting it together in her mind.

"What did your mom say about my test results?" Drax became silent as he met her intense stare evenly. Dianna swallowed hard.

"Oh my God!" She gagged. "Is that what my cold is? I'm pregnant!"

Drax nodded as he threaded his fingers together on the table.

"I need a drink!" she said as her face paled. "Where's the waiter?" she searched the wide-open area for a server. He wanted to tell her that drinking could harm the baby, but he was pretty sure she would slap him good and hard. She snatched her clutch and got up clumsily from the table, almost pulling the tablecloth with her. He went after her.

"Dianna, wait!" He caught up with her outside the gazebo. The air was crisp, and he could hear the crickets chirping around them. He held her still as he noticed she was shivering. He encircled her with his arms. "I want this," he whispered in her ear. "More than you'll ever know," he said to her. He rocked her body soothingly. She pressed her face against his chest, clinging tightly to him, absorbing his strength. She hadn't stopped shivering, so he took his shirt off and wrapped it around her. Thankfully he had an undershirt under it. "I know this is unexpected," he said to her. "But I promise, it's not as bad as you think."

After a long silence, Dianna finally spoke. "How did we let this happen?" She sniffled against his now moist undershirt.

"You know how it happened." She punched his exposed muscular arm playfully and he kissed the top of her head.

"You know what I mean. I thought this was unlikely."

"Me too...but in case you haven't noticed, a lot of unlikely things have been happening where you're concerned."

"I can hear my mother in my head telling me to go into hiding or to get rid of it," she said letting him into her dark thoughts. He hoped she wasn't entertaining notions of abortion like his mother.

"You and I know it's different this time, Dianna... For both of us." She looked up at him.

"Your mom wasn't too thrilled, was she?"

"She was ecstatic! Her first three quarter Nagalian grandchild and we aren't even married! I would say she is brimming with pride," he said sarcastically. They both laughed.

"But it's not about your mom or mine," he assured her.

"You know you'll outlive us both; right?"

"You don't know that."

"But you said--"

"I said a lot of things, but I think there's a lot of unchartered territory here. Let's just take it one step at a time." Dianna nodded as she thought about the full extent of their circumstances. She shook her head. "If it's good with you, I'd rather not think about it," he said, his eyes smiling.

"You're everything," She stared into all-encompassing brown eyes and saw so much love there.

"Promise me something," he asked her. "Promise me that no matter how hard things get, this baby will be your number one priority." Her eyebrows knitted together as she pursed her lips tightly. He felt the change in her. *What the hell did I say wrong?* he immediately thought to himself.

"You think I'd hurt the baby?"

Shit! He cursed inwardly, wishing he could take back his words. Just then, her cell phone buzzed from her clutch. She slid his arms from around her and then took her phone from her purse. When she looked at the screen, it was a strange number from Alabama. She accepted the call.

"Hello!"

"Dianna, we know where you live. We know where your brother lives and we know your boyfriend thinks he can protect you from us, but he can't. We want to give you and your mother a chance to give yourselves up before things get any uglier." The voice was distorted, and there was a lot of crackling sounds on the other end of the line. She realized a little too late that she had accidentally hit the speaker button.

"How did you get my number?"

"Don't worry about that!" the voice snapped. She stared horrified at Drax. Drax snatched the phone from her, taking the call off of the speaker setting.

"Whoever you are," he seethed walking a few feet away from her. "I'm going to make you regret every fucking word that you just said." The person's laugh jarred him.

"If I were you, I would cut that bitch loose! She isn't worth half the chaos we're going to drop off at your front door." The voice was seething. There was a loud click and then dead air.

"Fuck!" He pushed the phone in his pants pocket.

"What are you doing?"

"I'm keeping it."

"Drax, if you don't give me my phone back, I will claw it from you!" She charged at him like a bull. She was trying to get inside his pocket to retrieve her phone.

"No!" he shouted at her. She was able to pull the phone out, but he wrestled it from her causing it to fall and break apart on the stone pathway.

"Noooooo!" Dianna screamed at the sight of her phone. She fell to her knees as she picked up the broken pieces.

"Don't be so dramatic. We can easily get you another one," he said walking toward her with her back turned to him.

"That's the only way my mom could get in touch with me!" she said realizing there was no use even trying to salvage it. The screen was shattered, the battery was broken. She found the memory card and placed it in her clutch. Clearly whatever was on it was important to her.

"You can't keep that number. They have it!"

"I don't care!" she shouted at him. Then her eyes widened with panic. "They are going to kill my brother! They know where he lives."

"No, they won't!" He tried to help her up, but she flinched away.

"YOU DON'T FUCKING KNOW THAT!"

"I do!" He took his phone out and dialed a number. She noticed that it wasn't his normal phone. "Hey, what's your position."

The person responded by telling him the street he was on. Dianna recognized the street name. It was the street Quinton lived on.

"Anything new?"

"No. Same old same old. Work, school and home."

"Are you alone?"

"Yeah. It's another slow night," the male voice said nonchalantly.

"Get a few other men out there. I just got confirmation tonight that the bounty hunters might be surveilling the house too."

"Shit!"

"Yeah! Stay alert." He ended the call. She looked warily at him.

"You think you have the answer to everything don't you?" He saw that she was looking for a reason to be angry and he was the perfect target to take the hit.

"I don't like loose ends! So, I do what I have to." He grabbed her up roughly and was leading her back to the gazebo.

"Stop pushing me around!" She managed to break free from him. "You've placed yourself in charge of my life and I never asked you to do that!"

"I'm pretty sure I'm in a position to know what's best for you!" he said trying to keep his voice contained. He wasn't in the mood right now. Like the distorted voice said on the phone, shit was getting ugly and he didn't want to waste time arguing with her. "You should be happy that your brother's family is safe."

"HAPPY! I should be happy? I wish you would just get the fuck out of my life!" she said pulling his shirt tightly around her shoulders.

"You know I can't do that," he said stoically. Her lips trembled. She started looking around wildly. He recognized that look in her eyes. It was the same look she gave him when she went down to his garage looking for her motorcycle. She was about to run. "Don't fucking think about it!" he warned her. "So, help me God, Dianna! I will transform and not only outrun you! I will drag you by your legs screaming and hollering back to our cabin and strap your ass to the living room table for the entire weekend if I have to."

Her eyes challenged his. "Do I look like I give a damn about what you will or won't do!"

"So, I guess we're doing this," he responded promptly. His face immediately transformed, and he was a menacing sight. He sneered at her. The rest of his muscles started ripping through his thin undershirt. He saw her looking around to see if anyone was watching as she backed away from him. He laughed at her. He stepped towards her as his pants ripped. She stopped dead in her tracks.

"I'm a little disappointed in you," he said goading her. He could taste the excess saliva on his teeth as his primal instincts were heightened. He started stalking her, waiting for her to run.

"You are always so worried about who's going to save you from the humans," he laughed derisively. "But have you ever wondered...who's going to save you from me?" He closed the gap so quickly between them she fell back into some bushes, her clutch falling from her hand. He grabbed her arm so tight; he was certain he was almost crushing it. She yelped in pain. He should've felt sorry but instead he smirked at how weak she was compared to his strength. He wasn't even fully transformed. "You think this is a game?" he shouted at her.

"No!" Her hair had uncoiled into snakes, but even they knew better than to try him. He realized that she was scared but he didn't care.

"Why do you keep testing me?" He yanked her up and she whimpered in pain. He slowly started transforming back to his human form. His clothes were shredded except for the bits that covered from his waist to his thighs. He couldn't walk back into the main restaurant in his disheveled state and neither could she. She was scratched up; her hair was a mess. It looked like they were chased by wild animals or worse, in some type of domestic dispute. That would certainly get everyone's attention.

She took off his shirt and flung it at him. There was a large purple bruise covering her entire arm from his grip when he had transformed. He loosened his grip. He flung the shirt back at her.

"You need it more than I do. Keep it." She looked at it petulantly. "PUT IT ON, DIANNA!" He had lost his patience with her. He waited for her to put on his shirt then he picked up her clutch and handed it to her before he pulled her with him to the gazebo. He had left his wallet on the table. He picked it up and awkwardly threw some cash on the table to pay his bill, since he was still holding Dianna's arm with his other hand. His pants were nothing but strips of cloth hanging from his legs. "Put this in your thing," he instructed in an agitated tone, giving her his wallet to put in her clutch. Dianna smirked at the fact that he didn't know what to call her accessory. "We're taking the long way back," he informed her. They both started walking along the path with him almost dragging her. As they walked on in silence, Drax felt his nerves calming with each step as they got closer to their cabin. He began to think of things he needed to do. Dianna's mom was in danger, but he couldn't help. No one knew where she was, but Dianna couldn't get her old number back. The bounty hunters would keep calling her until she did something stupid like searching for her mom. On the other hand, if he kept the number for a while longer, he could wait for her mother to call.

"Thinking of more ways to control my life!" she said angrily.

"Aren't you perceptive," he shot back unimpressed with her.

"I would like my arm back. My feet are killing me, and I would like to take my shoes off."

"You have another arm for that!" He said without looking at her. He yanked her forward as she tried to slow down.

"Can you at least stop so I can take them off?" He cursed and then stopped. She bent to the side and took both her shoes off with one hand. Then without warning she started pummeling him with her shoes. "Let go of my arm!" she said trying to pull her arm away. "Stop treating me like a fucking child!" He expertly gained control of her other arm as they stood facing each other, breathing heavily.

"Stop fighting me! I'm done with your cat and mouse bullshit. One minute your sane and the next minute you're a bipolar bitch!" he snapped at her.

"Well maybe you should give me back my motorcycle and let me return to what I'm used to."

"You're like a damn feral animal," he told her. "My dad was right about you." His eyes burned into hers.

"I'm a feral animal? You nearly ripped my fucking arm off back there!" She got closer to his face. "You're a spoilt, arrogant, controlling and abusive piece of shit!" He saw defiance blazing in her eyes. "You want to know the real reason you won't let me leave."

"Since you're so clever, Dianna. Why don't you tell me?"

"Because I'm so deep in here," she used her long nail to poke the left side of his chest. "If I ever leave, you will NEVER recover." She smiled tauntingly from ear to ear like a Cheshire cat. "Guys like you always fall for damaged women... or in my case the damaged half breed Nagalians," she taunted further. She was right. He was weak for her, but he wasn't weak, and he wasn't going to fall for whatever game she was playing at right now.

"For once, Dianna, be a standup person in your own life and stop living your life like a reckless teenager." He let go of one her arm. "Whether you like it or not, I'm the only one fully capable of protecting you. Are you dumb enough to try to do this alone...to raise our child on your own?" He released her other arm, and she went silent as the seconds stretched between them.

"SAY SOMETHING!" he demanded.

"No!"

"Then stop wasting my time with your childish games. If you want to save your brother's family...Adisa and your mother, you need to do exactly as I tell you."

She nodded compliantly. She stood helpless and defeated in front of him. He realized in that moment that she wasn't going anywhere...*at least not tonight.*

"It might take a while for me to recover...from us... if you leave, but you will die out there without me and the sooner you understand that, the easier it will be for the both of us," he offered her his hand. She looked at it and then placed her smaller hand inside his. She moved closer to him and he placed a protective arm around her shoulders, kissing the top of her head. "You're not damaged."

"You get to call me a bipolar bitch but now I'm not damaged," she said resting her head on his chest, having lost a few inches of height since she was no longer in her heels, and as the usual sequence of things...*they were back to normal.*

"You are a bipolar bitch! Doesn't mean you're damaged." He lifted her face. Her makeup was a little messy but that didn't stop him from kissing her beautiful red lips. He was itching to do it all night. "Besides, I'm probably the only guy that can handle it," he goaded her.

"Actually, I'm a little saner around human partners."

"That's only because you're usually hiding who you truly are, then you leave them," he said succinctly. He meant it as harmless banter, but he realized his words deeply affected her when Dianna averted his gaze. Sometimes, he was too frank for his own good. They arrived at the cabin, the porch light illuminating the red cedar wood of the large exterior. The aromatic smell of the wood lingered in the atmosphere as they walked through the door of their beautifully furnished luxury cabin. He went to the refrigerator for some ice. He wrapped it in a small, clean, lavender towel and walked to the bedroom where she was sprawled, out a little drained from their spat. He got ready to place the towel on her arm, but her bruise was already healing. "The beauty of being Nagalian," she said rubbing the spot. "It's fine," she told him, then took the towel from him and placed the towel on the side table. She took one of the ice cubes and placed it in her mouth. She then turned to him and placed her mouth on his, slipping the ice cube into his mouth. He was immediately turned on. He sucked on it indulgently and then slipped it back into her mouth. She moaned at the exchange. She ripped the remainder of what was left of his pants as she slipped the much smaller ice cube back into his mouth. "You don't need these," she said, throwing his pants aside. "When you change, I'm so terrified of you but so fucking turned on at the same time." He saw where her mind was going. "I don't think what you are implying is a good idea."

"But I think we should." She let her fangs grow out. He noticed she was getting better at dictating her physical changes. She allowed her elongated tongue to slip inside his mouth as she tasted the coldness from the now, melted ice cube. Her snakes uncoiled and hissed around her face. He slipped off her straps from her shoulders and pulled the dress over her head and his eyes traveled from her face blatantly to her breasts. He was ready to devour her, even though her condition was forefront in his mind. "Change," she whispered hypnotically.

"You're pregnant!"

"So?" He was about to say something more. She swung her legs over his legs, so she could sit in his lap and slowly sat on his aroused shaft. He grunted loudly, sweet pleasure coursing through his body as she moved up and down. "Change!" she repeated seductively. He wasn't going to make her beg. *Who was he kidding?* He loved having sex with her in his Nagalian form. He started changing and could feel himself expanding slowly within her. She gasped at his sudden change in size both inside her and outside of her. Then she gave him an evil grin. He pulled her hair and she moaned loudly. He inserted his tongue in her open mouth and licked every corner. Then he trailed his kisses to her long neck which he longed to taste. He moved onto her breasts and licked her dark nipples, one hard pointy bud at a time.

"Yesssss!" she hissed to him which intensified his need for her. He felt the sensations mounting as began to lose his sense of control. Everything was primal, everything. It was raw carnal desire. He grabbed her soft, shapely thighs and she winced slightly as his claws indented her flesh, but he couldn't stop himself...not this time. He lifted her body, slamming her harder and harder onto his shaft. Her smell, her taste was driving him to the brink of his arousal. He had to have her every way he wanted. Fucking her safely wasn't in the stars tonight. He pulled her off him and threw her on the bed.

"Turn around!" he growled lost in the moment. She did as she was told. He knew he should have entered her from behind delicately, but there was a disconnect between what he knew and what he felt. He was in his element and found himself ramming his dick into her instead. She screamed and he was instantly remorseful. He hissed and immediately pulled out. Her scream was a reminder that he didn't want to hurt her.

"Why did you stop?" she asked looking around at him.

"I thought you wanted me to stop" He felt a little helpless. She turned around so she could lay on her back as she ran her foot seductively over his hard, muscular body. He grabbed her ankle and sucked on her calf which tantalized her. "My safe word is 'bipolar'.

"What?"

"You don't stop until I say, 'bipolar'." She sat up, her legs wide apart and he could see the source of his impending downfall. She was facing his erecting. She leaned her head to the side and sucked hard. The suction as she moved her head forward and backward and the moistness of her mouth was enough to distract him from their conversation. He was now focused on the fact that he could barely fit in her mouth. He grabbed a handful of hair and guided her evenly onto him. He trembled from the pleasure.

After a while, she paused to whisper the word 'bipolar' and he stopped. "Good boy." She bent over and hoisted her butt in the air so he could see every inch of her exposed and wet vagina. He lost it again. As if he hadn't learned the last time, he slammed his dick inside her again. She screamed. He waited for her to say the safe word, but she didn't. He continued, stroking his dick against her wet walls. He held onto the side of her hip which seemed so much smaller in his claw now and he pulled her hair as her snakes wrapped tightly around his wrist. His strokes were hard, rough and punishing but she took it. Sometimes she screamed, sometimes she moaned but she never stopped him. He couldn't stop, his brain had turned off and it was his body taking from her. He closed his eyes as he felt it. He bit down as every cell in his body exploded in tiny bits, taking him to the volcanic eruption he wanted.

He moaned loudly as he felt the warm liquid spewing out of him into her, then, he collapsed on top of her. His chest expanding and falling as he tried to regulate his breathing. He rolled over as he became human again. "I'm going to kill you one day if we keep doing this," he said unable to hide the concern in his voice.

"It's a good thing you can't," she said snuggling up to him, placing her leg across both of his.

"Did you cum?" he said out of curiosity. He was so cocooned in his orgasm he had lost track of hers.

"And if I didn't, would you be willing to fuck me like that again," he laughed.

"Let's stick to the weird human stuff, like whips, ropes and toys. Much safer," he told her.

"No can do. I'd rather be almost fucked to death by a giant Nagalian guy!" she joked. He ran his hand over his face.

"God, I hope we didn't hurt the baby."

"I forgot about the little fetus," she said giggling at his expression. "Don't look so worried. The baby is fine...I think." She took his hand and placed it on her stomach. "Can you feel it?"

He waited. "No."

"Me neither. But I think there's a strong little girl in there."

"How do you know it's a girl?" She looked at his chest and gently stroked it.

"I just assumed." He understood that certain thoughts just came naturally to her. She looked exhausted. She closed her eyes. He got a pillow and placed it under her head. "Thank you," she mumbled. "By the way, I came. It's kind of hard not to. You make me so sensitive down there." He watched her drift off, but he couldn't sleep. Things had changed. The bounty hunters had made contact with her and he knew that an unforeseeable plan was now in motion. While they weren't sitting ducks, he knew there was no such thing as being overprepared. Then there was that one loose end that he couldn't string together no matter how hard he tried.

"Irene, where the fuck are you?"

* * *

She sat at the bar, her iridescent brown nails tapping the bar counter slowly as she calculated how to befriend the gay bartender with the pink hair. He had greeted her professionally and gave her what she requested, a Budweiser light, since she didn't want to drive inebriated, but he was so busy she could barely engage him. Just then, a man came beside her smelling like booze and cigarettes. He was a big, burly monster of a man.

"What's a pretty girl like you doing, sitting at a bar like this alone?"

"I'm waiting for my boyfriend, thanks," she said dismissively. He was definitely not her type plus; he was getting in the way of what she was trying to do. She decided to ignore him.

"Looks like your boyfriend stood you up, honey."

"He just texted. He'll be here faster than you can spell your name so I would disappear if I were you," she sassed.

"Like I said, A pretty girl like you shouldn't have to wait." He touched her wavy blonde hair with his clammy hand which immediately triggered her fighting instincts. She got up and kicked him in his scrotum. This sent him doubling to the ground with his hands between his legs grimacing from the pain.

"Don't fucking touch me you greasy piece of shit!"

"Yeah, we've got a situation," she heard the bartender saying. She turned to see him speaking into his walker-talkie. She then followed his gaze and saw another guy walking intimidatingly toward them. She assumed the other guy was a friend of the first guy.

"Bitch! Did you just assault my buddy!"

She didn't back down. She didn't cower. She hadn't meant to cause a scene but the last thing she would do was run from these two clowns. She could kill them both in less than five minutes. The bartender nimbly walked around the bar and stepped in between the two of them.

"Get the fuck out of my bar or I will call the police," he threatened. The man measured the bartender and laughed at his much smaller frame. Just then, there was a loud crackling sound as the bartender zapped the man with volts of electricity from his taser. The guy convulsed and fell to the ground. "I told you to get out of my damn bar. You've got some nerve scaring my customers!" the bartender said angrily. Security finally showed up. "Get them out of here," the bartender told them. They pulled the men to their feet and escorted them to the exit. He turned to face the green-eyed young lady in front of him.

"Are you okay?" His natural nurturing instincts kicking in. She smirked. The opportunity had just fallen right into her lap.

"I'm okay now. Hi, I'm Brooke." She shook his hand. "Thank you so much."

"It's Simon. Is your boyfriend really coming?"

"No. I just said that to get that guy off my back," she said, feigning a look of guilt. Simon was making this too easy for her. *Like taking candy from a baby.*

"Okay. Well, just sit by the bar and wait for security to come back. I'll have them escort you to your car. Trust me, I don't think you've seen the last of those two men tonight."

"Actually, I'd like to just talk to you if it's not too much."

Simon eyed her quizzically. "Why are beautiful women always flirting with me. I think It's the hair. It has to be," he joked. He placed his hand on his hip and looked at her seductively. "Sorry honey, but that ship has sailed since the 1990s."

"No. I know you're into men."

Simon clutched his chest, breathing out dramatically. "You had me worried."

"You seem like a nice person and I'm new in town." Simon peered at his unattended bar.

"Y'know. You remind me of someone. Has similar nails and streaks as you do. Well...except she's more cinnamon than vanilla."

"I'm guessing I'm the vanilla flavor," Brooke joked back.

"Have you noticed?" Simon said sarcastically. Brooke laughed. "Look! I'm a bit busy right now but maybe some other time when I'm not so busy, we can chat more," he explained sweetly.

"Of course. I understand. Take my number. Call me when you are free." Simon took the card she handed to him and stuffed into his back pocket. "And thank you again."

"Don't sweat it." He scurried behind the bar and threw a fresh towel over his shoulder. "Y'ALL MISSED ME!" he yelled to his waiting customers.

She hoped he would call soon. She would give him two days to reach out to her. If she heard nothing, she would come back to the bar...anything she needed to do to get closer to Dianna and Drax. She walked out of the bar and walked straight to her beautiful dark green sports car. She didn't need to wait for security. She could handle those two morons if she encountered them again. She adjusted her rear-view mirror to take a glance at herself. She let her snakes uncoil. They hissed at her reflection in the mirror.

"Okay, babies. It's just a matter of time."

She sped out of the parking lot in a haze of noise and dust as her plans were finally coming together.

***

Irene tried for the third time to call Dianna, but the call just kept going to voicemail. This worried her. She tried to keep a safe distance from Dianna's life so she wouldn't be baggage or make life harder for her in anyway. She was grateful that Dianna allowed her to stay in touch just enough to assure her that she was alive and doing well. For the most part, she let Dianna call her on her terms. After moving to Canada, she had gotten a job as a live-in nurse, caring for an elderly woman who lived alone. It was good money, much better than Alaska, so she was able to quickly get back on her feet. She also had some money from the sale she made on her house. She was starting fresh again and she hoped that this time, she could finally stay put and grow old in peace.

Yet, she couldn't shake the terrible feeling in her gut since of late. She wondered if helping Mack was the right thing to do. She tried so hard to stay undercover and all it took was one mistake to bring the house of cards down. She thought back to the day she first realized she could heal someone.

He had caught her eyes when he came inside the medic tent with a fellow soldier carrying a dying soldier by his arms and legs. They placed him on one of the beds. He was yelling at her to stop the bleeding, "save my brother, please!" but his brother had already lost too much blood. There was nothing she could do except to wrap as much bandage around the gaping wound on the wounded soldier. His leg was practically hanging by a bone. The smell of his blood lingered in the air and death wasn't far off.

213

"We can't save him," she said firmly to him. She could see the anguish on his face when she told him the truth.

"He's all I've got, ma'am! Please help him!" At that moment, the young man on the stretcher went into shock from the immense blood loss and died. This sent the handsome soldier in a delirium of grief. The only thing Irene could do in that moment was hold him as he cried out for his dead brother. Over the next few weeks, she had befriended the soldier so much so that her feelings began to extend beyond anything platonic.

"You're a good woman, Irene," Peter said to her as she stared into his deep blue eyes. "I'm gonna marry you one day when we make it out of this hellhole."

Many a night when he wasn't out fighting the enemy, they were making love. Eventually, the fantasy that they harbored together couldn't escape the prongs of war. On a stormy night, it was Peter who was brought to the medic tent on a stretcher bleeding from bullet holes on his body.

She watched him become delirious as she tried to remove as many bullet fragments from his body as possible, but he was doomed to the same fate as his brother. He was losing so much blood that the only thing that could save him was more blood. She was hit with the bright idea to attach the tubing to her arm and hoped that the direct blood transfusion would buy him some more time. What she didn't expect was for him to heal right before her very eyes. The other soldier there also watched the process in mesmerized confusion.

She quickly stopped the transfer, but it was too late. Peter looked as if he had someone else's blood on him as if he hadn't been shot multiple times. He had no visible injuries. The soldier present didn't waste any time detaining her before she could escape. They then took her to a medical center off base where they interrogated and tormented her to the brink of insanity for a year. They poked her with needles, took blood from her. Test after test after test. They had figured out that she could transform her physical features including her eyes, hair and fangs. They brought her back to the base often, using her as a healing remedy for dying soldiers, drawing so much blood from her, she would be unconscious days at a time as her body recuperated. She learned then that humans could be viler than she ever imagined. Yet, what hurt the most was when Peter turned on her, blaming her for his brother's death.

"You could've saved him!" he said with contempt for her as she lay strapped to a medic bed on base.

"Please listen to me Peter, I didn't know!" She was hoping his love for her was still strong. "You gotta let me go!"

"You're a damn monster, Irene. You're not going anywhere except to a mental asylum when they are finished with you here."

"YOU CAN'T DO THIS TO ME!" she screamed.

"You did this to yourself!" he spat with disgust

"I'm pregnant Peter! With your child!" He stared at her, horrified by her words.

"Ain't nothing growing inside of you belongs to me!" He then turned his back and walked away. She never saw him again.

"Dear, could you call Jeffrey. I haven't seen him all day." The old woman's voice trembled as she spoke.

Irene fluffed her pillow. "I'm sorry Mrs. Johnson, but your husband passed away two years ago. Mrs. Johnson pulled the covers up further to her chest as if she was getting cold.

"Oh, yes. You're right. I keep forgetting because of the dementia." She looked at Irene apologetically.

"It's no problem, Mrs. Johnson. I understand." Irene placed her warm hand on top of Mrs. Johnson's.

"Y'know, the husband and I never had kids."

"I know." They had this conversation almost every week. That seemed to be her one and only regret.

"What about you? Do you have any?"

Irene smiled patiently. "I do."

"They must be as sweet as you." Mrs. Johnson smile curiously.

"Now, now, Mrs. Johnson. Stop trying to poke around in my head. It's time to turn in." Mrs. Johnson chuckled.

"So secretive." She winked at Irene. "Look at the bright side of things. If you told me your secrets, I'd take it to the grave, so you won't have to."

"Okay. Sherlock. There are no secrets to tell." Mrs. Johnson lay on her side as Irene properly tucked her in.

"You look like a woman with many secrets," Mrs. Johnson rebutted, then she went silent. Irene liked Mrs. Johnson. In fact, she loved her job. It paid in cash. She was afforded boarding and it didn't require too much of a background check except to prove she was a licensed nurse. No one knew her or cared about where she came from. It was just her and Mrs. Johnson alone in the old Victorian style home. Occasionally, the agency that hired her would check in to make sure senior abuse wasn't taking place but that was it. Irene smiled at the thought that she finally found peace, but her smile faded as she thought of Dianna. This was the only crack in the paint. She left Mrs. Johnson's room silently closing the door behind her. She walked down the hall to her room where she tried to call her daughter again. "If only Dianna would answer her phone," she said feeling a little anxious.

"Hello!" A deep masculine voice answered the phone. Irene didn't respond. She immediately knew something was wrong. She was about to hand up the phone when the person spoke again.

"Irene don't hang up." There was some shuffling on his end. "This is Drax. I've been waiting for your call."

Chapter 11

"What did she say?"

"I told her I would give her your new information so you can talk to her directly." Dianna was getting annoyed with the way Drax had just taken control of her life after the gazebo incident. It was as if he forgot that she was on her own for 30 years and she was used to taking care of herself. It was as if he forgot that when they first met, she was a freelancer with independent drives and goals. Now, whenever he practically thought of her, she was someone that needed his help, his protection and his guidance. She rubbed her forehead agitated as she sat in his living room with her legs bent on the couch. Now, with the baby, things had gotten even worse. He insisted that she now only worked from home and not even hang out with Simon and Eric. She remained silent, avoiding his eye contact.

"I know that look, Dianna," he said to her.

"What look?" she deflected, then she got up and walked to the kitchen. She needed a drink so bad. She saw a bottle of wine inside the refrigerator and pulled it out.

"What are you doing?"

"Drax, don't start. It's safe. I promise." She pulled out a crystal wine glass from the cabinet and poured it halfway to the top. She then slowly swallowed the beverage, closing her eyes and savoring the taste. It was light but it had to do. She then started to head upstairs.

He called her name softly. She sighed before turning around to see him at the foot of the stairs looking up at her. She didn't want to be combative, but she was exhausted from it all. She hadn't needed anyone before and she wasn't sure if she needed him now but at the same time, she didn't want to be ungrateful. He tapped the banister as he seemed to be trying to find the right words to say.

"I'll take it down a notch."

"Will you?"

"I'm not sure how, but I'll try." He sat on the bottom step, maintaining the space between them. She folded her arms and gave him her best poker face.

"I want to work at the office on the days that I had originally chosen. I also want my motorcycle back and I want my old number back. I also want my friends to visit me, here at the house." Drax swore under his breath. "I knew you couldn't budge." She unfolded her arms turned to finish her trip upstairs.

"You can't have your old number. It's traceable. Your friends can't come here, no one can know our exact location." She waited for him to finish with her back turned. "but I will bring your motorcycle back and you can return to work at the office and you can visit your friends...minimally," he said to her as a smile crept across her face. "Under one condition." She spun around.

"What is it?" he chewed on his bottom lip, gaging her reaction.

"You must tell me exactly where you are going or where you are at all times."

"No!" she said vehemently. He threw both his hands up in the air. "Absolutely not!" She reinforced.

"Okay, fine." Dianna couldn't believe he didn't even challenge her but before she could question his response any further, he started chasing her up the stairs which made her squeal as she took flight. She ran into their bedroom and jumped onto the bed, covering herself with the comforter knowing it offered very little protection against him. She heard his footsteps as he entered the room but then there was silence. She waited for him to do something...anything but all was still. She peeped from under the blanket and at that very moment, he pounced on her. She screamed in delight as she felt his full weight on top of her. They wrestled for a second and she started hitting him with the pillow, but he maneuvered the pillow away from her easily and pinned her to the bed. They were both breathing heavy. He gave her a prolonged stare as they caught their breaths.

"What?" she asked him.

"You." She felt her face warm under his appreciative gaze. He kissed her lightly, then got up and went to his closet. He took out a green gift bag and then sat on the bed as he handed it to her. She looked from the bag to him and then she peered inside where she saw a box. She took it out and saw that it was a phone.

"I'm sorry for breaking your phone." She traced the outline of his lips with her thumb.

"It's okay." She then returned to opening the box. It was the latest iPhone. She admired its sleek design. It was already on.

"You're going to have to set it up with your personal details but--"

"I know," she said.

"I could've but I didn't. I wanted you to have your privacy."

"Thanks for being a thoughtful control freak."

A low laughter emitted from him. "Anyway, your mom seems like a really nice lady."

"Did she?"

"Yeah, she told me when you were a kid you had a nervous habit of picking your nose."

"No, she didn't!" she said rolling her eyes at his blatant lie. He laid his head in her lap and looked up at her as Dianna looked down at his gorgeous face. She couldn't help the strong connection she felt with for him. She loved that he felt so comfortable with her.

"Sometimes, I wish I had met you sooner."

"What do you mean?"

"The stuff that you guys must have gone through...alone." Dianna felt a lump in her throat. She didn't want to think about it, but he was right. It was tough. It was hard for her mom to maintain a job. Never being able to hire a babysitter so she could go to work was also tough. By the time she was twelve, she was so used to watching herself, making her own breakfast or dinner depending on the shift her mother was working. Homeschooling wasn't easy either. Her mom didn't always have the time to help her with her homework and whenever their location was compromised, moving and finding another place to settle was hard too. Birthday parties, prom, graduations, best friends, she missed out on everything. Her lips trembled.

"Drax, why did you have to go there?" She complained playfully, trying to quell the thick emotions that were awakening within her.

"My bad," he said as he stroked her arm comfortingly.

"You're here now and that's all that matters." She bent over to kiss his full lips. She then leaned her head against the headboard. She thought back to a moment when she thought she was truly going to be on her own at a tender age. She didn't know why but she decided to share it with him. "We were living in Chicago once, for a very short time. In a terrible neighborhood." She scoffed. "It was sort of the only place we could get quickly without too many questions being asked. This was after we left Georgia because she had lost her job...again." Drax's hand was resting on his chest and she used her finger to draw invisible circles on the back of his hand, unaware she was even doing it because she was so lost in her thoughts. "There was a guy that lived right next to us. Small time drug dealer and a felon. He gave me the creeps. He liked my mom though. Always trying to catch her outside of our apartment door but my mom wasn't interested. I think after she had me, she called it quits with relationships." She sighed deeply. "I guess she didn't want to risk it." Drax listened intently as she continued with the invisible circles, verbalizing the crazy cycle that used to be her life, which was something that she rarely did. "Anyway, one night, he may have been drunk or high or both and he tried to rape my mom right in front of our apartment door. I was right there, on the other side, hearing her struggle and not knowing what to do. I was fucking

10!" she said angrily. "What the fuck was I supposed to do except watch through a crack in the door?" She swallowed hard and then continued. "but he had the wrong one that day." She smiled proudly. "She fought so hard; he was completely fucked up by the time she was done with him. I mean slashes on his face, and she almost broke his arm. She left him in the hallway howling. I was so fucking proud of her." She pumped her fist slightly celebrating the small victory.

"Sounds like a strong Nagalian woman."

She looked down at him. "She is...but that's not the worst part. A week later because his pride was hurt, he called DFACS and made a complaint about child neglect. He ratted and told them that she left me alone at the apartment without any type of supervision when she went to work. They were at our apartment that same week, but she was at work." Dianna folded her lips as she fought back the tears. "They were banging on the door, telling me to let them in because they knew I was in there. I was so scared. I went out the backway and hid behind a dumpster until it was night. It smelled awful. and I remember being so hungry because I hadn't eaten anything. All the food was inside the apartment, but I had to wait. Finally, around 11:00 p.m., I heard her calling my name. I stepped out from behind the dumpster and she saw me and came running. I told her everything." She had managed not to cry but her face looked exhausted. "We weren't even there two months and we had to leave again." Drax rubbed his eye in a circular motion.

"Are you crying?"

"Hell no!" he responded vehemently, staring up at her with a guilty grin on his face.

She scrutinized him. "You were crying. Softie!" She laughed.

"Whatever makes you sleep better at nights," he commented, not appearing the least bit offended. Dianna was tickled but mostly touched that her story affected him so deeply. "I was thinking we should try to get your mom to come here."

"She's not going to come. I already tried."

"We can try again. She's more vulnerable alone."

"I'll talk to her, but I can't make any promises. She's a stubborn woman."

"The apple doesn't fall far from the tree."

"I guess not." He sat up, kissed her, and then rubbed her belly. "I hope she's the same way."

"You think it's a girl?" He shrugged his shoulders to show his uncertainty.

"You want a boy, don't you?"

"Am I that obvious?" His voice was deep and arousing. She couldn't help but to taste his lips.

"Yes, you are." He kissed her pushing her back on the bed then removed her robe to expose her breasts. He squeezed one as he controlled her mouth. He rushed to unbutton his shirt and began loosening his belt when his phone rang. He cursed angrily. "Ignore it!" Dianna said, her hormones raging. She pulled him down on top of her and trapped him with her legs. "Throw the phone away!" she said exasperated. He was unable to resist her as his hunger for her became more intense. But the phone kept ringing to the point of distraction. He stopped what he was doing. "You're going to answer it, aren't you?"

"It seems important," she yelled then released him.

"Go! Go do your important things!" She placed her robe on and started getting off the bed. He placed his hand on her lower back, and she paused. "I'll make it up to you later. I promise," he said searching her eyes for forgiveness. Her eyes softened.

"I understand. I know your work is important."

"Thank you," he sat on the side of the bed, placing his phone to his ear. Dianna used the opportunity to go to the bathroom. While in the bathroom, she could hear Drax's carefully worded conversation. She zoned out paying attention to her own inner thoughts. She started wondering how she could possibly convince her mother to come live with them when she heard Drax's voice getting louder.

"How could Norlan let this happen?!" she heard him shouting into the phone. "This is the fucking worst time!" It seemed the conversation had ended after that. Dianna returned to the bedroom eyeing him with concern. She sat beside him and started massaging his back. "What's wrong?" Drax was chewing on his lip again. "Babe, tell me."

"Jasmine."

Dianna racked her brain until she recognized the name. "The woman your parents wanted you to marry?"

Drax averted her gaze, staring intently at the floor. "Yes."

Dianna didn't want to talk about the woman that he could still potentially marry, and she was certain she wasn't going to like what he had to say. "What's the problem?" She asked cautiously, bracing herself.

"She was shot."

Dianna's eyes widened. "What?"

"With Apoptosyde."

***

He didn't want to bring her to the lab, but she insisted that he did. She knew what he wouldn't say. They needed her to help Jasmine. They needed a blood transfusion and even though no trials or tests were done, they had to use the only antidote they had to save Jasmine's life and that was her.

Someone in Jasmine's circle found out she was Nagalian and tipped off the bounty hunters. They waited until she was leaving work and walking to her car to shoot her with a tranquilizer gun and then they dumped her in a desert somewhere. It was her boyfriend, Clive, who noticed she hadn't been home for hours and that he couldn't get her on her phone. So, he did something he never thought he would do and reached out to her father. They began searching for her and finally, after tracking her cell phone signal, they found her half dead and freezing in the Mojave Desert.

It was 2:00 a.m. in the morning when they both barged into the patient room of his mother's medical facility to see Marvin, Norlan, Mrs. Ashton a few assisting staff members and another woman huddled around Jasmine who was lying in the hospital bed writhing and moaning in pain. She kept switching from her human form to Nagalian form every time the pain became worst. Her color was changing from her flesh color to a dead gray as her cells were slowly rotting and dying inside her. She was also foaming and bleeding from her mouth. There was also the putrid stench of her cells rotting. Dianna gasped and covered her mouth in utter shock at the sight that she saw. She couldn't believe this was what she wanted to do to herself only a few months ago. Drax immediately turned around and punched Norlan in his face and Mrs. Ashton screamed before running toward him, but Marvin held onto Drax and controlled him.

"You fucking piece of shit! You criticized me for utilizing personal security, and you weren't even making sure your own daughter was safe! At least I know how to take care of my responsibilities!" Norlan had fallen from the force of the punch and he licked the blood from the corner of his mouth as he staggered back to his feet. He was old but he looked like he had aged another century since the last time Dianna saw him. "Now you want her to risk her life to help you," Drax said trying to buck his father's stronghold so he could punch Norlan again. "You didn't even want to hear what she had to say at the meeting! Why the fuck should she help you?" Drax spat with daggers in his eyes.

"Because it's the right thing to do, Drax. You know this," his mother said calmly. He looked around at them with disdain.

"Is it? Is it the right thing?" he pushed his way out of his father's hold and walked over to his mom. His tall body and broad shoulders seemed quite imposing and intimidating in the enclosed observation room. "How much blood is she going to have to lose to save Jasmine?" His mother's gaze was unfaltering.

"I don't know, Drax. You told me to put off the research."

"You know why?" Then he was looking in Norlan's direction with murder in his eyes. "But you all had to come up with a way to force my hand!" Then he

224

dashed at Norlan again and punched him a second time for good measure. Norlan tried to defend himself against Drax's immense strength but it was futile. Drax wrestled him to the ground and was on top of him trying to strangle him as the women shrieked in the background.

"Get him off of me!" Norlan shouted trying to push Drax off him.

Marvin and some of the medical staff were barely able to pry Drax away from the target of his rage but they finally managed to get him in an upright position. "I'm good now!" Drax said shrugging them off him and straightening himself. It was obvious he needed to get his animosity toward Narlon out of his system.

"EVERYONE BE QUIET!" Dianna yelled. She didn't like the fact that they were treating her like an invisible furniture, talking about her as if she wasn't there. She walked over to Jasmine and touched her forehead. Even with a cooling blanket wrapped around her and whatever drugs were dripping through her IV fluids, she was burning up and she was dying.

Norlan walked over to her, his eyes were pleading. "Please don't let her die. She's my only child." Saliva sputtered from his mouth and tears ran down his face in his distraught state. Dianna looked from him to Mrs. Ashton and she touched her stomach thinking about the little grape that was growing inside her.

"Is there no other way?" she asked. "Why can't you use the blood of a full Nagalian? You guys have the same blood type, don't you?"

"It's not that simple and trust me I wish it was," Mrs. Ashton stated earnestly. "Each Nagalian's blood type is as signature as your fingerprint. It's completely rare that there is ever a match. That's why you are so unique. I don't know if it's a sick joke from nature or a blessing from God, but your blood type is compatible with all Nagalians and all humans. Essentially, your blood works like the O Negative blood type in humans. Anyone can receive it without causing adverse reactions but not only that, for full Nagalians, it acts as a booster kicking the regenerative effect into overdrive." Mrs. Ashton explain. Dianna could feel the high expectation in the entire room as they all waited to see what she would do. Everyone except Drax, who looked like he wanted to burn the entire facility to the ground with his eyes.

Dianna turned back to face Norlan, touching his left shoulder reassuringly. "I won't let her die." Norlan sobbed his gratitude. "We can't waste any more time. Mrs. Ashton, what do I need to do?" Dianna announced walking away from Norlan toward Drax's mother.

"Get the machine!" Mrs. Ashton said to her staff as she started getting into action. "NOW!!!!" She barked. It was obvious that her nerves were shot. She was less emotionally composed than usual. "Bring another bed over here. "She instructed, pointing to the space beside Jasmine's bed. She walked over to Dianna. "You don't have to do anything. We'll take care of it and I promise, I will make sure no harm comes to your baby...my grandchild," Mrs. Ashton said with conviction. Dianna held her hand and squeezed it.

"Am I hearing right? She's pregnant?" Marvin mumbled.

"Not now!" Drax said agitated.

They brought the second bed and Dianna sat on it. "Get her a hospital gown," Mrs. Ashton instructed. Dianna looked at Drax who stood there silently watching with his jaws clenched. She could see he didn't want her to do it but what choice did they have? The other men stood looking on helplessly. Mrs. Ashton looked annoyed by this. "Get out!" she ordered. The men shuffled out at her behest but the woman and Drax remained behind. Mrs. Ashton looked kindly at the Caucasian woman with short brown hair and sad eyes.

"Wyona, you mustn't stay."

"She's my daughter. I'm not leaving," Wyona retorted.

"And you know better than to ask me to leave." Drax brushed past her and went over to Dianna. He hugged her tightly. "Say the word and we'll leave now," he whispered to her. She wrapped her arms around him and squeezed tightly as she suddenly began feeling afraid.

"Just in case anything bad happens... I love you."

Drax was silent for a moment. "I was crying earlier," he said to her. She laughed remembering their conversation a few hours before. "And I'll be here the entire time...and I love you too," he finished, touching her hair and allowing her snakes to intertwine with his fingers.

"Drax we need to start," his mother prompted. Dianna changed into a hospital gown in seconds and lay on the bed. She felt a little chill and found herself wondering why hospitals, clinics and labs were always so cold. Drax got a chair and dragged it to the other side of the bed out of the way of the machine, IV poles and his mother. She worked quickly getting everything ready. She sanitized Dianna's arm before inserting the needle. Dianna flinched but Drax squeezed her other hand comfortingly. Dianna then heard the soft vibration of the machine when Mrs. Ashton started the process. She looked over at Jasmine who had stilled and looked almost lifeless except for her rhythmic breathing. Her mom was holding one of her hand with both of hers, hunched over in her chair looking tired and alone. She thought of her own mother and knew if anything happened to her, Irene would look the same as Wyona, tired and lost. She saw the red liquid moving through the tube, winding quickly as it travelled its way to Jasmine. They all waited as the minutes went on but there was no change...nothing. Not even her skin color changed. With Adisa it was immediate, only taking a few minutes.

"Maybe the poison is too far gone... maybe it's too late." Wyona sobbed.

"Maybe her blood was never a damn antidote to begin with." Drax glared at his mother. "Maybe you were wrong!"

Dianna could cut the tension with a knife. "Just wait," she said, realizing she was feeling a little depleted. She looked at the machine wondering how much blood she had already given. Drax seemed to have read her mind. "Mom, how much longer."

"Like I said Drax, I don't know." Dianna rested her head on the pillow and waited some more for what seemed like hours. She didn't realize it, but she had slowly drifted off to the humming of the machine.

She slowly opened her eyes to the sound of loud arguing. She moaned and tried to lift her head, but she felt light-headed. The smell of chlorine and sanitizer was strong in the air unlike before when the putridness of decaying flesh filled the room.

"Dianna!" Mrs. Ashton said running to her bedside. "Are you okay?" Dianna winced from the bright light. Mrs. Ashton knew immediately what she needed. She motioned to her assistants to dim the lights. "Is that better?"

Dianna nodded in response. "What happened, where's Drax?"

"Right here," he said getting up from a chair a little further away from where they were. He walked to the side of the bed then he threaded his fingers through hers, but she could see his jaw twitching as he ground his teeth and she knew something was wrong.

"Why were you guys arguing?"

"It doesn't matter. The most important thing is that you are okay. The baby is safe, and Jasmine is going to be okay."

Dianna's eyes widened. "It worked!"

"Yes!" Mrs. Ashton said with relief. "It worked. You saved her!"

Dianna looked over at Jasmine who was peacefully sleeping. Both Norlan and Wyona were standing by her bedside locked in their own world. Then she looked back at Drax who looked extremely tense. "Why don't you look happy?" She nudged him. He looked at his mom.

"Should I tell her?"

His mother's smile dissipated as she caved. "I'll leave you two alone." She then indicated to Norlan and his wife that they should leave as well, so they followed reluctantly behind her. Drax refocused his attention to Dianna. She touched her stomach.

"The baby is okay; right?" He placed his hand over hers.

"Yes, but you went into cardiac arrest."

"I did what?" Dianna tried to sit but the flash of pain gripped her chest, she touched it gingerly suddenly feeling the immense soreness as if a ton of bricks had been laid on her.

"Don't!" He gently eased her back onto the bed. "Just be still."

"Why did I go into cardiac arrest?"

"The Apoptosyde had almost taken full course. Jasmine wasn't going to make it unless her system was completely flushed which took a lot from you. It was too much blood loss too quickly. So, your body went into shock and your heart...just stopped." Drax's face looked strained. It was obvious that what he witnessed almost destroyed him.

"Could I have died?"

"I don't know. It's hard to tell because you didn't but when it was happening, we were all convinced we were losing you." He pulled the chair close to her bed and sat down, resting his head against the back of the chair, clearly exhausted from the night. He stared at the ceiling, his arms hanging limply off the chair. "We thought you were dying," he said without looking at her. "I don't think you can survive another transfusion like that."

"Hopefully, it will go better next time or hopefully there won't be a next time," she said massaging her aching chest. Her entire body ached. He leaned forward, resting his head on his arms beside her on the bed.

He propped his head up and was pensive as he stared at her. "We'll cross that bridge when we get there." She rubbed his head. She wanted to take his mind off the crazy events of their early morning madness.

"You promised me that you would make things up to me." He stared at her with incredulity and then shook his head at the fact that she could be thinking about sex at a time like this. "I'm beginning to think you aren't a man of your word," she goaded him.

"You know there's nothing I wouldn't do for you but aren't you sore?" he said to her and her heart melted from his affectionate words.

"Come here," she said disregarding his statement and slowly scooting over so he could lay beside her on the bed. Even though Jasmine seemed to be sound asleep, Drax drew the curtain to give them some added privacy and climbed onto the bed to face her, warming her with his body. He kissed her and he gently lifted her leg so it could stretch across his side, giving him ample space to rub her sensitive spot. He first rubbed her clit through the fabric of her underwear, and he slipped it to the side and continued to rub rhythmically.

She opened her mouth and paced her breathing trying not to make a sound. He dipped his tongue into her mouth, and she sucked on it. She moistened and he dipped both his fingers inside. Her walls pulsated around his fingers and she moaned.

"Shhh." The light stubble on his face scraped her skin. He withdrew his moist fingers and used his thumb to make circular motions on her very sensitive pearl.

He again inserted his fingers while kissing her neck. He pulled his fingers out and spread her juices on the outside of her labia and continued to rub her clit. She tried to reach for his belt to loosen his pants, but he stopped her.

"No," he whispered capturing her hand with his free hand. "Touch yourself," he instructed her with ravenous desire and hunger in his eyes. She stared at him innocently, unsure of what he wanted. "I want you to touch yourself the way you do when you think I'm watching you on the surveillance camera in our bedroom." She could hear the raw emotion in his voice. He pressed a few buttons on the side of the remote-controlled bed and it eased up automatically to a 45-degree angle, so she didn't have to adjust herself. He then eased behind her so that her back was braced against his chest. Next, he then widened her legs, holding them firmly apart, exposing her. The gown had slipped off her shoulders, settling under her round breast so she was practically naked. It felt so wrong and so naughty, but she was enjoying the wantonness of the moment...

"What if someone comes back?" she whispered. He sucked a tender spot on her upper back with the perfect amount of pressure, his tongue was warm and moist on her skin. It was the exact thing that the exact spot needed. She licked her parched lips and surrendered her thoughts to the sensation.

"Go on," he whispered, and she massaged her clit while pacing her breathing. "That's it." He kissed her right shoulder sensually and she leaned her head forward so he could lick her along the length of her neck. She realized that he didn't want to have sex with her, he wanted to drive her crazy with foreplay. It didn't matter because the feeling was so deliciously exquisite, she was going to come all the same. She rubbed herself faster as she felt her climax getting closer. It may have been because of her excursions of the day or all the blood she lost, but her arm began to feel tired. She rested against him and felt him reposition one of his hand under her knee while he used his other hand to move her hand away. "I'll take it from here," he whispered seductively in her ear. He dipped his fingers inside again, over and over again, removing it at length to rub her clit then dipping back inside her. It was so hypnotic, so much more intense that she had to admit that she enjoyed it way better when he did it.

"How the heck are you better at this than I am?" she whispered. He smirked at her words and continued his delicious torment. He released her leg and brought his hand up to her round breast, gently pinching her nipple. She turned her head to the side and again he unexpectedly captured her mouth. He was doing so many things at once her senses couldn't differentiate between what felt good and what felt better. It was just an overwhelming amount of stimulation. She moaned loudly.

"Not so loud!" he told her as she felt herself slipping because her body weakened, and her senses were overwhelmed but then he held her thigh firmly in place and thrusted harder and faster inside her with his fingers. She panted louder and he also massaged her clit harder and faster until she came, squirting juices all over his fingers.

"Damn! Never told me you could do that," he said caught off guard.

But she couldn't respond. Her eyes had rolled over and her body convulsed, still riding the orgasmic wave. He kept his pace until her body jerked from the last of her convulsions. She relaxed all her weight on him and closed her eyes, satiated from the intense pleasure she just felt. Her sheets were soaked, and she was half naked, but her body tingled.

"You two should get a damn hotel!" Jasmine spoke up from behind the curtains. Dianna's eyes flew open as she quickly fixed her gown. Drax chuckled and jumped off the bed. He went and drew the curtain back just enough to look at Jasmine.

"Happy to see that you're up," he said to her.

"Imagine waking up to the sounds of sex noises."

"We weren't having sex."

"Could've fooled me!" she rebutted. Dianna was feeling so embarrassed that she really didn't mind not speaking to her.

"Is she the woman you ditched me for?" she said jokingly.

"Yeah. She saved your life too."

"Let me see her," Dianna heard Jasmine say. Drax pulled back the curtains despite the fact that Dianna was throwing him hints that he shouldn't. When Jasmine laid eyes on her, Dianna waved shyly.

"Jasmine, this is Dianna." Jasmine smiled sweetly at her.

"I'm sorry about what happened to you," Dianna offered feeling awkward.

"Yeah...sucks to be me," she said looking around her at the hospital equipment then back at Dianna. "but thank you for saving my life."

"No worries."

Jasmine yawned. "Think I could get some sleep or are you two going to go at it again like Jack rabbits?"

"Maybe." Drax smiled wickedly. Dianna shook her head silently. She was too embarrassed to even think about having sex. She started wondering how long Jasmine had been listening before she even said anything. Drax was only too amused at her embarrassment.

"I'm going to get one of the staff to get you some fresh sheets considering you soaked these," he said touching the soaked part of her bed. Dianna stared at him horrified that he would just say that within earshot of Jasmine.

"You're enjoying this aren't you?"

He gave her a wicked grin. "A little." He kissed her and then walked out of the patient area leaving her alone with Jasmine. She looked over and saw that Jasmine's eyes were closed and breathed a sigh of relief that she didn't have to force a conversation with her.

"You two were definitely not quiet," Jasmine teased her. To Dianna's chagrin, she realized that Jasmine was still awake.

"We didn't mean to wake you," Dianna said politely. Jasmine opened her eyes and turned on her side as she stared at her like a cat ready to pounce on a mouse.

"If I wasn't in such a bad shape, I might've joined you two," she confessed. Dianna couldn't believe the words that came out of Jasmine's mouth. She could only stare at her in shocked silence.

"No. I don't like girls, but it was a turn on to listen to you two. Had me question my sexuality." She winked salaciously and then chuckled. Dianna wasn't sure but she was almost convinced that Jasmine was flirting with her. "You've got you a good one," she said. Dianna smiled in response. The moment was kind of weird considering they both knew what sex was like with him.

"If I wasn't in love with someone else, I might've tried to steal him from you," Jasmine jabbed.

"I don't usually fight over men, but I might've have fought you for this one." Dianna fired back. Jasmine laughed loudly at Dianna's candor, then turned back onto her back and stared at the ceiling. Except for the fact that she was exhausted, there was no evidence that she had just been battling for her life. It was something that never ceased to amaze Dianna, the way they healed so well, leaving no physical scars of their ordeal. "You wouldn't have to. Trust me. He's really into you." Dianna was curious about why Jasmine would say such a thing. "It's all my father talks about and from what I hear, the entire Fraternity was really pissed at Drax." She eyed Dianna sideways. "...and you." Dianna remained silent. "But I think after this, no one will say a damn thing about you two again."

"I'm not so sure about that, especially because I'm pregnant," Dianna divulged.

"Wow! You two work fast don't you. Like freaking Jack rabbits." Her statement amused Dianna. "Takes the rest of the Nagalian world centuries to bear a child. You guys do it in less than a year.

"Nothing but dumb luck. We weren't trying." But something Jasmine said piqued her curiosity, "What about you? You seemed to have moved on from Drax pretty quickly," Dianna stated observantly.

"Moved on?" Jasmine scoffed. "Drax did me a favor. I could continue seeing Clive free of guilt. I literally need to thank him," Jasmine explained. "I couldn't do what he did. Stand up against tradition like that. He's a true hero. Doesn't change much though. Just bought me more time because I am pretty certain my father will find another Full Nagalian for me to marry." Dianna could appreciate Jasmine's dry humor since she had a dry sense of humor herself, but she knew Jasmine was serious about one thing. She was in love with her partner and it was sad that her father was trying to dictate her love life. Suddenly, Drax walked back in with a medical staff who was carrying some sheets and a fresh gown.

"Anyway, it was nice meeting you," Jasmine said yawning some more.

"Same." Dianna responded. Then she noticed that Jasmine had closed her eyes again. Dianna began yawning herself. "Are you going to spend the night?" She inquired to Drax.

"Not unless you don't want me to."

"I do. I don't want to sleep alone tonight." The staff tried to help Dianna off the bed so she could change the sheets. "No, it's okay. I've got it," she told the woman thinking about the drenched spot. The woman would probably think she urinated herself which was just as embarrassing.

"Are you sure?" the thin short-haired woman asked her, indicating she was bit confused. Dianna nodded her head. She didn't want the nurse touching the sheets she squirted on, at least not while she was there. Jasmine hearing her having an orgasm was bad enough.

The brunette eventually left and Drax help lift Dianna into a chair so he could change the sheets. He then helped her back onto the bed where she changed her gown. He stripped down to his undershirt and boxers and slid in beside her. She was immediately relaxed. She closed her eyes feeling the tiredness lulling her body to sleep and in the midst of that she felt Drax's warm fingers sliding between her legs.

"Drax, if you so much as touch my cooch, so help me, I will slice your fingers off!" she warned without opening her eyes. She was still utterly embarrassed from their previous foreplay session.

"Dianna, be nice," he said in an admonishing tone but did a poor job of hiding the amusement on his face. Then they heard a soft chuckle from Jasmine.

"I promise this time I'll join if you guys don't keep it down."

"Can't say I would refuse the extra company," Drax quipped back without missing a beat.

Dianna's eyes immediately shot open. "What the hell is wrong with you two?" She was beginning to feel as if she was stuck in the twilight zone.

"All in jest," Drax said lighted-heartedly, kissing her eyelids. "Isn't that right Jasmine."

"Uh-uh," she said unconvincingly. Drax laughed silently, too tickled from the moment.

"Not funny!" Dianna said punching his arm. Drax feigned pain but the only thing that was probably hurting was his face from all the grinning.

"You know I wouldn't, babe...as freaking good as it sounds." She punched him again and again he feigned pain but then he sobered up. He stared into her eyes unguarded. "You said it," he said, bringing her attention to something she had said earlier.

"What?"

"The three words I've waited to hear you say." She realized what he was talking about. Her eyes softened.

"You've been waiting?"

"I couldn't force you to say it, could I?"

"You're easy to love, Drax," she said sincerely. "I'm the hard one to love," she berated herself. Something she had promised herself repeatedly that she would stop doing.

"You couldn't be more wrong."

"I couldn't be more right." She knew herself inside and out and she knew she had a tendency to flee. After 30 years of doing it, it was too easy, and he knew it too. He sighed.

"I've given you my love, I've given you security. Why is it so hard for you to trust me?"

"Because it's not anything you are doing or not doing. It's psychologically embedded and I can't fight the urge when fear sets in."

"I don't want to keep chasing you or trying to convince you to stick this through. I need you to fight that urge, for yourself, for our child...for me." She knew he was right. "I'm returning your motorcycle. I don't want to, but I can't keep making certain decisions for you." He looked like he was holding something back.

"What?" she pushed him.

"If you ran off with our child, would you blame me for hating you?" She bit her lip, knowing that this was coming from a dark place. He knew her history, the way half Nagalian women usually raised their children alone. "I don't want to hate you," he said to her, "but I'm pretty sure I would if you left with my kid."

"I know... and I wouldn't blame you." She kissed him. It was hard living for someone else other than herself but for him, and the little Nagalian inside her, she had to fight her natural instincts and her selfish ways. She looked at his handsome face and felt the warmth of his hand as he touched her flat stomach. She knew he was worth it. "And I promise you I'll change...for us."

***

Dianna was at a glow in the dark indoor mini golf course with Eric, Simon, Alicia, Kacey which she was happy she had finally figured out her name. Kacey showed no hard feelings from their last little confrontation at the bar, but she apologized to her anyway to smooth things over. There was also an addition to their group, who Dianna found to be interesting and easy going. Brooke had also taken a liking to her immediately even though they only met that day, yet there was something so familiar about her that Dianna couldn't help relating to her. She had dark brown streaks in her hair and her nails were iridescent brown. Yet it wasn't herself that she reminded Dianna of, it was her mom.

"So, when are you due?" Brooke asked. Dianna putted her ball into the hole with her golf club. The ball rolled to the side of the hole and they both walked closer to the ball.

"About seven months from now," she responded poising herself to hit the ball. She then hit the ball and it rolled into the hole with a soft thud.

"You must be ecstatic. Especially considering who the father is," Brooke said cheekily. Dianna wasn't sure if Brooke meant because he was wealthy...or because he was in line to be the next president of the Nagalian Fraternity but since there was no way she could've known that, she chose to dismiss what she said as an innocent statement. She picked up the ball and they sauntered to another more challenging part of the golf course.

"I know he's going to be a great dad, which is more than I can say for myself," Dianna said candidly, unsure why she was so open with Brooke.

"You seem like a good mom in the making," Brooke placated humorously.

"Excellent way to put it. Lord knows the only think I can do is try."

"So, how do your parents feel about it?" Dianna thought about how she had been keeping the pregnancy from her mother. The last conversation resulted in an argument because even after she explained that bounty hunters were murdering Nagalians by the droves with Apoptosyde, her mother still insisted on staying where she was. She was adamant that it was safer than being around her own kind. Dianna was angry but she understood her mom's thought process because it was only a few months ago, she was the same way. Now, she couldn't imagine her life any differently. She wanted her child to go to an excellent private school, she wanted a stable dad in her child's life, and she craved stability in her own life. She was tired of living on the outskirts of society. In a way, she felt rehabilitated from that life and had to concede to the fact that her prior life was no way to live.

"No, she doesn't, but maybe it's for the best for now," Dianna explained.

"Relationship not so great with mom, huh?" It seemed like a distracted question from Brooke as she seemed intent on making a hole in one on the beautiful but bumpy green course they were on.

"You could say that. We're working on it though." Brooke scoffed and then hit the ball. She skillfully made the hole on her first try which Dianna found to be impressive. "You're good! Where did Simon find you?" Dianna said enthusiastically.

"At his bar. Apparently, I am one of his pets now."

Dianna laughed. "So am I." She shared. Their conversation seemed so effortless she honestly wanted to get to know Brooke some more.

"What about your mom? You guys get along?"

"I don't know my mom actually. She left me on a military base with strangers."

"That's terrible!" Dianna said feeling a sudden surge of disgust.

"Yeah. Always said, if I ever saw her, I would let her have it for the way she dumped me like a dirty pile of garbage."

"How could any mother do that? Y'know, my mom isn't perfect but at least she tried," Dianna said feeling a sense of gratitude. She watched Brooke continue with her precise shots.

"Your mom sounds like a saint," Brooke quipped. "Hopefully one day I can meet her."

"Pff! Impossible! Even I don't know where she lives." Dianna remained cautious about divulging anything about her mom's location. As nice as

Brooke was, she learned from Jasmine that most humans could not be trusted. "Y'know, speaking of my mom. You sort of look like her," Dianna said, finally realizing why Brooke seemed so familiar. Same brown eyes and sandy hair."

"I'm wearing contacts." Dianna examined Brooke's eyes closely but couldn't tell. "Plus, I get that a lot...that I look like a lot of people. I think I have one of those faces," Brooke explained.

"I guess."

"Why the heck are you guys all the way over here?" Eric said as he and Simon got closer to them.

"See, babe. I told you they would hit it off." Simon proclaimed before giving Eric a peck on his cheek. "You owe me $100."

"You guys bet on us?!"

"It was Simon's idea, and I couldn't resist a good bet so get over it!" Eric said shamelessly. He then took a crisp $100 bill out of his wallet and gave it to Simon. The women looked at each other, shaking their heads disapprovingly. "Where are the other ladies?"

"I think they went to get some food. They said they would catch up with us later," Brooke explained.

"I miss the good ol' days of bar hopping and drunk sex. When did we become so boring?" Simon said looking around at the venue with disdain. Dianna actually thought the spot was fun. She liked the music and the lights, not to mention different sculptures of famous band members propped up at different points inside the building but she knew Simon was into a more salacious type of entertainment.

"I know what that look means. No! We're not going to your bar to get drunk!" Eric said exasperated. "I've got work in the morning and Dianna is pregnant."

"I forgot. She's not even showing," Simon commented as he gestured to her stomach.

"It's still early. It's barely a grape," Dianna explained.

"You guys should go enjoy yourselves. I can take Dianna home," Brooke offered.

"That won't be necessary," Eric protested with a hint of facetiousness. Dianna could count on Eric to be protective of her. She didn't know when it happened, but Eric had become almost like a brother to her. With Quinton busy with his family and living in another state, it was hard to spend time with him, but Eric made up for that. "Besides, she rode her motorcycle here and if it's one thing I know about her, she is not leaving her baby," he continued matter-of-factly.

"Yeah, I suppose he's is right," Dianna added.

"You have a motorcycle?" Brooke said, staring at Dianna in awe. "What kind?"

"Harley Davidson Cruiser. I fucking love it!" Dianna beamed, barely able to hide her pride and excitement.

"Can you take me for a ride?" Brooke's question was similar to asking Dianna if she wanted to breathe air. She couldn't tell the last time she had simply ridden to any random place at high speed with the wind in her hair and streetlights blurring by because she was going so fast. The thought made her giddy. "Heck yeah!"

"What are you doing, Dianna?" Eric said firmly. "You know Drax will lose his shit!"

"Not if you don't tell him," Dianna said recklessly. Then she grabbed Brooke's hand and took off. Eric was shouting her name, but she ignored him. "I'll be quick! I promise!" she shouted back.

"Woah! That was intense," Brooke commented.

"I know right. He'll be okay," Dianna said flippantly. The temptation to show off the speed of her motorcycle had taken forefront in her mind and she decided to worry about the consequences later. They got to her cruiser parked on the side of the street near a meter. She unstrapped her helmet from the back of the bike and gave it to Brooke. "Put this on... for safety."

Brooke was breathless from their sprint. She grabbed the helmet and carefully fitted her head inside. "This is so exciting," she told Dianna.

"Wait until we're riding through these streets." Dianna got on first and then Brooke got on behind her. Dianna revved the bike loudly after turning it on. This made Brooke giggle like a schoolgirl as she held on to Dianna tightly. "Are you ready!"

"Yes!" Brooke threw her hands in the air then quickly returned them around Dianna's waist. Then they were off, roaring down the narrow street over the speed limit. Dianna deftly swerved the motorcycle around cars and even ran a red light because she was so high on her own adrenaline. She was like an uncaged lion doing what her heart was telling her. Brooke was enjoying every moment of it as they raced down the well paved street faster than a magnet train. She eventually slowed down when she found herself in a part of town that she was unfamiliar with and she turned around in an alley way and started heading back at a safer speed.

"Damn! That was wild. I can't believe you ran that light!"

"Me neither. I think these pregnancy hormones made me do it," she joked.

"You're amazing!" Brooke said admiring Dianna.

"What makes you say that?" Dianna probed, stopping at a red light this time.

"Nothing. Just happy I had a chance to meet you." Dianna was completely confused by her statement but chalked it up to euphoria.

"I'm glad I met you too," she said so she wouldn't seem rude. When they got back to the indoor mini golf course, Dianna walked her new friend back to her car in the parking lot and practically gawked at Brooke's dark green and black Bugatti Chiron.

"You think you're the only one with a need for speed?"

"Nice!" Dianna said walking around the car. She could see that there was a lot of modifications on it. "You're a damn adrenaline junkie like me. It all makes so much sense."

"Maybe I can show you how fast she goes on a desert road soon."

241

"Oh my gosh, yes. How can you afford this?"

"Perks of my job."

"Oh yeah! What do you do?"

"Fugitive Recovery." Dianna did a double take, but she didn't want to pry further. Her phone began ringing. She saw that Drax was calling her and ignored it. "Fuck! I have to go."

"Take my number," Brooke suggested and quickly spewed the numbers as Dianna keyed the details in her phone.

"I'll call you," Dianna promised. She hugged her and then headed back to the where she knew her other friends were waiting. She still had a smile plastered on her face when she saw Drax waiting in the spot she had left Eric and Simon. He was still wearing his long gray overcoat and black suit he had on this morning and by the look on his face, she knew she was in trouble.

"Where's Eric and Simon?" she said looking around.

"Did you expect them to wait after you took off?"

"Did Eric call you? He's such a wuss!" Dianna groused.

"He didn't need to. I called you and you didn't answer your phone. I thought something was wrong."

"I had a wild hair. I'm sorry," she said sweetly and sauntered over to him with one of her sexiest walks.

"Dianna, don't. We keep having this conversation and it's getting old," he told her with frustration evident on his face.

"Please don't be mad at me. Sometimes girls just wanna have fun," she told him wrapping her arms around his neck. He removed her hand and stepped away from her, but she wasn't deterred. Excitement was still running through her veins. She grabbed his shirt and pulled him to her, then she bent his head down so she could kiss him passionately. This time, he didn't resist. He moved his hand down the small of her back savoring the taste of her mouth.

"I can't get enough of you," he said, his anger melting away.

"Let's ride back home on my bike," she said breathlessly as he ravaged her mouth.

"I'm riding," he told her.

"You always have to control the situation don't you."

"Yes!"

"Eh-hem" They both turned around to see Brooke standing a few feet from them. "I'm sorry Dianna but I think you dropped your keys."

"Oh my God!" Dianna said taking them quickly from her. "Wow! Thank you!" she said holding them to her heart.

"Yeah, I saw them on the ground when I was driving away. Figured you would be stranded out here without them, but I guess not," she said eyeing Drax. Dianna quickly remembered that she hadn't introduced them and immediately did so. Drax nodded his head politely but he remained silent.

"Yeah. Dianna has told me a lot about you," Brooke exaggerated.

"Has she?"

"Yeah. She thinks you'll make a great dad." The compliment did little to change Drax's demeanor. Dianna also noticed his apprehension.

"Are you okay?" she asked him, a little disturbed by his unaffable demeanor. He looked at her and gave her a stiff smile.

"I'm sorry. Just had a long night." He responded.

"No, I'm sorry. I interrupted you guys." Brooke apologized. "I'm going to head back to my car. Call me!" she told Dianna, then walked away.

"I will," Dianna shouted after her. Drax placed his arm protectively around Dianna's waist as they walked out of the park.

"You seem keen about her. You're not usually like that around new people," Drax said observantly.

"She's really nice. I like her," Dianna said resting her head on his shoulder as they walked slowly.

"Something doesn't strike you as odd about her?"

"Well she bears an uncanny resemblance to my mom," Dianna said. Drax stopped and looked at Dianna.

"She practically looks like you, Dianna. You both have similar physical traits and I'm not talking about the human side." Dianna widened her eyes.

"You think she's Nagalian?"

"Half Nagalian. I can bet my bottom dollar on it!" he said to her.

Dianna thought about it, but she couldn't be absolutely sure yet Drax seemed certain. "Well if she is, that's a good thing...right?" Dianna said, searching his eyes for approval. He smiled down at her and stroked her cheek.

"I think your pregnancy is affecting your judgement," he patronized her. "I just want you to be careful. You don't know what it would do to me if anything happened to you guys," he said to her, rubbing her stomach. She was having a lot of issues focusing lately. Mrs. Ashton told her she was experiencing pregnancy fog which made her brain a little scattered which she hated but she was certain Drax was overreacting. He started looking for her motorcycle. "Keys!"

Dianna's expression immediately grew dark. "Why?"

He walked towards her motorcycle and jumped on it. Even in his human form he was towering man, and he made her bike look almost toy-like as he waited for her to give him the keys. "Because I'm riding remember." She sighed in relief and then threw him her keys. For a second, she thought he was thinking of taking her motorcycle away again. She put on her helmet, straddled the back of the motorcycle and held on tightly around his waist, pressing her face in his back. He started the ignition and revved the motor before taking off towards their home. By the time they made it to the dusty highway, the road was lonely, and the wind was strong, but she felt safe as she always did when she was with him. She knew in her heart that this was what she wanted and where she wanted to be. But a fear always followed her, always telling her that this was too perfect, and it wasn't forever. It was the fear that one day she was going to wake up and it would all be gone like wind blowing the dust away on the lonely highway. And as much as Drax wanted to pretend, she knew he had the same fear. It was a fear that became very real that morning that Jasmine was poisoned, and Dianna's heart stopped. It was a real reminder that danger was always just around the corner.

After Drax parked the motorcycle in the garage, they both walked to the living room where Dianna immediately went to the kitchen for some wine. Drax eyed her disapprovingly. "You make me worry when you drink." His tone was patriarchal which annoyed Dianna to no end. Dianna stared back at him defiantly. She swallowed the rest of her wine, pulled out her phone and googled "Wine and Pregnancies". She walked over to him in the dimness and showed him the information. The article confirmed she could drink about a glass a week. "Doesn't mean anything," Drax countered. "Just because you're half Nagalian doesn't mean you're invincible, Dianna." He looked down as he took off his shoes. "Doesn't mean you're not prone to miscarriages." Dianna sighed. He worried so much...too much. Drinking a glass of wine helped to take the edge off but she figured it was useless to explain it to him. She decided to drop the conversation. She noticed a large brown paper bag sitting in the middle of the floor. She walked over to it and got low enough to peep inside. Even though it was dim, her dilated pupils under her contact lens made it easy to see the contents inside. There was a rope, some old books like the ones in his parents' cellar and some type of linen, could've been a curtain or flag. It was neatly folded so she wasn't sure, but she could definitely make out the Nagalian emblem.

"Why do you have these?" she asked curiously. He looked over at her and then at the bag. His shirt was open, and his belt was loose as he tried to get more comfortable.

"It's not for me. It's for my dad. They were going to throw them out at the academy since they are remodeling the school." He walked over to where she stood and his chest and glorious six pack was visible. It was clear he wasn't even trying to be sexy but there was no denying his sex appeal. Dianna felt her mouth watering.

"My father likes these things so I thought it would be a good addition to his collection." Drax maundered on but Dianna was zoning out as she was wrapped up in her own fantasy. He knelt beside the bag and took out the rope. "I think this goes with this emblematic tapestry," he said, pulling the rope taut. It made a sharp sound as his muscles tensed under the crisp fabric of his white shirt. Without any rhyme or reason, he took his shirt off and fanned himself with it. *Oh...you're burning up,* she secretly lusted. She noticed that she was a little hot too but was sure it had nothing to do with the ambiance. She placed her finger in her mouth as she came to the conclusion that she wanted to play and play hard. He rested the rope on the tile, then took out the tapestry. He unfolded it and she saw that it was wide enough to cover his bed upstairs. She didn't know why but she wanted to defile it by having sex on it. The thought turned her on immensely.

"How good are you at tying ropes?" Her voice was low and seductive. He looked up at her, standing over him with her finger in her mouth and her hip cocked suggestively to the side, her legs wide apart with her black, patent leather boots and tight, latex pants, accentuating her silhouette in the dimly lit room and he immediately understood. He gave her a lopsided grin that told her he wanted to play too. He picked up the rope and inspected it.

"What's your safe word again?"

"Bipolar." She smiled wickedly.

"That's what I thought." He proceeded to get up, but she pushed him back down. He stared up at her confused, but she only stared back at him in silence. He tried to get up again, but she pushed him back down with her heavy boot on his bare chest. He swiped her foot away and was in her face in an instant. He grabbed her curly hair and pulled her head back as he positioned himself behind her.

"You're trying to piss me off, aren't you?" He slid his hand inside her latex pants, feeling her thin lace underwear beneath and he pressed hard against her clit in a circular motion. All sensation concentrated in that area and she felt herself getting wet for him. "You want it rough?" She nodded her response. "All you had to do was ask nicely."

"Please," she asked with a devilish grin. He let go of her hair and his hand traveled down to her left shoulder. Next, he pulled his other hand out of her pants and placed it on her curvy hip and without any warning, he bent her body forward. Dianna thought she was going to fall at the sudden movement, but he held her steadily. He removed his hand from her shoulder and pulled her pants down under her ass. Dianna felt the warm air caressing her round bottom. Then she felt his warm hand massaging her bouncy derriere. A sharp pain followed as he slapped her full on her ass. She sucked in her breath sharply, but she didn't scream. Her ass stung and she loved it. She bit her bottom lip as the pain eased. He then pulled up her pants, allowing her to stand upright. "Be a good girl, go upstairs and wait for me." He instructed her then let her go. As she walked away, her boots sounding heavy on the marble floor, she remembered something. She walked back toward him as he waited for her to make her move. She bent down and picked up the tapestry by his feet, her face only inches away from his groin. Before she rose, she unzipped his pants and pulled it down a bit along with his underwear. His beautiful dick sprang out, hard as cut diamond and she placed it in her mouth and sucked seductively, staring into his soul as she did so. He hissed loudly and moved his pelvis slowly to her pace, grunting from the pleasure.

"I thought I told you to go upstairs and wait for me," he whispered. She stopped and stood up. Then kissed him.

"Guess it's a good thing I don't listen." She turned her back and walked away. "Don't forget the rope," she said adjusting the tapestry over her shoulder as it dragged slowly behind her.

She meandered upstairs to the bedroom, stripped herself completely naked and spread the large tapestry on the bed with the emblem facing up. Now that she could inspect the fabric a little closer, she saw that the emblem was the face of a woman with the snake wrapped around her torso and its head resting on her shoulder as if it was an ally, not the enemy. In her left hand she held a shield and in her right hand a spear. It was beautiful and she was surprised at the gender choice since there were literally only men in the fraternity. The rest of the tapestry was black with silver fringes. She ran her fingers across the embroidered emblem and connected deeply with the symbol.

"I don't understand the tapestry part but I'm with it," Drax said leaning against the door post with his arms folded, holding the cloth rope in one hand. He had been watching her. Except for his boxers, he was naked. He stood tall and muscular like the sex symbol he was. She started to walk towards him, but he put a finger up indicating for her to stop. "Get on the bed," he told her.

She crawled onto the bed excitedly and centered herself right on top of the emblem. He followed after her and she could feel the mattress sink under his heaviness. "Be still," he said sternly when she tried to wiggle beneath him.

"Or else?" she dared him. He didn't say anything. He gently took her arms and crossed them above her head, then tied the rope around her wrists.

"Always such a gentleman," she taunted. When he was finished tying her wrists, he started tying the rope to the middle of the headboard, so her arms were raised slightly above her head.

"What's your safe word?"

"Bipolar." She giggled barely able to contain her excitement, but it was short-lived as only a few seconds later, he yanked the rope so hard she bellowed in pain.

"Don't forget it," he told her.

"Fuck!" She breathed out realizing that shit was about to get real. When he was finished, he lay beside her and looked at her for a few minutes silently with a sadistic look on his face. She smiled playfully. "You're enjoying this aren't you?" she said to him as she already felt her arms straining. He captured her mouth and kissed her roughly. She was so out of breath when he finished the kiss, she had to catch her breath. "Shut up, Dianna!" he told her. "None of your smack tonight." He opened one of her eyes wide and gently removed one lens then the other. He threw them away. She blinked rapidly as her eyes adjusted. "Don't worry about those. Ill replace them," he told her.

"Why did you take them out?" she questioned utterly confused. His behavior was unpredictable, and she was uncertain of his plans, but come what may, she refused to say 'bipolar'.

"Damn! You really don't listen, do you?" he said to her and she knew she fucked up.

"Shit!" she whispered to herself. He ran the rope under her body and then bent both her knees raised, so the bottom of her feet was flat on the bed and her knees were in the air. Both her legs were so wide apart, she was sure he could see every crease and crevice of her vagina. When he was done, she was tied so tight, she couldn't move anything without it hurting.

"I don't think these are tight enough," he observed as he walked around the bed checking out his handy work. "What do you think, babe?" She didn't respond, unsure if she should or should not speak.

"Okay. Guess, I'll have to test it to see." He held on to it getting ready to pull the rope.

"No, babe. It's tight enough!" She tried to assure him. He stared at her blankly as if her words went over his head then yanked the rope above her head. She screamed bloody murder. "What the fuck!"

"I'm confused. Are we using your safe word or not?" he said to her innocently, but she knew he was being the devil enjoying her predicament. She forgot to say 'bipolar'. She was beginning to think this wasn't his first time. It sure as hell was her first time trying something like this and she thought it was going to be less painful. She was wrong as hell! She felt like a turkey ready to be cut open. He had all the control with the devil in his eyes and she had nothing. She was certain beyond the shadow of a doubt that she was going to regret it. He always made her feel in control every time they had sex, but this time was completely different. He was going to punish her for testing him every single time she did. *Now would be a good time to say 'bipolar', Dianna. This is way out of the scope of what you expected,* she thought to herself then she started praying inwardly. When she opened her eyes, she saw him leaning against the wall looking at her intently yet amused.

"You look worried." She couldn't believe this asshole was fucking with her mind like this. 'Bipolar' was the last thing she was going to say...EVER! She licked her parched lips and stared at the ceiling. "Nothing to say, huh?" She shook her head keeping her eyes on the ceiling. He chuckled then climbed on the bed. She felt him center his thumb between her moist lips between her legs, then spreading her to expose her clit. She felt his warm tongue on her, as he licked from her entrance to her erogenous button, making sure to spend a little extra time on her clit then back down to her entrance. He was slow and deliberate. It felt so good she jerked forward pulling on the rope which hurt her wrists. She whimpered a lot from the pleasure and a little from the pain.

"Stop moving!" he whispered, his breath was warm on her vagina, but she couldn't help herself and he knew it. He knew exactly what he was doing. He continued licking her, picking up the pace as time went on. She couldn't move, she couldn't hold onto to anything. The only thing she could do was moan in pleasure and she got louder and louder. He placed both his fingers inside her like he did at his mother's medical facility and fingered her with the same intensity. The only difference was he was sucking on her clit at the same time. She felt herself quivering. "I want you to squirt in my mouth so I can taste you." She heard him say. She could barely speak because once the words were said, he returned to her extremely sensitive clit.

"I don't know how to do it on purpose," she confessed, her breathing was erratic as she arched her back and yelled because what he was doing felt unbearably good. At one point she felt his long, slippery tongue inside her then his slippery fingers again. "Makes the reward even better," he said. Then she felt it. The vaginal spasm as she felt her walls tightening around his fingers, then the explosion in her body and then the explosion in his mouth as she squirted. She closed her eyes as everything culminated together. When it was over, she felt him kiss the side of her leg gently, then sucked it hard and she knew it was going to bruise. She watched him reposition himself, so his face was hovering over hers. "You are a fucking turn on!" She heard him say before he thrusted his dick inside her. She squeezed her eyes shut. He was so hard.

"Open your eyes!" His tone was aggressive. She opened her eyes. His pupils were completely dilated, and he sounded primal as he fucked her harder and harder. But she had to take it, and she wanted to. "Do you know what your eyes look like during sex?" His voice was course.

"I don't," her voice was soft, and she closed her eyes again as he thrusted inside her.

"They look like mine." He slapped her ass hard. She yelped, opened her eyes again. "Keep them open. I want to see how much you enjoy being fucked by me." His eyes were so dark she felt like she was falling into an abyss just looking into them. "I want to change." He confessed. She could see the glistening sweat, maddening desire and gripping ecstasy on his face. He waited for her to tell him. It was crazy that he could've changed but still waited. She wasn't going to deny him.

"Please," she asked nicely. He changed. She felt even more girth inside her as he fucked her without much restraint. It hurt but it felt so fucking good at the same time. She turned her head to the side and saw his large claws gripping the tapestry as the fabric bunched together. He slowed his thrust and she arched even more which was his undoing.

He groaned and slammed into her. She screamed but she didn't say bipolar. Sweat dripped from him onto her. He was in a pleasure trance and so was she. She felt it building. He paused momentarily to bend his neck so he could suck her nipples and with her walls stretching tightly around him and his wet tongue on her nipple, her clit sensitive from the oral stimulation earlier and her hands tied above her head, it was over. She came. He picked up his thrusts until he came too. Dianna had no energy and was happy when she felt the rope being untied so her blood could circulate properly. Her muscles were noodles.

"Best sex I ever had," she heard him say. She smiled and waited to feel his arms around her as both their breathing subsided.

"You lost, Jasmine!" was the last thing she said to him and he might've responded but she didn't hear what he said or cared to hear. She had earned his title of best lover even though she wasn't full Nagalian and as stupid as she knew it sounded, she slept well knowing that Jasmine hadn't even come close to her sexual appetite or shenanigans. Dianna had saved her life...*but fuck that bitch!*

Chapter 12

"Everything is going according to plan. Don't rush it," Brooke said to the person on the other line. Her boss was pressing her to wrap up the job, but she needed more time.

"Don't go soft on me, Brooke. Bring her in. We don't need her mother," he said to her patiently.

"Understood." Brooke hung up the phone and focused her attention on the details on her computer. Everything was going to plan. She had her sights on one, but she wanted them both to sweeten the deal. She spent her entire life knowing her mother had abandoned her but to find out she had another daughter that she protected with every breath in her body made Brooke's blood curdle. Dianna was a crazy bitch, but the good kind of crazy since she was more 'good than crazy'. She was the kind of bitch that would make a powerful Nagalian like Drax stick his neck out for her even though she was literally a nobody. Brooke scoffed with cynicism. "How you did that, Dianna, the world will never know." Brooke had to admit that even she liked her lovable baby sister. She thought her innocence was cute and she liked her sense of style. Plus, that bike ride was wild as hell. Under different circumstances, they would have been close. *Inseparable even.* But like her boss said, this is no time to go soft. She had to take her in. She literally had the ultimate cure-all vaccine running through her veins and she would go to the highest bidder. Pharmaceutical moguls had been hearing the rumors about her and they were waiting for the proof.

She thought how happy she was she never ended up with the trait, or she would've been a highly sought-after lab rat too. That was a life she never wanted to revisit. Irene left her as a new-born in Vietnam in 1955. From what she knew, they wanted to give her away to the locals and see what they could do with her but they eventually decided to keep her on base to see if she had the same blood type as her mother. They found out pretty early that she didn't when she was five and they did a blood transfusion. The soldier ended up reacting so badly to her blood he died in a few days. After realizing she was useless, they returned her to the US and handed her over to bounty hunters. It may have been luck, but her boss thought it would've been a good idea to raise her as his own and as a bounty hunter as well and they did. As she grew older, she proved herself useful by using herself as bait to befriend half and full Nagalians and usually the bounty hunters came in after her and did the dirty work. Thanks to her, her squad was able to capture and kill over a hundred half and full Nagalians. She had formed such a deep hatred for them because of Irene, she didn't care that they were dying or that she was making it easier for the bounty hunters to murder them. If they were living in groups, she felt like she had hit the motherload as they were picked off one by one with the Apoptosyde. Hatred wasn't her only incentive. They paid well too. She had a nice beach house in Florida and a few sweet rides to complement her beach front property.

It was no secret to her that she was dead inside. She didn't care about anything but her job and the money rolling in but when they gave her this job to bring her sister in, something within her came alive and it was worse than evil but she had to bide her time. For now, she had to keep up the charade with Dianna and her airy friends until she had Dianna exactly where she wanted her.

***

Drax was at his parents' house dropping off the tapestry and books he had for his dad. He was on the patio watching the sunset and driving himself crazy with his thoughts. He couldn't get Brooke off his mind. She had popped up out of nowhere and had just taken a keen interest in Dianna and his pregnant girlfriend was just naively going along with it. He couldn't find anything about Brooke. No paperwork, no family. Even her license plate traced back to someone else who was also a dead end. He had his private investigator follow her around, but she seemed very low key. She was staying at a high-end hotel and she was paying cash, no credit cards. It's as if she just had no prior life. He didn't want to scare Dianna, so he didn't bombard her with his suspicions, but he worried every time they went out together. For the most part, Dianna stuck to her promise to him that she would only socialize in a group setting which included Eric and he also had another person tailing them just in case but until he could get some sound information about Brooke, he was walking on eggshells.

Another thing he was keeping from Dianna was how he truly reacted the day she had the cardiac arrest. He had ripped the transfusion needle from her arm to stop the process and started yelling at his mother to do something. He went bat shit crazy and his dad and four other men had to drag him out of the room. Even thinking back, he couldn't believe how quickly he became a raving maniac. Finally, when her condition stabilized, they allowed him back into the observatory area under the condition that he would remain calm. Even though she hadn't awoken until half an hour later, he managed to wait in a corner silently until he and his mother got into it again.

"Is this your way of ensuring that I don't squander my life?"

"Drax, keep it up and I'll have them put you out again! What has gotten into you?" his mother said, baffled at his behavior. *"Never in my life have I seen you act this way before."* He couldn't explain it to himself much less to her.

"Stop deflecting mom! You almost killed her," he argued.

"You think it was intentional? That I wanted to harm her and my grandchild?" He had laughed in her face when she said that.

"A few weeks ago, you were suggesting an abortion?"

"I'm sorry Drax. I was out of line." Just then Dianna had started waking up and he had walked away to cool off. He didn't want her to see him so angry.

His mother was right. He had never behaved like this over a Nagalian woman, let alone a half Nagalian woman but how could he not? Not only had she gotten to the deepest part of him, but she was also carrying his child. Everything had happened so fast. When he had just met her, he thought she was just another half Nagalian he needed to save, or help, like the others or like Eric or Suzanne but she turned out to be so much more. He thought about his work and the community he had built over time. When he met Eric, he was homeless and begging for scraps on the street. He was leaving work and getting into his Limo when Eric stopped him begging for spare change. He saw his eyes and knew right away what he was. He took him in, gave him a place to stay. He cleaned up pretty well. Drax trained him and gave him a job at his company and he never looked back.

Suzanne, also a full Nagalian, was always a part of the family. It was his parents that raised her since both her parents were killed by bounty hunters. He hired her as his personal aid as soon as she finished college and she had been taking his memos, arranging his meetings, and made every single business trip with him ever since. He didn't know much about Simon since it was Eric that found him. All he knew was that Simon was a drug addict and Eric helped him to get back on his feet. That's what they did. That was their purpose. To restore the Nagalian communities to their rightful status. His company helped to hide their true work and also helped to provide jobs to help Nagalians get back on their feet. He also found it beneficial to keep a few humans on the payroll too.

He hadn't really known about Dianna until he had to produce an ad campaign for one of the biggest beer companies in Nevada. He decided to personally oversee the operations and when he saw Dianna's editing skills he was completely impressed. He inquired about her and was told she was a freelancer which Eric used sometimes when things got too overwhelming at the office. He thought it was strange that she was so good at what she did and didn't work at the company, which made him think that if she was a freelancer, it was only a matter of time before someone offered her a binding contract. So, he asked Suzanne to set up a meeting. He was more than bewildered when she told him it had to be done through Skype, but he went along with it.

There were certain things that struck him as strange during the meeting. The way she was constantly lowering her gaze or trying to avoid looking into the camera, or how guarded she was or even the way she refused his invitation to come into the office. Yet when she did look at him, her gaze was smoldering. To be honest, he enjoyed pushing her buttons during the meeting which he knew he did, just enough. Then she showed up at the office out of the blue trying to hide behind ugly sunglasses. At that point, it was becoming a scent trail for him. He couldn't stop thinking about her. She had an account on LinkedIn which also didn't give too much away. He soon realized that he had a growing obsession with her. He didn't know how he was going to arrange a one-on-one with her but he knew it needed to be done and it was as if someone, somewhere was listening because the opportunity presented itself when she liked his picture on social media. It was downhill from there.

When he picked her up at her place and she walked out in the green sheer dress with her nipples poking through the fabric, he knew he wanted her. She was gorgeous. Her skin was golden, and her eyes had specks of green, her mouth was pouty and inviting and he wanted to fit her ass right in the palm of his hand. He wondered if she was wearing underwear the entire night. However, it wasn't as if she was trying too hard to hide her desires. She was practically eye fucking him and by the time he dropped her off, it was 'a go'. She turned out to be a good little romp in bed but their first time sleeping together was only the tip of the iceberg compared to what came after.

"Hey, darling." His mother came out with some champagne to join him. He took the glass from her and downed it quickly. "Do you want the entire bottle?" she said a little flabbergasted. He quickly poured himself another glass.

"Okay, what's on your mind?" she asked him.

"Nothing," he lied.

She sighed feeling the weight of his silence. "We never finished our conversation we were having at the lab the other day."

"Maye it's better we don't?" he said in a hoarse voice. He swallowed the alcohol in his glass in one gulp then refilled his glass again. "Don't you have anything stronger?" He wasn't up for a heated argument. She continued anyway. "Drax, I'm sorry. I realized how much I hurt you when I suggested the abortion. I was just so wrapped up with doing the appropriate thing versus the right thing," she said. He held her gaze as her words healed the rift between them.

"I don't regret it, but I never expected her to get pregnant and I never expected to fall for her like this," he said candidly, looking like he did something wrong. "the situation just took on a life of its own." He scratched his stubble and reminded himself that he needed to shave.

"I know," his mom said as she sipped her drink slowly, looking at the fading light of the sky.

"The last thing, I wanted to do was to abscond my obligations."

"You're not doing that, Drax. You have taken up this mantle to save our kind and safeguard our communities and you've done just that...and the fact is, there is more than one way to do it. Trying to force you to marry Jasmine was an awful thing," his mom said apologetically. "Trying to force her to marry you was shameful." She crossed her legs and tugged at her earlobe as she mused over something in her mind. "And I should've known better...should've known that you wouldn't be any less different when it came to being a father."

His mother saying the word 'father' created a surreal moment for him. It made his obligations to his child and to Dianna much more palpable since the truth was now set in stone.

"...and I should've said this a long time ago...congratulations," she said softly and with pride brimming in her eyes. Drax didn't expect the change in her attitude but it settled his spirit to know that they were no longer at odds about his child. He nodded his head in acceptance of her peace offering.

"What did dad say about Dianna being pregnant?"

"What is there to say? He just has to accept it."

"Y'know, Dianna might be different. She may live longer than other Half Nagalians," he said. The tiny modicum of faith he had was wavering even as he spoke the words.

"I wouldn't be too hopeful if I were you. I think it's more likely that the baby might live longer," she rested her hand on top of his. "Let's just make the best of the situation and enjoy the good moments while they last," Drax agreed inwardly with his mother but deep down, he hoped she was wrong about Dianna. He wanted to believe that they had more than just a few hundred years together. It was better not to think about it.

"I brought this for dad," he said handing her the brown bag. She looked inside and took out the books, then the tapestry.

"Where's the rope?"

"What rope?" Drax asked innocently knowing very well that the rope was in his bedroom where he had been doing obscene things to Dianna. The memory flashed across his mind and he couldn't help chewing on his lip to stop himself from smiling. He had tried light BDSM before and wasn't really into that kind of scene, since the whole idea seemed a little violent. However, when he did it with Dianna, he felt really good giving her, her due reward and punishment. The controlled dominance he had over her was invigorating and he was already thinking of ways he could convince her to do it again... *But did she need convincing,* he thought to himself, as he rubbed his chin in deep contemplation.

"The rope that it's supposed to hang from."

Drax couldn't believe his mother was still gabbing about the damn rope. "I'll see if it's at the house somewhere," he said dismissively. His mother looked at the emblem and smiled.

"Y'know this symbol means we'll always protect our own. No matter how great or small." He nodded his head.

"I lost sight of that. Dianna saving Jasmine's life reminded me though of why we do what we do." She drank the rest of her champagne, neatly placed the tapestry inside the brown bag and took it inside since it had gotten dark, leaving Drax to his thoughts again. He stared into the darkness knowing he took that oath more seriously now more than ever and he had to protect Dianna at all cost, and it may have been just a gut feeling but Brooke seemed like a bad omen.

***

"Mom, I'm doing my first ultrasound next week."

"Isn't that too soon?"

"They just want to make sure everything is moving along fine, considering." Dianna said cryptically, as she thought about the cardiac arrest and the blood loss, she experienced a few weeks before.

"Considering what?"

"Nothing. It would be nice if you could be there with me."

"I'll think about it,"

"Just say yes."

Irene thought about it. As much as she wanted to visit Dianna, she would be taking such a risk, but she missed her and on top of that, her daughter was pregnant. "Okay, okay! I'll book a ticket today."

"Are you going to take the plane?"

"No, too risky. I'll call you once I'm in Nevada."

"Okay. I love you." Irene was shocked to hear Dianna say that. She was so shocked she found herself sobbing. "Mom, don't! Please don't. You always start crying for no reason."

"I love you too, sweetie," she responded then hung up the phone. She heard Mrs. Johnson's walker scraping the floor as she made her way to the kitchen. Irene quickly dabbed her eyes to get rid of the tears.

"Irene!" Mrs. Johnson sang her name sweetly. Irene ran to her. "Oh, there you are, dear."

"Mrs. Johnson why are you walking around. Shouldn't you be resting."

"I can rest when I'm dead!" Mrs. Johnson snapped facetiously. Irene couldn't help but laugh at Mrs. Johnson's dark joke. Clearly, she still had some fire in her. "Anyway, I'm just looking for my glasses, dear. Have you seen it?" Irene looked at the old lady's soft white hair and saw the glasses perched on top of her head.

"Your glasses are right here, Mrs. Johnson," she said reaching for her glasses and then handing it to her.

"Oh, my goodness!" Mrs. Johnson quickly put on her glasses. "I'm so silly."

"No, you're not. Let me walk you back to your room." She helped to turn the old woman around and started taking her back to her room. "I'm going to visit my daughter in the US, next week."

"The one with the boyfriend or the one in Vietnam?" Irene thought that for someone with dementia, her memory was very selective.

"The one with the boyfriend."

"Do you think he's going to marry your daughter?"

Irene laughed. "I have no idea and I really don't think it's any of my business."

"Pff! These young people today. They don't know anything about getting married and staying married."

Irene chuckled, "different times," Irene said opening the door so Mrs. Johnson could enter the room.

"Some things should never change!"

"but somethings do and that's not a bad thing." Irene bantered with the old woman as she finally got her back in bed for her afternoon nap, but she was sure that Mrs. Johnson would do some crossword puzzles or something similar since she needed her glasses. She had finally opened up to Mrs. Johnson and told her about her first child that she had to leave in Vietnam. She had explained to Mrs. Johnson that they had been separated and she didn't know if she was alive. Mrs. Johnson was hopeful that she was, but Irene knew better than to hope as her thoughts went back to the day they were separated.

She was sweaty, dirty and bloody from childbirth. They had just left her in the little backroom with only a blanket like a damn animal to give birth to her baby without any medical assistance. But she did it, and her baby girl was beautiful. She had wiped the blood off her and began breast feeding her when someone finally came to her assistance. Another nurse who told her that she needed to shower and gave her some antibiotics. She remembered looking at the antibiotics thinking she needed a shower more than she needed the pills.

"Where are you taking my baby?"

"We're just going to clean her up and bring her back." It was obvious the nurse was lying. Irene had burst into tears knowing they wouldn't return her baby. She grabbed the nurse's arm." Please don't let them hurt her!" The nurse stared back deathly frightened. The poor thing looked like she in her 20s. "Please don't let them hurt her!" Irene begged again, feeling weak from the labor. The nurse looked even more terrified that Irene wouldn't let go of her arm. "Her name is Brooke. She's just a baby." The nurse's eyes soften.

"Ma'am, I--I--I don't know what I can do." She stuttered nervously.

"Just make sure they don't harm her. Please!" The nurse was obviously disturbed. She looked at the baby and looked at Irene.

"I wish there was something I could do," she said, her innocent eyes wide with fear.

"Give me the baby and help me get out of here. What they are doing to me isn't right," Irene suggested sounding crazed. The woman's expression became sober and firm.

"I can't do that, Ma'am." Irene sobbed. Her face was grimy, and she smelled like a dead body rolled in pig feces. If anything good was going to happen, this nurse was her only chance.

"I don't care what they do to me. Just don't let them harm my beautiful little girl." She saw heartbreak in the nurse's blue eyes as she held the baby tightly.

"I'll see what I can do." Then she walked to the exit. She looked back at Irene briefly and then left with the door slightly ajar. Irene realized in that moment that she was helping her to escape. As soon as the young nurse was out of sight, she made her move. She snuck out of the facility not knowing how she would get back to America, but she knew she had to get out of Vietnam. She had to go into hiding and she had to hope that she could come back and rescue Brooke. She remembered seeing the exit and remembering how far away it seemed, but she was determined to get there. Once she was out, the fresh air had filled her lungs and she remembered feeling a sense of freedom. She wandered the streets for hours looking destitute and dirty when some

American soldiers found her. They thought she was victimized by the locals and immediately gave her some food, clothes, and a much-needed shower. They then arranged her flight out of Vietnam and never looked back...not even for Brooke.

She was never the same since again. For years she had waking nightmares and insomnia and she never felt like a whole person again. Her mother had warned her a long time ago that her life would never be normal around the humans, no matter how hard she tried, no matter how much good she did, no matter how much she looked like them. She learned the hard way and lost a very real part of herself because she wanted to be different from her mother. She wanted to be a nurse, to help with the war, to get married and to have a family. Instead, she was broken, used and abused by them and feared that her daughter would meet the same fate. She had never forgiven herself for leaving her daughter behind. She should have fought harder, taken her baby from the nurse and run but everything happened so fast and she was so weak and discombobulated at the time, her only instinct was to run through the door that the nurse left ajar.

Yet, she never returned. She never returned for her lost child and that is something that haunted her. Her yearlong trauma in Vietnam was so great, it crippled her from ever returning to that place. Sometimes, she thought it was karma that Dianna wanted to kill herself because the truth is, she didn't deserve a daughter at all.

***

Dianna trailed Brooke along the path as they jogged slowly together. Even though Brooke knew she could go faster, she had dropped her pace significantly to accommodate Dianna, but her pregnant sister was still lagging and having a hard time keeping up. She decided to slow her pace to a walk. Dianna's boyfriend had temporarily taken her off the leash and was allowing her to finally hang out with her alone without his watch dogs Eric and Simon. Brooke found herself wondering if Dianna was obliviously ignorant of some of the things happening around her or if she was just too comfortable to care. She noted that Dianna legitimately had no idea that Simon and Eric were essentially her bodyguards. She overheard them talking the other night they were at the indoor mini golf course by the gift shop when she was on her way from the bathroom.

"How long do you think we can keep this up?"

"Keep your voice down. And to answer your question, as long as Drax needs us to," Eric said.

"I never signed up for this."

"I know. He's like family to me though. How could I seriously say no?"

"Let's be honest, Eric. By the time you're taking money, it's business, not family. It's low that he used your friendship with her to his advantage."

"Are you trying to make me feel bad, because it's damn sure working." Eric sounded frustrated. "You know how he is. If it wasn't me, it would be someone else."

Simon sighed loudly. "You're right but paying you to keep an eye on her. That changes everything. When she finds out, she's going to hate you...us." Eric was silent. "Now he's telling you not to trust Brooke. How does he sleep at night with that level of paranoia?"

"With his woman safe by side," Eric quipped. "I mean, he's got his reasons. Look at what happened to Jasmine."

"Don't remind me."

"Then this chick just pops up out of nowhere," Eric continued. "it does make you wonder a little."

"Maybe she's like Dianna. She kind of popped up out of nowhere and ended up in my bar."

"You're always adopting grown-ass adults. Anyway, you know I would pay your friends to keep an eye on you too," Eric joked.

"Is that so?"

"Yes! Especially at that dangerous bar of yours..." The voices faded and she realized they were taking the conversation elsewhere.

Dianna's head was stuck so far up her ass, she didn't even know that Eric and Simon were Nagalians.

"Wait, I can't keep up. I need to rest," Dianna said blowing hard through her nostrils. She rested on a bench close by. Brooke was surveilling the area and as usual, there were a few of Drax's men following them at a distance. She began thinking it would be harder than she thought to get Dianna to a secluded area. She knew security would be deep but this by her standards was excessive for an ordinary day.

"Drax ever struck you as extremely paranoid?" she said sitting down beside Dianna and handing her a cold bottle of water from her backpack.

"Oh, you mean the security?" Dianna said casually, letting the cold water cool her throat. "He thinks I don't see them, but I do." Brooke realized that she had to renege her statement. Clearly her head wasn't so far up her ass, she was just used to it. "Don't let them spook you."

"Doesn't it bother you?"

"With Drax, he either lets you go and forget about you or keep you around and protect you with everything he has. There's no middle ground for him and I guess I understand why. The 'why' matters."

Brooke scoffed and decided to play devil's advocate, "Oppressive much! I mean, give a lady some breathing room!" Dianna laughed then placed the bottle to her lips again. "I mean seriously, can you fart without someone watching?" Dianna couldn't help spitting out a mouthful of water as she laughed harder at Brooke's joke. "I know you want your freedom."

"I was on my own for 32 years. Didn't seem to be working for me then," Dianna suddenly gasped and the look on her face told Brooke that she knew she had said too much. Brooke decided to use this to her advantage.

"I know you're half Nagalian, Dianna. Did you think these were natural streaks in my hair?" she said pointing to her hair and smiling. "I am too." Dianna covered her face and sighed with relief.

"I think Drax is right. My pregnancy is affecting my judgement."

"Fuck Drax!" Brooke said a little annoyed. "When you are around me, it's just us girls. You can tell me anything." Dianna had relaxed and seemed to have taken the bait. If it was one thing, she could count on with most women is that they need someone moan to, especially when their men started getting out of hand.

"Drax I can handle," Dianna said to her. "Irene, is a whole other nut basket!" Dianna confessed. Brooke's ears perked up at the sound of her mother's name. In fact, she wasn't expecting the conversation to take such a quick shift to her mother. She had to admit that she wasn't ready. "She's coming in next week. I wanted her to be at my first ultrasound."

"She's coming...here?"

"Yeah. I managed to convince her. She won't tell me the exact day so hey...surprise!" Dianna laughed uncomfortably. Brooke gave her a half smile and her eyes grew dark. Dianna noticed the change in her mood. "I'm sorry. I didn't mean to upset you."

"No, it's fine. It's just that hearing others speak about their moms always puts me in such a dark place," Brooke said sweetly. "May I come to your ultrasound appointment?" She noticed Dianna's hesitation. "You're right, It's a private moment. I didn't mean to impose."

"No imposition. It's just that I think Drax is probably going to want close family there only. He's kind of a stickler about those things."

"Ugh, the almighty Drax!" Brooke said sounding agitated. Dianna stared apologetically. "Are you guys arriving together?"

"No. He has somethings to take care of first before he stops by." Dianna stood up and started doing some stretches as she was preparing to continue her jog. Brooke noticed a little pudginess around her stomach area. She figured her stomach would start looking like a round ball in a few more months if she made it that far.

"How about I stop by a little earlier and then I'll be out before he's in."

"I don't know. Seems like a lot just to see a tiny grape," Dianna said standing up straight as she touched her belly.

"It's not. I promise. I'll come by with Simon," Brooke said placing her hand over Dianna's stomach. Dianna stretched her arms above her head as she contemplated and to Brooke's pleasure she conceded.

"Okay. I'll just let Mrs. Ashton know that you guys are dropping by." Brooke turned around and pretended to stretch her body as well while a devious smile played on her lips. It was like fishing in a bucket. This was her chance to net both Dianna and Irene and she would be damned if she let anybody screw up her chance.

***

He immediately recognized Irene from the pictures as she plodded her way from the Greyhound station to the corner of the street with her small suitcase in tow. She was wearing a baseball cap which partially hid her face, a blue sundress, and a pair of blue tennis shoes. He stared at Dianna who seemed a little nervous. He touched her hand and despite the weather being warm, her hand was cold and clammy.

"Why are you nervous?"

Dianna focused her gaze on him. "I always get this way when I see her." She looked back at Irene. "I never know, if she's going to say something to piss me off or vice versa."

"You're in charge of your emotions. Just keep a cool head."

"We're talking about me here." The corner of Drax's mouth curled into a smile as he admitted inwardly that this was something she struggled with. "It'll be okay," he said as he squeezed her hand reassuringly. She closed her eyes, breathed in and then exhaled slowly.

"Make a U-turn right here," Drax told the limo driver. The driver did as he was told, and they were pulling up a few feet from where Irene waited. She noticed the sleek black Mercedes S Long limo and couldn't help the curious look on her face. Dianna had thought a limo picking her mom up from the greyhound was ostentatious but since his driver was more than just a driver, he, on the other hand, thought it was ideal. He was about to step out of the car, but Dianna stopped him.

"Drax, no offense but you like secret services. You'll freak her out. I've got this!" Dianna said bracing her hand against his chest to stop him from exiting the vehicle. She hopped out of the car and her mom immediately recognized her. In a few quick steps, she was standing in front of Dianna and hugging her with Dianna stiffly hugging her back. It was an interesting exchange to watch. Dianna was about to get her suitcase when Drax indicated to the driver that he should get it as he remained in the car. The large driver took both women off guard when he emerged from the limo, took the suitcase and placed it in the trunk. He then professionally opened the limo door for them so they could get in. Drax was tickled at how uncomfortable they both looked, as his driver did what he was paid to do. By the time they got into the car, Dianna was glaring at him. "I was managing just fine," she admonished him. Drax couldn't help grinning at her.

"Can't be lifting heavy things in your condition, babe," he teased her. Dianna grounded her teeth, and he could see that she was visibly trying to calm herself.

"We'll discuss this later."

"Nothing to discuss," he asserted. Then he looked at Irene who seemed just a tad bit embarrassed to be there. She cleared her throat uncomfortably.

"Hi, I'm Irene. Dianna has told me so much about you," she said nervously. He extended his hand to her and she shook it. He noticed her hand was clammy too. He couldn't understand why their meeting was so anxiety-inducing for both of them. It struck him that she appeared to be just a little older than his mother even though his mother was older by centuries. It was a sad reminder of how short-lived their life was.

"Nice to meet you. I can see where Dianna gets her beauty from," he complimented her. Irene smiled at his flattery and began to relax. He looked over at Dianna who rolled her eyes and was bursting at the seams to say something cutting but she instead chose to be cordial.

"I've never met a male Nagalian before. You have no markings," Irene said assessing him.

"Mom!" Dianna was dismayed that her mother would be so direct.

"It's fine. I'm guessing you're in the dark where full Nagalians are concerned," he said, entertaining her curiosity.

"Afraid so," Irene admitted. "Dianna probably already told you how isolated we were from your-- our kind." Drax nodded his head. "You become so wrapped up with surviving the humans that other things like heritage." She looked at Dianna, "or self-acceptance becomes the furthest thing from your mind. It's becomes more about accepting the situation as it is than accepting who are you are." Dianna looked away and stared out the window, hiding her expression from him but he knew she related to every single word that her mother just said. "I'm sorry. That was a bit much." She apologized noticing Dianna's silence. Dianna rubbed her eyes and then turned around to face her mom.

"I got you something," she said trying to switch the subject. Irene looked surprised. She reached for a tiny bag on the floor and handed it to her.

"Sweetie...No. I can't accept this."

"Trust me. You're going to thank me." Irene opened the bag and took out a small box. Drax already knew what was inside. Irene opened the small box and saw that they were contacts. She was perplexed. "Put them in."

"You know they irritate my eyes." Dianna gave Drax a quick knowing glance.

"These won't."

Irene sighed and decided to go along with what her daughter said. She placed them in and blinked a few times. "Wow!"

Dianna took her baseball cap off her head and smoothed her hair. "Now you can stop wearing that ugly-ass hat!"

Irene inspected Dianna's eyes. "Are you wearing them too?" She inquired. Dianna nodded and laughed at her mother's awe. Irene looked at Drax's amused expression and turned a slight shade of pink. "I sound so outdated, don't I? I am pretty sure you guys have everything from organic contact lens to physiological suppressants."

"I know it's all new to you," he said patiently. "We do but no need to utilize the suppressants."

"Why don't you need them?"

"Uncontrollable physiological responses are mainly nuisances for Half Nagalians," he told her.

"Wait! You can suppress my physiological responses?" Dianna said looking at Drax incredulously. "Why am I just now hearing about this?"

"Because you would want the suppressants."

"And this is an issue because?"

"It's better to learn to control your impulses naturally instead of becoming reliant on suppressants." He touched her hair, and her snakes came alive. "Secondly, you steal things like suppressants and Apoptosyde." Dianna's mouth fell to the floor, ". ... and my most important reason is quite selfish and entirely for sexual reasons." He could see that he flustered her which was his main objective.

"You're insufferable!"

"So, I've heard."

"YOU STOLE FROM HIM?!" her mom pressed no doubt embarrassed by her daughter's behavior.

"You shouldn't act so surprised, mom! You stole my father's driver's license, remember?" Irene glowed red and Drax was tickled, realizing the apple indeed didn't fall far from the tree. Dianna fluffed her hair and allowed her snakes to disappear before proceeding. "Ignore what he just said and focus on me." Dianna secretly glared at Drax. "I'm really happy you're here."

"It means so much to hear you say that." Her eyes moved down to Dianna's stomach. "Can I feel it?"

"It's only stomach fat at this point." Dianna trivialized. Her mom looked a little disappointed, so Dianna took her hand and laid it on her stomach.

"I can't believe you're pregnant!" Her mom blurted out getting emotional. Drax couldn't help smiling at the sweet moment. His mind wandered off as he began thinking about the future. Dianna was in fact getting fuller around her stomach area and it made him wonder about marriage. Dianna hadn't mentioned it once, not even in a passing conversation. She seemed pretty at ease with being his 'pregnant girlfriend'. Yet he knew everyone, like his parents, were waiting to see what he would do next. *Imagine making vows to spend the rest of your life with someone you were absolutely certain was going to die hundreds of years before you do.* Yet, he couldn't imagine not spending his time with her for the rest of her years. He decided to put any thoughts of marriage on ice for the present moment and other priorities to the forefront. He had her and for now she wasn't dying or going anywhere.

Chapter 13

Dianna lay on the bed in Mrs. Ashton's medical facility waiting for the private obstetrician to come into the room to start the ultrasound. It dawned on her that the facility was literally a "one stop shop" for Nagalians in Las Vegas. It was crazy that if anything happened to them like pregnancies, poisoning, or any other types of ailments, most half Nagalians wouldn't know where to go but they knew where not to go. The one time she ended up at the hospital she ripped the IV needle from the back of her hand, got her things and left without even a second thought. Emergency rooms and hospitals for humans was a Nagalian's nightmare. Yet, here, they did tests, research and provided medical services if needed. It was as if the more submerged she became into the Nagalian subculture, the more she understood the need for a tight-knit, impenetrable community. They had to be organized and united for their own protection and progress. Unfortunately, not everyone was ready for the progress and as she watched her mother enter her room, she knew people like Irene harbored such a level of distrust, they would never adjust their mindset.

"Here you go, sweetie," Irene said handing Dianna a cup of room temperature water.

"Thanks," Dianna said, sitting up in her hospital gown to drink the water. They had been there for over half an hour now. She hated waiting and was getting a little antsy. But maybe it was for the best because Drax hadn't arrived yet and she didn't want him to miss the moment. It occurred to her that Drax may have instructed them to wait. She drank the water slowly as Irene took a seat. She didn't remember the last time her mother looked so radiant and happy.

"I didn't expect him to be so handsome!" Irene admitted cheekily. Dianna smiled at her mother turning a light shade of pink thinking about Drax.

"I could hook you guys up if you want," Dianna teased. Irene slapped Dianna's leg playfully.

"You know that's not what I meant. I just think he's so...regal." She looked at her daughter admiring her. "You guys are so perfect for each other."

"What makes you say that?"

"Because he knows how to push your buttons...keep you on your toes."

"I thought you would've wanted me with someone nice."

"He is nice," she reached over and rested her hand on Dianna's knee, "and I know you love him."

There was a knock on the door and they both turned around as Simon peeped his head in. Dianna waved eagerly, happy to see him. He walked in and went over to Dianna to hug her. Dianna introduced him to her mom, and he gave her a hug too.

"Where's Brooke?" Dianna asked.

"She was right behind me. I'm not sure where she went."

Just then, a blood curdling scream could be heard coming from outside the room. They all looked at each other silently praying it was nothing serious. They heard scuffling and then Brooke kicked open the door.

"Get in!" she said waving a gun at Mrs. Ashton who had her hands behind her head. She was shaking in fear.

"Brooke, what are doing?!" Dianna demanded, confused by what was happening.

"Shut up, bitch!" She spotted Dianna's clothes on a chair inside the room. She picked it up with her free hand and threw it at Dianna. "Put these on now! You both are coming with me," she said pointing the gun back and forth from Dianna to Irene.

"Brooke?" Irene said rising slowly.

"Bitch don't move! Or I swear I will shoot you with this Apoptosyd!"

"Sweetie, you don't need to do this," Irene continued, remaining where she was.

"Do you know her?" Dianna questioned becoming more confused by the minute. Irene looked at Dianna silently with untold truths in her eyes.

"Now is not the time for this! Put your fucking clothes on and let's go!" Brooke shouted, shifting from side to side anxiously as she kept the gun pointed at Mrs. Ashton.

"Brooke, please stop!" Dianna said with no intention to go with her. "These are innocent people. They'll take care of you and give you whatever you need."

"You're so stupid!" Brooke spurted. "I'm a bounty hunter! And in case you haven't figured it out, I am kidnapping you! LET'S GO!" Through the corner of her eye, Dianna saw Simon reaching for something but not before Brooke turned the gun on him and shot him. Dianna screamed his name. The syringe got him in the arm, he pulled it out quickly, but it was too late. The Apoptosyde was already in his system. He fell to the ground in excruciating pain. "Anymore of you want to try your luck!" Dianna was crying as she stared at Simon writhing and moaning in pain. She knew exactly what would happen to him. She had seen it with Jasmine.

"Please, we have to help him now! He needs my blood," Dianna begged. Brooke caught Irene's questioning expression and her eyes became inflamed with jealousy. Her snakes popped out wild and thrashing.

"Oh, you didn't know. Your golden child can heal both humans and Nagalians...like you." Her voice was sinister. "Isn't that sweet. Guess that's another thing for you two to bond over before they take every ounce of blood from you for drugs and vaccines to feed the beast aka Big Pharma." She sounded maniacal as it all became clear to Irene. "Now, if you don't put your clothes on or the next Nagalian that's going to be on the floor smelling her rotting flesh is her," Brooke said pointing the gun at Mrs. Ashton.

"Okay!" Dianna got up quickly, removed her gown and dressed in her ordinary clothes.

"Get in front of me!" She motioned to Dianna. "You too, MOM!" Brooke said with a wild look in her eyes. "Your precious baby girl didn't even know I existed. You made it so easy for me to just take her. You're fucking pathetic!" Irene was shaking as she walked slowly in front of Brooke. Dianna followed suite.

"FASTER!" Brooke bellowed like a deranged person. They all walked out of the room in a line, leaving Simon who had begun foaming at the mouth. Dianna couldn't believe Brooke was going to let him die but her hands were tied. If she did anything sudden, then Mrs. Ashton would be next in line to be killed.

They went out to the main area where they saw two more men holding guns at the other staff. Tears streamed down Dianna's face as the reality kicked in. Brooke was a fucking bounty hunter that befriended her so she could kidnap both her and Irene. She didn't want to acknowledge it, but the worst part was, she was possibly her sister. She heard Irene sobbing behind her and a deep hatred for her mother, formed inside her. *How could she have another daughter and not tell her about it* was the biggest question in her mind. They got outside and there was a black van waiting. The van door opened, and another man jumped out. "Get in!" Brooke shouted at Irene and Dianna. They clambered in and the man covered their heads with black cloths and tied their hands behind them with zip ties. Dianna couldn't see anything, but she could still hear. "No! You stay! I have a message I want you to give to Drax. Tell him not to look for Dianna or we're going to kill them both. He stays away, she lives. Got that!" Dianna assumed she was talking to Mrs. Ashton who she was relieved was being left behind. She heard feet shuffling about in the van then the door sliding shut. The engine chortled a few minutes later and she jerked as the van moved forward. She also heard her mother whimpering uncontrollably. She had stopped crying. It wasn't going to help. She found herself thinking about Simon and a sinking fear crept over her. She knew he was going to die. They wouldn't find her in time.

She couldn't see Brooke, but she could sense her watching them. "You lied to me, Brooke."

"Really? Is that your biggest concern right now? That I lied to you." She felt her head being yanked backwards as Brooke pulled her hair. "News flash Ms. Thing, everybody lied to you! Your mother lied to you about me. Simon and Eric lied to you about being your friends and Drax pays all the people around you, including your fake friends to make sure you don't run off with his kid and that special blood of yours. Does he really love you or is he manipulating you, Dianna? You're too damn gullible and weak to know the difference."

"You don't know what you are talking about?"

"Open your eyes, Dianna. The only thing special about you is your blood. It makes sense that this is practically the only reason Drax would want you, a damn nobody!"

"Enough!" Dianna heard Irene snap at Brooke. Then she heard a loud slapping sound and felt her mom falling beside her.

"Irene, if these people weren't paying me so much money to bring you both in alive, I would kill you my damn self." She heard her mom screaming some more and felt Irene's body being dragged like a ragdoll from beside her. "YOU FUCKING LEFT ME IN VIETNAM! Who leaves a newborn baby in a warzone? WHO DOES THAT!" Tears were flowing again down Dianna's cheeks as she thought about what Brooke was saying. Her family was a circus outfitted with freaks and stunts to keep people entertain for a lifetime.

"I didn't have a choice!" She heard Irene whisper.

"Everyone has a choice, Irene. You chose yourself!" Dianna heard a thud. Then silence.

"Mom!" Dianna yelled.

"She's fine! I just shot her with the tranquilizer. I wish I could have shot her with Apoptosyde instead."

"You're the epitome of evil."

"I'm sure of it." She paused momentarily before continuing. "For what it's worth Dianna. I genuinely liked you. That's not a lie." She heard another thud. This time she felt something piercing the skin on her neck and before she knew it, she was crashing to the floor of the van into darkness.

***

The medical facility was a wreck. Overturned trays and paper scattered everywhere. Terrified faces of both Nagalians and humans alike could be seen throughout the facility trying to restore order as they tried to make sense of everything that just happened. Simon was dying and no one could help him. Drax arrived with dread in his eyes. Even though he knew Brooke and her posse were long gone, he still did a walk-through just in case. He, however, didn't have time to dilly-dally. Dianna had the phone he bought for her in her possession. She didn't know he had inserted a secondary tracking device that worked even when the phone was turned off. He needed to gather the Fraternity members together to make some tough decisions. He walked over to his mom who was sitting on a bed, shaking with a blanket around her. He hugged her tightly.

"Dianna told me she was a friend, or I wouldn't have told security to let her in."

"It's my fault, mom. I let her get close to Dianna."

"How can you blame yourself?" his mother said looking up at him. "The woman is a deranged Nagalian bounty hunter. She would have stopped at nothing. No one would have thought she would do this to her own kind." His mother was right. He knew something was wasn't right, but never in a billion years would he have thought that she was working for bounty hunters. This was one mistake he would never make again.

"Let me in! Get your hands off me!" The sudden commotion caused Drax to turn around to see Eric trying to push his way past staff to get to Simon's room. "I want to see him!"

"That's not a good idea, Eric!" Drax stopped hugging his mother and started walking towards Eric. He knew how Eric felt. He was there when both Dianna and Jasmine almost lost their lives, but Eric wasn't listening and immediately went full Nagalian!

"GET THE FUCK OUT OF MY WAY!" He roared. Drax stopped in his tracks and the staff instinctively stepped away from him. Eric then returned to his normal form with his clothes tattered from the transformation and went inside the room. Drax went in after him. Eric stood by Simon's bed staring at his putrescent body writhing and moaning in pain and couldn't help the tears that flowed down his clean-shaven face. "Do you know how hard it is to find a gay Nagalian, willing to spend the rest of his life with you?" he said without looking at Drax. "While the rest of you are worried about producing offspring, I could only be grateful I had found someone as beautiful as he was to die with." Eric didn't seem squeamish about the putrid smell of rotting flesh or that his lifetime partner was decaying before his eyes. He held Simon's hand and squeezed it.

Simon stared up at him. The last bit of life beginning to drain from his eyes. He whispered to him with the blood and foam draining at the corner of his mouth. "Thank you. I didn't want to die alone." Eric sobbed and placed his other hand over Simon's enfolding it. "Not in a million years would I allow that." Simon smiled then closed his eyes and time stopped for Eric. Drax walked closer to him and placed his hand on his shoulder.

"I'm sorry, Eric."

"Yeah, me too." His face wet with tears. "But not as sorry as that bitch is going to be," he said turning to Drax.

"I'm going to handle this."

"Not without me you're not!" Eric was determined. Drax sighed. He didn't need this bullshit right now, but Eric was a mourning Nagalian. He couldn't deny him the chance to get even.

"Well, we can't waste any more time," Drax said heading out of the room.

"I guess that means we're taking my car," Eric responded.

***

Dianna woke up to blinding lights and a white ceiling. She squinted trying to adjust to the brightness. She saw a medical tray to her left with varying surgical tools and tubes. She turned to her right and saw her mother lying on a gurney parallel to hers. She tried to move but she realized that she was tightly strapped down. As she became more aware of her surroundings, Dianna realized that this was literally everything they were running from their entire lives. Her mother moaned and opened her eyes but immediately squinted from the blinding lights.

"Where are we?" lifting her head.

"I don't know, but by the looks of it, we're about to be guinea pigs." Irene groaned and rested her head back on the gurney. They both fell silent for a while.

"I'm sorry I didn't tell you about your sister," her mother said.
"How could you keep that from me?" Dianna responded.

"Because I didn't want you to think I was a bad person." Dianna remained silent. "I wanted to save her. I wanted to bring her with me, but they took her from me as soon as I gave birth to her. I was weak. I begged the nurse to let me escape with her but she kept Brooke and left the door open so I could escape."

"Escape from what?"

"A place like this?"

"They captured you?"

"Yes. I was a nurse on a military base in Vietnam and I accidentally saved a soldier and another soldier had witnessed it. They detained me and used me as a backup plan to heal wounded soldiers...soldiers that were on their dying bed." Dianna was horrified by what she was hearing. She hadn't known her mother had gone through so much.

"What about her father?" It was obvious they didn't share the same father since Brooke wasn't biracial like her.

"He was a soldier. The first person I ever saved. He rejected me and Brooke once he figured out what I was."

"Sounds like a real hard ass!" Dianna commented. "You should've told me." Dianna then looked over at her. "I don't think you're a bad person. I never did."

"Why didn't you tell me you could heal people...and Nagalians."

Dianna scoffed. "I was taking it in strides. It's sort of strange information to have about yourself." Irene nodded understanding the feeling.

"I didn't know what to think the first time I discovered I could heal people." Irene shared with Dianna.

Brook walked into the room. "See, I told you that you two would be bonding before they slice you both open." She walked around the gurneys leisurely inspecting the tools. "Cute story by the way."

"You heard us?"

"Yeah. See that window over there. It's a two-way window. Other people are observing you too."

"You must know that I would never willingly leave you behind." Irene tried to explain.

"Doesn't matter now and the damage is done. I'm dysfunctional and there's no way to unfuck it so I guess the moral of the story is...consequences?"

Dianna wondered if the beautiful but broken woman she saw in front of her was beyond repair. She had thought that she was beyond repair at one point. She had wanted to succumb to the darkness and kill herself. Yet Brooke had succumbed entirely to the darkness and become a monster. It was the worst timing, but she couldn't help thinking of Medusa. How she was a victim of her circumstances but then she succumbed to her vengefulness and became the monster, the Greek goddess, Athena had transformed her into.

"You can change," Dianna whispered as a last-ditch effort to get Brooke on their side.

Brooke pointed at her head, "There's no changing this," she said as she tapped herself on the side of her head. "Anyway, I just came to say, goodbye and good luck! And that I have no regrets." She walked out seductively; her hips swinging from side to side.

"She's nuts!" Dianna thought out loud as Brooke slipped through the door.

"It's my fault!" Irene said with trembling lips. "I scarred you both."

"We'll get through this mom."

"Do you think Drax is coming?"

"Damn, I hope so!" Dianna said praying that by now he knew what was going on. She hoped he would fight like hell to find her. Just then the door opened again and a man in a white lab coat came in. He walked around the room silently organizing things as he prepared to do something. She saw him open the cabinet to her left and take out some type of box and set it on the tray with the surgical tools. He opened it and pulled out a syringe with some kind of blue chemical in the slim barrel. He squeezed it and the chemical dripped out then he placed it back inside the box and left the box open.

"Listen to me. She's pregnant. Don't do this!" Irene begged.

"Pregnant?" The man laughed. "The gift that keeps giving," he continued to walk around the room checking charts. A few more people walked in and started hooking Irene and Dianna up to monitors. Panic began setting in for Dianna. Whatever they were about to do was already beginning.

"So, we have some investors that wants to see some proof of certain things. Y'know, things like how fast you can heal and if you can truly heal humans." He went back to the box and pulled out an empty syringe.

"I'm just going to take some blood samples, if you don't mind."

"No! No! No!" Irene screamed. Dianna started rocking from side to side hoping to topple her gurney, but she was strapped so tightly she was only wearing herself out.

"Sir, please. You can take my blood. Let her go! PLEASE!" Irene begged.

"Oh, don't worry. I am taking multiple samples from both of you. Don't worry. It won't hurt a bit." He walked over to Irene first and inserted the needle end of a long tube into her vein on her hand and pumped the blood into the beaker.

"MOM!" Dianna screamed. Dianna shook the gurney even more. By now she was changing. Her hair had become vicious snakes as she bared her fangs.

"Holy Fuck! Impressive!" the man in the white coat said with his hand on his chest. He looked at the window and nodded to whomever was behind the window.

"Stay calm, Dianna. I know it's hard but stay calm." Her mother implored her, but Dianna ignored her as she felt her strength gaining. She continued to rock the gurney violently and as her panic increased, so did her adrenaline. The straps on her wrists snapped and both her arms were free. She sat up and immediately started unstrapping her legs.

"SECURITY!" the man yelled, terrified that Dianna was escaping. Three large men ran into the room, one of them grabbed Dianna from behind and the other punched her face so hard, she started bleeding from her nose. Irene's scream was deafening. Brooke ran back into the room with her gun and shot it twice, tranquilizing Dianna. Her eyes rolled over as she became unconscious again.

***

Drax was at his parents' house which was filling up with more and more Nagalians as they slowly arrived one by one. Norlan was also there. He walked over to Drax.

"Anything you need, Drax. Just ask. I have Nagalians waiting to take orders from you," he said to him. Drax shook his hand, grateful for the support, and in that moment, he gained maybe an ounce of respect for Norlan.

"We're going to need all the help we can get," Drax explained. "Bring them in. I want them to hear what I have to say."

Drax ushered for everyone to be quiet. The din in the large living room began to slowly die down.

"Listen. They found her cell phone and threw it on the side of the road but lucky for us it took them a while to find it. Based on the tracking signal, we were able to find the closest abandoned medical facility about 30 miles west of where the signal stopped in the middle of the desert and we think this is where they are holding them. I want to go in deep but stealthy. Wear your protective vest. They have Apoptosyde and some of us might get hit. Remember, they are humans. They only have one half Nagalian, Brooke, and she is no match for all of us. Use your guns and transform if you have to but we are going to tear that operation down and we are going to send a message. You fuck with one of us, you fuck with all of us. They have been doing this way too long and we have kept our peace for centuries. Not today!" He looked around the crowd, searching for his father. His father was in the back, with a proud look on his face. He spotted the tapestry he had given to him hanging on the wall. He pointed at it. "Remember this emblem. We fight for our own and we protect all of us, no matter how great or small." The men were riled up from his speech. "We are going to surround the building from all sides and smoke them out with tear gas. And then we are going to destroy everything, find Dianna and Irene as quickly as we can and get out."

"What about Brooke?" Eric piped up.

"We're going to try to bring her in alive, but if she stands in your way, you know what to do." Eric nodded his head as his eyes grew dark.

"What if they are not there?"

"Then we sweep the area for any type of details that can help us find them, but I am pretty sure they are there." The men murmured among themselves.

"Aright, we need about twenty of you. Who is coming?"

There were over fifty of them there and they all raised their hand.

Drax smiled. "More than I needed but the more the merrier. Let's move out!"

***

When Dianna opened her eyes again, this time she was alone. They had taken Irene and she didn't know where. She felt nauseous as a sick feeling entered the pit of her stomach. It frightened her that they may have taken Irene to another location and if they did, she would never know where. She was still strapped to the gurney, her jaw hurt, and she had a bandage on her nose. She looked to her left and saw machine numbers rising and falling on monitors as they beeped. Wires were attached to her chest and finger. She looked to her right and saw a glass window and the blinds were slightly open. She couldn't see any buildings outside the window from where she was as she tried hard to think of where they were located. It was getting dark outside and Drax hadn't found her. Her eyes watered as she began to think that maybe they were no longer in Nevada and Drax may never find her…and the baby. It made her think of her mother's terrifying moments in Vietnam. How alone and lost she must have felt. At least she could hope that Drax was coming, her mother had no one. Suddenly the door opened and the man from earlier walked in, chart in hand.

"Listen up! You pull that shit again and we're going to start cutting out tongues and cutting off eyelids from both you and your mother without anesthesia. We placed your mother in another room. I think it might be easier, that way you two aren't getting each other spirited."

He checked her nose. "The security broke your nose but it's healing pretty nicely and quickly." He noted and wrote something down on his chart. "Sorry about that by the way but you gave us all a scare."

"Who are you and what are you going to do with us?"

"Who I am is not important. As of right now, nothing but we are waiting for a helicopter to come in tonight to air lift you guys to a better, more equipped and secure facility. We have the basics here but for what we are trying to do, we definitely need more equipment and supplies."

"You can't do this to us!" Dianna protested.

"Think of it this way. The extent of the research that we're planning to do is going to be so groundbreaking, you will be saving lives long after you're dead." He then walked out and left her to her thoughts. She was out of tears and her inner fight was gone. She was also hungry, and she needed to use the bathroom. She stared at the ceiling realizing that the circumstances she was in now, answered the 'why' of Drax's paranoia. Why he did everything in his power to protect her. She chastised herself for making things so hard, even though he just wanted to ensure that she was safe.

Brooke walked in. She had a brown paper bag in her hand with a drink in the other. She placed it on the gurney next to Dianna. She pulled out her gun, "I've got Apoptosyde in here. If you try to run, I will shoot you." She then started unstrapping Dianna's arms. Dianna rubbed her aching wrist. "I got you a burger and some fries." Dianna picked up the bag and opened it silently. The tasty smell of the food tantalized her nose. She started eating the fries. Then she took a sip of the drink. It was a fruit smoothie. Strawberry pineapple to be exact and it was refreshingly delicious on her tongue.

"How did you know this was my favorite smoothie?"

"I didn't", Brooke confessed. "I bought it because it's my favorite." They stared at each other acknowledging the strange coincidence, but it changed nothing.

Dianna ate in silence not trusting herself to speak any further. She hated Brooke beyond words and the next thing she planned on saying would be the complete opposite of the moment that just shared.

"I should've been long gone but they want me to stay until the helicopter gets here just in case you try anything funny." Dianna chewed the food in her mouth slowly. "Irene is fine. They just took a little blood from her. I gave her some food earlier too." Dianna wasn't sure why she was telling her all of this. Brooke hung her head appearing exhausted.

"What you are doing is unforgivable," Dianna said, sucking through the straw and staring at Brooke with dead eyes.

"You wouldn't understand."

"You're working for humans who murder and massacre Nagalians and you turned in your own flesh and blood for experimental gains. What is there to understand?"

"I'd rather be helping them than be hunted by them. Clearly, if you can't beat them," She stared at Dianna's restrained ankles as if she would die than be in that position, "you join them." Just then there was a loud commotion. Dianna heard glass shattering and then there was a lot of yelling. Brooke began strapping Dianna back to the gurney, spilling the smoothie from her hand. Dianna struggled but Brooke pointed the gun to her throat and Dianna stopped. She finished strapping Dianna in and ran out of the room. Brooke got a glimpse of a lot of smoke when Brooke opened the door and some wafted into the room. There were more crashing noises as the smoke began to burn Dianna's eyes. The pain was so bad her eyes began to water profusely. Someone crashed through her window in their Nagalian form, she could barely see the person as they neared her bed with a tear gas mask on. He placed the tear gas mask he was carrying over her face and then changed back to his human form. Dianna's eyes widened as she saw it was Eric. She didn't know he was Nagalian. Never guessed it even once.

"Eric!" He started unstrapping her. She hugged him as soon as he was free. "Is Drax here?" He nodded.

"What about Simon. Is he still alive?" She saw the pain in his eyes as he shook his head.

"Get up, Dianna! We don't have much time."

"How did you know I was in this room?"

"Blind luck. I just chose a window. Drax might be a little mad I got to you first." He smiled but his attempt at mirth failed to reach his eyes. He helped Dianna off the bed and took her to the window.

"This is the safest way out," he said pointing to the window. Dianna climbed through, barely noticing that she cut herself on broken pieces of glass that jutted out from the window frame. She ran outside to the desert and Eric followed pointing to the vehicles parked in the distance. Once he got her close enough, someone else took her and escorted her to the Ford Explorer and locked her inside. She looked around but Eric was gone. "Fuck!"

She waited for what seemed like hours watching the horror unfold in front of her. Even though she was far away, she could still hear the gunshots and the screaming. Then the whirring noise of a helicopter propeller. She looked up and saw a helicopter trying to land and then she saw Brooke running out of the building with Irene. Brooke was obviously waiting for the helicopter to land so she could get in with Irene. Dianna tried to open the door, but she was locked inside the SUV. She tried kicking the door open but couldn't, so she started beating on the window, screaming her head off. The helicopter landed and Brooke started pulling Irene towards it. Then she saw Drax running from the building.

She screamed his name, but it was in vain. She was just a distant voice, barely audible outside the soundproof SUV. Brooke turned around in time to see him and pointed her gun at him the same time he pointed his gun at her with her mother in between them. Dianna's heart leapt into her throat. Brooke was saying something to Drax as she backed towards the helicopter, but Dianna could barely hear her. She saw other men coming out from the building, but she could barely tell if they were humans or Nagalians. They surrounded Drax and she realized they were humans. She felt helpless watching everything. He got on his knees, placed his gun carefully on the ground and placed his hands behind his head, but it was short-lived as Nagalian men in their true form came running from behind the building. It was pretty much an ambush. One of them shot Brooke with a sniper gun and she fell to her knees and Irene started running away from the epicenter of the activities. That's when she saw Brooke pointing the gun at her mom's back but before she could shoot the gun, Drax picked his gun up from the ground and shot her multiple times. She fell forward succumbing to her injuries. The Nagalians charged the helicopter and pulled the men out, while other Nagalians rounded up the rest of the humans from the building. Drax shouted some instructions and then he headed in her direction. He caught up with her mother and he guided her towards the SUV. Dianna started beating on the window and Drax saw her. He ran to the car and unlocked it. Dianna got out and jumped on him wrapping her legs around his waist.

"You shot her!" she said her arms squeezing his neck.

"I didn't have a choice." Dianna sobbed knowing it was the truth. "Are you hurt?" he asked, staring at the bandage on her nose. She shook her head in response.

"You put up a fight, huh?" He smirked knowingly.

"I tried," she admitted. He kissed her as if he were trying to make sure that she was really there.

"I couldn't find you. I thought they took you somewhere else."

"Eric found me, took me out here and locked me in the Explorer." Drax smiled. "Is he okay?"

Yes. I think we both got hit by regular bullets but--" Drax responded.

"What? Where?"

"I'm fine," he assured her. She kissed him tenderly and then got onto her feet. Her mom was standing behind them staring at the destruction in front of her. Dianna walked over to her and squeezed her hand. She looked at Drax, "Is she dead?"

"She was shot a few times with the Apoptosyde. If she isn't already dead, she's pretty close to it," Drax said pointedly. Dianne could tell that he felt no remorse, but she couldn't blame him. Brooke was the reason behind all this chaos.

"Is it bad that I don't want to save her even if I could?" her mom said.

"No, it's not," Dianna said reassuringly. Drax had walked back to the vehicle and opened the door.

"I'm going to handle a few things, so I need you guys to wait in here."

"I don't want to wait in the SUV!" Dianna said eyeing the vehicle with disdain. He pulled her close to him and kissed her.

"Please don't argue with me babe. Not now." Dianna's eyes softened at his soothing voice.

"Okay," she surrendered. She followed behind her mother inside the vehicle and waited. She touched her stomach, feeling overwhelmed with gratitude that she was alive, and her baby was also alive. She hadn't been surer in her life than she was in that moment that she wanted to live her life to the fullest. Two people had died today. Simon and Brooke, one didn't deserve to die and the other never got a chance to change. She had wanted to take her own life and if she had, she also wouldn't have gotten a chance to shed her old skin and change into the better version of herself or to experience love and bring a life into this world. She knew she would live her life, forever changed by things she saw that night and as she stared at her mother's distant eyes, she knew she wasn't the only one.

Chapter 14

Dianna, Drax and Eric stood together as they threw the red roses on top of Simon's coffin. It was pouring down and both Eric and Drax held an umbrella.

"The good ones die young," Dianna found herself saying as she stood between both men. They walked away as the funeral aides started shoveling dirt into the grave.

"So, I'm heading back to my place," Eric said his eyes were red and blood shot. She could tell that his nights were sleepless and agonizing.

"Okay," Dianna responded.

Eric stared at her for a while. "Hey, can I talk to you privately for a minute?" he requested.

Dianna gave Drax an uncertain glance and then walked away with Eric walking shoulder to shoulder under the large black umbrella to avoid getting wet from the rain. The large raindrops were beating down on them by now.

"I'm sorry for lying to you," he said earnestly. "Simon wanted me to come clean but...my loyalty to Drax stopped me." Dianna was silent as she contemplated his words. She wasn't mad at him. She couldn't be. His significant other and best friend just died, and Simon was her best friend too. "But our friendship wasn't fake. I was just a bodyguard friend if you want to call it that."

"I'm more surprised that you kept the fact that you were a Nagalian from me. You could have made my life so much easier." Eric gave her a half smile. "The bodyguard thing is expected from Drax." Eric couldn't help laughing at what they both knew was the truth. "Is there anyone else?"

"Yeah. Simon and Susanne."

"I should've known Susanne was full Nagalian. Imagine my surprise when I saw her at the Fraternity meeting. Both of our eyeballs nearly fell out of our sockets," Dianna became animated as she recounted the moment to him. Eric laughed lightly in response and she couldn't help cherishing his laughter. "But Simon!" she shook her head vehemently, "What about his parents? I thought…"

"Yeah, he talks about his parents a lot, but they disowned him for being a drug addict…and gay."

"Damn. That's harsh!" Dianna's heart lurched as she thought about Simon's wretched life before he finally found his peace.

"Yeah, producing offspring is like a damn religion to Nagalians and clearly if you are gay…" he trailed off as Dianna nodded her understanding.

"And you…what's your story?"

"I don't know. Drax found me wandering the streets, homeless, hungry and begging for scraps. I don't remember anything before that," she could see him fighting back the tears. "He's the only family I know."

She held his hand supportively. Eric's words came back to her and this time she understood the depth of his statement. *'That man is out here saving lives.'* "Thank you for everything Eric, especially for saving my life."

He squeezed her hand, "We stick together," he said to her and she nodded, affirming his words. After she released his hand, he gave her his umbrella. He waved goodbye, then walked towards his Bentley, looking like a sad, wet, lost puppy. It looked strange to not see Simon by his side. It was a stark reminder that nothing is ever permanent. Dianna walked back to Drax and they went in the opposite direction toward their limo.

"Do you think your mom will ever come back to visit?"

"If she doesn't want her grandparent privileges revoked, she better!" Dianna snapped. Drax laughed. They walked silently for a while and Dianna could sense that something was weighing on Drax's mind. "What's wrong?"

He looked at her and smiled patiently. "Nothing. Everything I need and want, I have right here." He placed his arm around Dianna's waist.

They got into the limo and started heading home. On their way, Dianna finally asked him the question that had been plaguing her for a while.

"When Brook was pointing her gun at you and dragging my mother back to the helicopter, what did she say to you?"

Drax stared at her a little bewildered and then it was as if his memories came flooding through his brain. His jaw ticked from the memory.

"She said anything to do with Irene isn't my fight and I should let her get on the helicopter with her."

"...and what did you say?"

Drax pulled Dianna close and kissed the top of her head.

"Anything to do with Irene was always my fight and I couldn't let her take her."

By the time they got home, Dianna was ready for a long bath. She went upstairs and drew herself a bath. She took off her clothes and stepped inside the warm frothy bubbles. She rested her head back and relaxed her shoulders, letting everything in her present surroundings melt away. She had attended two funerals this week. Her sister's funeral and then Simon's. Even as she thought about it, she couldn't believe that the loving, bubbly nurturing person Simon was would no longer grace the face of the Earth. It was heartbreaking.

Things had changed to some extent for the Nagalians nationally. Drax and his father became heavily involved in congress in an attempt to legislate sanctuary communities for Nagalians in each state. It was their hope that protective laws would lessen the occurrence of Nagalian murders. Yet even though legislations could be passed, laws didn't always change the hearts of men. The threat would still remain. Even so, she knew Drax would never give up his paranoid ways. He knew better than to believe he could trust the humans. She also knew that with the knowledge out there that her blood had mutated, the humans would always be looking for her and her mother ... and possibly her baby, which would only serve to make Drax even more paranoid.

Luckily for him, she had grown to be just as protective and embraced the need for excessive security. Too many lives were at stake and they could not risk losing anyone else even though they all knew it wasn't something they could control.

She had also wanted to play her part by donating blood for Mrs. Ashton's antidote research and to ramp up the manufacturing of the synthetic blood. She realized that there was a real urgency to start the process for the antidote and she didn't want to wait any longer. However, Mrs. Ashton protested, and Dianna only succeeded in donating enough to kickstart the research phase. Mrs. Ashton wanted her to remain healthy during the remainder of the pregnancy and was in no rush to receive pints and pints of blood.

"I know your heart is in the right place, Dianna. But right now, we are putting the baby first," Mrs. Ashton had said to her. "You've already been through enough."

Things had also changed on a personal level between her and Drax. She finally decided it wasn't smart to keep her apartment. She would be pregnant and exposed considering that her address was known. After she got it professionally cleaned, she broke her lease and moved in officially with Drax. It was still only a few weeks after Simon's death, but she noticed that their arguments became more and more infrequent and usually involved petty things like whether she should take the limo to work or drive herself. Dianna chuckled at the thought. She found herself wondering things like when she started aging like her mother, would he still be in love with her or when she died, would he fall crazy in love with someone else as he did with her? Or when she was well in her old years, would he cheat on her? It was a chance that they were taking yet what was the alternative? They break up and try to be with other people knowing that their hearts belonged to each other? She hated thinking about it, and she chose to live in the moment. Chose to love him without regret now and to bask in their happiness while they could. To make sure that when they raised their child, their child would never doubt the love that they have for each other.

She let the water out and got out of the bath. She wrapped the towel around herself when Drax walked up behind her. She closed her eyes as he planted his lips on her neck and sucked the water droplets remaining on her skin from her bath. She then felt something covering her eyes.

"What are you doing?"

"Shhh... Do you trust me?" Drax asked as he tied the blindfold behind her head. She paused and then smiled.

"Yes, I trust you."

He stripped away her towel and replaced it with a terry robe. Then he bent down in front of her and put on her boots. She wasn't sure what was happening, but her heart was racing from the suspense. He then slowly guided her out of the room, down the stairs and she felt the wind cool her face as he guided her out of the house.

She noticed that they were walking up an incline and she became even more confused than ever, but she remained quiet because she wanted to prove to him that she trusted him with every fiber of her being. They had walked for probably 10 minutes, as she stumbled and hesitated her way to their destination. They finally stopped. The cool air felt good on her chest, but she was otherwise warm from the robe he had placed around her. He removed the blindfold and she found herself standing close to the edge of a cliff.

"Sweet Mary and Joseph!" She gasped and grabbed on to him. "Why are we here?" she asked him utterly confused. He stepped behind her and used his arms to encircle her in his safe embrace. He was wearing his robe too.

"I've had this property for years and this is my first time coming out here."

Dianna eyed the highway below skittishly. "We are really close to the edge," she said holding on to his arms folded across her chest.

"I know." She couldn't help thinking he was connotating a deeper meaning to her words. "Don't be scared. Enjoy it." She calmed and just stared at the desert stretching out for miles. The highway was empty, and it was just them. If they wanted to strip completely naked, they could. It suddenly seemed so vast, with the starry sky hovering above their heads. It was breathtaking.

"I love it!" she whispered as if he had given her a gift.

"I had a gut feeling you would," he whispered back. He kissed the side of her face and let her go. She turned around and he was standing there, in his robe and tennis shoes holding a box with a beautiful amethyst ring. Her eyes widened as her brain grappled with what was unfolding in front of her. She covered her face trying to hide her emotions, but it was useless. The waterworks had already begun, and she felt overwhelmed with emotions.

"Why?" she asked her face still covered. It was imperative that she knew the 'why' behind the proposal. He removed her hand from her face so she could look at him.

"Well, obviously, you're pregnant with my child!" she scoffed at his dry humor but he continued," but more so because I watched Simon die and I've watched you almost lose your life a few times and I realized that I can handle you dying before me but I couldn't handle living without you while you're here."

She sobbed like a baby at his beautiful words, "Me neither," she confessed to him. She nodded her head emphatically. "Yes!" she said and watched him nervously put the ring on her finger with shaky hands.

"You were nervous?" she asked him through tears.

"Yeah."

"You never get nervous."

"That's what you think." He took her hand in his and they walked back to the house. When they stepped inside the house, there were candles lit in the living room and red and white rose petals led up the stairs.

"You did all of this?" she whispered. She continued up the stairs to the bedroom where more beautiful red and white rose petals were delicately placed in a circle around the bed and on the bed was a large spread with the green Nagalian emblem in the middle which seemed striking under the soft glow of aureate candles on both sides of the bed. She stared at the emblem captivated; called to it like a moth to a flame.

"I want to know why you are so drawn to the emblem," he said.

"Because she is so unafraid and she's a protector, a healer and a friend. And y'know how people are always telling you to never trust a snake."

"Yes."

"Well, it is the other way around here," she said pointing at the snake. "It's the snake that is placing its entire trust in her."

"Am I the snake?" he asked curiously.

She laughed at his question. "Everything has to be about you, huh?"

"Afraid so." He walked to her and started kissing her. She kissed him back and allowed her robe to fall to the ground as she slipped his off his shoulders. Their breathing became heavy as he lifted her and placed her in the middle of the bed on top of the emblem. He took her shoes off and kicked his own shoes off. He trailed kisses from her lips to her stomach and then captured one of her breasts in his mouth. She moaned and then pushed him off her and got on top of him, delicately feathering kisses on his chest. He lifted her gently and placed her beside him. He positioned himself behind her as he ran his ordinary nails along her beautiful soft skin.

"I don't want to change," he told her. "I want to be a gentleman tonight."

"Okay," she responded. It didn't matter what form he made love to her in. They were both him, the man she loved and trusted with every atom in her body.

He kissed her neck and then her shoulders. "I enjoy you so much either way," he told her, mirroring her own sentiments. Then he gently eased himself into her from behind. He encircled her with his arms and slowly thrusted inside her, watching her enjoy his strokes. She understood why he didn't want to be rough or punishing tonight, he just wanted to be intimate and she loved the slow, languidness of their lovemaking. He lifted her leg so he could access her sensitive pearl while he slowly pressed into her and she placed her hand on top of his as he massaged her rhythmically. She stretched her arm around his neck as the feeling became more and more exquisite and he enjoyed her erratic breathing as she got closer and closer to her climax. She got a glimpse of their reflection in the large dresser mirror and marveled at how much they looked like a Greek painting with their naked bodies entwined together. She watched him watching her as she came and he absorbed every moment of it with his eyes as if he wanted to remember her like that forever, then he strained as he finally came but he never took his gaze off her as she wanted every drop of him inside her. When they were finished, she turned around and faced him as he buried his face in the crook of her neck.

"I want to be yours always...whatever that means," she whispered, thinking about her short life compared to his very long life.

"You will be," he said possessively pulling her closer. "Let anyone try to take you away from me, they will have to come with hell's army." Dianna felt a chill run down her back at his words and knew that his protection was limitless. He was her army. She was his half Nagalian healer and he was right. They, no matter who they were, would have to come with everything they had to separate them.

***

"Did you recover the body?" The boss said in a low voice on the other line.

"Yes. There was no reviving her," Jack responded.

"I loved her like a daughter."

"Brooke was our best soldier, hands down." Jack used his switchblade to etch her name on the wooden table in front of him as he thought about Brooke. She was a tough nut to crack, but she had let him of all people in, and he loved her endlessly. They were supposed to be partners until the very end, but she let revenge get the best of her and now she was dead.

"I know she would've wanted us to continue our work."

"Agreed." He smoked his cigarette in the dimly lit room, allowing the smoke to fill his lungs trying to numb out his deep sense of loss. "How are we going to circumvent the involvement of the US government and their new laws?"

"Rules are meant to be broken. We continue as we were, only more covert." The boss coughed violently, and Jack knew that his health was getting worse, "...and we don't stop until we get them both," he continued before hanging up the phone. Jack turned on the light and looked at the file on his cluttered table sprinkled with cigarette butts and ashes. He stared at the picture of Drax, the reason Brooke was dead, and then stabbed it with the point of his knife. "Correction, we won't stop until we get all three of them dead or fucking alive!"

***

Made in the USA
Columbia, SC
29 October 2020

23372963R00163